SEASON ONE

YESTERDAY'S GONE

SEAN PLATT

DAVID WRIGHT

YESTERDAY'S GONE: SEASON ONE
(Episodes 1-6)

Copyright © 2011 by Sean Platt & David Wright. All rights reserved

Edited by: Jason Whited jason-whited.com
Email at: jasonhwhited@me.com

This is a work of fiction. Any resemblance to actual persons living or dead, businesses, events, or locales is purely coincidental. The authors have taken great liberties with locales including the creation of fictional towns. Reproduction in whole or part of this publication without express written consent is strictly prohibited.

The authors greatly appreciate you taking the time to read our work. Please consider leaving a review wherever you bought the book, or telling your friends or blog readers about this book to help us spread the word.

Thank you for supporting our work. You rock!

Published by Collective Inkwell
Visit: CollectiveInkwell.Com
First Print Edition August 2016

Layout and design by Collective Inkwell
CollectiveInkwell.Com

* * * *

WARNING: This book is intended for mature audiences. It is a dark book with many disturbing scenes and mature language.

To YOU, the reader.
Thank you for taking a chance on us.
Thank you for your support.
Thank you for the emails.
Thank you for the reviews.
Thank you for reading and joining us on this road.

* * * *

YESTERDAY'S GONE

SEASON ONE

SEAN PLATT

DAVID WRIGHT

YESTERDAY'S GONE
::EPISODE 1::
(FIRST EPISODE OF SEASON ONE)
"2:15"

CHAPTER 1
BRENT FOSTER

Saturday
Oct. 15, 2011
Morning
New York City

On the day everything changed, Brent Foster's biggest concern was getting an hour to himself. But hell if he wouldn't have settled for 15 minutes.

His head was pounding when he woke, as if he'd spent the night partying rather than staying late at the paper. Fortunately, it was his day off. He glanced at the alarm clock and saw that the blue numbers were black. The fan he used to drown out the sounds of his neighbors and traffic was off, too. The power must've gone out.

Great.

Judging from the morning sun coming through the opening in the curtains, he figured it was probably 9 a.m. And since he couldn't hear the sounds of his rambunctious

3-year-old at play, Gina must've taken Ben for a walk or play date at the park.

He smiled. He loved when he had the apartment to himself. Moments alone were so rare these days. He worked under constant deadlines in the newsroom, still always hustling and bustling, even with the layoffs. Then, at home, his son was *usually awake* and in need of some daddy time.

"He just wants to spend time with you," his wife would say, tugging at Brent's threadbare guilt strings. "You're always working."

Brent wasn't *completely* antisocial, even if Gina might argue otherwise; he just needed time to decompress when he woke and when he got home. He was just wired that way. If he didn't get time, he grew moody and anxious. And he was short with Ben, which carried the rough consequence of feeling shitty for hours, one hour for every second he was uncool to Ben. The last thing he wanted to be was like his own dad, yet some days, he was headed there with a full tank of gas and a brick on the pedal.

He was in a better mood when he could start the day alone. Today, it seemed, would start just right.

Brent walked into the living room, popped open the fridge, off but still cold. He grabbed a bottle of water and took a deep swig as his eyes scanned the counter for a note from his wife. She always left a note when she went somewhere. But apparently, not today. Brent took another swig of water and headed down the hall to his son's room. The door was closed; big, blue wooden letters spelled *BEN* on the door. Brent peered inside. The bed was unmade, curtains drawn, even though Gina always opened them when Ben first woke. Both pairs of Ben's sneakers were sitting on top of his blue, wooden toy box that doubled as a bench.

Brent was confused. Gina wouldn't take Ben from the apartment without shoes.

He went back into his room, fished the cell phone from his pants, and glanced at the time" 10:20 a.m. Later than he thought.

He dialed Gina's cell and put the phone to his ear.

No sound on the other line.

Phones are down, too?

Brent dialed again, same result.

Mrs. Goldman.

They had to be at the apartment across the hall, Mrs. Goldman's. Her husband had passed away a few months earlier. Gina had started bringing Ben over to keep her company. She loved Ben, and he loved eating her cookies — a perfect match.

Brent slipped on some sweatpants, then headed across the hall and knocked on the door. The lights in the hall were out, save for four emergency lights spaced every five doors along the ceiling.

Mrs. Goldman always took forever to answer the door. Brent suspected she was going deaf, even though she had a keen ear for neighborhood gossip. He knocked louder. Still, no answer.

Mrs. Goldman never went anywhere. Ever. Her only other family was her worthless son, Peter, who never visited. The few times Gina had invited her to the store or for a nice afternoon lunch, Mrs. Goldman declined. She didn't care much for the city. Was only there because her husband loved it. Now he was gone, and she was happy to spend her days watching TV, reading her mysteries, and playing bridge with some of the other ladies twice a week.

"Mrs. Goldman," Brent called, "Are you there?"

Nothing.

Weird.

Brent didn't know the other neighbors on his floor, but Gina had recently become friends with a young mother a few doors down. Maybe they went there, Brent figured. He walked toward the end of the hall, but couldn't remember if the woman lived in number 437 or 439.

He tried knocking on 437 first.

No answer.

He tried a couple more times, then went to 439.

No response.

What the hell?

People were always home, or at least it seemed that way. Brent was never able to sleep in because his neighbors were loud and the walls were thin. He'd wanted to move somewhere quieter for years, somewhere with neighbors who actually left the building every now and then. Brent turned and tried the door across the hall, 440.

No response.

What the hell?

Brent turned around and headed up the hallway, stopping to knock at each door along the way.

One, two, and then five more doors. Nothing. He continued down the hall, his heart thudding, knocks turning to pounding at each door.

By the time he reached the end of the hallway, he was hot and sweaty, yelling. "HELLO?! ANYONE?!"

Nothing but black silence. The darkened hall seemed to constrict as his mind started racing.

Impossible. There's no way that nobody's home. No fucking way. Unless . . .

Terrorists.

The word bubbled to the surface as an answer to a question he'd not yet had the courage to ask. They were in New York, so it wasn't implausible. He raced back to his apartment, door still open, went to the windows and pulled the curtains aside, then looked down on the city streets. The empty city streets.

Brent was speechless, his heart on pause, eyes swimming in and out of focus.

"What the fuck?"

It didn't add up. If there were an attack, there would be bodies. If there was an evacuation, surely his wife would've woken him. Unless maybe it happened while she was out and unable to get back.

That thought died on the vine when he spotted Gina's purse and keys on the kitchen table, right where she put them every night before bed, ready for the next morning.

He looked back down. No people. No cars on the street. Well, none that was moving, anyway. Brent could see a handful that were either in the middle of the street, or had crashed into the cars parked on the opposite side of the street. He could see exhaust from some of the cars, their lights still on.

It was as if everyone on his block just simultaneously vanished. Everyone except Brent.

He went to Ben's room again to get a look from his son's window, which had a slightly better angle at the cross street. Something sharp stung his foot. He cursed as he stumbled, glancing at the carpet to see a small, blue train.

Stanley Train, Ben's favorite toy, which he carried with him everywhere, including to bed. It was there, just setting on the floor. Brent bent and picked it up. Its wide eyes and eternally giant smile stared back at him. Wherever his little boy was, he was without his favorite toy.

He set the train on Ben's pillow and returned to his room. He got dressed, then grabbed his keys, wallet, and phone. He shoved everything in his jeans, then went to the kitchen, found the notepad and a pen and left a note for Gina.

Where did you go? Went outside to look for you. Knocked on doors at our neighbors, nobody's home. I'll be back at 1 p.m. If you come home, wait for me.

Love,
Brent

Halfway through the front door, Brent thought of something, then went back to his son's room, grabbed Stanley Train from the pillow and put it in his pocket.

**

Brent took the stairs down to the next floor, and started knocking on those doors, despite not knowing *anyone* on this floor.

At the sixth door without any response, he worked up the courage to try a doorknob. Locked.

Halfway down the hall, he got an idea. He found the fire alarm and pulled it. The alarm blared; a banshee shriek amid the quiet. Brent covered his ears, watching the hall, waiting for people to flee.

Not a single door opened.

"Fuck it," Brent said, and went to apartment 310, tried the knob. It was locked. He backed up a bit, kicked at a spot right below the doorknob and was surprised at how easily the door burst open. *Why even have locks?*

"Hello?!" he shouted.

No response.

The apartment was as vacant as his own. Pictures on the wall showed a Puerto Rican family of four. Parents with two twin boys, about 10 years old. He was about to leave the apartment, but movement grabbed him. Something just beyond the sheer curtains covering the living room window. He moved closer and saw the slinky silhouette of a cat sunning on the windowsill. How it could relax with the alarm blaring was beyond Brent, but then again, so were most things feline.

He went to the curtain, pulled it aside, and saw the white, long-haired cat stretched out, face nuzzled against the warm windowsill. As he reached out to pet the cat, it started to roll over to show its belly. As it turned, Brent jumped back.

The cat's face had no eyes or mouth.

Brent fell back two steps, letting the curtain fall into place, his heart racing, half expecting the monstrosity to jump on him or worse. He stared at the curtains, dread creeping up his spine.

What the hell is that?

He watched the cat's silhouette as it lay back down. He worked up the courage to pull the curtain aside again to make sure he'd seen what he thought he'd seen. The cat's face was turned down, so he had to reach out, hesitantly, again and pet its head to get it to look back up at him. As his fingers touched the cat's fur, he felt a slight shock, like static electricity. The cat didn't seem to notice the shock. It began purring in response to the touch, then lifted its chin to meet Brent.

Only this time, the cat had eyes, wide blue ones, and a mouth.

Brent shook his head, feeling stupid. He continued to pet the cat's head as the alarm kept ringing.

"You deaf, kitty?" Brent asked.

No response. Which was a good thing, or Brent might have just jumped right out the window.

He glanced out at the street below to see if tenants were pouring from the building's lower floors because of the fire alarm. If so, he didn't see anyone.

As the curtain drifted back into place, he saw movement on the street below.

He snatched the curtain aside again, and glanced down at the apartment building across the street. A man in a dark sweater, baseball cap, and pants emerged from beneath the green awning and onto the street, looking around. He was too far away to get a good look at, particularly under a baseball cap, but something about his gait suggested he was nervous.

Brent jumped up, excited, and began smacking the window, yelling, "HEY! HEY!"

The cat leaped down and scurried out of sight.

The man on the street didn't seem to hear Brent. He was walking north along the street, sticking to the sidewalk. Brent stopped trying to get his attention. While the man did glance over at the building a couple of times, likely drawn by the sound of the siren, his attention was mostly on something further down the road that Brent couldn't see.

Brent watched, waiting to see where the man would go.

He seemed to be looking for someone. The man pulled a pair of binoculars out of his jacket and scanned the street in both directions. Then, he raised his binoculars up toward Brent. Brent waved frantically. For a moment, the man paused, and Brent was certain that he'd seen him. But he put the binoculars down and turned quickly to the north side of the street as if he'd heard or seen something.

The man lifted the binoculars to his eyes and focused to get a better look at whatever had his attention.

Brent turned, pushing his face against the window, struggling to see whatever the man was now staring at, but the angle was marred. He looked back down at the man, only to see him running as fast as he could in the opposite direction, and back into the apartment building he'd come from.

Brent pressed his face against the window again, struggling to see what scared the hell out of the guy. Whatever it was, he couldn't see it.

Hide, a voice in Brent's head said. *Hide now.*

It's coming.

* * * *

CHAPTER 2
MARY OLSON

Saturday
Oct. 15, 2011
Morning
Warson Woods, Missouri

Mary woke up sticky.

Another dream about Ryan, the sixth one in the last two weeks. *Weird.* She probably hadn't thought of him for a month before that. Or longer. Though she couldn't help but picture her ex from time to time since their daughter was his spitting image — well, a cuter, girly version, anyway.

Mary turned over and buried her face in the pillow. She hated dreaming about him, and *really hated* when they were sex dreams.

He'd never stop being *inside her*, but he hadn't actually been there in three years. They'd been divorced for two, but once she found out about Natalie Farmer, the bitch that was 10 years too young and as perky as a sitcom schoolgirl, she couldn't touch him without a shudder.

She hated him for the innocence he stole and the lives he abused. But a large part of her could never forget the way he made her feel — the way he made her laugh, the way that, for no reason at all, he used to slip behind her and whisper treasures in her ear. The way he truly seemed to love her and their daughter, Paola. And the way he always reassured her that everything would be okay, even if he only did so in her dreams.

Mary rarely slept past 7. During the week, Paola had to be at school by 9 and they usually left by 8 because Paola liked to go early. Unlike most 12-year-olds, Paola would wake early even on the weekends. Sometimes, Paola would join Mary for some early morning yoga before Mary worked a few hours on the greeting cards that paid for the $1.1 million house high on a hill in Warson Woods, just outside St. Louis - no thanks to Ryan.

A million dollars bought a palace in Warson Woods, the kind of house Mary liked most, even though it made her feel guilty all the time. Her cousin lived outside L.A. He said nothing was for less than $350,000 unless you were willing to settle for bullet holes.

It was probably thinking about bullet holes that made Mary realize how quiet the house was. More than usual. She sat up in bed. More than quiet - eerie. The trees were swaying, but that was it. No birds chirping. No dogs barking. And no lawnmowers. In Warson Woods, people loved lawns like children, and spoiled them the same, either themselves or through their teams of landscapers. Mary started calling lawnmowers the "Missouri Symphony" the second week she moved in. To *not* hear lawnmowers on a Saturday morning made her briefly question whether she'd slept straight through to Monday.

Mary left the bed and padded toward the stairs. She needed coffee. That would help the oddness fade. The hallway was dark. Mary flicked a light but nothing happened.

She sighed and kept walking. *One million for a house, fine, but everything should work.*

She would have a hard enough time this morning without light, but being without caffeine might make it impossible. So, she wasn't happy when her new Keurig wouldn't work either. *Maybe there was an outage in the neighborhood?* A sudden chill iced her insides. It wasn't logical, but it came from the place that keeps its eyes peeled for the stuff logical doesn't.

"Paola?"

Paola didn't answer, but the Keurig rumbled to life and started warming its water as the hall light came on and the air conditioner cycled on. She would've called for Paola a second time, but she didn't have to. Paola called for her instead. "Mom!!!" *Mom* sounded like a war cry rattling from the throat of a warrior who knew she was about to die.

Mary was at the foot of the stairs in less than a second and all the way to the top in two after that. She flew through Paola's open door. Her daughter was screaming at something out of view.

It was gone before Mary got there, but it had left Paola a vibrating mess. Mary tried to soothe her, but Paola pushed her away. "It's okay, Honey." Mary pulled her closer. Paola surrendered, and Mary's hands fell in a familiar pattern behind her daughter's head.

"What was it?" Mary asked.

"I don't know," Paola shook her head. "I don't know the words."

"Try."

"It was like," Paola fell into a second fit of sobs. Mary continued to pet her. "It was like ... " more sobbing, then, "It was like Daddy."

"What? What do you mean, it was like your father?"

Paola shook her head. Her cheeks burned. "It was Daddy. He was in my room, but he wasn't. It was just him, but not all of him."

"Your father was here?!" Mary could feel her white face making Paola's redder.

"No." Paola started to say something, then closed her mouth. A long three seconds passed, then, "It was like if a ghost was there without the ghost. Daddy, but not Daddy."

"How do you know it was a ghost, or your father, if you couldn't see anything?"

Paola just stared at her mother. "I'd know Daddy anywhere."

Her face cracked, and she started to cry again as the power went off again.

**

It seemed to take longer than normal for Mary to calm Paola's whimpers down to heavy breathing. Right when inhales and exhales were starting to meet, Paola broke the rhythm.

"Why is it so quiet?"

Mary had almost forgotten. "I'm not sure, honey. The power's out and everything feels … "

"Wrong," Paola finished.

"Yeah, *wrong*." Mary stood and held out her hand for Paola. She was almost as tall as her mom, and would likely tower over her in another year or two. Paola followed her mom downstairs and into the kitchen. The coffee machine had died before it could produce enough for a cup. Frustrated, Mary went to the fridge and grabbed a Diet Coke for herself and poured some OJ for her daughter.

When they finished, Mary looked out the front window. "Let's go look outside."

They walked the neighborhood that had gone from posh to ghost town overnight.

They peered through windows and into cars, and crossed well-manicured yards, starting at Mrs. Parker's house on the corner, because she was the first to move into the subdivision and had made it family business to know everything about everyone every day since. She wasn't home.

After two empty streets, they rounded the hill and hit the hiking trail, thinking there might be a neighborhood gathering they didn't know about. The trails were empty, too. Odd for the weekend, when the housewives and retirees were usually out en masse.

They followed the trail, then rounded the avenue back to their street. They were surprised, and thrilled, to see someone standing in front of their house. It was their neighbor, Jimmy Martin - Jim, as he'd been introducing himself since eighth grade, even though no one would listen. He was a head too tall for his age. That, along with his long, dark hair that he let hang in his eyes, made him look a bit older than his 16 years. Any advantage he had in looking older was usurped by his immaturity. While he was generally a good kid, as far as Mary knew, he got into frequent trouble for skateboarding in the shopping center, trespassing at the pool after hours, skipping school, and the stuff that unfocussed kids generally did to pass away the time.

"What'd you find out, Mrs. Olson?"

"Nothing," Mary shook her head. "Do you know what's going on?"

"Other than the entire world going *POOF!?*" Jimmy made jazz hands, "I've no idea. I woke up, my mom and dad were AWOL. So were both my brothers. I figured they were fu ... messing with me, but I can't figure out the angle, plus there'd be no way they'd get the whole neighborhood to play the reindeer games."

Jimmy seemed oddly unfazed by events.

Mary was about to ask him if the electricity was working in his house when her neighbor from the other side, John, appeared in the distance. He was walking fast, directly toward them. Mary closed her mouth mid-sentence, Jimmy and Paola turned to see why.

"Thank God!" John was running toward them.

"What's going on?" All three asked, hard to tell who was first.

"No idea. Jenny's gone. No note. Nothing. She doesn't even go downstairs without kissing me goodbye."

It was true. With any other couple it would've been disgusting. But John and Jenny were probably the two nicest people alive. And so adorable and doting, it was almost creepy.

No one had a chance to console John, or consider Jenny, before a smoke-colored Audi appeared on the drive coming toward them. It was Desmond Armstrong, the neighbor from across the street. The Audi's engine died, but Desmond stayed inside. They could see him through the tinted windows, sitting and staring into space. It was an endless minute with no one knowing what to do. Finally, the door opened, and Desmond put his boot on the grass.

"There's no other way to say it," Desmond shook his head. "The world is dead."

* * * *

CHAPTER 3
CHARLIE WILKENS

Saturday
Oct. 15, 2011
Morning
Jacksonville, Florida

Charlie Wilkens wasn't upset when he woke to find an empty world. In fact, it was the best damned thing that had happened in his 17 years on the planet.

He was frightened at first, of course, when he woke to find his house empty, both cars in the driveway, and no sign of his mother or asstard stepdad, Bob. But when he went door to door and discovered his entire block was as empty as his house, he was a few planets past the moon.

As he tottered down the street on his 12 speed, he stopped to knock at each house, considering its occupants and the offenses they'd committed against him over the years. He knocked on the bully Eddie Houghton's house, remembering the time the fat, red head made Charlie eat dirt in front of his classmates in sixth grade.

Good riddance.

He stopped at Josie Robinson's house, a girl he had a crush on since kindergarten, and who had been his friend until last year, before she started hanging out with Shayanne and the rest of the cheerleaders in the Bitch Clique. It was bad enough that she'd shunned him, but at one point, she called him "pizza face" in front of half the lunchroom. It was all he could do to keep from crying.

Bye bye, Josie.

Then there was that asshole, Mr. Lawrence, at the end of the block. A short, creepy dude who once hired Charlie to go door to door and hand out flyers for his painting business. Mr. Lawrence had promised Charlie $40 for the job. But after Charlie spent the entire weekend canvassing the neighborhood with the ads, Mr. Lawrence claimed someone saw him dumping a box of the flyers in a dumpster at the Quick Stop (which was bullshit). So, he refused to pay Charlie.

Sayonara, asshole.

Charlie laughed as he raced to the next block and repeated the process, growing more giddy with every empty house.

"Goodbye, assholes! Fuckers! Motherfuckers!" he shouted from the top of his lungs. It was an amazing release, even if no one was around to hear him.

For too many years, he'd had to bottle his emotions and take shit from everybody. He'd been the world's doormat for most of his life, through no fault of his own. He just happened to be a bit geekier, a bit paler, and had a few more zits than everyone else in his class. If he didn't have the zits, got tan instead of turned pink in the sun, and his hair was straight instead of a curly, blond mop, maybe people would have seen him a bit differently.

All he wanted to do was get through adolescence under the radar. But ever since middle school, it was as if he had some sort of homing signal which seemed particularly honed to attract unwanted attention. And when you stood out, the wolves licked their chops.

Growing up a momma's boy had made him soft.

He spent the first eleven years of his life practicing ways to make his mother happy. She'd been depressed since his father died, so it was his mission to bring her smile back. He'd put on puppet shows, tell her jokes, and would even go to painting classes with her on weekends. While most kids avoided their parents, Charlie was best friends with his mom.

But having no father figure in his life had made him meek and a magnet for the aggro assholes wanting to vent their frustrations and call him momma's boy, faggot, and anything else their tiny intellects could muster.

He *might* have been able to cope, if it weren't for Bob.

Charlie's mom met Bob four years back. They began dating immediately. Dating turned into an impromptu wedding. Everything was good for a few months. That's when Bob dropped the mask and let his drunken, violent colors bleed into Charlie's world. In a land of bullies, Bob was their king. And there was nothing Charlie could do. And nothing his mother *would do*.

And for that, he was glad she was gone.

Smell ya later, Mommy.

**

Charlie rode around a while longer until he circled back to Josie's. He knocked again. When nobody answered, he tried the doorknob. To his surprise, it was unlocked.

Hot damn!

He opened the door and stepped inside "Hello? Josie? Are you here?"

When nobody answered, he closed the door.

The house was cool, despite the loss of power. And it was well lit by all the large windows and open blinds. He hadn't been in Josie's house in three years, but it was as nice as ever. Her mother was in real estate, made good money, and routinely indulged in her premium tastes.

Josie's dad had left her mother a few years earlier, but the a-hole was an investment banker, so the monthly checks were fat.

Despite her family's wealth, money didn't seem to affect Josie all that much. In fact, she seemed embarrassed by her mother's extravagance, which was probably the thing Charlie liked most about her, other than how she was cuter than an anime character. She didn't act like the other rich kids in the school, and had never treated him like the poor kid he was.

Well, at least until she started hanging out with the Bitch Clique.

Charlie trudged up the stairs to Josie's room, and opened the door.

She had redecorated since he'd last seen it. She used to be obsessed with stuffed penguins, which once lined her shelves, closet, and even her bed. Now, her room was more adult with pinks, blues, and the sort of furniture his mom circled in the catalogue but never bought. No childish stuff anywhere, save for one lone penguin standing guard at the foot of her unmade bed. His name was Percy, Josie had once told Charlie. That was something else he'd liked about her. She wasn't afraid to be goofy, one of her most endearing qualities, actually.

Charlie sat by the headboard and picked up her pillow. He lifted it to his nose and took a deep breath. It was soft, fluffy, and smelled just as he remembered her.

He closed his eyes and sent his mind to a time when they were sitting on the floor in the room. They were both 12, and she'd asked Charlie to give her a neck massage. It wasn't sexual of course, he'd barely even thought about sex at that age. And she wasn't *that* kind of girl. But sitting behind her, with her long hair spilled in his face and his hands on her shoulders, along with a glimpse down her shirt, gave him a raging erection.

When she lifted her shirt, and asked him to rub her back, he was painfully erect. Then, to his utter horror, he ejaculated in his pants, and had to make an excuse to rush home.

So, technically, Josie was his first, and only sexual experience *with another person*, even if she never knew.

Thinking about Josie as he sat on her bed, he was hard again.

He began to look around her room and found a photo album she'd made. He thumbed through the book and saw pictures of her, taken recently at the beach. Her lips were full, her skin the color of honey, and her breasts practically falling out of the pink bikini. He was rock hard.

He went to her dresser and thumbed through her drawers, investigating her underwear, surprised to find such lacy numbers. He wondered if her mother knew what Josie was wearing under her skirts. In the mirror, he caught a glimpse of the expandable hamper in the corner, pink, of course.

Charlie retrieved a pair of pink, silky panties from the top and smelled them. The faint scent of piss and perfume made him wince, then smile. He closed his eyes, imagining the prettiest of her pink that he'd never see, then went to her bed, dropped his pants, wrapped her underwear around his staff and started stroking.

He lasted three seconds longer than he had when he'd given her a back massage.

Charlie caught a glimpse of himself in the mirror, denim snaked around his ankles and wiping himself with her underwear. Shame flushed his face. He threw the panties into the hamper and yanked up his pants, then glared at himself in the mirror, angry at his lack of self-control. Josie was right to shun him — maybe some part of her had sensed his perverted thoughts. Maybe she'd only become a bitch to him because he was such a creepy geek.

The thought depressed him, and he went downstairs to her fridge. Rich people always had good food.

He grabbed a piece of birthday cake. It was half gone, but enough remained for Charlie to imagine the *Happy Birthday, Mom!* scrawled across the top. It had a chocolate ganache frosting, at least he thought that's what it was called, and it tasted better than delicious. Maybe even the best cake he'd ever had. He was about to grab a glass of milk, when he thought better. Though the contents of the fridge were still cold, the milk (even though it was soy milk, whatever the hell that was) might've already started to spoil. The last thing he wanted to do was get sick, especially if no doctors were left in the town, or hell, maybe the world!

Instead, he found himself eyeing a four pack of red wine coolers.

He'd never drank alcohol before. As a child, he'd never had the urge. And Bob was a living poster for why NOT to drink. But he knew a lot of the kids in school *did* drink. Mostly the dumb jocks, cheerleaders, and the "Fiesta Crowd," as they were called. Charlie considered them all about as smart as a hot dog and didn't want to be anything like them, even if that meant being a pizza-faced geek, but they *did seem* to enjoy their lives. His life, on the other hand, was a constant broadcast of misery.

It didn't take long to do the math. Charlie grabbed the four pack, locked the front door (just in case), and headed back to Josie's room.

He decided there were worse places to hang out at the end of the world. He sure as hell wasn't going to go back home to *his* shitty, little house.

**

Three bottles in, Charlie wondered what all the fuss was about. He didn't feel all that different. If anything, he felt worse. His head was hurting, and he was feeling sad.

He decided to take a nap. He slid off his jeans and shoes and laid down in Josie's bed, nestling his head into the cool, perfumed pillow.

Josie was so beautiful. Why did she have to be such a bitch?

Charlie began to think about where the world had gone. Or rather, where all the people had gone. Whether this was a localized thing or if maybe people were missing in India, too. He'd thought about it earlier, of course, when he realized something was wrong. But now, a bit tipsy, he found himself sinking deeper into the thought.

He decided that though he hated most of the world, or at least the people he'd met, he didn't want to see *everybody* gone. He'd be awfully lonely. In fact, he was lonely now. Hell, he'd even be happy to see Josie, even if she were mean to him.

Charlie cried himself to sleep. Fortunately, he faded fast.

**

A loud knocking downstairs woke Charlie from his sleep.

"Charlie? Are you in there?!" a man's voice.

What the fuck?

Charlie leaped from the bed, nervous, looking around until he found his jeans and shoes.

Oh shit, oh shit, oh shit.

He was busted. This had all been a dream; he sleepwalked and broke into Josie's house. The police were outside!

His heart raced as someone shouted his name again. The voice was deep, angry, and familiar. He ducked low on his way to the curtains, then slid them aside just an inch to peek at who was outside. It was the devil himself — Bob.

* * * *

CHAPTER 4
EDWARD KEENAN

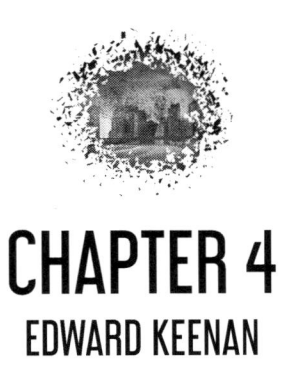

Saturday
Oct. 15, 2011
2:18 a.m.

The first thing Edward Keenan felt was rain, cold and splashing his face, snapping him from the darkness and into the bright light beaming through a thick canopy of trees.

The next thing he felt was pain — everywhere, as if his entire body had been thrown from a building and slammed against every awning on the way down and then picked up again and thrown off the building once more to hit the awnings he missed the first go-round. A high-pitched whistle pierced his throbbing eardrums. He reached up to cover his ears, before realizing his wrists were still bound together by plasticuffs.

Ed stood clumsily, pain shooting through his legs, back, and arms, then glanced around. A faint, flickering glow broke through the tree line. He made his way forward tentatively, stumbling several times, but managing to stay upright.

As he got closer to the glow, he could hear the crackle of fire. Could smell the fuel. And there, as he pressed into the clearing, he saw the mangled, fiery wreckage of Flight 519.

Ed raced forward, searching for any sign of survivors. The plane was split in half, swallowed by billowing smoke and a quick-spreading curtain of flame.

Suitcases, clothing, papers, chunks of the plane, and other debris littered the field, with some of the smaller scraps sailing low in the sky. From what he could see of the cabin, nobody survived other than himself. Yet, there weren't any bodies. He looked back into the woods, wondering if perhaps all the passengers had been ejected from their seats as he had. Perhaps some, but not all of them.

Where the hell is everyone?

The last thing he remembered was his escort, Agent Grant, telling him to shut the fuck up. They'd be in Washington soon enough. Ed decided to take a nap, but didn't think he'd actually fall asleep. He must have. Next thing he knew, he was on the ground.

He was torn — go back into the woods and search for survivors, or run as far and fast as he fucking could. Last thing he wanted was to run into Grant — assuming Grant was alive.

He took a chance. "Hello?!" he called.

As he stood at the edge of the woods, another high-pitched sound sailed over the drone in his ears, sounding as if the sky was ripping to shreds above him. He instinctively ducked, glancing up as another airplane shot by maybe 10 stories from the forest floor, on a sharp dive, soaring past the tree line before disappearing into a deafening explosion just out of sight.

Christ on a cross. What's happening?

Ed raced toward the crashed plane as fast as he could, pain shooting through his legs. He stumbled into the woods, but stopped short when he reached a partition of flames where a large, unidentifiable chunk of the plane had set the surrounding trees on fire.

There's no way anyone survived that.

He retreated, away from both crash sites, following a winding path that led uphill, where he spotted power poles and lines leading toward civilization, he hoped.

"Happy 44th birthday," he said to himself as he slipped into the black of night.

**

Despite being in top physical shape, Ed was exhausted by the time he reached the first row of homes. Falling out of the sky will do that to you.

Two-story, faux New England architecture lined either side of the street, barely illuminated by the half-concealed moon. Was one of those new gated communities in the suburbs, designed to look nice, but they were usually shit quality with tiny lots. As he stepped onto the first street, he realized not a single light was on. Not a streetlight, nor a light in any of the windows of the 20 or so homes on the street.

A blackout?

Ed rolled his neck, sighed, and headed toward the closest house, a neatly manicured, two-story home with a large, double door and windows on either side. Judging from the moon's position, he figured it was around 3 a.m. Not a great time to be knocking on doors, especially when you're bloody and in handcuffs. But options were scarce — he had to find a phone and contact Jade. No doubt news of the crashed plane would've already reached her.

Perhaps, though, it was best that he not contact her. *Maybe she's better off this way, thinking I'm dead.*

The more he thought about it, the more it made sense. He should just disappear. It was what he did best. He had a safe house in Florida that *nobody* knew about. He'd just fall off the radar. Again. And this time he knew better than to trust the agents he used to work with. Maybe the plane crash was the best thing that could have happened. Nobody would be looking for him. Not hard, anyway. This was his chance at a fresh start.

Ed would live like a ghost. No relationships, no friends — just live out his life until someone found him or he died of old age. As much as he'd love to hear his daughter's voice one more time, to let her know he was alive, he knew he'd lose what might be a golden opportunity to finally make things right. She was a big girl; she'd get over his "death."

But he still needed to get to a phone to contact Xavier, the only person left (other than his daughter) he could truly trust. Xavier would help him get out of town.

He knocked on the first door, lightly at first. No response. Raindrops grew larger and started to fall faster, but he was mostly sheltered under the gable roof. He knocked again, louder, watching through the window into the dark house for any sign of movement or light.

Nothing.

He knocked a third time, this time with authority, like the law.

Still nothing.

Ed glanced around at the house across the street to see if he'd attracted any attention. All the windows were dark, showing no movement.

On the ground, Ed spotted a garden with large, decorative rocks. He grabbed one, gripped it tightly on the end, and tapped it hard against the window to the right of the doorknob. The glass crashed loudly, and Ed glanced around to see if anyone had taken notice.

Nothing, still.

Crackerjack gated community security, hard at work.

Ed smashed a large swath of glass away; he'd need plenty of room to reach inside the doorway with his hands bound. He swept the last shards of glass from the frame until he had room to safely reach in and twist the locks. He opened the door and rushed inside, closing the door behind him.

"Hello?" he called out, wishing he'd thought to bring the rock. "This is Officer Grant. Anybody here?"

Nothing.

He knew, from years of experience, that he was alone in the house. Houses harbored a specific brand of quiet when empty. A still you could sense immediately. This house wasn't only silent, it was dead. No electricity meant no humming fans, electronics, air conditioning, or any other heartbeats of the average home. Sounds you didn't even notice until their voices were taken away.

Ed made his way toward the kitchen, scanning outlets for any sign of plug-in lights. Finding nothing, he rifled through drawers until he found a flashlight heavy with batteries. To his relief, they weren't dead, and the light was bright. He waved the spotlight around the kitchen, finding the phone. A fucking cordless, meaning it wouldn't work with the power out.

He tried it anyway, just in case.

Nothing.

Fuck, doesn't anyone use regular phones anymore?

He clicked the light off, thinking about his next step, then headed back upstairs, light on. Two doors were on either side of the hall, and a large, double door was at the end, which he assumed would take him to the master bedroom.

The first two rooms weren't bedrooms at all — one was a converted office. The second was a monument to clutter, tons of boxes leaving little room to walk. Finally, he reached the double doors, drew a deep breath, and pushed one of the doors open, training his light on the king-sized bed.

Unmade, nobody in it.

He figured whoever lived here was out of town, maybe on vacation. But something reflected back as he swept his light over the nightstand — a glass of ice water. As he moved closer, he saw beads of sweat, a small pool of water around the glass, and the last remnants of ice floating.

His heart stopped as he spun the light around toward the bathroom door, which was shut.

Had they heard him and ducked inside?

Ed squinted his eyes, searching for any signs of movement. He was too old for this shit. And not at all ready to die at the hands of some yuppie with a Beretta playing *Die Hard*.

He considered turning around and leaving, but something rooted him in place.

The house was empty. He could *feel it*. And he was never wrong about these things. Yeah, the loss of power might have been screwing with his instincts, but he didn't think that was the case. Whoever was here was gone.

He clicked off the light and began to creep toward the closed bathroom door. A closet was to his left, but it was open, and he could see it was empty. If anyone *was* with him, they were likely in the bathroom.

He was nearly five steps away when he rolled his neck again, then spoke.

"Hello? This is officer Grant. We're investigating a break-in at your neighbor's house and we saw your front door was wide open. You okay?"

Nothing.

He turned on his light again.

"I'm coming into the bathroom now. My partner is in the hallway, checking out your other rooms. Do NOT shoot me. I repeat, do NOT shoot."

He twisted the knob, pushed open the door, and thrust his light into the bathroom.

Nothing.

He caught his reflection in the mirror: dirty, banged up, bloody, and a huge knot sticking out from his closely-cropped dome. He laughed grimly at the reflection, then checked the closet for clean clothes. He would be stuck with his dark trousers, but he grabbed a black tee from the closet, which he'd put on as soon as he got the cuffs off. The shirt looked like it would be tight on his muscular build, and a bit short, but it would have to do.

Ed returned to the bed and felt the sheets. They weren't warm — whoever had been sleeping in them had been gone at least a few minutes before he'd entered the house. He grabbed the glass, picked it up, cool to the touch. He took a long drink, the water soaking his dry throat. He chewed the remnants of ice, placed the glass down, and opened both nightstands, hoping to find a gun. No luck.

Ed moved from room to room, searching the house for anybody. At last, he reached the door leading to the two-car garage. If anyone was here, this was the last place they could be hiding, unless they sneaked into an attic or something. He did the police routine another time, with the same lack of response, then opened the door. Clutter filled one side of the garage, though more neatly arranged, and all of it boxed. The other half of the garage housed an SUV.

He flashed his light to make sure the vehicle was empty, then doubled back to the kitchen, found a pegboard with keys and an automatic car lock, alarm attached. He glanced at the fridge, where a photo in a magnetic frame showed a middle-aged guy, a middle-aged woman, and a 20-year-old girl wearing an Ohio State sweater. He pocketed the keys, headed back to the garage and was relieved to see a workbench on the far wall with a large, red Craftsmen toolbox beside it.

Thank God some people still do shit themselves.

He found a hacksaw, fastened the blade on a C-clamp, then proceeded to saw his restraints away. Once he had the middle part cut, he found some bolt cutters, sheared the bracelets the rest of the way, and massaged the red from his wrists. He slipped on the tee shirt, which fit him better than he thought it would, and balled up the shirt he'd been wearing and tossed it in the SUV.

Ed went to the fridge. Stuff was still cold. He inhaled a Coke, then grabbed a box of cookies from the pantry and threw them on the passenger seat of the SUV as he climbed in the driver's side. He turned on the radio to a static assault and hit the scan button, watching the digital display race through the FM spectrum without slowing.

All the stations are down?

Something was very wrong.

Ed hit the garage door opener before remembering it ran on electricity. He hopped out of the SUV and flashed the light at the ceiling, finding the motor for the garage door opener. A red cord dangled from the center. He yanked it, disengaging the opener, opened the door manually, got back in the SUV, and backed out of the driveway.

He figured he had maybe two hours until the state was crawling with feds.

* * * *

CHAPTER 5
LUCA HARDING

Saturday
Oct. 15, 2011
Morning
Las Orillas, California

Luca's skin was burning. He opened his eyes and put an end to the dream where Mommy was making eggs on his arms.

But he was still too hot. The sun outside was brighter than it was supposed to be. It looked like the last day of school, but it was only a week before Halloween. Light poured through the window like Daddy was hosing it down with sunlight like he did with water sometimes when he washed the car.

Luca never slept past 6, but it definitely felt later than that. Dad got up at 5:30, even when he wasn't working. Luca had been no more than a half hour behind him for all but one of his eight years.

I don't like the feeling in my arms. Tingly bad and burny. I want to scratch them, but maybe it's like the bites that Mommy says I shouldn't scratch because it always makes it worse. The itchy hot burny will probably go away if I ignore it.

His *Cars* alarm clock wasn't working, and the screen on the computer was black. The house sounded like when Mommy went across the street to talk to Mrs. Susan, only quieter. Luca went to the closet and peeled off his Lego pajamas, replaced them with jeans and his favorite *Star Wars* T-shirt, then went to the window, and stared at the rainbow.

It was brighter than usual. Most rainbows looked like they were already erasing. But this rainbow looked like someone just plugged it in.

The sun was past the start of the rainbow, so it was maybe as late as 8. Mom was gone, he could tell. But he couldn't hear his dad either, even though it was his day off. Anna should be up, but he couldn't hear her either. And he could *always* hear his sister.

Luca left the bedroom and looked around the house, even though he knew he'd find no one. "Mom, Dad, Anna?" Luca waited for an answer, counting to 10 as he always did when Mom said to wait.

After 10 seconds of less than nothing, Luca opened the door to a blanket of heat. The air felt like hot sand and made his hot burny feel worse. Something moved at the corner of his eyes. He turned to see his cat, Lucky, leap to the front porch, where it settled a stare on Luca and licked its paws. The cat looked somehow different than it did the day before. Luca would swear. But he didn't know how.

Inside out. Yeah, the cat feels sorta inside out. It looks normal, but feels like someone made all its thoughts go on the outside.

Luca crossed the street to Mrs. Susan's house, put his nose to the window, and saw exactly what he expected. Since Mom didn't like him on that side of the street unless he was visiting Mrs. Susan, he went back home.

Instead of going back in the house, Luca decided to walk to the mailbox under the stop sign, all the way at the corner. That's where Mr. Hassell lived. Mr. Hassell probably didn't know everything about the entire world, but he knew a lot of things about people on Oregon Avenue. That's probably why he was always talking about it.

Mr. Hassell's empty house was the farthest Luca had ever walked alone. Mr. Hassel wasn't on his porch like usual, so he rounded the corner and kept going, all the way around the block. When he got back to his own number at 314 Oregon, he sat on the stoop and looked at the rainbow.

I should go to Coach Michael's. Mommy and Daddy said he's safe. And he is driving close. We even walked there two times before, like that time last June. His house will be easy to find because the rainbow is pointing right at it.

The rainbow was pointing toward the coach's house, but it wasn't the big, bright one Luca saw when he first woke. This smaller rainbow was brighter, and sat just beneath its big brother, spilling sideways instead of south.

Luca went back in the house and filled his *Star Wars* backpack with two granola bars, a banana, and two bottles of Smartwater from his mom's side of the refrigerator. The house was getting warmer, a lot warmer, but it was still cooler than it was outside.

Luca started walking toward the rainbow. He made it six blocks before he felt the headache start to hammer his skull. At least he thought it was a headache. The ouchy tingle sure seemed like the stuff mommy was always talking about.

**

It was easy to keep from getting lost with the rainbow showing him where to go. Luca passed all the places where no one was anymore on the way to his coach's house. But the only things home at the corner of Appian and Monrovia were the coach's collection of vintage cars.

Luca looked in the window. The lights were on, like most of the houses for the last few blocks. A purr at his feet pulled Luca's attention to Champion, the coach's cat, rubbing itself on his ankle.

Champion felt weird just like Lucky had. Comparing the two led Luca to realize that besides Lucky and Champion, he hadn't seen a single animal since waking. Which was weird since some dog in the neighborhood was *always* barking.

All Luca wanted was someone to explain what was happening. Like his dad always did. In simple sentences that would be easy to understand. But no one was around, and after following the rainbow 17 blocks to the coach's house and not seeing anyone, Luca felt the sad spiders start to crawl inside him. His mom could usually get them to leave with tickles, or the promise of a salami sandwich. But his mom wasn't there to make him a sandwich any more than his dad was standing by with an explanation.

Luca leaned against the door, slid to his bottom, put his face in his palm, and cried. He tried rubbing the headache from his head, but the headache said no. A dog cried out from somewhere in the distance. Luca was glad to hear it.

He felt a sudden icy chill beneath his burning skin, but shrugged it off and stood.

Luca looked around the neighborhood. White spots were everywhere, but he looked past them to get a good look at the brand-new rainbow. It was telling him to listen to the trees. And though Luca was old enough to know that trees couldn't talk, they *did* seem to be whispering something or other.

Trees aren't supposed to talk, but they keep telling me to follow the wind. And the wind won't stop talking about the water. I think they like the place we go each summer, the beach in Mexico where the man makes the lobster tacos.

Mexico it was. And it made perfect sense. His parents were probably there at the small house already – that's what the rainbow said. And rainbows were too colorful to lie.

Luca didn't know how to drive, but he *did* know a car was better than walking. He would've gone back to his house, but his dad's truck was way too big and his mom's car was a stick shift she'd had since her 20s. He definitely didn't think he could drive that.

One of the cars in Coach's collection was a red Porsche that looked like a bathtub. Luca had ridden in it before. It was parked on the street, and he needed it, so Coach Michael would understand if he took it. His mom said that in emergencies, like when you're bleeding or vomiting, there were special rules. Luca wasn't bleeding or vomiting, but he was definitely having the biggest emergency of his life.

Luca looked but couldn't find any keys. They weren't in any of the cars, even though people in movies found them tucked inside the thing you use to keep the sun from getting in your eyes. Then, he tried Coach's door and was surprised to find it unlocked. He went inside and called for Coach, but nobody answered. Luca started searching for the keys.

He looked for over an hour, until his skin was burning and head pounding enough to make him stop. He was about to walk back home when he heard a meow coming from the kitchen. He went to the kitchen where Champion sat beside the cooking island, patting his paws against the wood.

Luca walked straight to the drawer above Champion's head, slid it open, and removed a small, rectangular, cobalt-blue box with three keys inside. He removed the middle key, because it was the one that worked in the small Porsche that looked like a bathtub. Luca knew it, just as he knew what was in the box as soon as the cat told him.

**

Even though they were supposed to have sticks in the middle like his mom's car, the coach's Porsche didn't. That was because it was a model car for grown-ups. And it wasn't as old as it looked. Coach said it was a replica. It had a Volkswagen engine and an auto something transmission. He said that even though it was all sizzle and no steak, he loved driving it just the same.

Luca opened the door, sat behind the wheel, turned the engine, and scooted down until his foot was on the brake. He put the car in drive and moved his foot to the gas. The Porsche lurched forward and threw Luca against the seat. He had to scurry down to hit the brake before the car rolled too far.

He tried a few versions of the same thing several times before realizing that though he was big enough to ride in the Porsche, he wasn't yet tall enough to drive it.

He returned to the house and ran upstairs to Matthew's room. Matthew had more Legos than anyone Luca knew. He pulled the largest bucket from Lego Island, the one with all the odds and ends and oversized pieces. For five minutes, he didn't think about burny skin or white spots in the sky or rainbows. For five minutes, he did nothing but stack Legos, wearing a rare smile for that morning, on a face that usually looked naked without one.

Once he had created two, neat cubes about 15 bricks high, Luca went to Matthew's closet and grabbed a pair of shoes, size 12, same as him. He used duct tape from the garage to tape the two cubes to the bottom of Matthew's shoes. He put them on and smiled.

Luca climbed into the car and drove toward the end of the smaller rainbow at a comfortable 20 mph. He was a robot, with super-cool, handmade, ninja robot feet.

**

He drove slow but exactly where the rainbow told him, winding down the hill until he hit a mostly empty Pacific Coast Highway where he made a left. Luca wove through the occasionally idle traffic as if playing a slowed down PS3 game with his daddy.

He had driven for three hours and 41 miles when he noticed the animals. At first, it was just a cat or two, then three. The math got harder as he drove, and by the third hour Luca was noticing all sorts of animals trotting along both sides of the highway.

Like animals that aren't really animals anymore.
BAM!!!

Luca was lost in thought when he smashed the back of a pitch-black truck dead on the highway. Luca hadn't seen a car for two miles, just long enough to send his attention elsewhere.

The empty hood of the bathtub crinkled like paper and threw Luca back hard against his seat and out cold on impact. The last thing he sensed as he slipped into darkness was the fire, not on his skin, but starting in the back of the car.

* * * *

CHAPTER 6
BORICIO WOLFE

Saturday
Oct. 15, 2011
1:17 a.m.
New Orleans, Louisiana

There were no explosions. No crashing concrete, crackling electricity, or menacing reverb to blanket the city. No screams. Just that hollow pause that sits in the seconds between ignition and detonation.

Except this one came and never left.

Boricio woke a second after *It* started, wide awake even though he'd been tangled in a fat thick of sleep — the kind you get after a night spent doing all the things he'd just finished doing. He wasn't sure *how* he knew the end had begun. He just knew.

His feet hit the floor and felt colder than they should have. That didn't bother him. At least not like the air. Stale. Though he could still smell the restaurant below, there were no sounds. And there were *always* fucking sounds.

This is some beer-battered bullshit.

Boricio looked around the loft — nothing out of place, at least not that he could put his finger on. Just the smell that didn't smell right and the crazy feeling of empty that seemed to swallow the entire apartment like the fat lips on a French Quarter whore.

And the crazy-as-a-cat on crack dream.

Boricio looked outside. Sky wasn't right.

He opened the window, and *yup*, same beer-battered bullshit outside, but stronger. He didn't bother to shut the window, heading outside and grabbing a beer from the fridge on the way out instead. The fridge was still cold, though it'd gone as dark as the always-blinking alarm. Boricio stepped into the hallway and grabbed the time from the beat-to-shit clock with the three missing Romans — 2:17 am.

Fuck that.

Boricio hit the bottom stair and opened the door. He could smell the beer-battered bullshit before it was halfway open. *Yup*, the restaurant was dead. The restaurant hadn't been empty once in the four months he lived upstairs, but Boricio could see through the glass: no cooks, no customers, no servers. He walked outside into the night.

And on the corner, Lucy was gone, which was equally weird. Lucy was never gone. Fucking mystery when she slept; stood on the corner day in, day out, except if cops were on the beat or she was filling the mayonnaise jar. Even then, she was only gone for five to nine minutes at a time. Lucy had a way of taking guys into the room and giving them more than they expected in less than a quarter of the time.

Like his apartment, the motel across the street was dark. But the humming light from the restaurant's sign (which was lit) illuminated the split crack of Room #112. Boricio crossed the street, then opened the door the rest of the way to a whole mess of *what-the-fuck?*

The room was neat. Ready for the next five to nine minutes neat anyway. And the air was so cold, it wasn't like Lucy had stepped out so much as she'd never even been there. Boricio had smelled that room most days ending in Y for four months straight, and it had never smelled like that.

The motel room was dead. Just like the alley. And the stairwell. And his fucking apartment. And just like that, the restaurant sign went dark, the humming ceased, leaving everything quiet. Like no animals or insects quiet. The kinda quiet you sometimes got right before a hurricane, but even quieter.

A flirt's worth of fear fluttered through Boricio's body. It almost made him smile; it'd been so long since he'd felt it, but his beading temple kept the grimace fixed. Boricio stepped back into the alley, drawing a deep breath and inhaling a perfumed gust from the Mississippi.

The river.

Fuck yeah, that's where he'd go. Something had happened, and he'd missed it. People were evacuating and would have to meet in one place. The river made sense. Besides, if it really was the end of the world, the Mississippi would look him in the eye and tell him the truth.

Boricio crossed the street, hopped in his 10-year-old, 2-ton Ford, then gunned the engine, and tore into the street with a roar thundering over dead earth. He was only a half mile from the river but didn't even make it a block before braking hard enough to burn his nostrils with the scent of burned rubber.

FUCK.

Maybe the world had been shingled in shit and maybe it hadn't, but a sudden memory from his previous night's adventure filled Boricio's brain with a planet and a half's worth of *fuck this!*

The world had disappeared. The thought of *her* disappearing, despite the neat slit that ran beneath her chin from ear to ear, was about as much as Boricio could take. He flipped the pickup in a U and sent it flying toward the Village de L'Est where that little bitch Brianna had kept her tidy apartment, at least until he'd made her breathing impossible.

He'd see if the body was still there. If so, he'd deal with it.

Him, too.

**

Boricio coated the back of his hand with brow sweat and pushed the pickup harder. Less than a mile to go.

Fucking bitch. I wanted to wait until Christmas. She was my present. And if it wasn't for that ancient fuck, or the punk ass with the pink glasses, I would've. Still, she'd been yummier'n a Hurricane and a heap of hot wings. Didn't even scream. Not once. Just wheezed at the end a little, like a dying vacuum cleaner.

Boricio broke into a cracked laugh at the memory.

Punk ass with the sunglasses, though, he cried like a stuck pig. Would've died fast no matter, but the squealing made it easy. She was worth savoring every second. Too bad about the rush. Happy fucking Halloween.

Now I need something new for Christmas.

Boricio rounded the corner at Dauphine and killed the engine at the second curb so he could walk the rest of the way. Like always. *Just in case.* From a block back, he knew everything he needed to, but kept on going anyway. The old man, same fucker who had been sitting on the stoop since early September when Boricio first started scoping the place, was gone. He'd been half the reason Boricio had to hurry his Christmas, and now he wasn't even around to celebrate the end of the world.

The door to the apartment was unlocked just as he left it. He could almost smell her as he crossed the apartment toward the bathroom where his first surprise was waiting. Boricio had left precisely one body in the bathtub with all its limbs in place. He'd even left the head on since an extra body was all the cops needed to open-and-shut his ritual into an easy-to-swallow murder-suicide.

The punk-ass dude had bled out, coating the tub in a thick mottle of red, but his body was gone and the gallons of blood looked like they'd been replaced with fresh water.

The fuck is this?

And *she* was missing, too.

The bed was rumpled from where she'd been taking her final nap, but the buckets of blood that were beneath her when Boricio closed the door three hours earlier, now looked suspiciously like bleach stains. Same for the drops leading from bed to bathroom. The white against the brown of the hard wood was clear, even with only one light working.

Someone turned the world inside-fucking-out ...

Boricio tore through the apartment, trying to pull sense from the impossible. He wasn't worried about getting caught at all. It hadn't happened in 20 years and sure as shit wasn't about to happen an hour into the Apocalypse, but he wasn't a guy to flip a bitch on Answer Road.

After 15 minutes, Boricio couldn't find a single thing, except for the panty drawer he'd rifled through 73 times before.

Those aren't her panties. Ain't a single pair in that drawer was ever worn.

Thing about beer-battered bullshit is it doesn't taste different until you spit it out, so Boricio threw a final scowl around the room, then headed for the door, pausing at the threshold. He could swear he felt faster, stronger. And not just like he usually did after a good kill and a great night's sleep.

Like a few lines of coke gone permanent. Must be the adrenaline. Feels good. Could get used to this shit in a hurry.

Boricio bounded down the stairs and kicked the door with a giggle. Maybe it was the end of the world, and maybe that shit wasn't too bad. Humanity was mostly made of assholes anyway, and that was scientific fucking fact.

Boricio was practically skipping across the street, but broke into a full run when he saw the police cruiser sitting in the ghost lot of a usually hopping Circle K.

The meek don't inherit shit. Earth belongs to the wolves.

* * * *

CHAPTER 7
EDWARD KEENAN

Darkness bathed every block.

Not a single light or car on the street. Nor a single person in sight.

The shit was downright spooky. He followed the streets until they led him out of the neighborhood and into town, wherever the hell he was. He didn't think to look at an address while in the house. That was the second mistake he'd made this evening. He'd have to stay sharp if he planned to get back home. He was about to lean over, open the glove compartment, and dig out whatever paperwork was in there, when he saw the glow of lights from a gas station's lit canopy ahead.

Excited, he floored the gas, and raced to the station. A red Honda was parked at the pump, and a blue Mazda was parked in a space at the back of the store.

The gas station was in the lot of a small shopping plaza, which had gone completely dark. As he got closer to the gas station, he looked inside the store. It was lit, but dimly. Backup lighting, no doubt.

Ed parked behind the Honda, hopped out of the SUV, and went inside the store, which was haunted by the same vacant feeling of the oddly abandoned house.

"Hello?" No cashier at the register; no one in the store. He walked towards the walk-in cooler, which was muted from its usual hum, and peered inside the window. Nobody in there, either.

He headed to the back of the store, checked the bathrooms and a back storage room doubling as an office. He saw a closed-circuit TV, its broadcast dark. He was about to leave the back room when he spotted something on the desk — a phone! And not one of those wireless fuckers, but a landline.

His heart leaped in his chest. He raised the receiver to his ear, heart beating faster and excited fingers ready to dance the 11 digits on their way to Xavier.

Except he heard no dial tone.

He clicked the disconnect a few times, nothing in return. The line was as dead as the lights. It didn't make sense. Even during a total power outage, phone lines had enough power to make calls. Perhaps, he considered, the phone company's power was out?

Nope, they'd have backup generators up the ass and back. Something is definitely sideways.

The voice in his head told him to get the hell out of the store and back on the road. Because at this hour only stoners with the munchies and cops frequented gas stations. He needed to find a highway and head to Florida, A-fucking-SAP. First, though, he had to figure out where he was. A newspaper rack at the front counter spilled the beans – he was in Ohio. Made sense given the girl's sweater in the photo.

He grabbed a 5-pound spiral book that included a map of the United States. He glanced around the station, then outside again. Still no signs of another soul. He went behind the counter and approached the register. It ran on power, and was off, but when he twisted a key in the bottom, the drawer sprang open. Inside the drawer he found four stacks of bills, from 20s to singles. He grabbed them all, shoved them in his pocket, figured there was about $250 total. He was about to leave, when he spotted a black backpack nudged in the corner, probably belonging to the missing cashier. He glanced around again, then retrieved the bag. There it was — a Smith and Wesson 9mm. Automatic in a holster.

He was surprised to find such a decent gun just laying out in the open.

Ed grabbed the backpack, a few snacks and drinks for the road, and got back in the SUV. He was about to reverse, when he realized the Honda was gone.

What the fuck? It must've left while I was in the back of the store.

He spun around, scanning the parking lot and the street. No sign of the car. He glanced back to the parking lot behind the station. The blue car was still there, seemingly empty. He didn't know what was happening, but knew enough to know Ohio was creeping him the fuck out. He had to bail. Now.

He put the truck in drive and hit the gas.

**

Ed had driven nearly three miles, and the entire town was pitch-black, save for the occasional emergency lights at gas stations. Nobody was on the streets, in car, or on foot. He found the freeway ramp that would take him out of state, and merged in a hurry. The lights along the highway were dim, but not out, also running on backup power, he figured.

How big is this blackout? Something's not right.

His head was still pounding, and his thoughts still jumbled from the crash. Once he got some sleep he'd be able to think more clearly, suss out what the hell was happening. Falling planes, blackouts, missing people — this wasn't all coincidence. Something bigger was at play. And while he could see someone downing the plane to free him — he still had some fans at the agency and killing a bunch of innocent people was nothing to them — a second plane and the blackouts made no sense.

Something big is happening.

Maybe he *would* call Jade — if he could find a working phone.

Would be nice to know she's okay.

He'd been driving nearly 10 minutes and had yet to see another driver, but was careful to keep under the speed limit, anyway. He let the radio continue its scan, waiting for something other than static.

White lines raced by as the sound of rain splattered against the thumping of his windshield wipers. The quiet drone threatened to send him into sleep. His eyes were heavy, and he wanted nothing more than to pull over and grab a quick nap. But he couldn't stop. He had to press the advantage of his newfound freedom before they came looking for him.

His eyes grew heavier as he strained to see through the thickening rain, which was now a blinding, white squall in front of him. He had to slow the truck to ensure he didn't run off the road. His eyes were dry, and he wanted to close them, but had to concentrate on the rain to see anything in this mess.

That's when he heard it.

"Sssaaiirr," a voice echoed in some faraway place over the radio waves.

Ed's eyes shot wide open, and he sat upright, attention on the radio's face as the numbers escalated from the 101s to the 105s, and then the voice again.

" ... again ... "

There! The word was clear as day. The digital channel locked on a station. 88.8 FM, a spot on the dial reserved for public airwaves, religious stations, and talk radio. Ed hit the button to stop the scan, waiting for another sound. Still static, but busy static, something just out of range, trying to come through.

His eyes were glued to the radio as if he'd *see* whoever it was he was waiting to hear. So, he didn't see the car until it was nearly too late.

On the side of the highway, the soft, red glow of taillights broke through the white wall of rain.

"Fuck!" Ed screamed, yanking on the steering wheel sharply, sending the SUV sliding.

Ed rotated the wheel in the direction of the spin, praying the SUV wouldn't roll. The truck spun, faster out of control, as it crossed into the opposite lanes. Ed's eyes were wide, adrenaline shooting through every cell, as he somehow turned through the skid and managed to come to a full stop.

His body shaking, he let out a deep breath he didn't even know he'd been holding, and glanced ahead, his car now facing the original direction. Twenty yards ahead, a light-colored Buick sat on the side of the road, its front passenger side crushed against the side rail. Its front driver light and taillights were on, but the cabin was dark.

Ed leaned forward, trying to see into the car.

Is there someone in there?

He thought he saw movement, but couldn't be certain.

Every instinct told him to get the hell out of there, but something else tugged at his brain, pushing him forward.

He grabbed the gun from the backpack and checked the clip.

He drove toward the car, slowly, with high beams on. Nobody was in the driver or passenger seats.

He saw movement again. This time for certain. Someone was in the backseat, just out of view. He pulled the SUV in front of the car, aiming the lights inside, and stepped from the truck, into the rain, gun in hand.

He approached the car carefully, eyes on the backseat and its just-out-of-sight inhabitant. He brushed the hard-falling rain from his eyes, and inched closer to the car until he saw a shape in the back seat. He trained the gun on the vehicle as he approached the back driver's side door and peered inside. As he moved closer, his eyes widened.

Sitting in the backseat, with her hands over her pregnant stomach was a ghost-white girl, no more than 16.

* * * *

CHAPTER 8
LUCA HARDING

Luca woke alone, sore, and somewhere with a lot of confusing. Trees surrounded him, but he could still hear waves from the Pacific. The rainbow was gone. His Lego shoes had been taken off, his other shoes sat beside him. A dog, a husky, was panting beside him.

Luca grabbed his shoes and started to put them on. His head was still pounding, though less than before. His arms were painted in purple, and a long gash ran along most of his right leg. It was bigger than the cut on his left ankle, though the cut on his ankle hurt a lot, lot more.

It was painful to stand, so Luca stayed sitting, rubbing his wounds. The heat in his body was easing the pain. So was the air, which had cooled down enough to feel a little like a kiss.

The Husky didn't seem weird like the other animals he'd seen; it was pretty normal. The dog whimpered and nudged his nose at the bottle of water beside him. It was warm, but Luca drank it all in a few furious swallows.

"Did you help me?" he asked, half expecting an answer. The husky nudged him and Luca looked up. The rainbow was back, still pointing south, slightly brighter.

Luca's leg throbbed. "What am I supposed to do now?" He looked at the husky. "No way I'm driving."

"I don't like driving without the controller. Or Daddy. It's pretty sort of scary. Especially because I can't look around me like I can when we're going somewhere as a family. But we can't go anywhere as a family now because I don't know where anyone is and the phones don't want the numbers to work."

The husky trotted to the edge of the clearing and stuck his nose at something Luca couldn't see. Luca slowly followed. In 10 steps the dirt ended in concrete. On the other side of the yellow paint sat a rundown shack that looked like it sold milkshakes. And they were probably great milkshakes, because a lot of bikes were in the bike rack.

Luca looked both ways and crossed the street. He felt a bristle on the other side. He turned back and looked toward the trees, but saw none of the eyes he felt peering from behind them.

They're there. But I don't know how many because the math is hard when it gets to a lot.

Luca looked another moment, then turned and headed for the employee entrance of the ice cream shack. It was locked, but the window wasn't. Inside, he looked for the white, plastic box with the big, red cross, like the one in Mrs. Engler's office.

He found it in a cabinet a lot like Mrs. Engler's, the first place he tried. It looked mostly the same, though it didn't have the peeling Transformers sticker that Johnny Bryson put on the back when Mrs. Engler wasn't looking.

Luca split the square into a rectangle, then made a pile of the stuff people used when ambulance men were saving people in the movies. He finished cleaning his wounds and suddenly felt hungry. A little at first, but then the hungry grew really, really big. It grew into the kind of hungry his dad called "alligator hungry."

He made a bowl of ice cream and a big sandwich. He didn't eat enough ice cream to get sick later, like he had at Billy's birthday when he ate so many scoops he threw up in the pool. He ate just enough to know his mom would be happy if she was sitting right beside him. After all, maybe she was.

Maybe everyone else is here, and I'm the one who's not?

He removed the one bike without a lock, the red one with a white stripe, then swung on the seat and looked into the sky. Sure enough, the rainbow was back. Luca started to pedal, struggling through the pain, leaving the eyes behind him.

**

Luca stayed on the bike, but the next several hours were mean.

His leg looked like it had a layer of Rice Krispies coated in blood. His head felt like when he hung upside down on the monkey bars and fell, and his tummy was like the time Greg Moore punched him in the stomach because he had accidentally dropped and cracked his Super Soaker. Except worse.

He stopped four times, seven counting the places that were locked. The entire time he still hadn't seen a single person. Probably about 500 cars, though that stuff was hard to count. All the empty made it easy to feel the something following behind him. A lot more animals were here than at the ice cream shack, maybe times two. But Luca didn't mind. They felt like less alone. And besides, they probably knew a lot of stuff he didn't. Like where his mom and dad might be. If the rainbow knew, maybe they did, too.

It was only after his fifth stop when Luca finally realized he had a hard time seeing the rainbow when he was thirsty. The rainbow had started to flicker alongside a roll in his belly when he saw another one of the shacks that looked busy like it was open but was empty like it was closed.

A few yards from the front of the shack, Luca's bike hit a sharp rock jutting from the dirt. The bike's front tire came to a dead stop while the rear wheel lifted from the back. Luca's short stint as Superman lasted only a second.

He hurt. A lot. A million galaxies worse than when Greg Moore had punched him. He wanted to close his eyes but couldn't. The big rainbow was back, leapfrogging over the little one.

I'm supposed to go. I'm supposed to go now.

Luca stood. But only for a moment. His knees wobbled, then quit. His cheek met the thin side of a rock on its way to the dirt, and a little river of blood ran toward the highway.

**

Luca woke in another small clearing. He felt different. Looked different, too. His mottled arms had returned to their normal olive color and his legs were free of their bloody Rice Krispie layer. His face, which he remembered falling on, didn't hurt either.

The Husky was there, looking at Luca with large, sad eyes that looked even larger and sadder beneath the bright light of the full moon. In front of Luca sat a small pile of broken twigs and brittle leaves, gathered like the mini-mountains Dad made for the family campfires, just smaller.

And water was there. A lot of it. All the bottles were warm, but at least 20 were sitting in a big pile of plastic just a few feet away.

Luca looked at the sky. The rainbow was gone.

"It's coming back," the dog said, though its mouth didn't move.

Luca shivered. That was un-possible. Dogs didn't think loud enough to hear.

"Sometimes, we do."

This doesn't feel like my pretending reading mind imagination. This is different. Like someone scratched me on my thoughts.

Luca didn't like his thoughts being scratched. At least not without being asked first. Mom and Dad wouldn't like it. So he refused out-loud dialogue with the dog, but was willing to follow the husky as it trotted back toward the highway. He grabbed two bottles of water and opened one. Warm, but refreshing.

Luca followed, hearing the rustling of more padded feet slapping the dirt behind him.

He walked for hours, feeling stronger the entire time. He was still warm, warmer than he should be, but a whole lot cooler than he'd been a few hours before. Before he fell down, before he woke to a dog that could talk to his thoughts. Before he woke to a ready-to-go campfire.

Luca didn't get thirsty again. Every time he felt his mouth start to dry, the husky would appear with another bottle of water.

"I think I'm going to have to name you," Luca finally said, drinking water and rubbing the husky on the snout. "How do you like the name Dog Vader?"

The dog whimpered. "It's good for now."

Luca stroked the Husky's fur.

He'd been walking for hours and though he wasn't really tired it was probably past middlenight or even next day. So, Luca stopped, lay his head on a smooth rock and closed his eyes. It was only a moment before he was in the twitchy part of dreams, where his body moves a little but his brain moves a lot.

He opened his eyes and saw an Indian. The kind like in the movies. The kind you're supposed to call Native Americans. The Indian was sitting on a stump looking at Luca right where Dog Vader had been just a moment before. The man smiled.

Luca sat up. "Am I dreaming?" he asked.

"What do you think?" the Indian spoke, his mouth not moving either. His voice didn't sound like the deep-voiced Indians from the movies though. It sounded like his own voice, a bit, just like the dog's had.

"Yes," Luca nodded. His floppy hair bounced up and down. "And no."

"You are correct," the Indian smiled.

"Are you Dog Vader?"

"I am your friend, yes, but I never agreed to that name."

"Can I call you Dog Vader?"

"No." The man smiled. "But you may call me something else. What would you like to call me?"

"Kick."

"Kick?"

"Yes, like sidekick. Like Robin. From Batman and Robin."

"Okay. But what makes you think that *I'm* the sidekick?" The Indian continued to smile.

"Because you're the one following me."

"Then Kick it is," he said with a laugh.

"Where are we going?" Luca asked.

"There," Kick pointed toward the far side of the coastline.

"Are we almost there?"

"Almost."

Luca believed him. He closed his eyes again and didn't open them until the bright light and white spots came back and told him to. Of course, the rainbow agreed. Kick, if Luca wasn't crazy, was sitting beside him, awake, snout pointed at the rainbow. Luca got up and followed. So did the countless animals behind him.

Luca looked both ways, crossed the street, then ambled over a thin row of rocks separating the road from the sand. He looked at the coastline, then gasped and fell to his knees.

Cats, dogs, birds, and plenty of other animals that weren't fancy enough for the zoo were there. They were everywhere. Maybe 1,000, though Luca was sorta bad at counting when the counting stuff was spread all over the place.

Luca turned back toward the highway and followed the rainbow. An army of beasts followed.

* * * *

CHAPTER 9
BORICIO WOLFE

Streetlights had flickered the entire way from his apartment to *Her Majesty's*, but unlike his apartment and the rest of Crap Alley, currents were crackling at the Circle K. Neon bathed the lot in a cheap glow, which looked especially bright against the backdrop of black.

Boricio laughed out loud at the unlocked cop car and held his grin while looking at the shotgun sitting upright in the back seat. *Shit sure is easy at the end of the world!* He opened the trunk of the cruiser and headed inside the Circle K for a bit of light early-morning shopping.

Beer, chips, protein bars, Excedrin, porn, everything Hostess makes, a few Cup-A-Soups, and some other sundries made it into the surprisingly large trunk. Boricio slammed the trunk shut, then went back in the store to empty the cash register, *just in case*. He took the snub-nosed revolver from under the counter and tucked it into his waistband next to his .45, also *just in case*. After a swift kick to a safe that wouldn't open and a *like it fucking matters*, Boricio was sitting in the *front* of a police cruiser for the first time in his life.

View's much better from here.

The few miles to the Mississippi were graveyard quiet, with less than nothing on the radio and the same empty hanging in the air outside. Though Boricio wasn't sure what he expected to see when he hit the river, it wasn't anything close to what he actually saw. He figured there'd either be no one or everyone, but a fat river void of boats — save for what looked like three ships sitting out as far as his eyes would go — wasn't on his radar at all.

If it had been bobbing in the middle of the Mississippi by last sundown, it was gone now.

Looks like it's time to get the fuck out of Dodge.

A minute later Boricio was back behind the wheel, with the siren at full bray and the cruiser's odometer kissing red, headed back into the business district. To see so many buildings, a city that was always busy like this, dead, was a mind fuck like no other.

**

After a few miles of nothing, Boricio found himself playing I Spy with his sanity. The empty outside was bad enough, but the shit he couldn't put his finger on was a chronic case of crabs worse. People were missing, but now it seemed like shit was missing, too. And he didn't know what. He could feel things gone, but couldn't put his finger on what they were. Like memories he couldn't withdraw from his bank.

He knew billboards were missing, but wasn't sure which. Seemed like all the chain shit was still there, though. Boricio flew by a billboard for Applebee's advertising their new Stacked, Stuffed, and Topped *Entrees You Deserve!*

That right there's a swinging sack of crap, especially in New Fucking Orleans. Not like the slop makes you sick, but it's always cold, crappy, or served by some curly cunt hair pimply faced fuck who spends 40 minutes giving you the WhatTheFuck? eye. Plus, the pussy up in there is always too old or too young. Never just right. If the world is dead, at least it took Applebee's with it.

Boricio whistled as he flew by the missing church that everyone knew wasn't really a church. That one he knew was missing. The big billboard was still there, but other than that, it was just a big, empty nothing sitting on the side of the street.

Well, how about that!! Crazy, fucking shit.

Boricio kept fiddling with the radio. Nothing. Hell, he'd settle for Top 40 right about now, but the nothing on the radio and the nothing on the scanner matched the nothing in the air and all the nothing he'd been driving by.

He was about to drive back home; he'd thought of a few people's places he'd like to break into if they weren't there. Some people that had some good shit that could keep him high for months. But then, in the middle of the street was a pickup. Unlike the countless other vehicles he'd passed, this one had a passenger standing next to it. The guy was waving for help.

Yee. Fucking. Haw.

Boricio slowed to a stop and gave the siren a celebratory blare as he pulled beside the stranded motorist. The pickup was less than a year old, and the dude with the fresh haircut standing next to it was wearing clothes that still held their store-bought creases.

What kind of asshole puts on new clothes to meet the seven fucking horsemen?

Boricio lowered the window, then leaned his head out and smiled. "Morning, Sir. Need any help?"

The motorist nodded. "Thanks officer, you're the first car I've seen pass in the last two hours. Any idea what's happening?"

"Haven't a clue," Boricio stepped from the cruiser, closed the door behind him, and leaned against the black and white. "Been responding to calls all morning. Didn't even have time to get my uniform on proper." Boricio gestured at his dirty jeans and the faded indigo polo with a tear on the collar. "Where you from?"

"Gretna, but there's no one there now. Whole city seems to have disappeared. Same here, I see?"

"'Bout half the town's gone missing," Boricio chewed on the lie, "They sent the rest of us south on reconnaissance. I'm sure happy to have found you. I was about to turn around."

"Any idea what's going on?"

"Nothing for sure, though we got a call from the feds around 4 a.m. saying there was some strange happenings started last night over in Nevada. Nothing certain, but you can imagine how the rumors are flying." Boricio had to swallow his grin, looking at the idiot with the brand-new clothes wrestling the idea he'd put there.

"You think it's some kinda ... alien thing?"

"Probably. Seems like Hollywood's been predicting somethin' like this forever." Boricio ran his hands through his thick hair then looked up and down both sides of the street. Nobody else in sight.

Time to figure out if this fuck knows anything worth knowing.

"I need to check in with dispatch. Anything you can think of for me to tell them?"

"Not much to say. I woke up this morning, and everyone was gone. Thought my girlfriend was pissed since we had a big blowup last night. Same brand that happens every 28 days or so and she's never left before, but I've never slept on the couch either, so I didn't think anything of it at first. But then the air got so heavy, know what I mean?"

"No, not sure. We didn't have anything like that up north, just a bunch of people running and screaming in the streets. What sorta feeling you mean?"

"Well, it was like … " the motorist swallowed hard, "Don't think I'm crazy or nothing, but it was like the air weighed more, or maybe less, I'm not sure, but it was *different*. And I could feel it so I knew something was wrong."

"What'd you do?"

"At first, nothing. Turned on the TV, but there was nothing on. Not a single station."

"You mean the TV was dead?"

"No, it was working, but all the channels were blue, except the ones with snow. Oh, and one channel that was showing some old show from the '50s. Might've been *Leave it to Beaver*, but I'm not sure. Didn't leave it on long enough to find out."

"What'd you do after the TV wasn't working?" Boricio looked at the motorist with kind eyes, waiting to kill.

"Went outside to see what I could see, you know? And I could just *feel* it, the whole neighborhood gone. And sure enough, it was like someone had shaken the city and dumped the people out. So I changed my clothes, grabbed my keys, and started heading north."

"Why north?"

"Got some family here, brother and his kids, wanted to check on them. But my truck was near empty, hadn't gassed it in a week, and the gas stations I ran into are all down. No power, no people."

Fuck. No gas. That was gonna be a BIG time, beer-battered bullshit of a problem. Good thing the cruiser was still three-quarters full.

"Well, you're welcome to ride along with me," Boricio jerked his thumb at the cruiser. "I can drop you off at your brother's, if you like. Anything else you can think of before I check in with dispatch? Anything that might help us figure what this is all about?"

The motorist looked far off, half swallowing what he didn't want to say. Boricio put a reassuring hand on his shoulder.

"It's okay, you're not alone. Tell me anything you think dispatch might wanna know, and don't worry if you think it sounds weird." Boricio smiled as wide as he could. "This is the season of weird after all."

The motorist returned the smile and swallowed again. "Okay, you know that church up the road? The big one with that sign that says, *The Perfect Place For Imperfect People*

Boricio felt a bristle at the back of his neck. "Yeah?"

"Well, it was still there, but it wasn't. Know what I mean?"

Boricio wished he didn't, but he mostly did. "No, not sure I do."

"I could see it like it was there, and I felt like if I got out of the pickup I'd be able to feel it beneath my fingers, but it was gone, just like my girlfriend and everyone else in the city."

"Well, that *is* weird. I'll report that to dispatch."

It's official. This fucker has gone from worthless to boring.

"You ready to ride?"

"You bet!"

Boricio stuck out his hand. "Sorry I've not introduced myself yet. Must've left my manners back with the chaos. I'm Officer Thompson. Good to meet you."

The motorist took Boricio's hand. "Jim. Jim Silva. Good to meet you, too. Thanks for your help."

"My pleasure."

Jim Silva had exactly two seconds to notice the officer's face move from passive to predator before he felt the grip on his hand tighten.

"Hey, Jim?"

"Yeah?" Jim asked, confused by the tight grip on his hand, but too pussy to do anything about it.

"I'm not a cop, Jim."

"Huh?"

"No, I'm a hunter. I hunt people like you, Jim. Hunt 'em and kill 'em."

Jim's eyes widened as he tried to pull back his hand. Boricio locked his grip tighter. He loved the look in his victims' eyes in that moment when they first realized they were with a psychopath. It made him erect, even though he was no queer.

Boricio grabbed Jim by the back of his head, twisted him around, and thrust forward.

Silva's nose smashed into the top of the cruiser and rained a fountain of blood. He would've screamed if sudden knuckles hadn't beaten the possibility from his throat. Boricio released Jim on two unsteady feet, then let him wobble a few seconds before kicking them from under him with a maniacal laugh.

Another second and Boricio was on top of his new friend, Jim, banging his head on the asphalt like a stick on a snare drum. Jim heaved a few quivering shudders, already dying but a good stretch from dead. Boricio pulled the .45 from his belt, put it to the motorist's temple, then shook his head and put it back.

Bullets are better than money now.

He raised his boot above the motorist's head and Silva's final whimper was silenced with a squish and a new stain on the highway's old asphalt.

Adios, dipshit.

Boricio climbed back in the cruiser and floored the gas.

**

Boricio wondered if he'd killed his friend, Jim, too quickly. Sure, it felt good, but he'd never killed two days in a row. Maybe he should've added the crisp-clothed cocksucker to the stash of Ding Dongs in the trunk and saved him for later. Would be a shame to not have anything else for a while, which was probably how it would be.

He was relieved to find another breather, though; to know he wasn't alone on the big, blue marble, yet. That meant it was only a matter of time before he'd have someone else to play with. And hopefully the next time it'd be something he could fuck.

Boricio ran his hand along the sudden bulge beneath his denim. The hard-on made him think of pussy for sale, which sent his thoughts to his favorite strip club, Plan B, which made him realize their billboard had gone missing, too.

Why the fuck didn't I notice that?

For some reason, that bothered Boricio more than just about anything else. He loved that fucking billboard, and looked forward to it even if he wasn't gonna stop. Shit was obviously wrong with the world, but shit was wrong with him, too, if he didn't even notice his favorite pussy parade was AWOL.

Boricio pulled off the road at a Love's Travel Stop. If he couldn't get gas, then he'd get a fully-gassed car. The lot was lit like Christmas, but none of the pumps was working. Boricio traded his cruiser for a full tank and an empty Prius, then went inside and emptied the register of cash, *just in case*, before heading back to his brand new ride.

The door was halfway open when Boricio heard a muffled, "Help!"

The cry was female, causing the bulge in his jeans to resurface. It sounded like it came from the back of the store, maybe from the bathroom, but after 15 minutes of frustrating search and two more cries, Boricio gave up looking.

I'll be fucked if I start hearing things, too. If the world is fucked to pieces, fine. That's them. But if I'm hearing voices, well baby, that's all me.

Boricio flew back onto the highway and started fiddling with the stations, thinking maybe they'd be better than the ones in the police cruiser. For the first 15 minutes or so, they weren't, but then a crackle of static on 90.7 reversed the trend.

90.7 was the New Orleans "Original Local Jazz and Heritage Station," but if jazz was what was being broadcast, Boricio couldn't hear it through the hazy wall of static punctuated by the occasional beep or muffled word. And though he couldn't make anything out, the sound was still better than the eerie nothing outside. Besides, it was sorta fun trying to hear what he could, like trying to watch porn on a scrambled channel.

Boricio kept driving while the sky outside darkened. Daylight hadn't hit, though it had to be morning. But the gloom in the clouds looked less than normal and mostly like a bruise.

A loud POP! on the radio was followed by the word "Boricio," which despite its clarity, he knew he must've imagined. The world could disappear, sure, but some shit just wasn't possible.

Like the strength in his shoulders, it didn't make sense. Boricio felt like he could ditch the Prius and run the rest of the day, though he hadn't eaten since early yesterday and wasn't hungry enough to bother with any of the crap food piled in his trunk, even though he'd taken the time to move it from the cruiser to the Prius.

He was in mid-daydream, imagining pitting his new strength against some 250-pound pussy (the fat ones always liked to fight) when the broadcast from 90.7 suddenly jumped in volume. Boricio heard his name again, no doubt, followed by another 20 minutes of mostly silence seasoned with the muffled versions of the words *gone, absent, defunct, dead,* and *buried,* all crackling through the speakers.

Only one word repeated though, several times, in fact. *Extinct.*

* * * *

CHAPTER 10
CHARLIE WILKENS

"You in there, Charlie?" Bob shouted, rattling the door with his knuckles.

Charlie's head was still hurting, but Bob's sudden appearance had startled him to readiness.

The whole town ups and leaves, and this asshole is still here? The end of the world and it's me and Bob? Fu-uck me.

Bob caught a glimpse of Charlie peering through the curtains, so there was no point in hiding. He grabbed the empties and tossed them in Josie's closet, then headed downstairs and opened the front door.

"What the hell happened?" Bob asked, pushing his way into the house without invitation. "Where's your mother?"

"I dunno, I woke up, and you and Mom were gone, then I went around the neighborhood and everyone else is too."

"Your mom's gone?"

"Yeah," Charlie said, noticing that Bob looked genuinely concerned. "Where were you? I thought you were gone, too."

That's when Charlie noticed Bob was wearing his greasy work shirt and cap, with *Sal's Towing* in ugly, cursive letters.

"I had to cover someone's shift last night. I was bringing a car to the impound, and I must've nodded off waiting for the asshole to fill out the paperwork. Next thing I know, I woke up and everyone is gone."

"It's not just our neighborhood, then?"

"Dude," Bob said, his eyes wide and nervous, "it's the whole fucking world. Or at least everything I've seen for 50 miles on the highway."

Charlie stared, digesting the news.

"Why are you here? Anyone home?"

"No, I came looking for my friend Josie, and saw her door was open. So I came inside to see if she was here."

"So you broke into her house?" Bob said, his face showing a shadow of the asshole Bob hid beneath the surface.

"The door was open," Charlie explained. "I came in to see if anyone was here, maybe hurt or something."

Bob stared at him, likely trying to decide if he'd be a total fucking hard ass like he usually was or if he'd let it go on the count of it being the end of the world and all. He turned and headed out the door, "Come on; let's go home. Your bike's in the truck already."

Charlie wanted to protest, but knew he didn't have a choice. He was, by all accounts, Bob's bitch again. He walked like a dog behind him.

**

"So, what are we gonna do?" Charlie asked, sitting on the couch opposite Bob, who was in His Chair — the chair nobody else in the house dared to sit in — drinking his fifth Natty Light.

"Fuck if I know," Bob said, his voice slightly slurred. "Wait for someone, the Army, The Marines, fucking *X-Files*,

I dunno. If you ask me, it's the goddamned Rapture. God came and took the good folks to heaven so we degenerates could rot."

"Don't you think if it was the Rapture there'd be a lot more people *here* than vanished?"

Bob stared at Charlie for a moment, as if trying to figure out how he felt about Charlie's response.

"Shit, boy, that's the funniest damned thing you ever said."

Charlie glanced at the ground and shrugged.

"You ain't so bad," Bob said. "You should talk more instead of always staying up there in that room of yours."

Yeah, maybe I would if you didn't always call me dumbass or retard, or slap me around.

"How old are you now?"

Charlie squirmed a bit, not sure where this was going. "Almost 18."

"Well, hell, 'almost 18' is old enough for a beer. Shit, I was drinkin' when I was 13. Of course, times were different back then. Go get me another beer and get yourself one, too."

"You sure? I don't think mom would want me . . . "

"Your mom ain't here, now is she? She's probably up there in heaven and seeing as you and me *are* still here, means we're probably goin' to hell. So, we may as well have some good times 'til then, eh?"

"I guess."

Charlie went to the fridge and grabbed the last two cans of beer, then returned to the living room and handed them both to Bob, just in case Bob was testing him.

"Here, crack it open," Bob said, throwing it to Charlie.

Charlie pulled back the tab and beer sprayed all over his face and shirt. He let out a yelp before running into the kitchen so his beer could overflow into the sink. As Charlie cleaned himself, Bob was in the living room, laughing his ass off.

"Goddamn, you are funny, boy."

Charlie glanced at the beer, still about 70 percent full, then lowered the can into the sink, quietly spilling all but 10 percent or so down the drain. He returned to the living room taking a sip of the beer as he entered. The beer tasted disgusting. Like shit's shit, if shit could shit. Nowhere near as sweet as the wine coolers he'd downed at Josie's. He made an awful face, and Bob laughed again.

"Beer virgin!" Bob said like he was some kinda frat boy asshole. Charlie would've rolled his eyes if he didn't think Bob would knock one of them onto the floor.

Charlie took another swig, though most of it was thankfully gone. He pretended to drink longer than he had been, then put the empty can down and let out a loud burp. That ought to make ole Bob laugh his ass off.

And it did.

"Holy shit, you're done?" Bob said, grabbing the can and shaking it, "Wow, that's impressive."

Charlie smiled and sat back on the couch.

"You didn't pour it down the sink or anything, did ya?"

Charlie's heart sped up. He wondered if Bob had seen him, but the angle of the kitchen's opening killed the clear view into the living room.

"No, but I spilled half the can on myself. And . . . oh shit, the floor," he said, realizing some had gotten on the carpet, also.

"Hey, boy," Bob snapped, a serious glare flamed in his eyes, "you watch your mouth, ya hear."

Charlie paused, staring at Bob, waiting for him to crack a smile or laugh, or tell him he was just kidding. Hell, Bob had just told him to drink a beer and now he was gonna get all hardcore about a curse word? Sure, Charlie never cursed in the house before, but that was out of respect for his mom.

He never realized Bob would be Billy Bad Ass about a little foul language.

Hypocritical fuck.

Bob continued to glare, "You don't use that language under my roof."

"Yes," Charlie said, glancing at the floor, not even bothering to point out that it wasn't *his roof*, but his mother's, and that Bob barely contributed to anything, much less rent. God knew what he did with his money, but he sure didn't give any to Charlie's mom.

"Yes, what?"

"Yes, sir," Charlie said, and shrunk into the kitchen to get some paper towels to clean the mess.

As Charlie sprayed the beer stain with carpet cleaner, Bob got up and went to the kitchen. A moment later he yelled, "Hell, we're outta beer!"

Charlie cringed, wishing he'd mentioned that his was the last can. He was even more glad Bob hadn't seen him pour half the last beer down the sink. He dabbed at the stain, soaking it dry with the paper towels, pretending to be deep in concentration and hoping to avoid Bob's wrath.

Bob slammed the fridge, came into the living room, and said, "Come on, kid, we're gonna hit the store."

Charlie jumped up, threw the dirty paper towels away and told Bob he'd be right out, after he went pee, using the word *pee*, because if *shit* ticked off Bob, *piss* would probably make him go nuclear.

"Okay, hurry up, I'll be waiting in the truck."

Great, we're gonna go out and do some drunk driving in a tow truck. That should be a blast.

**

Bob was a surprisingly good drunk driver, though he still went too fast for Charlie's tastes. When Bob saw Charlie clenching the hand holder thingee above the passenger side window, he vented another one of his dirty, *ain't-I-an-asshole?* laughs.

"What? You think I'm gonna crash us? Shit, boy, I've been driving trucks since before you were an egg in your momma's snatch."

Wow, there's an image.

"I'm sure you're a great driver," Charlie said, "I was just thinking maybe the beers might impair your driving a bit."

Charlie regretted the words as soon as they left his mouth. He expected Bob to go ape shit.

Instead, Bob laughed.

"She-eeit, it takes more than a six pack of beers to get me intoxicated, kid. You ain't even *seen* me drunk."

Charlie laughed, uncomfortably. He still had a few bruises that said otherwise, but he wasn't about to say *that!*

The streets beyond their neighborhood were creepy enough to keep the hair on his arms high the entire time. Not a soul on the roads. They passed a few cars here and there, which had seemingly been left running in the middle of the road or crashed on the sides of the streets, but not enough to cause any congestion.

When they pulled up to Evergreen Square, the closest shopping plaza to their house, the emptiness got louder. The always-full parking lot had been reduced to just three cars. Bob pulled right up to the first spot in front of the Save-A-Lot.

"Let's go shopping," he grinned.

The store was dark inside, but not so dark you couldn't see between the daylight and the store's huge, glass facade. The automatic doors were dead, so Bob went back to his truck, opened a side panel and retrieved a crowbar.

"Stand back, kid, I've got a door to open."

Charlie thought Bob would pry the doors apart. Instead, being the subtle kinda guy he is, Bob smashed the glass with the crowbar, until he'd made a big enough hole for them to climb through.

**

The store was dark and damned creepy without people inside. While Bob grabbed a shopping cart and headed straight to the beer aisle, Charlie was tasked to fill another cart with as much water and food as he could fit. If any other people were left, it wouldn't be long before they'd be looting the store, too, Bob warned.

"Anyone too stupid to loot was just smart enough to die," he said.

As Charlie navigated the aisles, he couldn't help but feel a thrill from the all-you-can-grab shopping spree. Anything he wanted in the entire store — for free! He imagined Bob was filling his cart with nothing but beer. Maybe some canned meat products and pork rinds, too. The idea made him laugh. He could hear Bob on the other end of the store singing some country song about beer, which made him laugh harder. If Bob weren't such an asshole half the time, Charlie might actually get along with the prick.

He loaded up on water and soda on one aisle and was shoving every battery pack, flashlight, and battery powered gadget he could find into his cart when he heard a noise one aisle over.

He froze, listening. All he could hear was Bob's obnoxious singing. He was in the middle of his aisle, ready to run in either direction. He crouched down and moved closer to the source of the noise and then he heard footsteps.

Shit.

The barren store, hell, the *barren town*, the lack of power, and the general creepiness convinced Charlie he was about to come face to face with a zombie.

Shit, shit.

He crept toward the front of the store, abandoning the cart.

The footsteps, which were at the back of the store and heading away from him, reversed course, and were now following his path in the next aisle. He stopped. The other person stopped one step after.

Charlie was frozen in place, Bob's drunken singing sounded as though it were a mile away.

He scanned his aisle, looking for something, anything he might be able to use as a weapon. He wished he were in the cutlery aisle, but the small tool aisle would have to do. He grabbed a generic-looking hammer, orange with a black handle. It wasn't heavy, but it was metal, and he figured it could do a fair amount of damage.

He started toward the front of the store again, this time on tiptoe, hammer ready. Silence on the other aisle. He wondered if his stalker was staying put or creeping along with him. He gripped the hammer as he approached the end of the aisle. Once there, he'd have to make a decision whether to round the corner and confront whoever was there or start running and yell for Bob. He'd hate to be imagining things, then go running for Bob like a big baby, so he decided he'd turn the corner and let fate figure it out.

Bob was still singing, but now it sounded like the out-of-tune was coming from a mouthful of food. Fucker was probably chowing down on raw steaks.

Charlie inched toward the soda display at the end of the aisle, his heart in his throat as he rounded the corner. His shaky hand clutched the hammer, as he considered the ways he might use it when needed. Swinging it would require getting in close, and if the other person — or persons — had a better weapon, he was screwed. He could throw it, but if he missed, he'd be empty-handed. And he'd be facing an angry attacker.

He sat frozen and crouched at the end of the aisle, weighing his decision, and glancing toward the other end of the store to see if Bob was in sight. He wasn't.

Charlie heard the footsteps, now in full sprint toward him.

He ducked down, and got ready to swing the hammer. As trouble ran toward him, he cried out, "Bob!"

He stumbled back just as the figure in blue jeans and a black hoodie shot past him and darted toward the front doors.

Bob came running, crowbar in hand, and glanced down at Charlie who had fallen to the ground. The person had hopped into Bob's truck.

Bob raced from the store, yelling, "Hey, fucker!"

Charlie followed, gripping his hammer. As Charlie pushed through the front door, Bob yanked the hoodie-wearing punk from the cab and threw him to the ground. He brought the crowbar up and swung. The guy rolled out of the way at the last second and knocked Bob's legs out from under him. Bob fell to the ground.

The guy hopped up and raced across the parking lot. Charlie followed, driven by adrenaline, and a desire to do something good in Bob's eyes by catching the bastard who tried to steal his truck.

"Stop!" Charlie yelled, as he got closer, emboldened by both the hammer in his fist, and knowing Bob would surely be beside him in a moment and help him deal with the punk.

Though Charlie couldn't see anything beneath the hoodie, he could tell the guy was shorter and skinnier than him. So long as he didn't have a gun — and Charlie didn't see one — he figured he might have a chance to win a fight for once in his life.

Charlie was almost close enough to grab the guy. He considered throwing the hammer at the back of the guy's head, but didn't want to slow down as he was almost ... catching ... up.

Just inches away, Charlie dropped the hammer, reached out with both hands and grabbed the hoodie, then yanked the guy back. They collided in a rough roll to the ground that lacerated Charlie's arms and bruised his ribs and back, but he didn't release his grip, and the two rolled until they'd come to a stop with the guy on top of Charlie. Only it wasn't a guy, but rather, a young, black girl, close to his age, with short, curly hair and piercing, azure eyes.

He let go immediately. She stood, and their eyes locked in a tango of fear and survival. *I'm not a threat, are you?*

Just then, Charlie heard Bob's thundering footsteps, then looked up to see him running up behind the girl, screaming with the crowbar raised.

"No!" Charlie screamed. The girl spun around just as the crowbar came down. It narrowly missed her head, but hit her hard in her right shoulder, sending her sprawling to the ground as she cried out.

Bob immediately brought the crowbar up again and was about to take another, surely lethal swing, when Charlie leaped at Bob, pushing him back, and sending the crowbar back where it bounced off the ground with a hollow metal thud.

"She's just a kid!" Charlie yelled as Bob stumbled back, but didn't fall.

Bob's bloodshot eyes were crazy, his nostrils flaring. He was out of breath.

"She's a kid, man. Relax," Charlie gasped, leaning on his knees to catch his breath.

Bob's eyes relaxed a bit and Charlie turned to the fallen girl, lying unconscious on the ground.

"Did I kill her?" Bob asked.

"I don't think so," Charlie said, leaning down to feel for a pulse.

Charlie wasn't sure whether or not Bob was disappointed.

* * * *

CHAPTER 11
BRENT FOSTER

Brent wasn't sure how long he hid in the pitch black, waiting for a looming dread to fade from the apartment. Maybe 20 minutes. Probably two hours. Hard to tell in the dark and with nothing to count.

He wasn't sure what he was hiding from, either, but something in his lizard brain made him run from the downstairs apartment. Something told him if he stayed, he'd die. He hadn't even worked up the courage to look out his windows.

What did he see?

Though he couldn't see the man on the street's face well enough to see his expression, his run told Brent all he needed to know. The man was fleeing death.

Maybe the city *had* suffered a terrorist attack, and the man saw the bad guys coming. Or, Brent suddenly thought, perhaps the man had something to do with what happened and was running from the police or Army or whoever the hell was now in control of the city.

Brent had only recently moved to New York, so he was a tourist to 9/11, not a citizen. But he knew enough to know someone was surely out there evacuating people, searching for survivors, or both. He couldn't expect someone to find him; he'd have to find *them*. And that meant leaving the building.

He went back into the living room, glanced out the window and down to the street below. The city, or what he could see of it, was a morgue. He went to the fridge and grabbed another water, sat on his couch, and put his feet up on the coffee table, where a framed photo of his family faced him.

They took the picture last Christmas, just in time for cards. Brent thought sending family photos for cards was smarmy, but Gina insisted. He wondered if it was something women did to compete with their friends to prove who really had a nicer-looking or happier family. All Brent saw in 90 percent of the photos were uncomfortable children and miserable spouses holding tight to a veneer of love.

Merry Christmas, indeed.

He held the photo, eyes fixed on Ben's joyous smile.

Brent hadn't wanted kids, not really. The world was far too fucked for that. Ben was an accident. Gina's plumbing made him a one in a million shot at best. Same as Ben's odds when Gina was rushed to the hospital bleeding at seven and a half months.

Only then did Brent realize how much he'd come to love the thought of having a son, and let his cynicism face the light of hope. When the doctors came out to update him on the status of the emergency C-section and told him he had a son, he was nothing but tears. And when he finally saw his son in the Neonatal Intensive Care Unit, his heart melted. Ben was their miracle. And for one not inclined to believe in miracles, that was no small statement.

Sitting there on the couch, Brent felt guiltier than ever about trading his family for work.

He'd always wanted to be a reporter. When he landed a gig in New York, his dream came true. Sure, it wasn't *The Times*, just *The Apple Tribune*, but still, he was in the heart of it all, covering features in the city of a million stories. But the newspaper business was dying: the Internet, evaporating advertising, and a cast and crew that couldn't stop the bleeding. As the cuts came, he was always spared (so far), but it meant working that much harder to survive the next round.

He rarely saw his family.

It was a temporary sacrifice, he told himself, and a necessary one. He was working toward something, and getting there a word at a time. And he knew good writers, damned good writers, who were unemployed, hungry, and writing anything they could just to keep food in their fridge.

And while he used to dream of the life of a newspaper writer in New York, as something close to being famous, or at least respected, the reality of his role was a slap in the face. Most people treated him like shit. Especially people who disagreed with the politics of his paper, something he had nothing to do with. He was a features guy, telling nice, little stories about the city and its eclectic denizens.

But most people didn't care. You work for the wrong paper, they treat you like a lying, thieving, evil bastard. And even when they didn't hate him for the paper's politics, they often bitched when he got some little facet of a story wrong, or more often, didn't stick with the narrative they imagined the story would take. It never ceased to amaze him how many people would get bent out of shape or threaten lawsuits over a *nice story!*

Now, sitting alone with no idea where his family was, the vanity of his job was apparent. He was too busy trying to impress strangers and win their love, while neglecting his family who *already* loved him.

Brent pulled Stanley Train from his pocket, looked at the train's big, goofy smile, and he felt his heart fade into an ache. Ben was gone. The thought that he might never play with his toy train again shattered Brent into tears.

**

Brent spent about half an hour feeling sorry for himself while fear ran rampant in his head. Then something swelled inside him. Anger. Anger at himself and his inaction. His family was out there — he hoped — and it was his job to find them.

He grabbed a backpack from his closet, filled it with food, drinks, and clothes, wrote his wife another note — this one saying he'd be back at midnight — and headed out the door. He left it unlocked since Gina left her keys inside. If someone broke in, let 'em. Halfway down the hall, he raced back to his apartment, grabbed the framed photo from the couch, put it in his backpack, and headed out into the city.

First, though, he'd need a gun. He found one in the fourth apartment he kicked in. A revolver with a box of bullets. He'd fired a gun twice at a range, but never owned one. No matter, he knew enough to be dangerous.

He stepped out of his apartment building and onto the street. The air was cool, and a fog was rolling in, like a wooly icing atop the haunted hallways of the abandoned, concrete empire. Brent couldn't smell any smoke, or anything out of the ordinary. A good sign, he guessed.

He stared off in the same direction as the man had been staring before losing his shit, but saw nothing odd. Well, no odder than the ghost streets, and buildings getting swallowed by the fog descending on the city. The fog was different than normal, though Brent couldn't quite place *what* the difference was.

He crossed the four lanes of West End Avenue to the apartment building the man had ducked into. It was roughly the same size as his, 15 stories tall. He wasn't sure how he'd find the guy, or if he'd be dangerous, but Brent had to establish contact with the only person he'd seen.

When he reached the double doors that would normally be locked or tended by a doorman, he noticed that one of the two windows was shattered. Glass covered the red doormat inside. Brent put his hand on the gun tucked inside his jacket and stepped through the doorway. Glass crunched beneath his sneakers. The lobby desk was deserted, and the elevators were dead, which meant he had to take the stairs and begin his ascent.

The stairwell was dimly lit by emergency lights. His footsteps echoed off the walls. He didn't bother with stealth. He hoped the guy, if he were still around, would show himself so Brent wouldn't have to search the whole damned building.

Brent got his wish as he opened the door to the second-floor landing and came face to face with a pistol. On the other end of the gun, a wild-haired, disheveled, skinny guy in his late 40s or early 50s wearing thick, black-rimmed glasses. Brent's hand held his gun tight in his pocket, but made no move to reveal it. Instead, he aimed it at the guy, through his jacket.

"Anyone see you come in here?"

Brent shook his head, "No, I don't think so. I didn't see anyone out there."

"Who sent you?" the guy asked, his voice tuned to nervous.

"Nobody, my name is Brent Foster, I live across the street. I'm looking for my family."

"Brent Foster?" the guy said, his eyes darting up for a moment, accessing memory. "Brent Foster who writes for the *Tribune?*"

Great, the moment he'd always hoped would never happen. Some wacko with a gun recognizing him as a reporter. *Hope he's a fan.*

"Yes," Brent said, reluctantly, bracing for reaction.

The guy lowered the gun, and a broad smile crossed his face.

"Stanley Byrd, but you can call me Stan. I'm a big fan of your work, sir." the guy said, putting the gun awkwardly in a jacket that was about 20 years out of fashion.

Brent let go of his own gun and shook Stan's clammy hand.

"What have you heard? Did you see anything?"

"Nothing," Brent said, "I woke up, and my wife and son were gone. And apparently, the whole damned apartment building, and everyone on the streets is gone, too."

"Yeah, the whole city is gone, but not just the city." Stan said with the certainty of someone who took such things in stride.

"What do you mean?"

"Come, come, I want to introduce you to some people," Stan said, turning and heading down the hall. "I can't believe you're here. I read that story you did on the blind jazz guy who plays in the subways to put his son through college. Goddamn, that was beautiful stuff."

"Thanks," Brent said, following, hand in his jacket. Just in case.

Stan brought him to the last apartment in the hallway, knocked three times, paused, then knocked twice, paused again, then two more quick knocks.

Bolts, several of them by the sounds of it, unbolted, and the door opened. A bald, buffed, stone-faced Hispanic in a tight, black tee greeted them, arms drowning in ink. He nodded and let them in.

All charm, this one.

Sitting on a sofa even older than Stan's clothes, was a blonde-haired woman in her early 40s or so. She reminded Brent of a doctor or scientist, and he was rarely wrong when judging people by appearance. Stan was nuts, muscles was angry, and the lady, well, she was probably the brains of the bunch.

Muscles locked the door, and Stan introduced everyone.

"Everyone, this is Brent Foster, from the Tribune. Brent, this is Luis Torres, who lives five floors up. And this is Melora Mitchell, who lives in your building, actually."

Luis nodded. Melora stood up and reached out to shake Brent's hand. Her hand was cold, thin. She retreated quickly — or perhaps Brent was just imagining things — as if she were aware of Brent's judgment of her hand's temperature.

"Have a seat, Brent," Stan said.

Brent took a seat in one of two recliners across from the couch. Stan took the other, while Luis stood up, arms crossed.

"We didn't think we'd find another," Melora said. "How long have you been having the dream?"

Brent didn't have a chance to ask what she was talking about.

"Where were you at 2:15 a.m.?" Stan asked. It seemed as if he were waiting for a specific response to the time.

"In bed. Why?"

"What do you remember?"

"Nothing. I went to bed dog-ass tired, woke up this morning with a headache, and the world was gone. Why are you asking me about that time?"

"Because that's when The Collapse first started."

"What do you mean, Collapse?" Brent asked, glancing now at Melora to see if she were also buying into Stan's weirdo speak. Her face was all business.

"At 2:15 a.m. Eastern Standard Time, nearly 99.9 percent of the population of the planet vanished. Gone, poof, into the unknown."

"What are you talking about?" Brent asked, now glancing at Luis, also stone-faced.

"We're calling it The Collapse. And we've known it was going to happen for years."

Brent stayed silent. He was certain his expression was louder than words, anyway.

"The four of us have been dreaming of this day and hour since we were children. We found one another five years ago on some message boards, and started researching this thing, trying to prepare. We even came up with a name for ourselves," Stan said with a laugh, "We call ourselves the 215 Society."

Okay, that's it, I'm outta here. Brent began to think of a way to get the hell out of the room without offending Luis.

"We're not crazy," Melora said with a professorial smile. "We've been dreaming of this moment for most of our lives. Something in the dream told us that the world would be gone and we had to prepare."

"Prepare? How?" Brent asked, his curiosity getting the better of him even if he was chasing delusion. It wouldn't be the first time he entertained some loon with crazy, tin foil hat stories.

"Well, we never really knew, to be honest," Stan said, "At first, we thought we were supposed to warn people. We tried that, but nobody listens to you when you say the world's gonna end. And we didn't want to lose our jobs or get thrown in the loony bin. So we kept mum, just trying to be ready in whatever ways we could."

"Wait," Brent said, looking around the room, and trying to see into the hall, which likely led to a single bedroom and bath. "You said there were four of you; where's the fourth?"

"We haven't seen her yet," Melora said. "She was supposed to come here last night to wait with us. But she never showed."

"So, you all stayed here for the end of the world? What happened at 2:15 a.m.?" Brent asked. "Did you see people vanish? Was there some big light from a UFO? Was God here? What happened?"

Melora smiled one of those smiles that someone gives you when they're looking down on you. "You think we're crazy, don't you?"

"I don't know what to think," Brent said, "I'm just looking for my family and would like to know what the hell happened."

"They're gone," Luis said from behind. "They're all gone."

Brent was getting pissed, but kept his attention on Melora as he spoke. "They're not gone. I'm going to find them."

"I'm afraid Luis is right," Melora said. "Everyone is gone. Which is why I'm confused. You didn't answer my question before. Have you not had the dreams, too?"

"No," Brent said, standing. "I didn't have any crazy dreams. I told you what happened, and now I'm going to go out to find my family. Thank you for your time and your . . . *stories*."

Brent pushed his way past Luis, who didn't bother to stop him.

"Wait," Stan called out, his voice hyper. "There's something you've gotta see."

Brent was going to ignore him, just head the hell out of there, get back out on the street and leave Crazy Town. But again, his reporter's curiosity tugged at him. Even if these people didn't know what the hell was happening, he wanted to understand what they *thought* was going down.

"What?" Brent asked, going to the kitchen where Stan and Melora were pulling something from a box. A small video recorder.

Stan handed it to Brent.

"Press play."

He did.

The camera showed the time in the bottom right corner: 2:14 a.m. The scene was the room he was in now, except the chairs and couch were all moved aside, and the three 215ers were sitting on the floor talking.

"Should be any minute now," Stan said in the video.

Melora started to say something and then the power went out.

The camera switched to night vision green and showed all three fall to the ground, unconscious. There was some static. Brent watched the screen, waiting for them to move, but they didn't. They were out cold. If he didn't know better, he'd think they dropped dead right there.

"That's it until an hour later, when we woke up," Stan said. "Then we went out and drove around the city to confirm what we thought."

"*I* drove around the city," Luis corrected him.

"Yes," Stan agreed.

"Okay, so you recorded yourselves 'passing out' at the same time; what's that supposed to prove?" Brent asked.

Melora reached into the box and pulled out another recorder. "This is the one we put in an apartment two doors down. One of several we placed in other apartments, I might add. Without anyone's knowledge, of course."

She handed it to Brent, and he pressed play.

The recording started at 2:14 a.m.

The scene was inside someone's bedroom, a king-sized bed. The camera was already on night vision. Next to the bed, Brent saw a clock's face that read 2:10. He could see the shapes of a man and woman in bed, the guy hogging the blankets, the woman curled against him. He could hear one of them snoring.

The alarm clock went black.

"That's the power outage," Melora said.

Brent kept watching.

More static, this time accompanied by a five-second burst of a high-pitched whistle like a tea kettle if the tea kettle's sound were filtered through a high-velocity fan.

And then something came into view of the camera and Brent jumped. The camera fell from his hands.

"What the fuck was that?!"

Stan, surprisingly agile, grabbed the camera before it hit the ground. He rewound it to where Brent had left off and handed it back.

Something that looked like a dark cloud had formed all at once over the bed, a swirling mass of slow-moving, smoky tendrils. Except it moved more like smoke in liquid form. Brent stared in horror as two long tentacles of darkness twisted and snaked down toward the sleeping bodies. Just as one of the tentacles crept toward the woman's head, the image flickered.

More static and the high-pitched weird teakettle noise whistled for the longest five seconds of Brent's entire life. The static cleared. When it did, the bed was empty.

The time in the corner read 2:15 a.m.

* * * *

CHAPTER 12
MARY OLSON

Desmond was a fun neighborhood mystery. Everyone loved to guess where he got his money. No one knew what he did, but everyone knew he had to be one of the best. His house, directly across the street from Mary's, wasn't larger than hers. But it was just as big and 10 times as impressive. You could tell that she was someone who was struggling to stay in such a grand home; he was likely living beneath his means.

Desmond rarely wore anything other than jeans and a simple shirt, but on him, everything looked custom tailored. Even jeans and tees. He always had new toys, including cars. And new women, or so rumor went. And the one time Mary had been inside his house, she left thinking it was the most beautiful interior she'd ever seen. And his garden inspired jealousy from everyone in the neighborhood. She'd dreamt of the garden more than once.

Mary had known a few guys who could mint money, all of them assholes. Desmond wasn't. He was a good guy with a great sense of humor, though he spent most of the time quiet, at least at the neighborhood gatherings. He had honest eyes and was a great listener; rarely broke eye contact and usually waited his turn to speak. When he spoke, people listened.

"What do you mean *the world* is dead?" John asked.

"Exactly that. May not be the entire world, but St. Louis is gone for sure. If there's a rest of the world, we need to get to it now."

"People are missing, or do you mean the town itself?"

"A little of both," Desmond said. "All the people, definitely. But a lot of the town, too."

"How do you know?" John's bottom lip started to dance.

"Because I've been driving the city since 3:30 this morning. It's a ghost town, and I can't get a signal from anywhere in the world. If *I* can't get a signal, no one in this city can."

Jimmy lost his tongue for the first time in years.

Mary said, "What do you think we should do?"

"Pack some supplies; we're gonna head southwest to Fort Leonard Wood. If the world's gone to shit, you can bet the Army base is the best place to be."

Jimmy's tongue came back. "What if the Army is gone?"

John stepped in front of Jimmy. "I'm not going. I'm waiting for Jenny here."

Desmond said, "Jenny's gone."

"She'll be back."

A sadness shuddered through the tiny circle. Desmond put his hand on John's shoulder. "We'll be safer together. And have a better chance at finding Jenny."

Jimmy agreed. "Yeah man, better together."

Mary turned to John. "I know how you feel. But right now, we don't know what's happened or what that means for tomorrow. All we know is, yesterday's gone. Whatever happened, we were hit hard. If our numbers were cut, then every number matters. We need to stick together and figure out what's going on."

John was silent. Desmond thanked Mary with his eyes then opened his mouth. "I suggest we're packed and ready to hit the road hard in 30. Take only what you know you need. No computers or large items. I only have so much room in the cargo van for our supplies. We can also use the Escalade."

John said, "I'll go. We can take my Suburban. Just cleaned it yesterday."

Desmond smiled. "Okay then, let's hustle. Everyone back here in 30."

"Why the hurry?" Jimmy wasn't being flip, just wanted to know. "Looks like we've got all the time in the world."

A shadow smudged Desmond's face. "Time might not mean what it used to. But if the sky is falling, every minute matters."

Mary and Paola went back into the house. Paola ran upstairs to pack clothes; Mary stayed downstairs in the kitchen tossing a medley of foods into two, 30-gallon trash bags. She packed all the dries, then made a cooler of perishables and set it by the front door beside the two plastic bags.

Paola met her mom at the front door with two suitcases, stuffed with Mary's favorite jeans, cammies, and sweaters, with 15 minutes to spare.

"Anything else?"

Paola was sweet this morning. And it was early.

"Not sure. Other than are we dreaming, is this real, or any other way of saying, *this can't be happening*. Most of all I just want to know you're okay. Are you?"

Paola smiled. "Would it be weird if I said yes?"

"A little," Mary hugged her daughter and laughed. "But you've always been a little weird and a lot tough!"

"Mom?"

"Yeah?"

"What do you think happened?"

Mary had no idea and couldn't possibly guess. "I don't know, but I think we'll be okay. *That* feels right. And you know I'd tell you if it didn't. Whatever happened, we're okay. That has to be enough for us right now, got it?"

Paola gave her mom her hand. "Pinky promise."

Mary wrapped her pinky around Paola's. They spent several minutes rocking back and forth, then opened the door to the sudden future waiting outside.

**

Desmond's cargo van was nice but nondescript from the outside. New, tall, and shiny. Black. The back doors were open. Mary saw custom cabinets and shelving inside, sitting beside a small bank of computers, every screen black. Her face must have looked louder than she thought.

"I'm not crazy," Desmond laughed. "I'm just always prepared and can afford to do it well. Come on, let's get packed." He took the bags from Mary and Paola and loaded them into the van.

"Mind if I take a look?" Mary asked.

"By all means," Desmond stood behind the swinging door and bowed his head.

Mary climbed in and started opening cabinets. They were packed with an end-of-the-world picnic: juice, dried fruits, condensed milk, canned meats, peanut butter, jelly, crackers, granola bars, baby food, coffee, tea, hard candy, cereal, salt, pepper, sugar. There was a giant first aid kit, the biggest Mary had ever seen, a portable toilet, light sticks, a stack of 5-gallon buckets, plastic trash bags, bleach, a disaster supply kit, and tons of water, though it looked like it would run out quick.

Mary looked at her two plastic bags and felt like she was watering her lawn while looking at Desmond's copper piping.

"One more," Desmond said, straining to lift a small footlocker into the van. A padlock secured the lock.

"What's in there?" Mary asked, even though she anticipated the response.

"Guns," Desmond said matter-of-factly.

"Who's riding with me?" John opened the door to his Suburban and climbed in. Mary and Paola climbed in back.

"I'll go with Desmond," Jimmy said.

Desmond shook his head. "You should ride in the Suburban. I'll hit the front line."

Jimmy didn't disagree, just opened the passenger side of the Suburban and climbed inside.

The cargo van left Warson Woods. The Suburban followed.

**

The Suburban was a coffin of silence as its occupants surveyed the city beyond their neighborhood.

It was gone.

In its place, torn trees jutted up from the debris-strewn earth consisting of splintered remnants of houses, destroyed vehicles, broken glass, and paper. Lots and lots of paper, as if a million office buildings exploded, and paper rained from the sky, as if a super-tornado had wiped out miles and miles of the city.

Paola burst into tears, and Mary hugged her tight.

"What happened?"

"Jesus," John said. "Everything is ... gone."

Mary held Paola tightly, unable to think of anything to say that would soothe her this time. As they drove along, Mary saw that Jimmy, who had his face buried in a fantasy book, was starting to tear up. She turned away, so as not to embarrass him.

**

Fortunately, the on-ramp to the highway was intact and the streets remarkably, and eerily, were free of vehicles. If a mass exodus occurred, everyone either got out in time, or took other means of escape.

And the sky had a gauze. It made her think, *opposite of Colorado,* and that managed a smile. They'd driven nearly 20 minutes before the trees began to appear along the side of the road again. The tornado, or whatever it was, hadn't reached this far. In another 15 minutes or so, they would reach the next major city. She hoped it was still standing.

As they drove in relative silence, something gnawed in Mary's brain. Something she should either remember, or notice. That's when it occurred to her — something was *off* about the trees. She realized what it was before Jimmy said a thing.

"You hear them?" Jimmy turned to the back seat.

"Who?" Paola asked.

"The trees."

Paola did, though she hadn't realized it until that moment. That they were able to hear anything from inside the cabin of the Suburban, let alone trees, confused her. That she and Jimmy agreed it was the trees they heard, even odder.

"Yeah," Jimmy drummed his fingers on the dashboard, "they're definitely talking."

John turned his head to the right and raised an eyebrow. "The trees are talking? What are you smoking?"

"Nothing yet," Jimmy laughed. He pulled a small Ziploc baggie from the inside of his jacket and opened it. The sweet, skunky scent of herb filled the Suburban.

"What is that?" Paola asked.

"Nothing," Mary said. Then, after a second, "It's marijuana."

"Oh," Paola said. "It smells sorta good."

"Yes, it sorta does," Mary laughed, then traced the memory of her and Ryan in their old days losing hours to the fog.

"I don't want that in my car," John said, eyes on the road.

"Relax, yo. It's the end of the world. This might be the last baggie we ever gonna smoke... until we start planting it. Until then, I'm willing to share. You have the car, I bring the weed. It's fair. Besides, what're you worried about — getting a ticket?"

John didn't care anyway, but the argument turned to vapor when they saw the cargo van slowing to a standstill.

Desmond got out, and the temperature in the Suburban rose a degree.

"I wish my brothers were here," Jimmy said. "Mom and Dad, too."

Mary and Paola exchanged the same knowing look: Everything was different, except that they were all that mattered.

**

Desmond was looking down, his right hand raised at the Suburban in a silent *stop*. "What should we do?" Paola said.

"Nothing yet," Mary said, then, "Stay inside."

"I'm going to take a look." John put the Suburban in park, then climbed outside and headed for Desmond.

"Yee-haw. Me, too." Jimmy opened his door and hit the concrete. John and Jimmy were just shy of Desmond when

Paola opened the door and ran past the boys, in front of Desmond, then face first into a scream.

Desmond pulled Paola back, already hysterical. Mary rushed to her daughter. In front of the van, Mary saw what caused her daughter to shriek. It was all she could do not to follow suit.

The twitching creature on the highway was human — mostly. Its face was pale-black, with bright, white balls of light pulsating under the glistening, mottled flesh. It had no mouth, eyes, or nose, and its legs were longer than they should've been. The body was moving, gasping in its death throes.

The sky got ashy, and the twitcher started twitching more. As the sky grew darker, the thing's jaw began to push out, stretching its head until a slash ripped horizontally above its jaw — forming a rudimentary mouth. From its newfound orifice, it gasped and groaned, as if trying to form words.

Desmond stepped toward the creature, and turned to Mary, "Cover her eyes."

Paola buried her face in her mother's shoulder as Desmond aimed a pistol, a Glock, Mary believed, at the twitcher.

"What are you doing?" John screamed, knocking his hand away.

Desmond lowered the gun, then turned to John with a glare, "You *won't be* touching me when I'm aiming a loaded gun."

"He needs help. You can't just kill whoever you want. None of us agree to that."

Desmond raised the Glock and pulled the trigger. Twice. The light in the creature's body seemed to flicker just before its head exploded in gore. Then, the lights went out, and its body went limp and still.

The shot sounded like a rolling detonation as it caromed across the emptiness.

"This is the Apocalypse, not a democracy," Desmond said, "Let's go."

Desmond got back in the van and drove around the body without another word.

**

Nothing but silence in the Suburban for several minutes. Mary wondered what Desmond knew that he wasn't telling anyone else.

Sure, people had vanished, and an entire town wiped off the planet, but who said anything about an Apocalypse? There was no way to know how far spread this event was. No reason not to think that once they reached the Army base, they'd be transported somewhere where everything was still normal.

Apocalypse?

As much as she wanted to believe her hopes, something told her she was wrong, that Desmond was right, and everything had indeed changed. Forever.

She wanted to cry, too, but she had to be strong for Paola. And for Jimmy, to an extent. Though he was practically an adult, so much about him was still a child. An orphan.

"Where do you think everyone is?" Jimmy asked, breaking the silence.

"I dunno," Mary said. "I'm thinking of some sort of evacuation or something."

"No," John said, "I mean, maybe if everyone from the same homes were gone. But my wife is gone, Jimmy's family is gone. There's no way the Army or anyone would be able to evacuate half of a family without waking the others. It doesn't make any sense."

"Maybe they were all Raptured?" Paola offered. "God called all the believers home?"

"That's all bullshit make believe," Jimmy said, "And besides, if there was a heaven, no fu ... friggin' way my dad was on the list. Believe you, me."

"Maybe aliens?" Paola said.

Jimmy thought on that for a moment. "Now that I wouldn't rule out. Though, that would be an awful lot of UFOs to take all those people away."

"Maybe they didn't take them away?" Paola countered. "Maybe they just killed everyone."

Mary flinched, catching a look from John. She made an "I'm sorry" face, and his expression changed from scorn to understanding.

"Let's change the subject, huh? Why don't we talk about ... I dunno, you all pick a topic."

Before they picked a topic, John slowed the Suburban. Desmond had stopped again, in the middle of a bridge, which ran maybe 50 yards, a few hundred feet above ground.

"Why's he stopping here? We're nowhere near Fort Leonard Wood."

Desmond got out of the van and was looking up at the sky. And that's when they saw them — birds. Lots of them, swarming and diving overhead to the river below. Desmond walked toward the guardrail and looked down, then turned back to the Suburban and held up a hand, telling the others to stay put.

Jimmy ignored the signal and jumped from the car. John followed. Mary looked at Paola and told her to stay put, she'd be right back. Surprisingly, Paola didn't argue, and Mary stepped out of the car and joined the rest of the gang looking down over the guardrail.

As she drew closer, she noticed an overpowering, sickly-sweet smell that seemed somehow familiar, though she couldn't quite place it. The sound of a river rushing beneath them was barely audible over the squawking of birds as they continued to circle and dive.

John turned toward her and leaned over, vomiting on the road.

Jimmy and Desmond simply stared. Mary reached the guardrail, looked down below and immediately wished she'd stayed in the car.

Corpses filled the river, in the hundreds, if not thousands, bobbing up and down, floating like logs as birds feasted on their rotting flesh.

"Well, I think we know where all the people went," Jimmy said, his face ashen.

* * * *

::EPISODE 2::
(SECOND EPISODE OF SEASON ONE)
"DOWN THE RABBIT HOLE"

CHAPTER 1
CHARLIE WILKENS

Oct. 15, 2011
Early evening
Jacksonville, Florida

It had been two hours, but the girl was still passed out in Charlie's bed. He started to wonder if she had fallen into a coma — maybe she'd die.

He'd removed her hoodie when they first got home. She was wearing a charcoal tee underneath, and Charlie cut the sleeve from her shirt to dress the wound. It was more bruise than torn flesh, which was good because he didn't think he'd be able to stitch someone. He didn't understand why the girl was still out, but he also wasn't in a hurry for her to wake. Because then he'd have to deal with her reaction to being abducted, which could get violent.

He kept flashing back to that moment when they'd fallen in the shopping plaza parking lot, and he first realized she was a girl and not some dude looking to jack their truck. Something in her eyes said she wasn't a threat. But what was she doing in the store? The doors were locked when he and Bob arrived, so she must've followed them in for some reason. But why?

If her goal was to take the truck, she could have done that without going into the store. Hell, she could've taken anything with four wheels; the streets were plenty full. Then again, he guessed she could have entered the store through a side door or service entrance.

He thought of her beautiful eyes again. He only knew a handful of black girls, and none with blue eyes. Bob searched her for ID, but came up empty. While he had thought she was close to his age, closer inspection put her closer to 20.

"Who are you?" Charlie asked, neither expecting, nor getting, a response.

The light outside, bleeding through the thick and slightly-parted curtain, was starting to dim. It would be night soon. It wouldn't be long before they'd have to switch to some of the battery-operated lamps they'd lifted from the store. He wasn't sure what he'd do if she didn't wake soon. If he went to sleep and wasn't awake when she came to, she might freak. He wasn't worried that she'd hurt him, even though it was a distinct possibility. His main concern was that Bob would see her as a threat and put a bullet in her before Charlie could calm the situation.

Charlie stared at the shape of her breasts beneath her T-shirt. They were on the small side, but still quite nice. He had resisted the urge to "accidentally" brush against them when they were carrying her to his bed, then again when he was dressing her wounds, even though Bob made some sort of joke about Charlie keeping himself a "little, chocolate sex slave."

What an asshole.

As he kept watch over the girl, Bob stayed in the living room drinking his beer. Not Natty-Light, either. He'd looted good shit. Beside him, on the couch, a shotgun. Usually, he'd watch TV as he got good and drunk. Without TV, Charlie wondered what Bob would do for entertainment. He didn't strike Charlie as much of a reader.

He hoped Bob didn't plan to continue using him as a dartboard for his amusement. He didn't mind pretending to drink and burp to keep Bob in good humor, but he wasn't Bob's court jester, and wasn't willing to play one in front of a girl. But if Charlie's history with bullies had taught him anything, it was that bullies loved to humiliate others. An audience was just fuel to a fire.

Bob was originally going to abandon the girl to die in the parking lot, but Charlie begged him to show compassion. They couldn't just leave someone — especially a girl — behind to die.

"Well, she's your responsibility," Bob said as if she were a stray mutt. "But if she gets outta line, I'm putting her to sleep again, and she ain't waking up."

Charlie hoped it wouldn't come to that. He had no idea what they'd do with the girl once she came to. Obviously, he'd see if she had any friends or family. If not, he'd probably invite her to stay until things got sorted. Whether Bob would go for that was another story.

He stared as she slept. Her eyes were rolling beneath their lids, deep in dreams. The room grew colder as the sun started to set. He pulled a blanket over her and lay on the floor to rest his eyes.

**

"Where am I?" the girl groaned.

Charlie's eyes snapped open, and he sat up. The room was pitch-black. He'd slept too long. Why the hell hadn't Bob woken him?

Must be passed out drunk again.

Charlie fumbled in the dark until his hands found the portable lamp and clicked it on. She was crouched on the bed, ready to pounce but blinded by the light. Charlie pulled the lamp back and lit his face.

"It's okay; you were hurt."

Her eyes darted to the closed door then back at Charlie, weighing her next move. He stepped between her and the door, praying she wouldn't run, wake Bob, and end up with a bullet or two inside her head.

"Please, hear me out," Charlie whispered, "My drunken stepdad thought you were a thief and hit you with the crowbar before seeing you were a girl. I'm so sorry."

"A girl can't be a thief?" she said, eyes blazing, almost challenging him.

"No, I mean, yeah, they can be, but ... "

"It's okay," she said, relaxing a bit and sitting on the bed. "Did you do this?" she asked, running a hand over her bandaged right shoulder.

"Yeah, though I'm not sure I helped much."

She pulled the bandage aside without flinching, then looked at Charlie. "Where am I? How long was I out?"

"My house; on Charleston Street. We didn't want to leave you alone. And I'm not sure what time it is, but it's been at least five or six hours."

She closed her eyes and looked like she was going to add an encore to her original fade to black. But she took a deep breath and steadied herself, then opened her eyes again.

"What's wrong?" he asked, "You okay?"

"I dunno," she said. "I have these horrible headaches that make me black out every now and then. Doctors don't know why. They think it's probably migraines."

"I thought you were in a coma," Charlie said.

"Where's the dude that hit me?"

"I'm guessing he's passed out, drunk."

"Okay," she said, standing, flinching a bit as she did. "I need to get out of here before he comes to."

"Why?" Charlie asked, "He's not gonna hurt you again. I told him to back off."

She stared at him, "Was that before or after he knocked me out?"

"After," Charlie said, looking down, "But you're safe now."

"No, I'm not. And neither are you."

"What?" Charlie asked.

"You're not safe here. Neither of us are. We need to get the hell out of here before they come."

"Who?"

"The ones that took everyone away," she said.

"What do you mean?"

"We weren't supposed to survive," she said, "They're gonna come back for us. Just like they came for my neighbor."

"Wait, you *saw* them? Who took the people away?"

"Not when it happened, no. But I saw them today. They attacked my neighbor right in front of me."

Her eyes were wet, as if she might cry, but she continued.

"My neighbor Tom was outside loading his car with supplies. We were gonna drive until we found other survivors. I was in his living room, filling the last of the duffel bags with supplies when I heard him scream. I looked out the window and that's when I saw them. These ... *things*. They were like people, but like ... *undone* or something. One of them was missing eyes, and the other was missing a mouth. And they just started attacking him, and ... one was eating him while the one without a mouth was shoving Tom's guts all over the front of his face where his mouth should've been."

She paused, "Did you hear that?"

Charlie looked around, "What?"

She leaped on him, falling on top of him. At first, he thought she was attacking him, but she was after the lantern. She clicked it off, threw the room into darkness, and slapped a cool hand over his warm mouth.

"Shhh. Can you hear that?"

He did — a clicking sound, faint, but constant, just outside his bedroom window. He glanced at the curtain, but it was closed, mercifully.

"They're here," she whispered.

* * * *

CHAPTER 2
BRENT FOSTER

Oct. 15, 2011
Afternoon
New York City

Brent couldn't stop watching the video.

One minute the couple was in bed, sound asleep. The next, an impossible, smoky-looking liquid cloud appeared from nowhere, killed the video and filled the screen with static. And then the sleepers disappeared — vanished, vaporized, gone.

Stan, as requested, showed him three other videos they'd recorded in their neighbors' apartments. Each video showed the same song, different tune.

"What is it?" Brent asked.

"We have no idea," Melora said. "Though we suspect it's extraterrestrial, and that the dreams we've shared the past few decades were some sort of alien broadcast meant for us."

Brent shook his head, trying to shake the thought of the black, liquid cloud hovering above his wife and child, desperately wanting to ignore the lunacy. Yet, without a better explanation for where everyone except them had evaporated to at 2:15 a.m. the night before, he clearly had little choice but to play along.

"Why us? Why didn't they take us?" Brent asked. "Why would they take a ... " he wanted to finish the sentence, but fell short at the word *child*, as though murdering the word would take the reality with it. He HAD to believe Gina and Ben were out there, somewhere.

"There have to be others," Brent said, glancing at the self-proclaimed 215 Society. "I mean, you all had the dreams, so yeah, you're still here. But I *didn't*. And I'm here, too. So there must be something else which kept me around. Something which may have kept others, too?"

"You probably don't remember your dreams," Melora said, the professor's tone starting to piss off Brent. "In fact, most people only remember a small percentage of their actual dreams. Isn't it possible you had the dreams and don't remember?"

"Nah," Luis said, "He'd have to remember at least *one* of them, right? Maybe there *are* others out there like he says. Makes sense."

Brent nodded as if endorsement built the road to reality.

"Even if there are others," Melora said, in her parochial voice, "it's safe to assume his family isn't among them, or else they would have been in his house this morning."

Brent stared at her. Her face was blank, clinically detached from her words. He was pretty good at guessing people's histories, what made them the way they were. Melora, however, was beyond him. He felt like punching some color into the pasty white of her face.

Brent suddenly remembered seeing one of them on the street. "Wait a second. Was one of you out on the street earlier? Wearing a dark jacket and a hat?"

"Yeah," Luis said, "why?"

"You saw something. I saw you looking north with your binoculars, then you ran. What was it; what did you see?"

"You don't want to know," Luis said, taking a sudden interest in his boots.

"We may as well tell him," Melora said, "He's going to find out sooner or later."

Luis shook his head, as if delivering this news was more painful to him than it would be to Brent. The sensitivity seemed a bit odd coming from such a muscle-bound tough guy.

"Tell me," Brent asked more than said.

"You sure you wanna know? I mean, you might have a wife and child out there and when I tell you this, you're gonna wanna go after them."

"Tell me."

"You're right on one thing … we're not alone. There's something else out there. These … things. Not quite human, but not quite anything I've ever seen either. Maybe aliens, I dunno. I saw a few of them when I was driving around the city before the sun came up. They look like people, if you stretched them out and burned them black, then dumped them in some kinda gel. And they move all weird and shit. When I drove past, a few of them chased after me. And they were faster than any human I ever saw."

"And you saw one out on our street?" Brent asked, shaking his head, as if it would help him digest the impossible.

"More than one," Luis said, "A whole mess of 'em. They looked like they were searching for something or someone. Maybe to come and get the ones who had been left behind."

Brent stared at Luis, his mind reeling.

"I've gotta go out there. I *will* find my family. I feel it in my gut."

"That's hope you're feeling," Melora said, "but it's not informed by fact. And chasing hope is an empty pursuit."

Brent glared at her, wondering if it was still never okay to hit a woman, even at the end of the world.

"So, what? I'm just supposed to give up? Hole away in an apartment and hide day and night while my family might be out there and in danger? Then what? What's the plan after that, huh?"

"We don't have one," Luis said.

Brent thought the comment almost sounded like a criticism of the group, then Melora threw Luis a dirty look that confirmed it.

"Listen," Stan said, trying to make peace, "We're as much in the dark here as you are. Sure, we have theories and ideas, but we don't know what's next, what's out there, or where anyone went. If you want to check it out, I understand. Really, I do. But I think Melora is right about your family. You saw the video. You *saw* the people vanish."

"Yeah, but we don't know *where* they went, right? I mean, when people vanish, they *go somewhere*, right? You can't just make matter disappear without a trace. We haven't found any bodies or mysterious piles of ash or anything, correct?"

"No," Melora said. "The beds are all empty. No trace of anything."

"So," Brent continued, his hands were everywhere as he worked through the ideas taking shape in his head. "All we know is that all the people went somewhere. But we don't know *where*. Which means they might still be in the city somewhere."

"Or in spaceships," Stan suggested.

"Maybe," Brent gave him that, "But if that's the case, maybe we'll see them. Or maybe the aliens will come and take us, too, and we'll be reunited. Did any of you lose anyone last night?"

"I did," Luis said, "My little girl, Gracie. She's 7."

"And do you *really* want to sit here and do nothing?"

Luis looked at the others then shook his head no.

"You're talking millions of people," Melora said, "The odds of millions of people being somewhere in the city ... no. That doesn't make sense. I'm more inclined to believe they all got called to heaven in a Rapture, than walking around the city or being held somewhere by aliens. And I'm an atheist."

"I don't think they were Raptured," Brent said, "And maybe they *are* in UFOs, for all we know. But sitting here isn't going to answer any questions. I'm going out there. And if any of you wants to come, I'd love the help. Otherwise, I'm going solo."

"What about those things?" Stan asked, his voice shaky, "What do we do if we run into them? How do we fight?"

"I don't know," Brent said, "But I'd rather go down fighting than cower in here waiting to die." He headed toward the door, then turned back midway and said, "You don't have to stay here and wait for fate to find you."

"I'll go," Luis said, "We just need to go to my place and grab some shit."

"Anyone else?" Brent asked.

Stan said nothing, but looked at Melora for direction.

"There's nothing out there for me," she said. "I wish you luck. And when you give up, our door is open to you both. We have enough supplies to last a long while, and we're happy to share with you."

"Thank you," Brent said, "And good luck."

"I'll keep in touch with you all via the two-way radios," Luis said. "Turn them on every half hour, and I'll do the same. Anything happens, anything at all, we contact the others."

"Good luck," Stan said, shaking both men's hands.
"Be careful," Melora said.

**

Upstairs, Luis grabbed a black duffel bag full of supplies, most of which were of the shooting variety.

"You any good with a firearm?" Luis asked as they walked down the stairwell to his car outside.

"Eh," a regular gun, maybe, not those submachine guns. "You?"

Luis smiled, "Those two up there, they say they've been preparing for this day, but neither one of 'em ever really got ready to fight. I did nothing *but prepare* to fight for the past 10 years. I'm ready for anything and everything, and all of it at once."

Brent found himself liking his new friend. A lot.

**

The fog had descended, blanketing the street and reducing visibility to less than 20 yards. The New York streets had fallen mute for the first time in centuries. Every step echoed not just off the buildings, but off the fog as well. They climbed into Luis's car, a black BMW.

"This should keep us somewhat safe," he said proudly. "Polycarbonate sandwiched between two panes of glass for the windows, and ballistic steel armor on the body. As close to bulletproof as you can get without being in the belly of a tank."

"But," Brent said, "Can it keep out whatever the fuck was in those videos?"

"The company I ordered this from was fresh outta alien-proof materials."

Brent laughed as Luis put the car in gear and hit the gas.

"Where are we going?"

"Gonna look around, see what's doing. See if we can find our families and wipe that look offa Melora's face."

Brent was surprised by how hard he laughed.

**

If the streets were eerie when empty, the fog took them close to terrifying. It hung thinner on the ground, giving limited visibility. But above the streets, the fog swirled in thick clouds that seemed to swallow buildings like a sentient being. Though the city had never seemed less populated, nor the streets more wide open, Brent felt an intense claustrophobia, as though the fog held unseen mass that might crush them at any moment.

After minutes of silence, Brent had to fill the cabin with idle chatter to distract his mind from the looming danger above.

"Is it just you and your daughter?"

"Yeah" Luis said, "My old lady died last year. Cancer."

"Oh shit, I'm sorry," Brent said. He never knew what to say when someone mentioned death. And he always felt like "sorry" was one of the worst things you could say. It was so … trite. Yet, he could never think of anything better. He'd tried other phrases, like "sorry for your loss," but that felt like a cheesy cop show line, even if it was slightly better than "sorry." If he were being honest, he'd simply say, "that sucks," because death truly did exactly that. But "that sucks" seemed almost flippant. So, he always fell to the old uncomfortable standby, "I'm sorry."

"It's okay," Luis said.

And they always say that, too. 'It's okay.' No, it's NOT okay. It's never fucking okay.

"I hope you don't mind me asking," Brent began, "But if you'd been having these dreams, and you knew some shit was gonna go down, and were even preparing for it, why did you settle down and start a family?"

"Way I see it, we have a limited amount of time on the planet, right? I just happened to know how limited mine might be. You can spend your time fearing inevitable death, I mean, shit, we're *all* gonna die, right? Or you can make the most of the time you've got. Live the fuck outta those years! Do everything you can. Live, learn, laugh, love. Dance like no one's watching, you know, all that shit."

Brent smiled.

"Though, to be honest, I didn't intend to have Gracie. She just kinda came along. And that shit weighed on me, knowing we'd brought a child into this world for such a limited time. It seemed so fucked up. But what was I gonna do?"

"Did you tell your family about the dreams? I mean, how did you prepare? What did you do last night with Gracie?"

"No, I didn't tell my wife. I wanted to a million times, but she had her own shit to deal with. She'd had cancer as a teen and it was in remission for years. I don't know if stuff like worry can cause cancer to come back, but I always felt like it sure as hell couldn't *help*. So, I tried to make things as easy as I could for her, make sure cancer never came back. But, as it turned out, shit came back anyway."

Luis' jaw clenched on some misery just beneath the surface, but he kept talking.

"Last night, I thought about telling Gracie, but I didn't want to scare her. So, I took her out of school for the day, and we went to the park, saw a movie, and had dinner and ice cream. All her favorite stuff. When we got home, I read to her. And we made a tent in the living room with blankets and couch cushions, and then went camping. We talked for hours. I asked her stuff I'd never thought to ask her before, so I could really know her. I asked her about her earliest memories, what she wanted to be when she got older ... "

At this, Luis paused, blinking back the tears.

"It was a magical night. She fell to sleep on my chest. I remembered thinking I had to go to the bathroom, but I passed out. I wasn't going to meet the others last night, but I was wide awake, and I thought maybe there would be safety in numbers or something, so I brought Gracie over and let her sleep on the couch. She slept the entire time. And then 2:15 hit. I woke up, and she was gone."

"Jesus," Brent said, not knowing a single word worthy enough to follow, except maybe "Christ."

"Now here's the thing I didn't tell the others," Luis said, turning to Brent, eyes red. "They'd all been dreaming about the whole world disappearing and the four of our group surviving, right? Well, I had, too. Until a few weeks ago when the dreams started to change."

Brent was only vaguely aware of the white, blurred world outside the car.

"In my dreams, we didn't survive. Nobody did."

* * * *

CHAPTER 3
MARY OLSON

Oct. 15, 2011
Afternoon
Somewhere in Missouri

The huddled survivors shrank from the railing, frozen with fear.

Mary glanced at Paola, who had left the car despite her mother's warning. Her daughter shouldn't have to see this. They should be back home, arguing about her constant attitude and whether or not she could manage three days in a row without losing something new to the growing pile of contraband and consequences Mary had started to stockpile in the basement.

But Paola *had seen it*, and was a bleached sheet because of it. So was Jimmy. John had already emptied a few gallons of his home-brewed ralph over the railing and into the river, but his insides must have been bottomless because he was still going strong.

"They look so neat," Jimmy said.

"No," Desmond was still staring at the bodies, "Not neat; stacked."

And they *did* look stacked. The bodies had a barracks-like organization, lined in orderly rows the river's current had yet to separate. John sent another liquid scream over the railing, but some of the chunky cargo caught wind, flying behind him and into Paola's hair. Mary drew her daughter closer and pulled her hair into a loose ponytail.

Everyone waited quietly while John finished throwing up. But it just kept going and going, stripping his organs by the sound of it.

"She's dead. Gone and slaughtered. Probably stacked somewhere just like this, maybe in that floating cemetery, or another just as awful." John's jaw had hardened.

He looked more angry than sad, fierce even. Mary always thought John looked a little pretty and on the soft side of masculine, but now he looked mean. Like he could kill, maybe even like he *wanted to*. She wondered how long it would be before they all turned into the worst type of animals. Only thing separating man from beast was civilization, after all. Once that disappeared, they were little more than talking bears in a Saturday morning cartoon.

"We'll find her, man." It sounded almost sweet, the way Jimmy nearly believed the sound of his voice. "We just have to start looking."

John probably wouldn't have yelled at Jimmy, but he couldn't yell at Paola. She was too young. And someone had to get yelled at after Paola chimed, "It's okay, sometimes you just have to believe."

John stared at Paola for a long second, then pounced on Jimmy. "I don't need any goddamned platitudes. We won't just *find her*. HOW are we going to find her? At the next rest stop? Don't you realize what's happening? Everything is gone, and everyone is dead. And we're next. This probably isn't just here, it's probably everywhere." He reeled around to face Desmond. "You seem to know everything about everything. What do *you* think? Is this global?"

Desmond chewed on the answer. "Yeah, I think whatever this is, it's probably everywhere."

Jimmy's brief spark of hopefulness was gone. Paola's, too. Mary probably would've cracked, but she had to keep her fractured psyche fused for her daughter's sake. John was already well beyond shattered; hollow, not quite there, a bit like the thing they had found twitching on the side of the road.

"See," John turned to the rest of them. "We're all just days from dead, if we're lucky."

"That's not what I said," Desmond was firm, but his kind eyes met John's and his right hand was resting on the grieving man's shoulder. "But we need to go now if we want to play our odds."

"I want to be alone," John said. "I'll drive the van."

Desmond shook his head and lowered his arm. "You can't do that."

John clenched his teeth. "Why?"

"Because you're distraught, and rightfully so, but that van has 100 percent of our supplies and weapons. Without our gear, we go from bad to worse, fast. Our cargo gives us a better chance of facing whatever's out there. I'm really sorry for what you're going through right now. I can't even imagine, but you've gotta man up. That's all there is to it."

Desmond leaned in and spoke to John in a near whisper. Mary took the cue and led Paola and Jimmy back toward the Suburban. As the kids situated themselves, she watched the exchange between the men, trying to decipher what was being said, via body language alone.

After a few minutes, Desmond put an arm on John's shoulder again, said something, and John met the man's eyes, then nodded. John turned toward the car, and Mary hurried inside, trying to avoid getting caught spying.

John settled into the driver's side and slapped his hand hard against the door. "Well then, let's go."

They drove in relative silence, everyone lost in their own charred, dark tumble of thoughts. Paola was likely thinking about her father, wondering if he maybe somehow survived. She'd asked Mary a few times, and each time Mary said they'd have to wait to find out, but he was probably fine. But right now, they had to travel with the others if they wanted to find safety and answers.

Whether Mary believed Ryan was alive was another story. It wasn't impossible, especially if whatever had happened was only local. He lived a good 80 miles away, so it wasn't as though they could run across the street to check on him. She knew how Paola felt. Despite her many issues with Ryan, she'd rather see him than anyone else in the world.

Mary had no idea what Jimmy was thinking, though he was probably taking a much needed respite from the usual adolescent fantasies that most often painted his brain. John's thoughts were evident by the curl in his lip and the furrow on his brow.

Mary wished she could see Desmond's face. You could tell a lot about a person by watching them drive. So, it didn't surprise her that Desmond wanted to drive alone. He was smart and charming, quite a guy really, but not the person she'd expect to lead a ragtag group of survivors to safety at the end of the world. Yet, he seemed well prepared, more than a guy like that should've been really. His level of prep went beyond hobby, bordering on compulsion. Maybe he wasn't really who he said he was, not that he'd ever said much of anything in the first place.

Desmond had tried to tell her how he made his money, on several occasions actually, but his many explanations made almost no sense, at least not to her. He spent all his time online, including a few hours each day on social media websites. She knew many people who spent countless hours on the Internet, but none of them were doing as well as Desmond. They certainly weren't buying shiny, new models of precision German engineering every month from their efforts.

And what about the guns — who needed an entire trunk of them? Maybe that's what happened when you got bored with regular toys and had more money than God, but it still seemed off. Yet, as weird as it was, she trusted Desmond. And she and Paola certainly owed their lives to his fortunate proximity.

Mary tore from her thoughts when Jimmy started wondering out loud about the end of the world. "You think it was aliens?"

"No," John said. He sounded far stronger than he had just 20 minutes before. "There are no ships in the sky or anything like that. It was probably some sort of poison. You watch too many movies."

"Poison doesn't make sense," Jimmy shook his head. "Where did the bodies go? I mean, yeah there were lots in that river, but that can't be *all of them*. That's probably not even half a town's worth. And poison doesn't make stuff disappear. Look around, man. Everything's just ... gone. Cars, too. Have you noticed how we keep seeing fewer and fewer? Where are they all going? I think they're being moved, just like the bodies in the river."

Paola spoke up from the backseat. A small voice, but in no way timid. "Then that means there are bad guys, probably a lot of them."

"She's right," Jimmy agreed. "Anyone who's moving stuff or making it disappear would have to know what happened. And they would need some crazy technology to make it happen, which is why I'm putting my chips on aliens."

"You're not old enough to lay your chips on anything," John said. "Might be the Army; that wouldn't surprise me at all. And if *that's* the case, Desmond's leading us down the highway in the worst possible direction."

"It's not the Army." Mary didn't know how she knew, but it felt right and given her instincts, that meant it probably was. Besides, she didn't like what John was insinuating about Desmond's decision, or perhaps his intentions.

"We don't know what's going on." John said. "It's best to be prepared for anything, including an Army that's also an enemy."

"It's a zombie outbreak, or maybe some weird interdimensional shit. Maybe something's happening to time." Jimmy had three theories in three seconds.

"Maybe it was nature," again from Paola in the back seat.

John took his eyes off the road and moved them to Paola. "What do you mean?"

"Well, maybe the planet is the bad guy, and it's taking itself back from all the people. It's not like the people have been very nice to it."

Silence filled the car as everyone considered Paola's theory. It was her father speaking, Mary thought, thinking from an angle no one else saw, yet was somehow so tangibly practical. John was something of an environmentalist, or at least the kind who tried, so he seemed to be giving Paola's idea some weight.

A thick silence lingered for a few minutes, interrupted by a slight rattle that sounded like it was coming from under the hood, followed by a heavy blanket of ... atmosphere, or something; a sudden weight — gravity growing thick and fattening the air around them.

"See," Paola said. "The trees are mad."

Something stole the flush from John's face.

"You hear them now, don't you?" Jimmy asked.

John nodded. He could hear the trees, at least until they fell silent a moment later. The dense clusters started to thin. They passed a patch of twisting, blackened branches, then the green was suddenly, shockingly, all gone.

Everything grew darker over the next few miles: the sky, the surroundings, the ground. The entire drive had seen the five of them sailing through the great big empty, but the long miles were nothing compared to the rather abrupt dead man's walk now surrounding them.

There was nothing — no trees, no cars, no people, no houses. Nothing but ashen ground and empty air. Corpses would've been a welcome sight over this. At least it would've been something.

Everyone in the car was wondering the same thing: Was Missouri gone forever, and was this the tundra of their new, dead world?

They drove for another few minutes in awed, toxic silence, wondering where everything had gone. Then they drove right into the answer. No words could describe the devastation before them. Storm, squall, tempest, tsunami — none would do.

If the world had ended, it looked as though they'd surely found the center.

* * * *

CHAPTER 4
LUCA HARDING

Oct. 17, 2011
Morning
Somewhere in California

Luca woke up mostly happy, though he still felt slightly scared. The itchy burny was gone. It started to fade when he woke up and now almost felt nice. Warm all over, like being by the fire naked.

The invisible fire kept him from getting tired. It was his third day walking, yet Luca could still have easily played a full game of soccer, or several. He saw another dead dog on the side of the road, and his sad spiders started to crawl.

Luca shuddered, but didn't stop his stride, or even slow. He missed his family, and the world. But he would find everyone soon. Probably as soon as he found the man who made the lobster tacos. Luca had been thinking about him a lot lately. Whenever he went to sleep, usually after he was finished talking to the Indian.

Luca didn't remember what the man who made the lobster tacos looked like, so his brain made up a brand new face. Now he was tall, taller than most people, but not quite as tall as his dad. The lobster man was older than his dad, though. His skinny body swam inside an extra large, lime-colored T-shirt. It billowed beneath his blue apron as it battled the beach wind that whipped around them.

The taco man looked happy enough to play the good guy in a cartoon, and his smile was so nice it made Luca feel like he'd find his mom and dad as soon as he finished eating his taco.

The spiders weren't there because he missed his mom and dad, even though he did. They were there because so many of the animals had started to disappear. There had been hundreds, and though there were just as many now, the ones on the side of the road weren't moving. And when they stopped moving, they got bugs all over their faces. Dog Vader, or Kick (as he preferred to be called even though Dog Vader was a much cooler name), was okay, but a lot of the other animals weren't. And the bad numbers were getting too high to count.

Luca could've kept walking through the night last night, but the dark was terrible scary to walk in, especially when the animals didn't move. Luca would walk until he couldn't take it anymore, then he would stop on the beach side of the highway and sleep in the sand. The other side was too close to the terrible scary — the only thing that made Luca feel like he might never see his family again.

I don't like the terrible scary. If Mom and Dad and Anna aren't coming back, then they might be hiding deep inside the terrible scary. Animals stop moving forever once the bugs are on their faces. If Mom and Dad and Anna are deep inside the terrible scary, they'll probably have bugs on their faces, too.

Sleeping wasn't too bad, though. Because that's where he got to see his new friend. It only took seconds last night before he was out and talking to Dog Vader, who once again looked like an Indian. He wasn't *really* an Indian; Luca knew that was un-possible. Dogs didn't just turn into people. But talking to the Indian in his dream was the only way he could understand stuff, since Luca couldn't speak barky, which is why Luca always wondered if he could really trust the husky's thoughts in the daylight.

"Why are all the animals dying?" he asked.

The Indian had grown more outlandish each time Luca napped. He now wore a giant headdress, earrings that hung half as low as a Hula-hoop, and a necklace made from what looked like the teeth of a saber tooth tiger. He also held in his lap a giant red, plastic pipe with a white ring around the top.

The Indian took a giant puff, then said, "They are not dying."

Luca thought about the animals, both dead and alive, and how they all looked so strange. Like they weren't really there, even though they were — equally un-possible.

Luca wished the Indian wouldn't use so much of the confusing talk. He was trying to think of a different way to ask the same question when a second ring of smoke curled through the air, followed by, "Dying closes a circle. The animals still move in a line."

More confusing talk. Luca didn't care about shapes. He knew the animals were dying, plus he could see pieces of their realness missing. He wished the Indian would just tell him why, but sometimes he liked to answer questions Luca didn't even ask.

"Where did the rainbows go?" Luca tried a totally different question, hoping the Indian wouldn't use confusing talk in his answer.

"They are there," he said, "but you don't need them like you did."

Luca would have asked another question but was suddenly eating a lobster taco and staring at the one smile that swore everything would be okay. He swallowed his taco and closed his eyes, then opened them to a beautiful sky that was the exact same blue as the bubblegum ice cream he wasn't allowed to try until he turned 10. Because bubblegum ice cream was two digits worth of sweet, at least according to his dad.

He rubbed his eyes and felt the invisible fire on his body. He was safe, even though the animals were all dying.

When Dad goes to the store and then comes back, that's a circle. When Mom says, "Let's go to the store together," we are moving in a line.

Dog Vader wasn't around when he woke in the morning, but Luca wasn't worried. They always managed to find each other. Luca began to wonder where the husky had gone when he realized he hadn't seen him in a whole lot of hours. It had to be close to lunch time, but Luca didn't want to stop just yet and eat any of the food in his backpack.

He had to be getting close to Mexico because Luca saw one of those signs with the family running across the street. That meant they weren't too much farther from the man with the lobster tacos.

Luca passed a cat with bugs on its face and felt an ouchy inside, but his attention wasn't on the cat for long. He heard the husky's unmistakable whine and saw Dog Vader a few yards up the road, nudging his nose against something on the ground.

Luca was standing beside the dog, just as a man was starting to wake up. He opened his eyes slowly, then smiled, leaping to his feet at the sight of Luca.

"It's you!"

Luca took a big step back. He was NEVER supposed to talk to strangers. *NO, NO, G.I. Joe.* But this was definitely an emergency, even if he wasn't bleeding or vomiting. He needed help, and how else was he supposed to get it if he couldn't ask? But there was a big problem. The man didn't look like just any old stranger.

He's a jumbo stranger. If I talk to him, he might take me far, far away. He might even make me live inside the terrible scary, since that's where he probably lives himself.

The man kept jumping up and down. "It's you, it's you, HA, it's finally you!" Luca looked past the scary, white hair and fixed his gaze on the man's smile. It made Luca feel safe, just like the man's large, lime-green T-shirt. The memory of lobster lingered on his tongue, and Luca took a small step toward the tall man.

Dog Vader whined. The stranger cleared his throat and ran his hands through a thick carpet's worth of hair. "I didn't mean to startle you," he said. "It's just so great to see someone else. Are you alone?"

Luca thought he should say probably no, but lying made his tummy feel terrible. "Yes."

The tall man looked disappointed, though not at all surprised. He held his hand out to Luca. "I'm Will, Will Bishop."

Luca took his hand. "Luca, Luca Harding."

"Where're you from, Luca?"

"Las Orillas."

Will looked impressed. "You walked down here yourself?"

"Yeah, most of the way. I drove a little, but I had to stop because I didn't like it when I crashed the car."

"Had a fender bender, eh? Well, looks like you made it out okay."

Luca didn't want to tell him about the invisible magic that made him better. He wondered where Will was from.

He looked a-lot-of homeless. More than just the few days' worth since everyone went away. He also looked a little like Santa Claus, if he were skinnier and his beard was less bushy.

"Did you drive down here?" Luca asked.

"Nope. I live here."

"Where?"

"Wherever I can."

"You ARE homeless!"

Will laughed. "Well, you don't have to sound so happy about it! Yeah, I'm homeless. And apparently, now so are you. But I have the edge since I've been doing it for a while. So, I say we stick together. Strength in numbers and all that. What do you think?"

His hair is scary, but his smile is from the man with the tacos.

"You recognize me, don't you, Luca?"

The boy nodded.

"Well, I'd like to tell you a story."

Will sat and crossed his legs. "You're a smart kid, Luca. And if we're gonna travel together, I figure we've gotta start out right."

Luca sat in front of him with his hands in his lap.

Will said, "I've been waiting for you. And I mean *you specifically*, not just anyone. And I haven't been waiting just three days. It's been nearly a year. That's why I came down here to live in the first place."

Will rubbed his temples, chewed his lip, lowered his voice, then dropped to one knee, and looked Luca in the eye. "The world is gone, Luca. And it's never coming back. I've known this was going to happen for a while. Told everyone I could, too. But that only made me lose everything I had, including a world's worth of friends and colleagues, each one thinking I was batty. Of course, I'm the one who ended up with the beachfront property."

Will winked at Luca and leaned in closer. "You see, I've been having dreams since forever. Bigger than big dreams, really. You know, like a Beatles song. You *do* know the Beatles, right?"

Luca nodded.

"Well, these dreams are all packed with color. More color than what seems possible to see normally, even when your eyes are wide open. Crazy colors, too. But even though they're all out of this world, the rest of the dream feels just as real as the school year. Well, Luca, in one of those dreams, several actually, I've been spending some time with you. Though I must say you look a lot different in person."

"What do I look like in the dream?"

Will studied Luca for a moment, "Different, that's all. But your colors, they're exactly the same."

"What do you mean my colors?"

"Everyone is made up of sound and color. Sometimes, I can hear people's sounds, but not all the time. But I can *always* see the colors."

"What do my colors look like?"

Will's smile was all over his face. "They're the most amazing colors I've ever seen! The sort of colors that might just make everything okay."

Will started to laugh so hard he came a little close to crying. His laughter slowed, then eventually stopped. He stood and said, "Come on; there's a ton to tell you. We'll get caught up on the way."

"I'm supposed to go there," Luca pointed toward Mexico.

"Nope," Will shook his head, "You were just supposed to meet me. And now you have. It's time to head east, and we're not gonna want to waste a lot of time. Are you ready?"

Luca nodded. "Do you have a car, Mr. Bishop?"

"It's Will, now and forever. And no, I don't have a car. But I do have something better." Will smiled and jerked his thumb toward a helicopter just sitting there in the middle of the sand.

First, though, they'd dine on some food. Not lobster tacos, to Luca's disappointment, but rather some peanut butter sandwiches and water from the nearby gas station.

Dog Vader chowed down on people food because Luca wasn't sure if Dog Vader was supposed to eat dog food or not. And he didn't want to insult him.

Luca thought about telling Will about Dog Vader's Indian side and his mind talking, but decided to keep it secret for now. For one, it was his special secret. For two, he didn't want Will to think he was crazy.

* * * *

CHAPTER 5
BORICIO WOLFE

Oct. 16, 2011
New Orleans, Louisiana

Boricio wasn't looking for anything in particular when he happened upon a living room packed full of shit he didn't understand. He had spent the day seeing how rich folks lived, specifically on the waterfront. He found himself in a fancy eight-bedroom, six-bathroom, two-story house with three boat slips, two of them occupied, in Gulfport, Mississippi.

He'd already been through four or five of the houses on the stretch, and sure as shit, rich fuckers knew how to live: alcohol, clothes, guns, jewelry, lots of pills, pounds of weed, loads of money, and plenty of food. What surprised him were some of the fetishes these homeowners seemed to engage in. One house had a secret room devoted to sex toys. A wheel on a wall, bondage gear, and a wall full of sex devices that looked almost like weapons.

They look at me like I'm some degenerate; these people are sicker than me! They just hide their dark side under shit tons of money and fuckin' Armani.

The stuff in the secret room was strange, but not as weird as the shit in the house he was in now. Like the other houses, the mansion was practically hermetically sealed. So he blew in the glass from the front door with a shotgun. He had a backpack filled with shells and sorta enjoyed the noise.

The foyer was the usual look-at-me, fancy-pants bullshit with too much white space. Past the foyer into the living room, though, that's where the walls were practically painted in the strangest shit Boricio had ever seen, rich people or no.

The living room was massive, with all the posh furniture pushed to one side. Eight bedrolls sat in a large circle in the middle of the floor. Each bedroll had a large bank of pillows, several bottles of water, and a medium-sized red bucket. The buckets contained what looked and smelled like vomit. The vomit was black, and every bucket was filled with the same shit that was on the walls.

The air was thick, and smelled alien to Boricio.

The fuck is that shit in the air? Smells like some sorta back bayou black-ass water from one of them fake-ass shamans who likes to fuck with the tourists. Difference is, back alley shit smells fake; this black-magic snatch right here smells like the real deal. Yessiree, some weird-ass shit went down in this room.

Two buckets had been kicked to the side. Scabs of black vomit crusted the lacquered hardwood floor. Rich people were willing to pay a chunky hunk of fat cash for thrills you couldn't score in a back alley, but the bad trips that had happened in the living room had practically scarred the air.

A red and white bedroll was in the center of the circle, with wooden instruments, spirit sticks burned to a nub, and a large, two-liter jug of what looked like sludge. It had been filled to the top, as evidenced by the thick coat of green and brown the bottle wore at its lip, but now it was mostly empty. A shot glass on the floor shared the ghost of whatever had been inside.

Well fuck me four times on a Friday if that ain't some million-dollar mind fuck right there. Giddy-up. I might as well make myself nice and cozy. The world is over, and there's some liquid fucking juju just waiting to get swallowed.

Boricio picked up the two-liter jug and shot glass, then went upstairs, found the master bedroom and lay on the bed. He had no idea on the dosage, so he filled the glass to the top, put it to his lips, held his breath, and spilled the entire psychedelic mess down his throat.

For a few moments, he didn't feel anything. He wondered if it wasn't some sort of drug in the jars but rather some perverted, sick-ass rich, weirdo bodily-fluid-ingesting ceremony.

Something moved in his guts.

Seconds later, without warning, Boricio lost it all. Vomit spewed from his mouth like an unholy sprinkler. The sudden acid in his nostrils made him wince. It was liquid death and smelled the part.

Boricio lay face down on the Egyptian cotton as the toxic stew leaked from his mouth and marred the ivory-colored rug. He noticed it in a detached, almost whimsical way. He smiled, moving to touch the stuff, but his hand felt weird, as if he was directing someone else's body from a distance. He started to laugh as his fingers opened and closed on his cue — a bottomless, retching chainsaw of a guffaw. Whatever he puked up, he was glad it was gone.

He felt so much lighter, so much stronger, so much *better.*

And besides, only once the blackness was gone could Boricio see all the colors around him. They bled and expanded and spun around, dancing in his mind and threatening to smother him in an endless torrent of mile-long thoughts.

It wasn't like drugs he'd used before. Those drugs made you feel things that weren't there. This shit made you realize the things that were right in front of you but you were usually unable to see.

He was normally able to control himself no matter what he was on. Sure, he might get higher, lower, but he never really let go of the steering wheel.

Something bad was happening here, though. He could feel it in the back of his skull, threatening to take the wheel and kick him right out the passenger door.

He snarled, had to fight.

Thoughts overwhelmed him, too many to sort, voices, images, and a million colors, *fuck, the colors,* as the world seemed to spin and cave in on him.

He could feel the end coming, might've died right there. *What's the point in going on? Just let go of it all.*

He wanted to wake so he could stand and run, but whatever universe he drank was crawling up through his body and infecting every corner of his mind. And as it raced through his memories and dreams, it forced him to watch what it saw, forcing him to witness the darkest shit inside him.

Hate, rage, violence, murder, rape, robbing, maiming, and all the perverted shit he'd ever done or thought to do. This thing inside dragged it all into the light — a bright light as big as fucking Christmas.

This is you. You are all of this.

But no one tells Boricio what to do, *not even other parts of Boricio.*

So, he battled his way through a thick haze of muddy time, swimming through an angry abyss of forever. He ran, not even sure if he were really running or if it were only in his head. Yet, he kept at it. Just as he got far enough away, and was about to get back in the driver's seat of his brain, he slipped, fell on his back, and slid down a steep hill of wet grass. Wet, bloody grass.

As he tumbled out of control, he could hear the sound of water rushing below, and knew he was about to slide right off a cliff and into the rapids.

Before he could roll right off the edge of the abyss, he jammed an elbow into the ground hard, causing his body to flip over and break momentum, stopping just at the edge of the cliff.

Below was a river, flowing fast and full of corpses.

Boricio had seen some fucked-up shit, even made a few *artistic* displays himself, but he'd never been anything so soul bleaching as that. Whatever was inside him had won. His head swam, the colors came back, and Boricio fell.

**

When he woke, he was back in the house, his liquid nightmare covering the white room like spilled ink in snow. He smiled.

Yeah, that was some scary shit, but hell if it wasn't the near side of fan-fucking-tastic, too. Like the trippiest movie ever, no ticket required.

**

Boricio spent the next day taking tiny swigs from what was left of a second two-liter bottle of slop while tearing down the highway. He remembered the colors, but none of the hundreds of miles of distance, the full tank of gas, or the two bodies that somehow found their way into his trunk.

The one with the nose ring looked like she would've been a Ferris wheel and a funnel cake full of fun. Looked like a screamer, and sorta mean. But it doesn't look like I took much time, what with that hole in the middle of her forehead.

Whatever was inside the green/brown sludge wasn't near as powerful on the second day. Or maybe Boricio was getting stronger or building resistance. The trips were definitely shorter, and time wasn't so fucking tangled. Plus, they ended with something a helluva lot less fucked-up than a river full of bodies. Boricio stopped at a hotel, made himself at home in the best suite he could find, and decided to get another ticket to the Magical Mystery Tour.

This time, he found himself at an abandoned gas station with an old man with crazy hair standing next to a kid. This weird dog was there, too. While neither the old man nor the boy could see Boricio, as he wasn't *really* there, the dog stared right at him, growling.

"Evil!" the dog said.

What the fuck?!

Boricio opened his eyes, his head swimming with the strongest sense of déjà vu he'd ever felt.

This is some weird-ass, third-eye shit, that's what it is. Ain't nothing to prove it, but I know it just the same. Shit I'm seeing in my head is somehow real, shit I could see now maybe, if I was in the right place.

Boricio was agitated that he had just a swallow of the liquid magic, but he took it in one gulp and spent the next several hours hovering just above reality.

I'm not alone.

Something on this planet wants me gone.

When the world is dying, even the hunters get hunted.

Boricio smiled.

He'd always been a hunter, but the world had always deprived him of a challenge. Sure, he kept on the move because he sure as fuck wasn't ever gonna get caught. But he'd be lying if he said the kills had the same joy they once did, the same sweet taste. It was still nice, but a bit like fucking the same redhead in the back of the same Impala for five years running. Only so long could you keep getting it up for the fuck.

There weren't many like him in the world. There couldn't be. Only room for a few kings in the world. And now, it seemed, even fewer to challenge him.

**

Oct. 17
8:14 p.m.
Somewhere in Alabama

Boricio flew by the *Welcome to Alabama* sign going 106mph. The highway was dead, had been for a while. No people, no cars. No billboards, no buildings. Just streets going dark as the world turned out the lights.

Vanished people were enough *what-the-fuck* already, vanished cars were just plain, beer-battered bullshit. When the seven horsemen first started galloping a couple days back, abandoned cars were everywhere. Boricio even saw several with their engines still running. But now, it seemed the cars weren't nearly as plentiful.

Boricio sneered and stepped on the gas, frustrated that his own thoughts were a brew of confusion. He was feeling paranoid, like the springs of some trap had been sprung, and its claws were about to close on him. He was kinda glad that the liquid was gone. As good as the trips were, the ride down was a bitch.

Signs of civilization were shifting, if not disappearing entirely, and Boricio was starting to worry that he'd run out of gas right out there in the middle of the big empty. The radio was still mostly silent, except for the single station broadcasting the occasional static punctuated by the even rarer "Boricio."

The needle was dancing just above the red when Boricio saw the impossible — a dull-red Ford F150 pulled to the side of the road. An attractive, slightly heavy woman with a sheer, sky-blue T-shirt and denim skirt was waving at Boricio as he slowed to a stop behind the open tailgate.

Fry me a fresh tortilla full of fuck yeah; are those her nipples pokin' through? Day-um, they must be the size of a quarter and the goddamned thumb holding it!

Boricio licked his lips and stepped from the late-model Honda Civic he had no memory of getting.

"Boy, am I glad to see you," the woman said, relief coating her dusty face. She smelled like a perfume this waitress he once fucked used to wear. Couldn't remember the name of it, or the waitress, though.

"Likewise, Ma'am. Been out here long? Need help? What can I do? I'm about on empty myself. You outta gas?" Boricio smiled behind his friendly rat-a-tat-tat.

"I have close to a full tank. But the truck started rattling about 15 miles back, and I got worried. Don't know what I'd do if it flat out quit on me out here."

"Yeah, you don't wanna be stuck out here alone. Not with them creepers out there."

"The creepers?" Splotches of white bled through the blotches of red on her face.

"Yeah, the creepers. They must be what up and replaced the people" Boricio tipped his head forward and then looked down. Ignorant yokel was one of his favorite masks. Seemed people liked believing that one, and Boricio liked to make it easy when appropriate.

"What do they look like?"

"Well, that I don't know," Boricio scratched his head. "I haven't actually seen them. But I know they're there." It was true, he hadn't actually seen them, so much as sensed them in one of his many trips.

The woman was scared, her eyes moving rapidly. Her voice rose an octave, and fresh sweat beaded her forehead. Her breasts were heavy, covered in sweat and full against the tee. Boricio felt himself getting stiff, but he couldn't rush it. This one had to last.

"You seen anyone else?" Boricio took a step back and leaned against the side of the Honda.

"Not since," the woman choked, then fell to her knees and started to cry.

Boricio didn't like this at all. No fun if they didn't fight.

"Now, now," Boricio knelt to one knee and put a hand on her back. "Everything's gonna be okay; you'll see." Boricio moved in closer. "I've got a plan. Come with me. Everything will be okay."

"What's your name?"

"Emil, Emil Branson." Boricio held out his hand, and the woman took it.

"Do you know where anyone else is?" she asked. He could tell she wanted a yes, to know he knew where others were. No problem there. He'd give her what she wanted, then take what was his.

"Sure do! Just heard a distress call on the CB. Small group, not more than 20 miles from here. Was racing to get there just as fast as this car'll fly, until I happened on you."

The woman met Boricio's eyes. And that's when he saw it. That ever-so-slight shift in the woman's eyes. The same shift so many of his victims saw just before the end. He didn't hear the person behind him until the last second.

Christ.

"I'm sorry," she said.

He felt the impact in the back of his skull and blacked out before he hit the ground.

* * * *

CHAPTER 6
EDWARD KEENAN

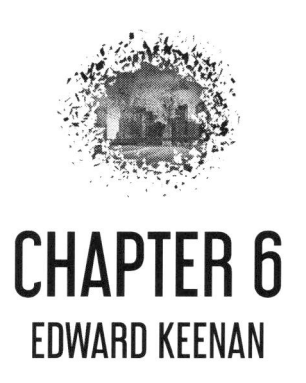

Oct. 15, 2011
Early morning
Somewhere in Ohio

Ed put the gun in his pants as soon as he saw that the only person in the abandoned car was an obviously unarmed and pregnant teenager. She was skinny (save for the belly) and on the mousy side, with long, auburn hair covering most of her face. When she finally looked up, he did a double take. The girl was nearly the spitting image, though a younger version, of his daughter, Jade.

"Are you okay?" he asked through the closed window. He didn't want to spook her by opening the door.

She was crying and mouthing something he couldn't hear through the rain, which was drenching him.

"I'm going to open the door, okay?"

She nodded her head yes, and he opened the front door, rather than the back, then leaned inside the car. The first thing he noticed was the purse on the floor in the front passenger seat. Then he saw keys dangling from the ignition, not much of a surprise considering the car was still running.

"Are you okay?" he asked again.

She shook her head no, wiping tears from her face. "They're gone."

"Who's gone?" he asked.

"My parents. They d ... disappeared."

"What do you mean, disappeared?"

She waved her shaking hands at the front seat as if it should be evident, then explained, through a quickly rising tide of tears.

"We were driving home from vacation. But Dad didn't want to stop at a hotel because he has to get back to work in the morning and we'd already left too late. So, he decided to drive straight through. I was sleeping. Mom was, too, in the front seat. Then I heard this loud whistling sound that woke me."

She lost her voice to a sudden torrent of tears.

"It's okay," Ed said in his calmest voice. He would have put a comforting hand on her shoulder, but was too far from reach in the front seat. It was probably for the best; she might see the move as a threat and then she'd *really* lose her mind.

She found her breath and finished her story. "I heard this whistling sound, and woke up. There was ... something else in the car."

Her green eyes were wide, wet, and tinged in red.

"It was like a dark cloud or something, but it moved weird, like it was alive. Pulsating. It moved over me, and I could feel it, cold and filled with some sort of electricity. It even zapped me a bit, but it didn't hurt exactly ... Then I noticed my dad was asleep at the wheel. And the car wasn't moving. The cloud thing moved faster and faster like we were inside a mini-tornado. The whistling grew so loud I had to cover my ears. And ... "

She cried again, then swallowed before continuing.

"There was this flash of light, and it was suddenly gone, just like that. My parents, too."

She surrendered to her tears as Ed tried to make sense of what she had laid out. He wanted to ask the girl if she were certain she saw what she saw. Maybe she'd been dreaming. But she was obviously fragile, and he knew from limited experience with his own daughter, as strong and independent as teenagers often appeared, they could easily and quickly regress to small children who needed reassurance that the monsters in their closets weren't real at all.

No, the real monsters are on the street. And they're often confused for the good guys.

As much as what she said seemed unbelievable, Ed had the honed instincts from years of training that told him when people were lying to him, or even themselves, with a shocking accuracy. It was part of what made him such a valuable asset to the agency. This girl wasn't lying. To him or herself.

Ed felt the unseen pieces of the night's puzzle slowly shift into place. Something had happened to the people on the plane, to the people in the house he'd been in, to the people in the store, and the cars, and everywhere else.

Something big went down.

Something his experience hadn't prepared him for.

It wasn't a terrorist attack or natural disaster. It was probably something that fell off the edge of his understanding.

"How long have they been gone?"

The girl looked at the clock on the radio face: 5:12 a.m.

"Three hours; it happened at 2:15 a.m. I remember looking at the clock because it kept flicking on and off while the cloud thing got faster: 2:15 over and over again."

That was about the time his plane went down, though he'd not had a watch to know exactly. He swallowed hard and asked the next question in his softest, most careful tone. "What do you wanna do?"

She looked up at him as if it hadn't occurred to her to do anything other than wait for her parents to return. She was shell-shocked, normal thoughts were canceled until further notice.

"What do you mean?"

"They've been gone almost three hours. You can't just sit here on the side of the road. I almost ran right into your car."

"I ... can't leave. What if they come back?"

This wasn't going to be easy, and time was a foe. He'd have to level with her.

"Three hours ago, I was flying in an airplane. I fell asleep. When I woke up, the plane had crashed. Somehow, I was thrown into the nearby woods. But when I went back to search for other survivors, there weren't any."

She looked at him. "None?"

"None. And no bodies. Everyone on that plane, except for me, had vanished. At exactly 2:15."

Her eyes widened as something inside her started to click.

"I drove through town and didn't see anyone there either," he continued, leaving out the part about breaking and entering.

"So, what are you saying? Everyone's gone?"

"I don't know about everyone; I mean, *we're* still here. But there's a lot of people missing."

"Where did they go? Are they coming back?"

Ed looked down at the purse on the floor, searching for the right words, but finding nothing. "I don't know."

The girl swallowed, wiping tears from her face. She seemed to be a bit less broken than she had a few minutes before. But he saw the familiar glimmer in her eyes — her brain was making the necessary adjustments to move on, even if it wasn't letting her know just yet.

Ed marveled at the brain's ability to sever emotions when necessary, to do what needed done despite emotional connections. He'd seen children become cold-blooded killers, soldiers mercifully end the lives of their fallen comrades, and agents turn on one another without hesitation. The Switch, as he called it, was in most people, though most would never discover it unless led there by circumstance. And it was almost never a good circumstance which showed you how to flick The Switch. It certainly wasn't in his case.

Sometimes, it was necessary to find The Switch in order to move forward. Those that couldn't *or wouldn't* flip it often paid a high price for their hesitance.

"My name is Ed," he offered, leaning closer and extending his hand.

"Teagan," she said, shaking his hand with a frail grip.

"Okay, Teagan. What do you want to do? Where's your home?"

"Cape Hope, North Carolina."

"Do you want to go there?"

"Do you think my parents might be there?"

"Honestly? No. I don't know where people went, but I definitely don't think they went home."

She stared out the window, then her hands went to her stomach, soothing her unborn child.

"How far along are you?"

She pulled her hands away, as if embarrassed by her condition.

"Five months," she said, then paused as if she were going to say something else, before deciding not to.

"Do you know if it's a boy or girl?"

"I hope so," she said, her face straight for a moment until he got the joke. Then she smiled.

She found The Switch.

Now she could move forward.

"I don't know; I want it to be a surprise," she said, staring into the dark. "Do you think there are still doctors left?"

"I don't know," Ed said. "But I'm sure we'll find someone who can help."

He thought to tell her that he could, in a pinch, deliver a baby. But decided not to. She was still three or four months away and there was no telling what would happen between now and then. They were stuck in a rather horrible present, and to count on anything beyond the moment was wishful thinking. For now, he would look after her. But he couldn't allow himself to get attached. If shit hit the fan, he'd have hard choices to make, and he needed to know he could find and flip his Switch without missing a beat.

**

They decided to drive to Cape Hope, even though it was sure to be a pointless trip. Ed hoped to find someone she knew she could stay with, and then he could go on his way.

She left a note in the car for her parents telling them where she was and that she was with "a guy named Ed" who was helping her. Ed hoped for her parents' sake they didn't come back to the car to find the note. He was sure that if roles were reversed, he'd be scared shitless to find his pregnant daughter running off with some "guy named Ed." She took her mom's purse and their suitcases from the trunk, so nobody would steal them, and loaded them into "his" SUV.

**

About 20 miles south, he decided they would need some sleep before the next day's travel. They stopped at a store and grabbed some clothes for him, along with a trio of portable lanterns and several packs of D-batteries. They filled the truck with food and drinks, then found a Trinity Suites Hotel, a place that normally charged $400 a night for its cheapest room. Though its sign wasn't lit, the lobby had a faint glow from the backup lighting.

They parked in the hotel's lot, which had a couple dozen cars. The lobby doors were open, just as Ed expected. "Hello?" he called, his voice echoing off the empty halls.

The hotel was silent, save the buzzing from the emergency lighting and the signs above the doors. They took the stairs to the second floor and knocked on a few doors. Satisfied nobody was inside, Ed kicked in one of the doors while Teagan lit the room with a lantern. It was large, with two queen-sized beds, a large flat screen TV hanging on the wall, and a broken mini-fridge, plus a separate bathroom and a mini-office setup against the windows.

The beds were made, meaning the room had likely not been occupied when the Big Vanish occurred.

"Nice room," Teagan said.

"Okay," Ed said, "Here's the deal. You can stay in the next room, and I won't take offense at all. I'm an old dude with a daughter older than you, so I'm sure you're nervous to stay in the room with me. On the other hand, I'm not sure what the hell is going on and I want to keep an eye on you to make sure you're safe."

Teagan thought about it for a moment. "Are you some

kind of cop?"

"I used to be ... something like that," he said, not wanting to tell her too much, just in case someone hit the cosmic pause button again and the world resumed as normal in the morning. The less Teagan knew, the better off they both would be. "You can trust me. Though I'm sure a homicidal maniac would tell you the same. Which is why I'm going to give you this."

He pulled out the pistol, and Teagan nearly jumped back when she saw it, eyes wide.

He quickly handed it to her, to strip any idea in her mind that he intended to use it on her.

"Here. Take it. Just click this button here; it's the safety. Aim and fire."

"No," she said, shaking her head, "I don't want ... need that."

"Okay, fair enough. Then you take this," he said, handing the gun to her.

She took it, if hesitantly. "Okay, I'll stay here. Which bed?"

"I'll take the one closest to the door," Ed said, "Just in case."

"In case of what?" she asked, sitting her lantern down on the nightstand.

"In case of anything."

**

After Teagan lay down, Ed went into the bathroom. The sink, shower, and toilet were still working to his rather large relief. He took a long shit and then a longer shower. The water was slightly warmer than ice, but after the night he'd had, he didn't mind at all. He was bruised and battered, but his injuries would heal quickly. A decent night's rest and he'd be ready to roar.

He dressed in his new clothes — jeans and a long-sleeved black shirt, a far better fit than the stolen clothes, then lay on top of the sheets on the bed closest to the door.

He looked over at Teagan, balled up under the comforter, then flicked the lantern and threw the room into darkness.

**

"Noooo!" Teagan's scream woke him violently from his sleep.

His hand was on his gun in less than a second, his eyes scanning the dimly lit room as he jumped out of bed to face whatever was there.

But they were alone.

Sunlight lit enough of the room that he could see Teagan sitting up in bed, crying.

"What is it?" he asked, sitting on the edge of her bed.

She fell against him.

"They were coming for the baby."

"Who?" he asked, putting his hand awkwardly on her shoulder.

"The men with the helicopters. They were hunting us because they want my baby."

* * * *

CHAPTER 7
LUCA HARDING

Luca had never been in a helicopter. And though he thought it would be exciting, it was mostly loud and a little bit scary. Fortunately, they wouldn't have to stay in the helicopter too long. Will said they would fly to the nearest airport where they could trade the copter for a fully fueled airplane.

"You can fly a plane?" Luca had never met a pilot before.

"Like you wouldn't believe," Will beamed, "Was in the U.S. Air Force for 14 years before we started thinking one another were crazy."

They did stop at the airport to trade the copter for a plane, but only after a small stop first.

"Been wanting to get down here for days, but I wasn't sure when you were gonna show, and I sure as a trip to Disney World didn't want to miss you."

Will winked at Luca as he lowered the helicopter into the mall parking lot, right in front of Nordstrom's front doors. "Do wish I could've looked a lick or two more presentable, though."

Will gave Luca an awkward smile then hopped from the helicopter and held his hand out. "Come on," he said, "I think you should come with me. The dog can stay in here if he wants. He'll be fine, and I'll be quick. Promise."

Will lowered Luca from the cockpit. He was gentle, squeezing the boy's shoulders as his feet hit the concrete. For a sliver of a second, Luca missed his dad a tiny bit less. His mom and sister, too.

They broke into Nordstrom by hurling a trashcan through the doors, but Will promised Luca it was okay emergency behavior. He took a grooming kit and a large pile of clothes into the men's restroom, where he stayed for a while. Luca thought it seemed like a long, long time, and it was, but the time made sense when Will came out of the bathroom looking almost exactly like the man who made the lobster tacos.

His scary hair and beard were gone. He was the same tall man as before, but looked even taller in jeans and a black T-shirt. His face was freshly shaven, and his scary hair was now shorter, though choppy in places he cut wrong. If Will had any idea how ridiculous his hair looked, he didn't care. He was all smiles.

"Alright, kid, let's go!"

**

After a quick swap at the airport, they were flying in a small plane that Will had arranged to be fueled and ready. Will explained that since there was no electricity in most places, they'd be tight on gas. So he outfitted the plane with some kind of fuel bibs which should give them enough gas to get where they were going. But if they ran out, Will warned, they'd need to land somewhere and find a car.

"Where are we going?" Luca asked.

"We need to get to the trees," Will said.

"Are we here?" Luca asked as they flew above Flagstaff, above a sudden, beautiful sea of green.

Will shook his head.

"You don't seem like you're an Army person," Luca said.

"I wasn't in the Army," Will smiled, "I was in the Air Force. But I see what you mean. I am a much cooler cat than they usually allow, what with my giant muscles and bottomless charm."

Dog Vader whined from the back of the plane, just like he'd been doing every 15 minutes or so since leaving the coast.

"I wasn't a normal officer," Will's voice rose just above the husky's wine. "The Air Force wouldn't have been my thing, but I was recruited young. Promises were made, and I was young enough to believe them. I was also naive enough to believe that if they wanted me bad enough they'd be willing to pay me what I was worth."

"What's Nai-Eve?"

"They needed something I have in here," Will tapped the side of his head. "You know what a one-horse-town is?"

Luca shook his head no.

"Well, it's small. My town was called Leonard. Sits so close between the Kentucky-Tennessee border, folks might argue over which was which, though the ones who said Leonard was in Tennessee would've been right. My cousin Jimmy called it a 'hoof town' on account of it being so small it didn't even have the one horse. The Air Force paid for everything, made me feel smart, and got me out of the hoof town."

"What did they want?"

Will pinched his nose, then stayed inside his thoughts for about a minute. "You know how I said I could see the colors of stuff, and sometimes their sounds? Well, it's like that, sorta. At least as close as I can manage to explain for now."

Will looked at Luca.

"Don't worry about getting it; you will. Wish it wasn't so, but it is. And you can take me to the bank on that. I've seen more in this life than I ever imagined I would, and I think a lot of that might have been just so I could get it all to you. A lot of what I've seen isn't fit to tell an 8-year-old boy, but I promise you'll know everything you need to know before you need to know it."

"Will?"

"Yeah."

"What happened?"

"To the world? I don't have a popped kernel of a clue, kid. Wish I did."

"But you said you knew it would happen?"

"I did. Even knew the day, time, and what I was supposed to do when it did."

"What did you do?"

"I went to live by the water. Slept by the border for most of a year, waiting for the post-modern Rapture, then eventually you. Night it happened, I went to the water and held my head under the ocean for a few minutes. By the time I'd surfaced, the world had gone hollow."

Luca could tell Will was wondering if he understood everything being said, but he kept quiet. Sometimes, the best way to let a grown up know you got what they meant was to nod and not say anything at all.

Will smiled at Luca then went on.

"There were a bunch of us this one time, and they sent us deep into the Alaskan wilderness. There was nothing but nothing around us. A little like this," he waved his hand across the empty beneath them. "We found something we didn't expect and weren't supposed to see."

This feels like listening time. No interruptions.

"We were deep in a cave on a crack of land I can't imagine anyone ever having stood on before. Yet we found technology in that cave that I'd never seen. None of us had. Venturing a guess, I'd say it was there to measure something, but what I can't even begin to guess without slamming hard into a wall of logic. My light was directly on it, whatever it was, but I couldn't get a good fix on the tech because the alloy was dull and the cave was so dark. I could see it, but I didn't know if anyone else could. You see," he looked at Luca, "sometimes I see stuff that isn't there, at least according to everyone else. That's why the Air Force sent me to Alaska in the first place."

I think I see stuff like that, too.

"Everyone saw it, though none of us knew what we were looking at. By the time we all agreed there were some strange things afoot among the ice floes, we saw a sharp flare of light, which looked a bit like the end of the world in the mean mouth of that cave. Then BAM!, we were out. No one remembers anything after the light. We woke up, and the tech was gone. Some of the guys remembered seeing it, most didn't. But I'm convinced whatever it was in that cave gave each of us 'The Sight.'"

"What's The Sight?"

"It's what let me see you about a year before I did. And lets me still see all the guys from the Alaskan adventure, except Renny since he's been dead for six years. Some of 'em see me right back. They all could if they knew how, but most of the guys never realized things had changed. Here's the thing." Will leaned closer. "All the guys who knew about The Sight, well they're all still alive. Right now, all four of them."

Luca gasped. *There are more people!* Maybe his mom and dad knew about The Sight, though even if they did, Anna probably didn't. "There are more people?"

"Of course!" Will slammed his hand on his knee. "There must be a ton. And that's just easy math. Even if we lost 99 percent of the population, and I'm not so sure the number's that high, we'd still have three million people in America alone. People will come together. We'll start over, and everything will be fine. Maybe even better than it was."

"Where are your friends?" Luca asked.

"Didn't say they were my friends," Will's mouth twitched, "and I'm looking for them every chance I get."

"You mean with The Sight?" Luca didn't wait for the answer. "I have The Sight, don't I?"

"I'd be as shocked as a man chewing on electric chocolate if you didn't!"

"How did I get it?"

"Born with it, most likely. End of the world just brought out the best in you."

Will hit Luca on the knee, but Luca wasn't feeling nearly as playful. From nowhere, he started to sob and cried himself to sleep.

**

Luca woke screaming from a nightmare unlike any he'd ever had in his whole life.

"You dreamt about her, too, didn't you? The girl Paola and her mom?"

Luca nodded.

"You've been dreaming about them, too?"

"Yes," Will said, "for almost as long as I've been dreaming about you."

"They're with the trees," Luca said, feeling like he might cry again. After a pause, he asked Will, "Does she have to die?"

Will shook his head. "No, that's what I call a tomorrowbility; it may or may not happen depending on the variables in the equation." Will shook his head and started over. "Sorry about that. I mean, no. It's a possibility, but it definitely doesn't *have to* happen."

"What can we do?"

"Get to the trees as fast as we can. We'll be there soon."

Luca said nothing. Will sank into his seat. An odd current crackled between them. Luca could tell that Will had dreamed more than he had said. Will was afraid to tell him something.

But Luca was starting to sense it.

Something bad was going to happen to the girl and her mom, real bad.

* * * *

CHAPTER 8
BORICO WOLFE

Boricio woke, lids gummed behind what felt like a thick wall of a cheesecloth blindfold. His head was buzzing, and the hallucinogenic sludge was still swimming its way out of his head. A thin strip of plastic was digging its teeth into his wrists, which were crushed between the floor and his back.

His nose twitched at the smell of prey. He couldn't tell how many people were in the room, but he definitely wasn't alone, and it was more than just that big-nippled bitch who had tricked him. In fact, he didn't smell her at all.

The room was slightly musty, and felt large. Boricio would lay a Benjamin that there weren't any windows. He felt the fabric beneath him. Burlap.

Well, where in the fuck-all am I?

Nope, Boricio don't like this one bit.

His ears prickled, and the short hairs on the back of his neck whispered that he was being watched. No way to know how many, but eyes were on him, no doubt.

He could either play it Sam Jackson and let the room know who was boss, or play smart and show the claws later.

"Where ... where are we?" Boricio stuttered weakly.

"He's awake." A man's voice said from Boricio's right.

"You're okay," a second man's voice, slightly farther and barely a whisper. "Keep your voice low, they'll be back any moment."

"Who is *they*, and how many are there?" Boricio let his bottom lip quiver, just in case he was the only one with his eyes covered.

"Don't know who *they* are, but they know what's going on. Three of 'em snuck up behind me while I was taking a shit. Next thing I knew, I was laying on the floor in here." This final voice was closest to Boricio, just a few inches away.

Predator's guess put five people in the room, including him. One to his left, another three to his right. Silent Bob was on his left, breathing like a lab with a belly full of pups.

"We're waiting to get processed." It was the guy farthest to Boricio's right again. "They come in here and take us out there to whatever's waiting. No clue what it is, but I'm pretty sure I'm next. They come in every five or six hours. And there's always five in here. One comes in, one goes out. So far, there ain't been any girls except the one I imagine brought you here, just like she brought all of us."

A click and a whine came as a door opened and a gust of stale heat rolled inside. And on that heat, a familiar scent of perfume.

Well, ain't that just a tall stack of pancakes worth of perfect. Big-nippled bitch was coming into the room. And someone with her. A guy. Smells like sweat and too much testosterone.

The mystery guest opened his mouth. "Well, lookie who's awake!" Boricio could smell the testosterone suddenly centimeters away. "You ready to tell us what you know?"

Boricio knew nothing, which is exactly what he said.

Testosterone cackled, "Fine by me, boy. You'll get to talking once you're outside and in the box." He finished his sentence with a slap at the back of Boricio's head.

Keep going, because when I'm through with you, I'll be staining this floor with slippers made from your face, you fuck.

Boricio must not have been able to keep his curled lip to himself, because before he knew it, bad breath was curling through his nose and Testosterone himself was snarling in his face.

"You got something you wanna say, boy?" The way he said "boy" was almost like the word had two syllables. *Redneck fuck.* "I know your mama told you if you ain't got nothin' nice to say then don't say nothin', but it isn't like that here." He laughed again. "We're friends here. You can say anything you want."

Something thrust into the back of Boricio's head. He let out a yelp, pissed to have given the man any pleasure in delivering the pain.

"So, anything?"

Part of Boricio believed he could free himself from his restraints, if he wanted to. He probably couldn't clear the room, though he'd be sure to end the fucker in front of him before anyone could stop him. But no, too many things he didn't know, and it was the end of the world. Besides, it'd be nice to make the fucker see the steel in his eyes before he killed him. It was that personal touch that was the trademark of Boricio's attention to detail.

"Nothing?"

Boricio stayed silent.

Boricio didn't see, or even sense, the giant fist until it smashed into his face. He felt the hollow thud rock through his head, then a ringing in his ears followed by stars in his eyes. Blood gushed from his nose and swallowed his face.

"Chew on that until you find your tongue, fucktard."

Boricio heard 15 steps, then a whine and a thud. Testosterone and the big-nippled bitch had left the building.

After a moment of silence, the heavy breather to Boricio's left tried to speak, but wasn't managing much outside a few labored rasps. The heavy breather went on breathing while Boricio continued to wrestle with his restraints.

Finally, as though pushing words from his throat with his entire body, the breather managed to make a few. "Drema buttle noggers son ... "

Well fuck if that didn't sound like baby talk.

The three men to Boricio's right were trading guesses, but it was still just pisses and babble. Boricio continued to twist at the plastic.

"Anything we can help you with?" It was the guy all the way to the right. His voice was full of compassion and Boricio wondered for a second what that must be like. More sounds came from the guy on the left, but the fucking idiot still wasn't saying anything, until he was.

Boricio froze.

"Boooorrrriiiiccccciiio," the heavy breather moaned.

Like his name on the radio surfacing through a sea of static, once there, it was unmistakable. Boricio was getting this broadcast loud and clear. It took a lot to scare him, and he never ran. But Boricio found himself in such a sudden twisted grip of terror, he would've charged from the room right then if he'd not manage to calm himself down.

Beer-battered fucking bullshit. What the fuck is going on here?

He'd need to run, even if he had to kill everyone in the room first. Not for pleasure, wouldn't be time for that, or anything else.

The restraints fell from his wrist, and Boricio smiled.

* * * *

CHAPTER 9
CHARLIE WILKENS

The clicking inched closer. It sounded just a step from Charlie's window. His body was shaking uncontrollably, and his eyes were starting to water.

He stared at the window, not remembering if he'd locked it and pretty sure that whoever, or *whatever*, was outside must have seen the glow of his light before the girl turned it off.

They'd been found.

Something was coming for them.

He opened his mouth, but the girl put her hand over it and shook her head and mouthed the words, "Do not let them hear us."

Her eyes scanned his room as the clicking sound outside intensified, then multiplied, as if drawing more clickers to his window. Charlie was frozen, listening helplessly, and waiting, his mind racing for some idea, *any idea*, of what to do.

A thump on the window.

Charlie jumped with a yelp.

The girl's eyes widened. Charlie immediately regretted the noise as clicking turned to shrieks outside his window. Another thump, and another, then a third, each one louder against the glass. Another came, and Charlie swore the pane was about to shatter.

"Run!" the girl screamed, out the door before he could get off his ass.

"Bob! Bob!" Charlie screamed, following the girl from his room.

Bob was sleeping on the sofa, in boxers, bare-chested. He looked up, startled by the girl running from the room with Charlie close behind. He had the shotgun in his hand and aimed at the girl in less than a second.

"No!" Charlie yelled, "There's something outside!"

"What?" Bob asked in a slur.

"They're monsters," the girl said, "They've come for us. We need to get outta here!"

Bob looked at the girl like she had a mouth full of Latin. Then he heard the shrieking and the sound of glass shattering in Charlie's room.

"What the fuck?" he said, more annoyed than scared, as he pushed past Charlie and into his room, shotgun cocked.

Charlie saw the bat by the front door, Bob's "Jehovah's Witnesses Be Gone Stick." He grabbed it and started toward his room as the sound of thunder ripped through the house.

"What the fuck?!" Bob shouted. He'd seen them.

Charlie raced into the room, bat raised, hands shaking.

Hanging from his window, a headless nude corpse of one of the things. A wide smear of blood painted his wall in a fresh coat of horror. Another of the things was tearing at the curtain and pushing itself inside. Charlie saw it — something that looked like a man, but ... undone. Its skin was dark, like a cross between burn and infection, but with a shiny, translucent coating. Its eyes were wide, and white, with no visible pupils. Its mouth was a mockery of actual form.

Click, click, click, click, click, the horrible rhythm clacked from the monster's maw of twisted teeth.

Bob fired the gun, clearing the creature's head from its shoulders.

From the living room, the girl screamed.

Charlie turned and saw one of the things burst through the living room window. It was fast, its head turning back and forth, ink-black eyes, scanning the room like a predator. It turned to Charlie and clicked, then back at the girl and moved to grab her.

The girl jumped back as the thing ran past her and tumbled into the living room. From the bedroom, Bob screamed something, shooting at another of the creatures trying to claw through Charlie's window.

The creature in the kitchen was back on its feet, glaring at the girl.

Charlie ran toward the monster, bat raised, and swung. The creature ducked as Charlie swung. The bat flew from his hands and into the living room.

Click, click, click, click.

The creature was on Charlie, open mouth spewing hot, putrid breath in his face, as the unholy click of its teeth shifted in its mouth.

Charlie screamed, hands digging into and slipping on the thing's wet neck, trying to keep its head back so it wouldn't bite him.

Click, click, click, click.

The girl let out a grunt as she swung the bat into the back of the thing's head.

It let out an unholy scream, louder than seemed possible, and rolled off of Charlie, and rose back up, dazed, but not out.

"Fuck!" the girl shouted as she swung the bat again, clocking it right in the face.

The creature fell to the ground, and the girl screamed. She brought the bat down again. And again. And again.

Charlie watched in a daze as the girl bashed its skull into chum.

"Holy shit!" Bob said, coming from the hallway.

The girl looked up, as if snapped from a daze, breathing rapidly, eyes wide and alive.

"You fucked that thing up good."

Bob went to the living room, then turned to them. "That seems to be the last of them."

"What the fuck were they?" Charlie asked, only realizing at the last second that he'd broken Bob's non-cursing rule. Bob didn't seem to notice.

"I dunno," the girl said, "but two of them killed my neighbor. And I've seen a few more walking the streets. Which is why I was trying to get the hell out of town when you guys found me."

Bob stared at her, as if just now remembering the incident at the store.

"Is that why you tried to steal my truck?"

"I didn't know who you were. I broke into the store about 20 minutes before you guys came. I snuck in through the warehouse door in back. I was getting stuff when I heard the glass break. Sorry, but I got scared. Two guys, the end of the world, and a young girl. You do the math. So I was trying to get outta the store before you realized I was in there. But when you all saw me, I was afraid you'd catch me, so I tried to take the truck."

She stared at them, either trying to read Bob's expression or waiting for one to read.

Bob glanced at the shotgun in his hand, then at the body on the floor, then broke into a grin. "It's alright. I woulda done the same shit if I was you."

Charlie sighed in relief, and hoped Bob wouldn't notice. He didn't; his attention was on the girl.

"I'm Callie," she said, offering her hand to Bob.

"Bob," he said, placing his shotgun against the wall, "And this is my stepson, Charlie."

Charlie shook her hand awkwardly.

"So," Callie said, "what now?"

"I think we need to get out of here. Sooner the better. Our place is compromised. And if there's any more of those fuckers out there, we're gonna need more protection."

"Amen," the girl said.

"Let's pack some shit and get outta here ASAP," Bob said.

**

They packed a few bags and searched the neighborhood for a better vehicle, something faster. They found a sports car one block over, though Charlie wasn't sure what kind it was. He never cared much for cars. This one was red, sleek, and cramped in the back seat, where Bob made Charlie sit. It was loud and seemed to impress Bob and Callie.

They drove farther into town and found a gun shop, surprised to see it wasn't already broken into. "Must not be too many more of us out here," Bob said before stopping.

The store wasn't easy to break into, with bars on the windows and glass doors. But of course, Bob was prepared. He had something called a bumper which could unlock any door.

They filled four duffel bags with as many pistols, shotguns, and ammo as they could stuff in the bags. Bob also grabbed a couple of semi-automatic assault rifles, the kind of shit Charlie had only seen in video games and movies.

"You ever use any of these?" Bob asked Callie as he handed her a pistol.

"No, but I'm a quick study."

"I'll take you out tomorrow and show you both how to use them. They're not hard, but there's some shit you need to know so you're not a danger to yourself or anyone else before you go off firing them. And depending on how many more monsters is out there, well, you're probably gonna need to learn how to aim. If we get caught up in a swarm of those fuckers, every shot's gonna count."

As Bob talked guns, Charlie found himself not hating the guy quite so much. Yes, he was a dick to Charlie for the past several years. Yes, he made Charlie's life a living hell and picked on him, beat on him, and made him feel like shit. But since earlier in the day, he'd been a bit cooler. Not all the way, he still had that weird freakout about the cursing, but he was treating Charlie more like an adult and less like a 'bratty kid,' which was what Bob always called him when speaking to Charlie's mom. "That bratty kid of yours."

And Bob's usefulness with guns and fixing stuff would no doubt come in handy if the whole world had gone to hell. Charlie wasn't sure how much longer things like plumbing and water would work, so they'd need creative solutions to things Charlie didn't know shit about.

Now that Charlie thought about it, maybe Bob wasn't off base in the way he treated him. Maybe he *was* a spoiled kid, even though he'd never considered himself one. What else would you call a 17-year-old who never had to do chores, didn't know the first thing about manual labor, and had never been forced to work an honest day's work in his life? Maybe, Charlie thought for the first time, Bob was trying to toughen him up. To get him ready to face the real world.

To face this new world.

**

As they drove the streets, searching for a place to sleep for rest of the night, Charlie couldn't help noticing the volume of the car's engine. The thing sounded like a fucking jet. Especially as it raced through the empty streets. The roar probably traveled for miles.

"Do you think we would've been better off with a car that wasn't so loud?"

Bob shot him a look in the rearview, "What?"

"I mean, this car is nice and all, but it kinda advertises to the zombies, or whatever the hell they are, 'Hey, we're over here, come get us!'"

Bob laughed. "Let 'em come; I'll run the fuckers over. VROOOOM VROOM, you fuckin' zombies!"

Callie laughed. Bob turned to her and smiled.

"Zombies or not, they go fucking down when you hit 'em with a bat, right, Callie?" he said, patting her on the knee.

"Hell yeah," she said, smiling, her eyes a bit glowing. And not at all reacting to Bob touching her knee.

Is he fucking flirting with her? He's old enough to be her dad!

"Only thing I don't get," Bob said, brow furrowed in the rearview mirror, "didn't *you* have the bat, Charlie? How the hell did the channel change to Callie here poundin' the fuck outta that thing, while you were in the corner pissing yourself like a little bitch?"

Bob looked into the rearview, smiling his asshole bully smile. No, he hadn't changed. He was still a major fucking bag of dicks.

"I dropped the bat when I went to take a swing," Charlie admitted sheepishly.

"DROPPED the bat? Jesus, kid, now I can see why you were always last picked in gym."

Fucker.

Callie turned back to Charlie, a kind look in her eyes.

"No, he saved me. If he hadn't come after that thing, it would've killed me."

Bob didn't say anything, just looked in the rearview, eyes locking onto Charlie's before returning to the road. Bob glanced up once more to meet Charlie's eyes, then accelerated, pushing the car faster, and louder.

As they drove into the unknown, Charlie felt the old, familiar feeling. The world had changed; its rules had not. The bullies still ruled while the weak cowered.

He glanced at Callie, who was closing her eyes and leaning back in her seat, and wished he wasn't so goddamned weak.

* * * *

CHAPTER 10
EDWARD KEENAN

They didn't get back to sleep after the nightmare, so they hit the road instead. The clock on the SUV's radio read 1:10 p.m., but the sky outside was darker than it should have been. The clouds were thick and low; thunderheads rolled in the distance, illuminated occasionally by pockets of lightning.

The highway stayed empty, save for the occasional abandoned car. Ed was surprised more cars weren't clogging the roads. At some point, he figured, they'd run into an area that was more heavily trafficked at 2:15 a.m. when the drivers all went poof, and they'd be forced to find an alternate route. But for now, at least, the highway was working.

They didn't talk much about the nightmare. The few times Ed asked about the helicopters and the men, Teagan brushed it off as a crazy dream that seemed silly in the rational light of day. And while the dream might have been, and probably was, perfectly innocent rather than some ominous sign of things to come, Ed couldn't shake the feeling that there was more to it than Teagan was saying. But he didn't want to upset the girl anymore than she already was.

Though he couldn't remember his own dreams at the hotel, he did remember an odd feeling when he woke, as if something else were in the room with them. Something that was probing his mind as he slept. Something he would have missed entirely if he'd not been snapped to battle by Teagan's scream. He couldn't put his finger on what it was, or whether or not it was something his mind had manufactured to help him stitch together the scattered clues found across a day packed full of mostly unknown.

Along with the human mind's ability to flip The Switch, it also worked constantly to find connections between disparate data. To make sense of the world and find connections. To learn through sleep and refine the animal mind. Nothing more, nothing less. It was the ultimate puzzle solver. Sometimes, though, the process, if closely monitored, led to more confusion than clarity.

It was in that confusion that many people attributed special meaning to ordinary things. Ed didn't believe dreams were magical, psychic gifts, divine province of the Gods, or anything other than the brain's hardwired response to stimuli. People who needed magic to explain science were simply not appreciative of the everyday magic of reality.

Still, even with his firm belief that psychic dreams were bullshit, he couldn't dismiss the *possibility* that someone could foresee things through some scientific means we had yet to comprehend. He'd once read a book by some scientist about quantum physics. Though the book was supposed to have been written for the layman, most of it was beyond Ed. The one thing he got from it, or at least he thought this was the scientist's point, was there is no past, present, or future, and all times co-exist in the same moment. In which case, perhaps some people were more tuned to such things — and saw these moments without realizing it, but our brains aren't wired to make sense of such things, as we're used to linear time, so our brains found other ways to make sense of the data — dreams.

Whatever the case, Ed figured it wouldn't hurt to keep an eye out for helicopters.

After a long silence, Teagan stirred from a nap in the passenger seat, "What's her name?"

"Who?"

"You said you had ... *have* a daughter. What's her name?"

"Jade. She's a little older than you, lives with a roommate in Georgia. Goes to college for art. A good kid."

"Do you know if she's okay?"

"No," Ed said, "I tried calling her a few times. But the lines are dead. Were dead at the hotel, too. So, I'm gonna drive out after I bring you home."

"Were you close?"

Ed glanced at Teagan, thought again how much she looked like his own daughter, and felt as if some ghost of Jade were asking questions, rather than this stranger he'd just met. A doppelganger who would transmit his answers to Jade, wherever she was. For a moment, he wondered if he hadn't died in the plane crash and he was in purgatory working through his issues with his demons, represented by the person he'd done the most damage to.

"Not as close as I would have liked," he said, in a rare, candid response, rather than the vague phrasing he usually used when discussing his daughter.

"Why not?"

"Were *you* close with your parents?" Ed asked, turning the tables and dodging the question.

"Not since this," she said, rubbing her tummy. "They're strict. My dad is super-religious, old-school religious, if you know what I mean."

Ed nodded.

"He called me a harlot, and actually brought me to the pastor, begging him to see if I'd been infected by Satan."

"Jesus."

"Yeah, good times. My mom isn't quite as bad, but she's afraid of him. And never really rocks the boat. I think she was even sort of happy I was pregnant, in some weird way. Like a baby in the house might bring some joy back into their otherwise miserable lives."

"And the father of your baby?" Ed asked.

"He doesn't know. This kid, Jesse Gold, that I liked, but dad wouldn't let me go out with him because he's Jewish. Dad asked me who the father was, but I wouldn't tell him. I don't know what he'd do if he knew the baby was Jesse's."

"You think he'd hurt him?"

"There's no telling. He might have even made me get an abortion, even though he doesn't believe in them and talks all the time about how abortionists are the devil's workers. I had an older sister, Becky, who got pregnant when she was 17 from this black guy she was dating. Dad made her get an abortion."

"What a fucking hypocrite," Ed said, shaking his head. "Wait a second ... what do you mean, *had* an older sister?"

"Becky killed herself last year," Teagan said, eyes wet again, but refusing to close them or wipe the tears. She just stared out the window.

"I'm sorry," Ed said, "Do you know why?"

"She left a note in my room which just said, 'I'm sorry,' with no explanation. It was about six months after her abortion. Her boyfriend got really mad that she went through with it, that she didn't ask him, that she let our father have so much control over her life, over *their* child. She was devastated."

"That's so awful," Ed said, not knowing what else to say.

They drove in silence for a full five minutes, until he spoke.

"Jade and I weren't close because I was a horrible father," he said.

Teagan turned to him as he continued his confession.

"I was never there for her. I told myself it had to be that way. I had a dangerous job and made enemies. I couldn't risk my family, so I had to leave. And it's all true. I was a threat to them. I needed to disappear. But it wasn't *always* like that. I could have quit the job before I got in so deep."

"So, you left for her?"

"I tell myself that. But truth is, I left because I was addicted to the job, the danger, and ... "

"What?" Teagan asked.

"Nothing. Some thoughts you shouldn't let out of their cage."

**

They drove for five hours and only had to turn off the highway a couple of times due to congestion, but each time they found their way back without incident. Though the storm clouds seemed distant, they drove into buckets as soon as they hit Beckley, West Virginia. The dark sky just opened up and dumped its deluge on them.

The rain was so bad, Ed could barely see out the window. He got off at an exit and searched for a place to ride out the storm. Teagan had to use the bathroom, so they stopped at the first gas station they found. He parked beneath the canopy, then led Teagan inside the store.

"What do you want to drink?" Ed asked, surveying the out-of-power cooler case as she went into the bathroom with one of the portable lanterns. "We've got warm Coke, warm Pepsi, warm Gatorade, warm water."

"Warm Gatorade sounds good; see if they have the purple one."

"Purple grape, or purple Ice, whatever the hell that is?"

"Ice," she said, "maybe it will make it a bit cooler."

Ed laughed. "Yeah, I'm sure."

The rain fell harder, and the wind howled as the storm grew teeth.

"We might be here a while," Ed said as he opened a purple Gatorade and took a swig. He wasn't sure what it tasted like cold. At room temperature, it was surprisingly okay.

There's an advertising campaign, "Slightly better than piss, try it today!"

Teagan left the bathroom just as Ed was going in. "Sorry," she said, her face red.

"Don't worry," he lied, "I've got a cold; can't smell a thing."

He was pissing, gun sitting in the sink, when he heard Teagan shout, "Ed!"

He shook the last of his piss, zipped, and ran out into the store, gun ready. Teagan was staring out the store windows.

A big, red pickup truck pulled into the station.

"Get in the cooler," he said, then followed her inside. The door into the cooler had a window where they could see all the way to the gas pumps. The red Chevy pulled up behind Ed's SUV and stopped.

Ed had his gun out and ready. The cooler was just dark enough that whoever was outside probably couldn't see in from their position. He could see them perfectly, though.

Two men, big guys with flannel shirts and caps, jumped from the truck and approached the SUV. Both had hunting rifles.

"Fuck," Ed said.

"What is it?"

"We've got company. A couple of men with guns, scouting our truck."

She pushed herself farther back into the cooler until she was pressed against a wall of beer cases.

One of the men glanced into the store as the other opened the SUV.

Why didn't I lock the damned doors?

The man looking in stared straight at Ed, then turned his gaze to the front of the store. Ed was sure the guy couldn't see him.

"What are we gonna do?" Teagan whispered.

If he were solo, as he *should have been*, the solution would have been easy. He would go outside, give them a chance to back down. If not, he'd end them both without a second's hesitation. But now, he had baggage. He had to worry about a child with child. If he made the wrong choice, she'd be left to deal with his consequences.

"Fuck," he said, forgetting what she'd asked.

He debated whether he should allow the men to take his truck, all their stuff, and let things go. They'd had no problem finding stuff so far, so he wasn't overly concerned. They would find another vehicle and more supplies, but it could be a big inconvenience, which would slow them down.

"Maybe they're friendly," Teagan offered.

"They've got guns; I doubt it."

"You've got a gun."

"Well," Ed said turning to her with a grin, "I'm not friendly."

While he was glad to see other people, he *wasn't* glad to see them with guns. He couldn't take a chance that they *might* be friendly. He would either have to engage and kill or stand down and ignore them. He was leaning toward the latter when one of the men opened the door and entered the store, rifle at the ready.

Ed glanced back at Teagan, who was frozen in place.

"Come out!" the man shouted as he aimed the rifle at the cooler. Ed could sense fear in the man's voice, which made him all the more likely to do something stupid.

The man was aiming blindly at the center of the cooler. He couldn't see inside to where Ed or Teagan was hiding. But Ed had a line on him. He aimed his pistol between the man's eyes and fired a single shot.

The gunshot thundered through the cooler. Teagan screamed as the man dropped to the ground, dead.

Ed pushed through the cooler door and rolled out of the cooler, just as the second target entered the store. The man was aiming high, but Ed was on the ground, aiming up, and shot him twice, once in the chest and then again in the head. The man fell back into the candy rack on the front of the cashier's counter, dropping the rifle, which sent a shell into the fountain drink station.

Ed jumped up, marched outside, gun aimed straight at the pickup, ready for anyone else.

No others were there.

He went back inside, opened the door to the cooler, and said, "Come on, we've gotta go. Hold my hand. Don't look down."

**

In the back of the pickup, Ed found a hose and some gas cans. He siphoned gas from the truck to the cans, then filled his SUV. He went back into the store, retrieved a few Cokes to wash away the taste of gasoline. He grabbed the Remington rifles and ammo, and tossed them into the back of the SUV.

Once in the truck, he saw Teagan in tears.

"Why did you shoot them? You didn't even find out if they were good or bad."

"I couldn't take the chance," Ed said matter-of-factly, as he left the gas station and headed back into the storm.

"You just ... shot them. Dead."

"Would you rather it was me? Or you?" Ed snapped, "Because those men had rifles. If they got my gun, then they had the advantage. They called the shots. And you'd have to do whatever the hell they told you to do. Men with power are hardly gentlemen in the normal world; you don't want to know what they're like when everything goes to shit."

Teagan shook her head, "I just can't believe you ... "

Ed didn't bother to say anything else. Either she'd get it, or she wouldn't. He didn't have time to convince her. And to be honest with himself, he'd be better off if he didn't have to worry about her. So, if she got pissed and took off on her own, his life would be that much easier.

He considered pushing her buttons, to get her to act, to get her to leave. Really piss her off. But when she looked at him again, so much like a younger Jade, and with such innocence in her eyes, and baby in her belly, he couldn't be a dick. Couldn't do what needed to be done.

He couldn't flip The Switch.

* * * *

CHAPTER 11
BRENT FOSTER

They took West End Avenue to West 93rd Street, then cut to Central Park, all the while, keeping an eye out for stranded cars, other people, or the nefarious creatures Brent had yet to see.

The fog had grown thicker, if that were even possible, turning Manhattan into an alien landscape where once globally recognized buildings and landmarks had moved from immediately identifiable to silhouettes of their original form. Everything had taken new shape — gloomy shadows shrouded in clouds of milky murk.

Luis stopped the car along Central Park West and took out the two-way radios. Static fuzzed in the car. "You guys alright?" he said to Stan and Melora on the other end.

"Yeah," Stan said, voice excited, "Did you hear the radio?"

"Don't have it on," Luis said. "What's up?"

"Turn it to 88.8 FM; there's a broadcast."

"Okay, hold on," Luis said, giving the radio life.

There was static, but it wasn't the empty static of a dead station. It was the lively static of an attempted broadcast.

A man's voice, loud and strong: "Attention, survivors. The Department of Homeland Security has set up a safe zone on Black Island. We are running ferries from East Hampton Docks every four hours starting at 8 a.m. We advise anyone traveling to do so only during the day. We've had reports of strange sightings at night. Repeat: It is not safe to stay in the city. If you are indoors at night, we advise you to wait until morning to travel."

A long pause followed, then the recording looped and started over.

"Black Island?" Brent said, "That's the place where Homeland Security has a complex and research facility, right?"

"One of a few islands like that out there, I think."

Luis picked up the two-way radio again, "Okay, Stan, we're gonna drive around the park once more, then head back if you all want to get ready to go with us."

"Melora isn't sure," Stan said, "She's thinking we should stay."

"Jesus," Luis said, venting the frustration Brent was already feeling with the woman. "You've gotta do what's right for you, Stanley. You think on it; try to talk her into coming. I'll call back in half an hour. If you haven't made up your mind by then, we're going without you."

Luis looked at Brent, as if only realizing at that moment he'd forgotten to ask if Brent was coming along.

Brent nodded, but as Luis ended the call, he remembered his midnight commitment.

"Shit, I can't go. Not tonight, anyway. I left a note for Gina saying I'd be back at midnight."

"Yeah, but if she's not there when you get home, you know she didn't see the note, and you can leave a new one telling her where we went."

"Yeah," Brent said, "but what if she came and then left? And she came back again at midnight looking for me?"

"You don't think she'd leave a note, or hell, just wait for you?"

"I suppose," Brent said. Luis made a good point. If Gina *had* come home, she wouldn't leave. And if she *did* leave, she would definitely write a note updating Brent on her status. She left notes for everything; she'd definitely leave one when the world was circling the drain.

Yeah, well where's the note when you woke up?
Not the same – she was probably outside when shit went down.
Outside at 2:15 a.m.? Come on, face the facts.
Well shit for dinner, you got me there.

"I'll think on it and have my mind made up by the time we get back. Worse comes to worst, I'll catch up with you next day."

"Um, hell no," Luis said, "We're in this shit together. You wait 'til tomorrow, I wait."

Brent smiled, "Thanks, man. I appreciate that."

**

Not seeing anyone, they decided to drive back to Brent's, listening to the radio the whole way, even if it was the same message on repeat. Something was reassuring about authority establishing some form of control and safety.

"Why do you think that's the only safe zone?" Luis asked. "I mean, there's a million easier places to get to than Black Island, right?"

"Maybe that's why. Maybe its remote location makes it the only safe place left? Maybe those creatures, aliens, whatever, can't cross water?"

"Can't cross water, but they can appear over people's beds and snatch them up in the middle of the night?"

"Well, that's assuming we're not dealing with two different things altogether," Brent suggested.

"Or maybe the cloud things are like those things on *Star Trek*, teleportation devices? They zap us up to their spaceships and then come down and hunt the rest of us?"

"I dunno," Brent said, shaking his head, "I'm just not thinking they're aliens. It just seems, I dunno, so unlikely."

"Any more unlikely than people vanishing?"

"No," Brent said, as they got out of the car and headed toward his building.

They glanced at Stan's apartment building. "Wanna meet me over there when you're done?"

Brent shook his head. "Nah, you can come up. Maybe you'll get to meet my family."

**

When they reached Brent's apartment, his heart swelled at the sight of his open door.

They're home!

He was halfway to the door when Luis yanked him back with one giant arm, "I take it your door was closed when you left?" he whispered.

"Yeah," Brent said, unable to wipe the goofy grin from his face.

"It might not be *them* in your house," Luis warned, his eyes void of any prior humor or warmth. Nothing but business.

Brent swallowed, embarrassed by his childish optimism. He was normally a cynical bastard, and should have known better than to see an open door as a sign of fortune.

"Call to them," Luis whispered, gun ready.

"Don't shoot until *you're sure* it's not people," Brent said, stepping in front of Luis. "Please. No accidents."

"Don't worry," Luis said, "I won't pull the trigger unless one of them is on you."

"Thanks," Brent said, as he moved closer to the door, looking inside, but seeing nobody in his apartment. "Hello? Gina? Ben? I'm home."

Nothing.

"Hello?!"

He stepped toward the doorway, acutely aware of Luis at his back. He moved with slow intent, maintaining distance between Luis and his family, as he navigated the entrance hall.

His heart choked when he saw the disaster scattered in his living room. The dining room table was on its side, chairs were everywhere, some broken. It was like a rugby team had run into the living room, trampled the table, grabbed a few chairs, and threw them across the room, smashing his TV along the way.

"What the hell?" Brent said, unable to make sense of the scene.

Luis pushed past Brent, gun raised, and stepped into the hall. "Stand back," he said to Brent.

"Be careful," Brent pleaded, getting his own gun ready.

Luis pushed open the first door, the bathroom, then headed to the master bedroom with the fluid movement of a well-trained SWAT officer. He left the bedroom, still intact, then headed toward Ben's room. Brent rushed to Luis's side and stepped in front of him, "Wait," he said, "I'll go."

Brent pushed the door open with the gun, and prayed his son wouldn't run out.

He'd never been so glad *not to see* his family.

"Whatever was here is gone," Luis said.

As if on cue, his radio beeped.

"Yeah?" Luis asked.

"Wh ... where are you?" Stan asked, his voice at a whisper, packed with fear.

"Across the street, why?"

"They're in here."

"*Who's* in there?"

"The creatures. I heard them in the hallway, making this God-awful sound."

"You have the guns, right?" Luis asked.

"Yes," Stan said, "Can you see anything outside?"

Luis and Brent rushed to the window in Ben's room and were met with wisps of white fog brushing the window panes.

"Can't see shit in this fog," Luis said.

"How many are there?"

"I dunno, sounds like a lot," Melora said.

"Wait, wait," Stan whispered loudly, "I think they might be leaving. Hold on, I'm gonna try and look through the peephole."

"No," Luis said, "Just stay put. Do NOT make a sound."

Too late, no answer.

Brent and Luis listened as silence seemed to stretch to eternity. Brent was pretty sure he could hear Melora's breathing over the light static.

And then all hell broke loose.

"Shit! Shit! Shit! Shit!" Stan screamed, as something pounded like thunder.

Melora screamed.

Stan's next scream was followed by the sound of ripping flesh and a rising chorus of "Click, click, click, click" sounds.

"Stan!" Luis yelled into the radio.

"They're eating him!" Melora screamed, but from a distance, as if she'd dropped the radio and was running into a room.

She fired two shots, three, and then screamed.

More flesh ripping, followed by what sounded like the splashing of blood and Melora's gurgling death cries.

Then nothing but silence, except for the clicking, like animals celebrating a kill.

Brent's heart felt like it missed every other beat as the drama played out over the radio, just a couple hundred yards and another world away.

"Stan!" Luis screamed, and suddenly the clicking stopped.

Brent's eyes shot wide open, waiting for what would come next over the radio as if he would see, not hear it. But they were met with silence.

They heard us!

And then footsteps.

Then the sound of a hand fumbling with the radio, followed by a ragged racket of breathing as it pulled the radio closer to its mouth.

Brent stared at Luis, as both men waited for the next sound.

Click, click, click, click, from one, at first, and then many.

* * * *

CHAPTER 12
MARY OLSON

It looked more like demolition than disaster.

The debris was centralized in a towering core, piled skyscraper-high in the center of the blackened tundra. Power lines, cars, splintered lumber, slabs of concrete, even cracked airplanes, and what looked like an entire freeway were laying in massive, oversized chunks.

Mary's voice was a prisoner in her throat. Jimmy's, as usual, wasn't. "Holy shit balls, this is some Roland Emmerich shit right here."

"Who?" It was amazing Paola cared.

"He's a shit director," Jimmy said laughing. "Crap movies, but cool looking most of the time. Aliens must've been looking at his storyboards."

John turned and glared at him, then pulled to the side of the road. All four survivors stepped from the SUV, wordless. Desmond was already out of the van.

The destruction gathered in the middle made no sense. It was as though the area had somehow imploded and exploded at the same time. Impossible, sure, but the reality was giving them the stink eye all the same.

It looked like the world had exploded before a massive tornado came and picked everything up then deposited it in a single location. No bodies were there, but no rubble was there either. Not exactly. The gravel and detritus that should've carpeted the ground wasn't there. Instead, they were ankle deep in some sort of charred rock, surprisingly uniform and each roughly the size of a golf ball, though the debris was angular, not round — volcanic looking, and almost beautiful.

"Do you think this is Ground Zero?" Mary asked.

John picked up a chunk of debris. "Looks like obsidian, feels like glass, but seems like … wood. I don't think this is Ground Zero. If this is what caused it all, the forest wouldn't have been so green just a few miles back."

"He's right," Desmond said. "Stuff would be scattered away from here, not gathered here if this were the point of origin. I've never seen anything like this."

Paola stared past the horizon. Mary wondered what kept her from crying. Her father cried like a baby when touched the right way. She'd seen it happen during commercials and sporting events. Especially when a player he liked did something historic.

"How long do you think all the black goes for?" Paola asked Desmond.

"No way of knowing," Desmond rose from his knee, dropped the hunk of rock, wood, or whatever it was, into the pile with a glassy thud, then looked at Paola. "But if I'm telling you what I think, I bet black crashes into green again just a few miles up the road."

"Do you think the Army Base will still be there?" Paola asked, her voice surprisingly strong. Mary was proud.

"You're old enough for me not to lie to you, so I won't say yes. I think the base and the people in it are probably gone like the rest of everything. I figure it'll be empty or worse. Whatever happened was probably something the Army couldn't have prepared for even if they knew it was coming. Might even be something we can't fully understand. What I *do know* is that it's our best hope at the moment. Even if there's no people, there may be supplies. And it could offer some safety."

"Safety from what?" Jimmy asked.

"Every environment has its predators, and predators like easy prey. We need to stick together. Our number is already too small, and we can't afford to let it shrink."

"Mr. Desmond," Paola said, "Can we find someplace to sleep? I don't want to drive after dark."

"Great idea," Jimmy said.

The sun was already a mean shade of orange, and it felt just a few feet away. It would be gone in minutes, even though it couldn't have been later than mid-afternoon. Desmond's chest rose and his nostrils flared as if he were going to let loose with a decisive NO. It was clear he wanted to keep driving. He opened his mouth, but closed it quickly. He opened it again, but before he could speak John interrupted.

"It's not a democracy. If the guy with the guns and supplies says GO, then around the board we shuffle."

Desmond smiled. "No need for that, John. Yes, of course, Paola. We'll stay at the first safe place we can find. Might as well take advantage of the full End-Of-Creation discount." He offered a wan smile at John and got into the van.

**

The Suburban followed Desmond for seven miles, then chased it down the first off-ramp with a bank of hotels waiting. Just as Desmond predicted, total devastation had ended just three miles past the pileup, meaning the obsidian rubble and mammoth pileup was definitely the evil eye of something.

The hotel was a Drury Inn, a nice one. And to their rather wonderful surprise, the electricity was working, with all locks set to "open."

They chose four rooms, next to and across from one another, all on the first floor. The five weary travelers took a much-needed three-hour rest, then showered, dressed in clean clothes, and met in the lobby bar for drinks. Four hours later, everyone was drunk, including Paola in a virgin Shirley Temple sorta way. Everyone was still wearing the shock, but the last few hours had stretched the fabric.

Mary sat with her daughter and Jimmy, but her attention was on the bar, a few feet away, where Desmond approached John.

"How're you doing, man?" Desmond placed his back to the bar and looked into John's fully toasted brown eyes with his slightly tipsy green ones.

John shrugged. "What can I say? We stared into the soul of absolute emptiness, and it just stared right back." He poured some fire down his throat, then emptied the rest of the bottle into an oversized glass.

"I won't tell you to stop, just remind you once more that every one of us matters right now. I'm sure I speak for the group when I say I'd prefer to not leave the hotel one man shy in the mañana."

John's face softened. "I'll be fine. A man has a right to grieve without the entire world getting in his way."

Desmond poured some of John's drink into his own glass, nodded at John, swallowed the fire in one large gulp, then set his glass on the bar and approached Jimmy, Paola, and Mary. The kids were cracking up.

"What'd I miss?"

"Paola says I smell like a marijuana skunk."

"She has a point," Desmond said.

"She always does, whether I like it or not." Mary laughed. Her wine glass was near empty, so she went to the bar to fill it. "It's getting warmer in here," she said walking back. "Do you feel that?"

"I do," Paola said. Jimmy nodded.

"Might be five degrees," Desmond said, "but the difference is definitely there."

They ignored the climbing thermostat and fell deeper into their drinks. Eventually, Paola made herself a bed by pulling two lounge chairs together. She was asleep seconds after her head touched the pillow they'd grabbed from a room. Jimmy managed a few minutes of small talk, then offered to pass the peace pipe with the rest of the grownups. When they declined, he smiled and slipped away to enjoy his stash, saying, "More for me," with a giggle.

Mary smiled at Desmond and said, "So, we're all alone, and it's the end of the world where money doesn't matter. Will you finally tell me how you made all yours?"

Desmond laughed. "I've told you before."

"How about telling me in a way I understand?"

"I use the Internet."

"So do I, so does everybody. My cards were wholesaled across the world on my own dot com. I know how *I* do it. How do *you* do it?"

"Well, there's no easy answer. Cool thing about the Internet is it's still mostly frontier. There's plenty of treasure for anyone who knows how to dig. Best part is, you can even learn how to make the treasure yourself."

They'd been down this road before. His answers, no matter how thorough, usually left her more confused than when he started, and sounded more like a rousing speech about online potential than a solid business model. "You make it sound like magic."

"It is, sorta. Just like any illusionist, Internet entrepreneurs can make the impossible look like downright inarguable." Desmond took a drink. "Money isn't hard to make. You just need to find a river and dip your bucket. But the Internet makes finding the rivers a whole hell of a lot easier."

"I don't care what you say. It's not that easy."

Desmond blushed. "Okay, it's not *that easy*. But it's easier than you think. People go online to look for stuff, right? If you have what they're looking for, can lead them toward it, or help them keep it organized once they get it, then there's good money to be made — and a neverending supply of leads."

"But what do *you do*?" Mary figured it had to be shady if he couldn't say what it was in 10 words or less.

"I don't do anything illegal, if that's what you're thinking."

Mary laughed and shook her head, "I never said *that*."

Desmond smiled with a blush, "I make a lot of stuff. I have a company that builds 'roads' that help users get from A to B quickly, software that helps people organize the growing assault on their digital lives, and a publishing company that releases heavily-researched white papers and reports. It used to be mostly Buyer Beware-type consumer lists we wrote for," he looked at Mary seriously. "People will pay to be informed, so we used to do a lot of work at the consumer level, but we've moved into science and alternative research. The dollars are exponentially larger, and some of our papers have commanded ... well, staggering fees."

"So what do you *do* all day?"

"Look for and evaluate new information, talk to my team, read, write, watch movies. Sometimes I play *Call Of Duty*." He smiled.

"Why don't you live someplace else? New York, Los Angeles, Sydney even! Why *Missouri?*"

"Missouri's where I grew up. It's my home, a great place to disappear and get lost in the quiet. But I love to travel, and fly out often. I get my fill of adventure, then come home to space and silence. My mom and dad lived over in Festus, close enough to visit, but far enough to leave me mostly alone."

Desmond noticed the final swirl sitting at the bottom of Mary's nearly empty glass. "May I?"

"No," Mary said. "Terrible idea. I can't believe I'm still standing as it is. But I'm glad we did this. Thanks for letting us stay here. It's nice to get off the road, and get some sleep in a decent place. And I think I might actually sleep." Paola snored loudly. Mary and Desmond traded a quiet smile.

"I didn't 'let' us do anything. We're a team, and I'm sorry about the democracy comment." He looked over at Paola. "Just know you're doing great. I can't imagine how hard it must be, worried about another life full-time like that."

"Thanks. It's the uncertainty that makes it so hard. I just want to know what she's thinking. It kills me to have no idea, and to feel so powerless to help her."

"She's doing great, too. You should be proud. She's strong and smart, just like her mom." He yawned, then said, "Ready for tomorrow?"

"Only if I get the sleep I need tonight," she said, following his cue again, and quietly thanking him for making it so easy.

Jimmy had his head against the wall, asleep in the corner. John was passed out, his cheek against the polished wood, fuel leaking from his open mouth. Paola was asleep in the middle of a row of chairs. Desmond made a bed to Paola's right; Mary stayed on her left.

"Good night, Mary."

"Good night, Desmond."

They were asleep in less than three minutes.

When Mary woke, her daughter was gone.

* * * *

::EPISODE 3::
(THIRD EPISODE OF SEASON ONE)
"THINGS THAT GO BUMP ..."

CHAPTER 1
PAOLA OLSON

Oct. 16
Early morning
Belle Springs, Missouri

Paola jolted awake as if she'd been falling in her dream. Only it wasn't gravity that snapped her back to reality, but rather the sound of her name being whispered in her ear.

She woke expecting to see somebody standing over her. However, nobody was there. The voice must've been an echo of her dream world that followed her to her waking life.

She strained to listen, in case someone *had* actually called her name. The only other sound in the eerily still hotel lobby was a low growl rolling from her mother's open mouth; a baby soft bark so familiar it was more lullaby than irritant to Paola. The world was a blur, and her mother was barely visible in the shadows that floated through the room like a dark cloud.

She blinked her eyes, trying to figure out which side of the dream she was on.

Must be a dream, the real world isn't so ... murky.

Paola laid her head on the pillow and closed her eyes. *Ninety-nine ... 98 ... 97 ... 96 ... 95 ...* On other nights, she rarely made it past 65 or so before sleep claimed her. *Ninety-four ... 93 ... 92 ... 91 ... 90 ...*

"Paola!" This time the voice was louder, and she had no doubt she'd heard it.

Paola sat up straight in bed. It was her father's voice, coming from the far side of the still-murky lobby.

"Paola, are you in there?"

This has to be a dream!

"Paola, please! Are you there?"

This was definitely a dream. She was sure of it now. Her father wouldn't be able to find her out here in the middle of nowhere unless it was a dream.

"Paola!"

Paola pushed the cushions aside and rose to her feet. It would be nice to see the real him, but that was okay if it wasn't. The Dream Daddy would have to do for now. Though the shadows scared her, she knew she had nothing to fear. When bad stuff happened in dreams, all you had to do was wake up. And she knew how to do that well; she did it all the time. It's how she could sometimes dream about the stuff she wanted to dream about, without having to dream about the stuff she didn't.

"Paola? Shortcake?"

Paola stopped at the side of her mom's makeshift bed. Up close, she could see her better through the shadows. Mary's eyes fluttered beneath their lids as she pulled the fat pillow in her arms and cradled it to her chest. Another low rumble came from her throat. It flirted with leaving her mouth but ended up whistling through her nose instead.

This is like the hide-n-seek dream. That was a good one.

Paola tiptoed toward her father's voice, past her mom and Desmond, past John, his face still pasted to the bar, then past Jimmy and into the dining room.

Paola loved the hide-n-seek dreams. She looked forward to them, even tried to make herself have them sometimes as she lay in bed counting down to the possibility, starting from 100.

She always played this in her dreams with Daddy, just the two of them. And in the dreams, she always felt a few years younger, before she began to feel too old to call her parents mommy and daddy. Before good feelings were replaced with the realization that her parents weren't the perfect people she used to idolize.

He'd usually call for her while she did her best to stay hidden. The longer she was gone, the more desperate he'd get to find her. He would call and call and chase her through the house, looking through windows and opening doors. "I love you, Paola. Please let me find you so we can be together. Don't make me wait any longer. As soon as I find you, we can go and find Mommy together!"

And they always did. He would find her first; under the bed, in the closet, behind the oak tree outside, behind the hot water heater in the basement, or in the pantry. Once he sniffed her out, he would open her hiding place door with a playful loud roar, then they would spend a few minutes laughing before holding hands and adventuring off together on a quest for Mommy.

He never took more than a few minutes to find her, and no matter how different the hide-n-seek dreams were, they always had the same sort of ending: the three of them eating ice cream, watching a movie, or doing any one of the million-and-one things Paola had gone from doing to missing each day in the real world.

Something was different about this dream, though.

The hide-n-seek dreams always started good and kept getting better. This one had just started and was already turning into a creeping kind of terrible. The shadow of something ugly twisted the familiarity of the usual dream, souring her warm nostalgia into something wretched.

Paola could've sworn she was in the kitchen, but was confused by the long hallway now in front of her. That made what was happening feel like even more like a dream. She was always retracing her steps in her sleep.

I was in the lobby, then I walked through the restaurant and into the kitchen. But now I'm in a long hallway. And it looks like it goes for miles, like the hotel in Vegas where we stayed when we were still a family.

Paola spun around. The endless hallway was mirrored on both sides, with 100 identical doors crowding each direction.

No, this was not the hide-n-seek dream. This was one of the other repeating dreams, where her daddy wanted to show her something, but never got around to it. In these dreams, she always felt lost and alone as she tried to keep up with him, following him for what felt like forever, through twisting halls and endless, winding stairwells. The buildings were always weird and never stayed the same shape for long.

This felt mostly like that, but this world wasn't soft like her dreams.

That's how she usually knew she was dreaming. Whenever she wondered whether or not she were dreaming, she could push hard on a wall, tree, or other inanimate objects to know for sure. If the object gave under pressure, she was dreaming.

The world she was walking through now was not soft, though. Despite the changing, impossible architecture, nothing budged under her touch.

"You're doing great, Shortcake. Almost there. Just a few more steps."

The hallway disappeared, and the doors went with it. Paola blinked and was back in the kitchen, standing in front of a long, steel table, a lot longer than it should have been. On top of the counter, directly in front of Paola, lay a large butcher knife, almost cartoonish in size.

Paola picked up the blade, its metal handle cold to the touch, and rotated it in her hand, staring at her warped reflection and wondering why she looked so real if this were only a dream. She looked at herself in dream mirrors all the time, but never had her reflection seemed so real.

She set the butcher knife back on the counter, then walked the half mile or so through the kitchen and into the milky clouds of fog that covered the world.

She walked for more than a mile, except now the distance had turned real. Not like the fake miles inside the hotel that acted like forever but were only a feeling.

Rocks, branches, and a shallow pool of shattered glass dug into her feet, stinging and tearing her flesh. She looked down, surprised to see blotches of red on her white skin, brown on the black asphalt.

The pain in her feet made the dream feeling fade.

She would have forced herself awake right there, but then she saw a square clearing in the night sky ahead with no fog at all, but rather a neon, blinking billboard that read, *DADDY THIS WAY* with a big, red arrow aimed in the direction she was walking. She would walk on.

Just past the billboard, Paola saw the bright, white canopy of a gas station, its rows of yellowed and aged fluorescent lights cutting through the fog. The station sat in the middle of all the light, making it look like an oil painting hanging from the middle of a big, black frame. The darkness surrounding the station made it seem as though all the world's light was concentrated under the canopy. Most of that light gathered in the middle, bathing a tall man slouched against a fuel pump.

A chill went through Paola.

The man was her father, only not quite. Same hair, same smile, same eyes, but different clothes, as though he were dressing up to play her daddy, but he'd missed the finer details that made her dad's style. He was even wearing one of those hats they wore in old films and *Indiana Jones* movies. The hat looked fake, but the stubble on her daddy's cheek was real so Paola raced forward, the pain in her feet all but a distant memory.

"Daddy?"

"Paola!" He took off his hat, fell to his knees, and wrapped his arms around her. "I've missed you so much, and I was so worried."

"I'm so glad you're okay!" Paola said. "Do you know what happened to everyone?"

"No, but I *do know* how we can find out. You have to come with me right now, then we'll come back and get your mom before she wakes up."

"We should go and get Mommy *first*."

"No, we can't, because she's sleeping right now and we'd have to wake her."

"She won't mind. Come on, Daddy." Paola waved her arms back toward the hotel.

He sighed, then shook his head. "It's okay, Shortcake, I promise. She won't even know you're gone. And as soon as we get back, we can all go out and get ice cream. Your new friends can come with us, and everyone will be happy. It's just like playing hide-n-seek, except right now your mom's sleeping instead of hiding."

Paola shook her head. "She won't mind if we wake her up. No one will. They'll be excited. And she'll probably be mad if I leave without telling her."

"But it's me, I'm your father. Besides, it's *my* week. You're supposed to be with me right now, anyway."

That doesn't sound like Daddy at all.

"I want to go back to the hotel, Daddy."

Paola's father rose to his feet, returned his hat to his head and flashed Paola a movie star smile. "Come on, Shortcake. We'll be 15 minutes tops."

Paola shook her head and took a step back. The dream part felt like it was fading.

"Okay then," he held his hand out for Paola, "We'll wake her first, but we'll have to be careful. You know how fucking awful she is when she doesn't get her sleep."

Paola froze.

Dream Daddy would never say anything mean about Mommy. Or use that kind of language. Neither would Real Daddy.

"Why did you say that, Daddy?"

Paola knew she'd never hear an answer because her father's face started to change right that second, mouth first as it drooped horribly. The nose went next; shifting, contorting, and folding itself inside out in an angry-looking, liquid motion. It looked like the devil was giving birth, like every bad thing Paola had ever seen, heard of, or thought up, was suddenly given two long and skinny legs.

Her father's skin grew bright-red, wet, shiny as the muscles and bones beneath the flesh seemed to churn like someone was running a mixer in the thing's insides. The monster looked kind of like the black thing they'd seen in the road, but different in ways Paola couldn't quite place as she had turned away from the creature in the road pretty quickly. It was then that Paola realized with horror that she could not look away from this thing that was not her father.

Its eyes, dark, black, and evil, were the only constant as its face shifted form again and again like it was searching for the right fit. Her head began to hurt as if something were pressing hard sticks against her skull. *Or fingers.*

And that's when she realized it had reached out and was clutching her skull, and somehow forcing its way into her mind.

Memories began to flicker past her mind's eye. Things she'd not thought about in years.

I'm 5, and we're sewing a pillow for the Tooth Fairy. We have to hurry because my tooth is hanging to my gums. Daddy comes in the room smiling. He just finished building a tiny bed for the Tooth Fairy, in case she gets tired and wants to rest before she finishes for the night.

Her headache grew worse as if her head were being crushed beneath the pressure of the monster's fingers. And just like that, she could no longer remember what her daddy had built for the Tooth Fairy. And a moment later, she could no longer remember what age she was when the Tooth Fairy visited. And then after that, the memory itself was gone, leaving her confused, as if trying to recall a name she'd heard once five years ago.

He's digging through my mind like when Mommy digs through her garden. He's filling his baskets with memories instead of flowers, and yanking them up by the roots. He's taking them with him.

She cried out and tried to smack the monster's arms away, but her body wouldn't cooperate. It wasn't hers to control any longer. She'd become little more than a puppet.

A few moments later, she lay on the cold, concrete ground of the gas station, unable to remember what happened, or how she'd gotten there. Nor could she remember her name.

The only thing she knew for certain was she was about to die.

* * * *

CHAPTER 2
CHARLIE WILKENS

Oct. 17
Early morning
Pensacola, Florida

As they got comfortable in the house in Pensacola, Charlie settled into the hope that things might be okay. They hadn't seen any creatures since leaving Jacksonville, but they also hadn't seen survivors. That was just fine by Charlie.

The house, a three-story mansion on the water, belonged to Bob's brother, Derek, who was gone to no one's surprise. Rather than be upset by the news, Bob was relieved to find the brother he hated was on the highway to heaven or hell or where-the-fuck-ever.

The house was easily the nicest Charlie had ever been inside. The photos of Derek and his family arranged in a neat row on the wall told Charlie exactly why Bob didn't care for his brother. He was gay, with a black boyfriend and an adopted Chinese toddler girl. Even if Bob weren't racist, the boyfriend wouldn't jive with Bob's hard-line, anti-queer views.

Charlie wondered how someone like Derek — successful, good-looking, gay, and who didn't hate minorities — could be related to Bob, who was the tail's side of the coin on all those things. Well, except the gay part. Charlie figured anyone as homophobic as Bob was probably deep in the closet hiding behind a pink taffeta gown or two.

Charlie had gotten a taste of Bob's homophobia the previous fall when he tried growing his hair out to look less geeky.

"What are you, a faggot?" Bob harangued him repeatedly.

One time, Charlie was feeling snarky, and answered, "Yeah, want a kiss?"

Bob answered with a swift smack in the mouth. That night at dinner, Bob demanded Charlie cut his hair or he would hold him down and shave him bald.

"You've got a choice," Bob said, "You have your mom take you to one of those faggy salons so you can get it cut nice and short or I will strap you down and shave you."

"Mom," Charlie pleaded, "He can't do this."

His mom had *that look*.

She wasn't willing to turn the burner up on Bob's temper. "You'll look handsome, honey. We'll take you to the place Chad's mom takes him. You like Chad's hair, don't you?"

Charlie just shook his head. He could hardly look at her. He was more pissed at her than Bob. She was his mother. She was supposed to fight for him, not help the enemy. Charlie fled from the table. The next morning, he took his bike and went to the barber he'd gone to for years and got a shorter haircut, vowing to grow it out the minute he turned 18.

Now, as he drifted in Derek's pool, Charlie considered growing his hair out again. It was already longer than it had been in years, though Bob hadn't seemed to notice in some time. The world was gone; Bob couldn't get too pissed. It wasn't like Charlie's haircut would cost him a job with some Fortune 500 company.

Charlie glanced at Bob, who manned the barbecue grill, cooking some recently-thawed burgers from Derek's deep freezer. He thought about mentioning his plans to grow his hair, but Bob had been in a decent mood today. No need to rock the boat.

Callie, who had been in the house reading, came out in blue fleece shorts and a gray T-shirt.

"Look out," she said, jumping in next to Charlie, causing him to go under and swallow a huge mouthful of chlorinated water.

He came up gagging, and saw Callie laughing.

"Thanks," he said, splashing water at her.

She splashed back, and moved closer to him, then jumped behind him, and pushed him under the water.

"Hey!" he said, coming up, and grabbing her shoulders.

For a moment, time seemed to slow, and their eyes locked again, as they had in the parking lot. He noticed her nipples poking through her tee, could see the outline of her breasts, as the wet shirt clung to her. He quickly glanced away, but not before she'd noticed. She smiled, then dunked him again.

He came up, this time behind her, and wrapped her head in a playful headlock. As their bodies touched underwater, Little Charlie was at full attention. As she tried to break free of the headlock, her ass rubbed against his cock, and he couldn't help but think she noticed. She pulled away, laughing, as she pushed off of him and swam away.

He went underwater, and closed his eyes trying to wish his embarrassing erection away.

Baseball ... Bea Arthur ... that old guy on those bran commercials WITH Bea Arthur.

When it was safe to come up, Callie was at the edge of the pool, Bob standing over her, chatting her up. Though he was clearly checking out her tits, Callie didn't seem to notice. She was either the coyest of flirts ever or naive to what men were always focused on. Bob was just smooth enough not to get busted by Callie, but more than a couple of times, Charlie had caught him sneaking peeks. Each time, Bob would wink at Charlie or make a crude gesture.

Bob said he was just encouraging Charlie to "tap that ass." But Charlie couldn't help but think Bob wanted to do some tapping, himself.

Charlie felt sick, watching Bob joke with Callie while she giggled in waves.

Is she flirting with Bob? Or is she so nice that she's oblivious to his creepiness?

It wasn't as if there were anything between him and Callie, though they had been getting closer — whenever Bob wasn't around as the third wheel.

While Callie was kind of a bad ass, she was also nice, funny, and kind of geeky. Not in a socially awkward way like Charlie, but in the things she liked — comics, video games, and sci-fi and fantasy books. All the same things Charlie liked. It was as if God, or whoever or whatever made everyone vanish, had picked the perfect girl to strand him with. He couldn't help but think fate had brought her to him. Or perhaps, fate's cruel sister, irony, to create and present someone so much like him, yet so much better looking that she'd never have anything to do with him.

Charlie had been relegated to the "friend" role far too many times with attractive girls. If you fell into the friend zone, you *never* escaped. One girl (who was rejecting him at the time) told him, "A girl knows within 10 seconds if she'll sleep with you. If you don't make a great impression right away, you'll never get with her."

Needless to say, Charlie had never made that kind of impression on any girls. He had too many things going against him. He was geeky and homely, with zits, and as more than a few girls had also told him bluntly, he was "too nice."

Charlie told himself that "too nice" didn't really mean *too nice*. It was code for *too ugly*, or perhaps the girl was too immature to appreciate a nice guy. Girls his age seemed to like so-called bad boys. And given the number of young women (even ten years older than him) who seemed to be attracted to losers, he wasn't sure when that infatuation with assholes ended. He hoped it was before they got old, or he was screwed.

Callie didn't seem like other girls, though. So, he had to be very careful not to miss his one chance at bat. He had to make a good impression *before* she could put him in the friends-only zone. The way he saw it, he had a couple of things going for him. They met in an emotionally charged moment. He saved her life (a brave and selfless act). And, as far as they knew, he was one of the last two men on Earth, and the other was an old, drunk asshole. Even if Charlie wore headgear, had uncontrollable, explosive diarrhea, and suffered from involuntary spasms, he was pretty sure he made a better match for a woman than Bob.

But Charlie also had things working against him.

Aside from not being Brad Pitt, he was also a white guy. A VERY white guy, so pale he would likely be a lobster after an hour in the pool. And he didn't know if Callie even liked white guys. He wasn't even sure what she was, if she were light-skinned black or mixed race, which the blue eyes made likely. In either event, white guys might not be her thing. He had never been attracted to a black girl before now. Nothing racial, just not something he'd ever considered, just like he wasn't attracted to redheads. You like who you like, not much you can do about it. But that also meant Callie liked who she liked, and geeky, pale guys might not be on that list.

And for all he knew, she might like assholes ... like Bob.

Yet, he felt something with Callie. When they spoke, when their eyes met, moments were there, just outside of time, when they seemed to connect on a deeper level. He didn't know if it was just his brain's way of lending importance to lust because he was experiencing it, or if it was something real and deep. And maybe Callie was feeling it, too?

He'd been trying to work up the courage to make some sort of move since last night, but each time they were alone and in deep conversation, Bob would show up to cock block Charlie. Either Bob was oblivious as hell or even more evil than Charlie thought.

Tonight, Charlie decided, as he watched Bob joking with Callie, would be the night he'd make a move.

It was, after all, the end of the world. Who knew how long they had?

**

Bob got weird at dinner.

They were sitting at Derek's fancy, dark, wooden table, which could have easily seated 10, when Bob set down the burgers on a giant plate, along with a bag of chips. He was bringing a baking dish from outside, which he'd cooked canned chili in, when it slipped from his hands and shattered on the floor.

"Dammit!" Bob shouted, his eyes quickly targeting Charlie, "Why can't you clean up when you track water in here?"

"What?" Charlie said, confused.

"Don't play stupid. You tracked water in here when you got out of the pool. And because you're too damned lazy to clean it up, I slipped, and dropped our fucking dinner!"

"No, I didn't," Charlie said defensively, "I came in through the bathroom door, and dried off in there."

"Are you calling me a liar, boy?" Bob said, his face redder than his bloodshot eyes.

"No," Charlie said, confusion turning to panic. "But I swear, I came in through the bathroom."

"Oh, so now I'm just imagining some spill on the floor, right? Next you're gonna say I didn't even drop the dish, I just threw it down on purpose, right?"

Charlie looked down at the floor and while a small puddle of water was next to the broken, blue baking dish and mess of chili all over the floor, it wasn't from him, meaning it had to be from Callie. He glanced at her, her tongue tied and eyes frightened, then back at Bob.

"Maybe it was me," he said, lying to protect her.

"I'm sorry," Callie said, "Actually, I think I might have come in through the door and forgot to wipe it down."

Bob stared at her, then back at Charlie, momentarily defused, and running a hand through his hair, then looked back at Charlie, "Clean this shit up, boy."

"What?" Charlie said, "Why me?"

He regretted the words even as the last one trailed from his mouth.

"Excuse me?" Bob said, inches from Charlie's face and reeking of alcohol, "Because I fucking said so. Things are gonna change around here. I worked my ass off so you and your momma could have a decent life. I worked night and day, busting my ass, and all you ever did was suckle on my tit, like a fucking parasite. You never did shit around the house, never contributed in any way, whatso-fucking-ever. But I got news for ya, boy, your momma ain't here no more. Time's are a changin' and you're gonna earn your keep if you wanna stay under my roof! It's time you grow the fuck up and be a man!"

Charlie's knee was bouncing as his throat tightened, and he struggled to hold back the tears of rage burning inside him. He couldn't even look at Callie after being ridiculed like that by Bob.

How can he?!

Charlie snapped.

"Under YOUR roof?! Your roof?! This is your brother's house! And the house before this? My mother's! Not yours! And according to her, you never paid your fair share! She had to beg you for money, because you held onto all yours and then had the balls to take hers, too! YOU are the FUCKING parasite, not me!"

Bob's eyes widened, his jaw dropped.

And though Charlie knew he'd made a huge mistake, the look on Bob's face, if for even a second, was worth the price of admission.

Bob screamed, throwing himself on Charlie. The two fell to the ground.

"You little fucker!" Bob screamed, punching Charlie square in the jaw.

Pain shot through Charlie's face. Another punch found him right beneath the left eye and left his face at the edge of explosion.

"No!" Callie screamed, pulling Bob away from Charlie. "Stop it!"

Bob reluctantly pulled away, glaring at Charlie.

Callie bent down to help him up, "Are you okay?"

Bob continued to glare as Charlie started to cry from pain and embarrassment. When Charlie responded in a sniffle, Bob smirked and walked to the fridge to get another beer. "Clean this shit up so we can eat like a family."

**

The rest of dinner was uncomfortably quiet, as Charlie and Callie exchanged nervous glances while Bob seemed to almost completely forget about the whole damned thing.

As Bob drank, he told crude jokes, and even made small talk with Charlie, telling him he'd done well with the pistol at target practice earlier.

Charlie played along. His pride was wounded, as was his face, but if Bob was being nice now, he'd not look a gift horse in the mouth. Charlie started to understand how his mother must've felt living with a ticking schizophrenic time bomb, never knowing what would set it off or what would defuse it.

Bob got up to take a piss upstairs. Callie looked at Charlie, her eyes gentle.

"Thank you for lying for me. I'm so sorry. I should've spoken up sooner."

"It's okay," Charlie said. "Better he take it out on me than you."

As Callie gave him a giant hug, Charlie felt, despite his weakness, like a momentary hero.

**

9:12 p.m.

Bob was in front of the TV in a drunken stupor, even though it wasn't working. Callie and Charlie were playing chess upstairs in the bedroom Callie had taken as hers for however long they planned (and there was very little planning involved with Bob) at Derek's house.

Thankfully, they hadn't spoken again of "the dinner incident," and Callie was being extra nice.

The house had five spare rooms in addition to the master bedroom, though only three had beds. While they'd each slept in separate rooms each night, Charlie was hoping tonight, Callie might stay with him.

He didn't even want to have sex with her — though he would in a heartbeat — so much as just lie beside her and hold her.

"Are you letting me win?" she asked as she took his black queen with her white bishop. "How could you have not seen that coming?"

"I dunno," he said, trying to work up courage. His stomach was butterflies. "I was just thinking about stuff."

"Like what?" she said, her beautiful eyes meeting his.

"Um, I dunno," he said, suddenly realizing that he didn't even know HOW to make a move on a girl.

Do I kiss her? Do I ask her out? Is asking someone out even possible now? I mean, how the hell are you gonna date when you don't even know if you'll be attacked by zombies tomorrow?

His head was spinning as he tried to think of something, *anything*, other than the rambling words falling awkwardly from his mouth. His mouth was moving a mile a minute, but he wasn't hearing the words. It was just small talk, meaningless gibberish, as panic moved to full steam.

He had to get control of the situation before his lunatic ramblings sent her running.

Be bold. Be assertive. Girls respect boldness.

"I like you," he said. His racing heart pushed out the three words, then stopped on a dime.

* * * *

CHAPTER 3
BRENT FOSTER

Oct. 15
9:47 p.m.
New York City

Brent's apartment was a fortress of darkness, barely illuminated by a single, battery-operated lantern. A second light sat in the hallway, turned off to keep the batteries fresh.

The refrigerator blocked the doorway, and the kitchen table blocked the living room window. Brent's mattress, dresser, and a trunk blocked the window in his and Gina's bedroom. The window in Ben's room was blocked, partly, by his mattress and dresser.

Their fortress wasn't impenetrable by any means. They hoped it would slow the creatures down long enough to defend the apartment with the small arsenal spread out on the coffee table.

It had been nearly an hour since the massacre at Stan's apartment. An hour of horrible silence and endless waiting.

"All this time, I was hoping Gina and Ben were out there, lost. But now I'm not so sure. If they're out there, with those things, there's ... " Brent couldn't finish. The mere thought of some monstrosity attacking his wife or child, especially his child, was something worse than unimaginable.

But even as he tried to squash the thoughts from his mind, his brain drew the image of Ben seeing one of the monsters, thinking it was a cool cartoon or toy come to life, and calling out to it. And then the look in his son's eyes as the thing came closer and then finally attacked.

Brent rose from the chair, pacing, wanting to do something, but not knowing what to do. What he *could* do.

"Do you think they'd be better off if they just vanished?" Luis asked.

"I don't know. If the same creatures who killed Stan and Melora are also behind the vanishings, then no. But maybe ... maybe whatever took all the people was actually saving them?"

"Saving them?"

"Yeah," Brent said, the idea starting to spin and gather speed in his head, "Maybe some benevolent force was calling people up before these creatures showed up."

"What? Like God or angels?"

"I dunno," Brent said, "I mean, the things in the video didn't seem all that godly, but would we know divine intervention if we saw it?"

"Then why didn't this ... *divine source* ... take us all? I mean, I could see if it was the Rapture and all the sinners or nonbelievers were left behind. But if that were the case, the city would be packed with people, right? As far as we know, it's just us four. Well, now two."

As darkness enveloped the city outside, Brent and Luis took turns taking naps. Luis told Brent to go first, lying on the sofa while Luis sat in the recliner. Brent didn't think he'd fall asleep. But as Luis was telling him a story from his life before the vanishings, Brent fell into the breath of nothing.

**

In Brent's dream, he found himself reliving a year-old memory.

Brent and Gina were in bed, listening to the baby monitor as Ben whined, not wanting to sleep. He was almost 3 years old, and had been sleeping on his own for almost two years, but had suddenly developed a fear of sleeping in his bedroom. Gina was trying to sleep. It was 10:20 p.m., and she had to be up early. Brent was typing story notes on his laptop. He didn't have to be to work until 11 a.m., but he had a few hours of work ahead of him still.

"How long do you want to let him cry it out?" Brent asked. "It's been 15 minutes."

Gina sighed, "We can't keep giving in, or he's not going to outgrow this."

Gina was right, and surely in stress listening to her son cry yet not going to him, but she was strong. Brent found it hard to listen to his son's cries without going to Ben's room.

Ben's recent night fears were likely inspired by Brent's absence at home as he worked later and later. Most nights, his son was asleep before Brent got home. He couldn't help but think if he went into Ben's room and cuddled with him a bit, it would do more good than the harm Gina felt would come from surrender.

"I'm going in," Brent said, closing his laptop.

"Sucker," Gina said, playfully, and half asleep. He was glad she wasn't going to argue with him. Raising a son was tough, but not agreeing on things with your wife made it harder. They didn't have huge disagreements, just lots of little things, which added to the stress he already felt under the insanity of his workload.

He slipped from their room, laptop in hand, and set it on the dining room table before going into Ben's room, dimly lit by the blue Stanley Train nightlight on the wall.

Ben was sitting up in bed, mouth wide open in full cry.

"Hey, buddy," Brent said, "What's wrong?"

"I want Daddy," he said, his voice tired, ragged from crying.

"I'm here, buddy," Brent said, "Want me to lay down with you for a few minutes?"

"Yeah," Ben said, wiping tears from his cheeks.

Brent scooted his son over, slid next to him in the bed, put an arm around him, then rubbed his hair, which often soothed the boy to sleep. Ben relaxed almost immediately.

"Daddy loves you so much," he said, hugging his son tighter and kissing the back of his head.

Usually, Ben would ask "how much" and they'd play a game where Brent would hold his hands apart in ever increasing amounts, saying, "this much."

Ben fell asleep without response. It never failed to amaze Brent how quickly his son could go from fully alert to fast asleep. Or in the mornings, when he rose at the crack of dawn, from comatose to running around the house at warp speed.

As Brent lay beside his son, listening to his breathing slow and deep, he was tempted to get up and go back to working on his laptop. That was what he usually did after his son fell asleep, went right back to work.

But this time, something compelled him to stay.

As he stared at the back of his son's head, and his soft, round cheeks, he was suddenly overwhelmed with tears. How Ben must feel never seeing his daddy, or being brushed aside when Brent had work to finish? He wondered how much damage he'd already done to his child's psyche, self-esteem, and overall level of happiness by being such an absent father.

In that moment, his arm around his son, listening to him sleep, Brent started to see things with a clarity he'd never had.

Time was flying faster by the day, month, and year. Soon, his son would be older and wouldn't want hugs from Daddy, and certainly wouldn't want to snuggle with him in bed. And they'd probably wind up battling in the teen years, if Brent's relationship with his own father was the normal trajectory for father/son relationships.

Moments like this, where Brent was everything in his son's eyes, where Daddy could make everything alright with a hug, would soon be gone and lost forever.

This was it, now or never.

He decided to change, to make more of an effort to be home for his family. To live his life to the fullest.

Of course, that's not what happened. The next day was the first of several staff meetings announcing deep newsroom cuts. Reporters would need to work harder, better, and more hours per week than ever before. Or they'd find themselves next on the list.

So, Brent kept running on the hamster wheel while another year flew by.

**

Brent woke with regret drowning his eyes.

As he wiped his tears, he looked at the recliner and saw that Luis had fallen asleep, a shotgun in his lap.

What time is it?

He glanced at his watch, an old-fashioned pocket watch Gina had given him when Ben was born. It was nearing midnight.

He was wondering if maybe Gina had already tried to get in the apartment, but was unable to.

As Brent rose from his seat, someone knocked on the door.

Luis snapped awake, gun ready.

* * * *

CHAPTER 4
MARY OLSON

Oct. 16
Just after dawn
Belle Springs, Missouri

Mary screamed.

Desmond, John and Jimmy were all awake and by her side in seconds. "What happened to her, do you know?" Desmond asked.

Mary shook her head, hysterical. She opened her mouth but her tongue was trapped. She tried to push a few words out, but the only things to leave were three long strings of guttural moans, followed by a soul-stripped bellow.

Desmond tried to calm her, but didn't have the first clue how. Jimmy stared, his verbal cascade uncharacteristically still. Nothing in his upper-class adolescence had prepared him for an unannounced end of the world, or the bottomless torment of a grieving, panicked mother. John's three miscarriages in six years of marriage gave him the sharpest tools in the room, but he was still too hazy from liquid poison to pull anyone from the abyss.

Desmond turned to Jimmy and John.

"John, I need you to sweep the lobby, everywhere across the common area on the first floor. Jimmy, go outside and look for anything unusual. Check the pool and trash areas. I'll stay with Mary." Jimmy nodded and turned toward the door. John was already on his way.

Mary tried to catch her breath, fighting against the 900-pound weight that sat in her stomach and plugged her throat.

She'd been in the wooly midst of a wonderful dream, where everything was okay — before her fate collided with an unimaginable future where her life's work went from giving the country's lovers the right words to say when they didn't have their own, to keeping her daughter from the edge of oblivion. Life's work that lasted all of a day before driving Mary to failure.

No. She couldn't, *wouldn't* allow that to happen.

"She's gone ... " Two words, but the ending of the second was swallowed by a wave of heaving, shattered sobs.

"We will find her," Desmond said in a soothing whisper. "She couldn't have gone far. We just have to start looking."

"You don't understand," Mary cried. "I can't feel her anywhere. Not at all. It's like she's *gone* gone. No thoughts, no energy, nothing. It's like ... " Mary fell into another pit of hysterics.

I have to stop. Paola needs me. She's in danger every second it takes me to get myself together. And if I don't stop freaking out, things will get worse.

Get it together, Mary. Now.

If she's dead, you killed her.

Ninety-nine ... 98 ... 97 ... 96 ... 95 ...

Mary blended the rhythm of her breathing with the numbers in her head, slowly aligning her internal chaos with the new impossible reality.

Eighty-four ... 83 ... 82 .... 81 ... 80 ...

She took a long breath, then looked Desmond in the eye. "What do you think we should do?"

Relief colored his face. Desmond pulled Mary into a sudden, surprising embrace, held her for a short moment, then pushed her softly away. "We're going to find her, and everything will be okay," he said, holding her eyes. "But we've gotta be smart right now, and make sure we're not letting fear drive the bus. Okay?"

Mary nodded, then collapsed into a minute-long fit of coughing.

John and Jimmy were back, standing a few feet away while waiting for their cue. "John, I want you to comb every corner of the first-floor offices. Bathrooms, office stalls, under the cushions, everywhere. Leave nothing out." He turned to Jimmy. "I need you to check the rooms."

"I already did," he said. "Twice, she's not in her room, or any of ours."

"No," Desmond said. "I want you to check every room on the first floor. The locks are off so the doors should open. If they don't open, make a list of rooms we need to check. We'll go back and kick those doors in one by one."

"Mary," his face softened, "You should check the restaurant area. Go through the dining room and kitchen. Maybe Paola got hungry, went to find something to eat, and fell asleep. She was awfully tired, and the kitchen is the one area on the first floor where she might not have been able to hear us, even with all the screaming."

"I'll check the exits, inside and outside, and we'll all meet back here as soon as we can."

More words weren't needed. The men went off, each hunter going to gather on his own, hoping he'd be the one to return a happy girl to her panicked mother and likely praying he wouldn't find something that would haunt her forever.

Mary examined the dining area. The end of the world must have happened pretty early in the morning, because the entire first floor of the hotel had few signs of life. Tables were cleared, chairs pushed in, and not a single item of clothing draped the furniture. She turned around and gave the dining area a final glance, waved to John who caught her eye from the other side of the lobby, then pushed the kitchen doors open to a powerful gust of her daughter's emotional scent.

She inched through the kitchen. Paola had been here. Mary took another step and was nearly knocked sideways by a powerful, unexpected wave of emotion featuring her ex-husband.

Her throat closed, and her head pounded. Her knees started to shake.

Why do I feel Ryan in here? I can almost hear his voice and smell the sweat on his collar. But that's not possible.

A lone butcher knife resting on the counter sent an arctic chill through Mary. She picked it up, the chill grew colder. Paola had held the knife, maybe for a while.

She shuddered, tossed the butcher knife on the counter with an angry clatter, then traded the cool, stale air of the kitchen for the crisp, early morning Missouri air.

Desmond was also outside, 30 feet away, inspecting an exit. "Any luck?" he called.

Mary shook her head.

"Let's head back inside," Desmond said, walking toward her. "I don't think Paola is in the hotel, but we need to know for sure before we split up and look out here."

Mary felt like she was on the edge, about to fall.

Demond said, "It's going to be okay."

Mary nodded.

Inside, everyone echoed the same report — they'd all seen more of the same — nothing.

"There are five floors in the hotel," Desmond said. "John, you take the second. Mary takes the third. And I'll take four and five. Jimmy stays down here in case Paola slips in or out. When we're done, we meet back here. If we find nothing, then we clear out immediately."

Desmond handed each of them a flashlight.

They headed up the stairwell, which was dimly lit by emergency lights just as the hallways were. Mary got off on the 3rd floor, and started with the first door on the right. Desmond was right. It was smart to search the hotel first, but hard to do when every molecule inside her wanted to run from the hotel on a hunt to pick up Paola's scent and trail. Because if there was one thing Mary knew in this moment full of unknowns, it was this — her daughter was not in the Drury.

All the rooms in the first and second hallways were vacant, as were most of the rooms in the third. Then she opened the door to something so terrifying it managed to nudge a new thought in front of her missing daughter.

Lying on the floor in the middle of two queen-sized beds was another of the charred-looking creatures they'd found twitching on the side of the road the day before. Though it looked different — the creature from the day before had been mostly still, quietly vibrating until Desmond and a pair of bullets stopped it forever.

This one was alive, animated, waiting.

Mary had no time to measure the differences between the nightmares before the one at her feet was off the floor and lurching toward her. She screamed, then ran, but not before kicking the creature in its torso, knocking a piece of its flesh to the floor where it splattered in wet chunks.

Mary slammed the door behind her and screamed, hoping she'd draw attention from the others. The creature hit the door with a hard thud, then wailed in what sounded like a cruel attempt at human agony.

It's in pain.

The thought gave Mary a chill. *What if the creatures are victims, fallout from whatever atrocity had obliterated the world?* Not that it mattered. Sympathy wouldn't keep her or Paola alive, and though she felt certain the creature had nothing to do with her daughter's disappearance, it was a threat.

Mary opened the door to the stairwell and took the stairs two at a time. She could hear the creature behind her on the other side of the stairwell door. She had a daughter to find and a team to protect; she couldn't very well lead the creature to them, which is exactly what she'd be doing if she ran to the ground floor.

The door opened one flight above, and the creature writhed into the stairwell. It looked down, saw Mary, then stepped on the first step. She opened the door to the second floor, ran into the hallway, and slammed the door behind her.

"John!" she yelled. No answer, the floor felt empty. Mary ducked into the first door across from the stairwell — a moderately-sized supply closet with shelves stocked full with tiny soaps, shampoos, and conditioners. But unless she planned on stabbing the creature with a sewing kit, nothing was useful as a weapon.

Three rolling carts were there, however, each fully stocked for a fresh day of cleanup. Mary stepped inside, flicked off her flashlight, and shoved the closest cart against the door.

Just in time.

THUD ... THUD ... THUD ...

The creature threw its body repeatedly against the door, pushing the cart, and Mary, back.

THUD ... THUD ... THUD ...

The door inched open, edging the supply cart forward and spilling a seam of warm light into the dark supply room. Mary fell back against the rear wall of the supply closet, and pressed her legs against the cart closest to her, attempting to leverage them against the door to keep the monster out.

She closed her eyes and thought of Paola.

If you're dead it's all my fault.

THUD ... THUD ... THUD ...

The door opened and closed again, pushing the carts forward before Mary kicked them back, forcing the door shut again.

THUD ... THUD ... And then nothing.

For a moment, silence filled the air as Mary dared to hope the monster went on its way. She held her breath, trying to listen beyond the sound of her thumping heart.

And then she heard a terrible clicking sound.

THUD!

The door smashed open, the carts rolled forward, banging into Mary, as the creature fell into the supply closet screaming and making that God-awful clicking sound. Its head swung back and forth, as if it were searching for Mary, then froze, its black eyes narrowing on her.

Fuck.

She screamed, gripping the handle of the cart closest to her, and thrust the cart forward repeatedly against a second cart, which slammed into the creature.

The thing screamed, as Mary kept slamming the carts forward, until the creature stopped thrashing and fell forward onto the first cart, injured and squirming.

Mary gripped the flashlight, and swung down, slamming it into the thing's skull over and over, warm blood spraying her.

It screamed. Terror, anger, agony as it pulled back, head half caved in, mouth still intact.

The creature's wail sent Mary three steps back, just as a hunk of its face fell to the floor. Mary swallowed the bile in her throat, then launched a second assault at the creature's head, bashing it repeatedly until the thing stopped screaming, clicking, and squirming, and collapsed to the ground.

Mary didn't know if the creature was dead, or even if it *could* die, but it was down for a moment and that was enough. She swallowed again, keeping the bile in her belly, then squeezed past the carts and creature, and out into the hall. She dropped the bloodied light and raced through the stairwell door and down to the lobby where Jimmy, John, and Desmond were standing.

The terror on her face sent the men to her side in seconds. "You okay?" Jimmy asked.

Mary swallowed, unable to talk at first, staring back at the stairwell door in shock, and amazed that she'd gotten away.

"What happened?" John asked, eyes wide and fearful.

"I just saw another one of those things, you know, like the dead thing we saw on the highway. The thing Desmond shot." She looked at Desmond with a weak smile, then down at her shaking hands and the front of her shirt, covered in black blood. "I'm fine. I think I killed it."

Desmond raced into the stairwell, grabbing a pistol from his waistband.

"What about Paola? Anyone find anything?" Mary asked.

Mary could read the NO written on their empty faces. She was right, at least about Paola. No one found a trace. But John had seen one of the twitching creatures lying on the floor in one of the rooms. Almost pissed himself when he saw it, but the beast was either sleeping or dead so he closed the door and counted himself lucky.

"I need to know which rooms the creatures are in," Desmond said returning to them, "So we can make sure they're dead. And then we move out and search outside for Paola."

"Someone needs to stay here and wait in case she comes back," Mary said.

"Mary, I understand how you feel right now," Desmond said, "but we have to stick together. We can't afford for our numbers to get split. We'll be able to help Paola better together, so let's go outside and look. If we don't find anything, we'll come back."

"No. Somebody needs to stay here," she said.

Jimmy and John seemed willing, but both were looking to Desmond.

Desmond sighed. "Please, Mary. Let's stick together and canvas the area. Chances are, she's close. If not, we'll be back in a few minutes. It's what's best, not just for all of us, but for Paola, too. I promise."

"And what if we're all out there looking for her and she comes back and, whoops, there's another monster in the hotel and nobody here to protect her?"

"I'll stay," Jimmy offered, "As long as you give me a gun."

* * * *

CHAPTER 5
BORICIO WOLFE

Somewhere in Alabama

Boricio gnashed his teeth at the injustice of his blindfolded captivity.

Unfortunately for his captors, the beast had already freed himself from his chains, breaking out of the plastic restraints which had bound his wrists behind his back. His blood was boiling, kinetic violence waiting to crackle, holding for the time when no movement would be wasted on his return to the rotting corpse of the world outside.

He wasn't sure how long he'd been out, but figured he hadn't lost more than a day already. Still, that was a day longer than anyone had ever held Boricio. Unfortunately, he would have to lie on the burlap mat a bit longer, until he'd sussed out the situation.

Danger was in the room, and dangers were outside. Outside was probably worse. Much worse. Difference was, outside Boricio made some of the rules. He was busting out one way or another. Question was how many fuckers would have to die before he was rolling down the highway, windows down, and dialing into the latest on Boricio FM.

Way he smelled it, he had six ways to end everyone in the room, and three of 'em made a helluva lot of sense. One wouldn't work, at least not until he could get a clearer picture of the distances between the last body and the wall, and the first body and the door. Of the remaining two, one was as easy as tenderizing a few pounds of meat.

None of the prisoners was armed, Boricio figured. He'd need to rip off his blindfold, survey the room, then get clear to his far right within the first second. He had no way of knowing for certain whether the four "prisoners" were friendly or not, but he'd have to assume they were all cozy with Testosterone and the Big Nipple Bitch, because as Boricio had learned long ago, you never take anything as a given.

He'd start with the prisoner on the far right, snap his neck before anyone in the room knew what was happening. He'd move straight in a row, ending each of the blindfolded pigeons until he hit Silent Bob at the end.

Bitch of it was, the strategy would have to flip a bitch in a second if any of the four prisoners were instead a guard. He'd still start with the guy on the far right, but would have to immediately grab the second guy so he could use his body as a shield while he figured out what to do with the other two fucktards.

It wouldn't be quiet, and that meant just seconds until Testosterone and Big Nipple Bitch came busting in with their Superdome-sized home court advantage and whatever weapons they carried.

Much as he hated to soak in the saltwater *suck on this* that came with murdering time, it was college cool to play the room until the right time. It would happen, and when it did, he'd let everyone in the room, dead and alive, know he was their new lord and savior, least for the six or so seconds they had the chance to swear allegiance. They were already on their knees at the end of the world; ain't no better time than that to switch up deities.

Boricio would've already snapped a whole lot of spinal cords, but the shit that came falling from Silent Bob's mouth a few minutes earlier had tripped him way the fuck out.

He didn't understand the dude's words, but his tone was all wrong — sent an arrow straight into the bull's-eye of Boricio's terror like few things he'd ever heard.

The Chinese had a weird ass ching chong ramma lamma ding dong of a language, but there was shit about it that just made good sense, way it was once explained to Boricio. Like the way they used the same words to mean different things, difference being in tone.

"Tiger" "four" and "death" were all the same exact fucking word in Chinese, just the tone the chinks said it that made the difference. Most people in America would be too stupid to hear that shit; everyone would end up confusing one another all the time. But if a fucker can learn how to listen over there, then they can do it over here. Boricio knew everything he needed to know 99 percent of the time, and he got there with his ears and his eyes, and sometimes his nose. That's what instincts were: listening to the music of the world around and never missing a note. When it came to hearing the fear in another man's throat, Boricio had perfect pitch.

Silent Bob was scared as fuck about something.

He saw something out there that he don't know how to explain. His mind is turning it over and trying to measure it, but there's too much and not enough and he can't stir that shit up enough to make no sorta sense. And it's mixed with the kinda fear a man gets when there ain't no way he's got more than 100 breaths left inside him.

Whatever he saw, there was a chance it wasn't human. A week ago that would've sounded like some science fiction bullshit to Boricio, but not anymore. Something soured the planet to memory — had to be global, otherwise some sort of cavalry would've been rolling in by now.

Something pointed the barrel at humanity. And it forgot to empty the chamber, or ran out of bullets. Either way, aliens, government, who-the-fuck ever — someone let the fires burn. And Boricio had a feeling that something was being done to clean up the mess. That something is probably what Silent Bob saw. It was something that Boricio had sensed more than knew, as a predator senses when a new breed has risen to the top of the food chain.

Whatever Silent Bob saw, must've fucked with his head big-time. Made sense. Boricio's head was fucked with, above and beyond his usual internal bullshit transmissions. It felt real, sure, but he sure as shit knew a Boricio FM wasn't broadcasting his name across all hours of fuck all.

If that were all true, and Boricio figured it was, he was safer in this room, even if it meant staying on his knees a little longer. He was a king now; this was his kingdom. It just might take a bit longer to claim the throne.

Another click and whine from the door, followed by a fresh gust of warm, stale air. A new scent entered the room. This scent had teeth. Boricio could smell it, under the sweat: mean, sadistic, and cruel. If Testosterone reeked of asshole, this guy was steeped in the scent of pain and misery. He was cock of the walk, and was all too happy to strut his stuff.

"Time to eat," Boricio heard the voice a split second before something was forced into his mouth. Earthy and unfamiliar.

Boricio spit it out, then heard the sticky THWAP!! as it hit the man's face. "Not hungry," Boricio said.

It was nice to hear the guard's laughter, good to know a nice kitty cat was there who wanted to play.

A sudden slap at the side of each of Boricio's ears rolled thunder through his head.

"You dropped something from your cockhole," the voice said. "Good thing I'm a generous teacher willing to help you learn more control."

Boricio's lips and jaw exploded in pain as the asshole took a cheap shot, and for a moment he wasn't sure whether or not he'd have to swallow a tooth. Between his nose and lips, he probably looked like Halloween. Not good. Boricio gave exactly two shits and a half a tinkle about his good looks, but knew the value of an effective weapon and a convincing disguise. His looks were both, and in a dead world, a pretty face looked like an angel.

Boricio laughed. A crazy, cracked, drunken alligator of a laugh.

Dead Guard Walking, that's what I'll call this special breed of fucker. Bag of shit won't just be any old corpse either. I'll be taking as much of my sweet time as I can afford. Won't have the minutes I need to make it biblical, but I'm gonna get creative, believe it, bitch. That's all I need, one minute to make this bag of shit wish he'd died as a child.

Boricio's laughter quieted to a dying rumble.

The voice cackled back. "Glad to see you've got a bit of fight in ya. This might just be fun," he said. "The rest of you fuckers were a bit vanilla for my taste."

Boricio felt a slap at his throat, not too hard but hard enough to make him open his mouth in reflex. The earthy shit was back, followed by a second slap to the throat. "Chew on it, fucker. I'll be back."

A whine, a thud, then seven or so minutes of silence followed by, "I think that asshole's name is Jackson," from the voice all the way to Boricio's right. "And I don't know it for sure, but I think he's the one who killed the guy who was sitting right where I'm sitting, 'round this time yesterday. I don't think he meant to, and I think he may have even gotten in some trouble from Brock, that was the other asshole who was in here earlier, but he gets carried away and they let him. Might even be his job. Gave me a gash on my right cheek. Feels creek deep, too. My name is Moe, by the way."

Moe paused, as if he were waiting for someone to say something. When nobody spoke, he continued.

"You all can't see it, but it's a bad one, and bled so much I expected I'd die right there. Happened right when that asshole Jackson hauled me in. And ain't no reason, neither. Asked me why I was smirking, and I said I wasn't smirking. Guess he didn't like me talking back 'cuz he started whooping me on the top of my head. I was just gonna take it, but then I got to hearing my daddy in my ear telling me not to be such a bitch, so I tried to swing, but forgot my hands were tied behind my back so I fell flat on my ass. That Jackson fucker just started laughing his ass off. He told me he'd teach me not to fight. A second later, I felt the worst pain I ever felt, no warning or nothing. My cheek was in a couple of pieces, and blood was spilling from my face like a busted faucet. I started screaming like a hog. Even pissed myself; ain't no shame in it either way, 'cuz I was bleeding. They gave me some sort of shot, I guess to sedate me. Next thing I knew I was in here, same as I am now."

"Shit!" another man to Boricio's left said. "My name is Jack. They didn't do nothing to me, least that I remember. I just woke up in here with my eyes covered and hands tied, about as scared as I've ever been."

"What about you?" Moe asked.

"Me?" Boricio said.

"Yeah, how'd you end up at the End of the World Inn?"

"Not much to tell. I spent most of the last few days hiding in a basement. Woulda stayed there, too, least if I hadn't got so goddamned hungry. You all are the first people I've seen since whatever happened happened, least if you don't count the bitch that brought us all together."

"And you, heavy breathing dude?" Moe asked. "You ain't said shit that makes sense yet. Someone fuck you up bad when you got here?"

"My name's Adam, sir, And no, not hardly. I've had no problems other than getting tossed in here to start with. And I may be a prisoner, but them folks out there saved me from something that was pure, pitch-black evil, I tell you what."

Silent Bob's name is Adam. Shit, and he ain't so silent now, way to fuck up a nickname. Oh well, not like I'll need to remember his name much longer.

Manny asked Adam, "What do you mean? That what you were trying to say earlier?"

"Yeah," his voice about cracked in half. Something in the tone made Boricio uneasy. "I seen some things that I don't even know how to explain, though I expect I'll try once they make sense inside my head. Are you okay, Mister ... what did you say your name was?"

"Boricio," he said. No sense in lying, as none of these fuckers were likely to get out of here alive. "And yeah, I've dealt with tougher women than that prick."

"That Jackson guy seems like a real sore wound of a fella," Adam said. "But I swear on everything I know we're better off in here than we are out there, unless these guys are as crazy as the things I've seen. And they were horrible, but a fat step up from my old man. World's gone; I'm a prisoner of who knows who, and I seen evil walking on two legs sure as I'm breathing earlier today, and I still say this is a better than the average week."

Boricio should've known the second he referred to Moe as "sir," but hadn't realized until just that moment — Adam was only a boy.

"How old are you, Adam?" Boricio asked, no disguise.

"I'm 16, but big for my age. Was my job to get the beer, no matter who was asking."

"Your old man sounds like a ripe old gash of an asshole."

Adam made a sound, might've laughed, though Boricio wasn't sure. "Yeah, have to say I'm not sorry to see him go at all. Gary was an asshole and beat the shit out of me on days ending in Y and fucking my little sister once a month when my mom wouldn't put out. Ma was busy pretending she didn't have a clue what was going on, when the truth was she was just too scared to do anything about it."

"How old was your sister?" Moe wanted to know, as if it mattered.

"Just turned 15 last week of September."

"How many times have you imagined killing him?" Boricio asked.

"Not once until last year, but once I started, every day since. Before then, I thought things were maybe somehow my fault. After that, it was clear he was some sorta demon."

Boricio felt something, maybe curiosity. He hoped it wasn't anything bullshit like compassion, though he'd guessed he could understand it if it was. "What happened?"

"We had just moved to St. Pete. Grandpa, the original asshole you might say, died and left Gary some land. A real dump, but paid for. There was a big trophy case in the house from when he was a kid. I was looking at the trophies, trying to see what the big one on top was for. I accidentally fell against the case and brought the whole thing down. I swear it was an accident, but before I knew it, all the trophies were on the ground, broken, and Gary came running in the room."

"He grabbed me by the hair and dragged me through the house, kicking me the whole way. When we got to the kitchen, he flicked on the garbage disposal and grabbed my hand and shoved it into the drain, and I thought for sure, my fingers were gonna get caught up in it." Adam started to cry, and *fucking beer-battered bullshit*, Boricio kinda felt bad for the kid.

"He kept calling me a liar and yelling at me to tell him what really happened. I kept telling him I wasn't lying. He told me if I ever lied again, he'd bring me right back to that same spot and let the blades tear my fingers up."

This day was getting all full up with fuckers to kill. Would be nice to find Gary and build a whole new kind of fire to hold his ass to. Would bring back the sweet taste for sure.

Boricio had a special place in his dark heart for evil fuck fathers ever since he paid his dear ole dad back for his childhood of hell.

Ears burned with cigarettes. Forced to drink shampoo. Three toes bent so bad the doctors considered amputation. A third-degree burn by way of blow dryer. A miserable fucking childhood raped of every molecule of joy. Yeah, it'd be nice to skull fuck some other asshole just as deserving.

"So, Adam," Boricio asked. "What do you think happens when they take you out of here, then? What's in the box?"

"World's been shit miserable so far; maybe outside is some sort of hallelujah to make up for it, you know, if you're the right kind of person."

"What kind of person is that?" Boricio asked.

"Maybe the world owes some of us a new beginning."

The room went silent, as if in the aftermath of an uncomfortable truth. Boricio wanted to laugh at the kid's delusional pipe dreams because as sure as shit, there was no God in the sky, no angels waiting to take you to heaven, and the world never gave you what it owed you. No, the only thing on the menu was shit and more shit.

However, perhaps fortune had smiled on Adam, as Boricio reconsidered his plans to kill every fucker in the room.

No reason he couldn't take out most of the room, leave one soldier behind. Maybe a second set of hands was just what Boricio needed. Maybe Boricio could be a mentor. A special kind of mentor, like Boricio had while growing up.

It felt good to think about Tom again. It had been a long time since he allowed himself to remember the man who taught him to kill and never get caught.

* * * *

CHAPTER 6
EDWARD KEENAN

Oct. 15
Early evening
Somewhere in North Carolina

Ed and Teagan were 60 miles from her home in Cape Hope, North Carolina, when she finally decided to break the ice that had frosted their air since the fallen bodies at the gas station.
"Why aren't we going to find your daughter first?"
"What?"
"Well, if my dad were looking for me, I don't think he'd stop to help a stranger and get sidetracked from doing what he set out to do."
"It's complicated," he said. "Can we talk about something else? Anything. Like your favorite bands or what movies you like, or what you like to do? Do you play any sports?"
"Had to give up football with the baby and all," Teagan said with a laugh, patting her belly. Another moment of

silence passed before she finally said what she'd wanted to say in the first place. "You killed those people like it was nothing. I mean, no hesitation whatsoever. How can you do that? What *are you?*"

"What do you mean, what *am I?*"

"You said you were kinda like a cop, but cops have to go by rules, right? Even now. My cousin, Jeb, was a cop, and I can't imagine him, or any of his cop buddies, pulling the trigger like that, no questions asked."

"I can't really say what it was that I did, but I worked for our government. And I was one of the *good guys*. And despite what you see on TV and in the movies, the good guys aren't necessarily the same as the nice guys."

"So, you're not a nice guy, then?"

He kept his eyes on the road. Teagan's resemblance to his daughter made the conversation every bit the biting through nails it would've been if it were Jade's mouth moving instead, so he tried not to look at her any more than he had to.

"I'm just a guy who does what needs to be done. You said your cousin, Jeb, was a cop? What do you mean *was?*"

"He was killed by a drunk driver a year ago. Tell me, why were you arrested?" she asked, so out of the blue he nearly swerved off the road.

"What?" he asked, playing stupid.

"The rings on your wrist, someone had you in cuffs, I assume?"

Ed smiled.

"You're observant."

"So, are you going to tell me?"

"Man, you just cut right to the chase, eh?"

Teagan was smiling, but just barely.

"You're right, I was arrested. But I didn't do anything I wasn't told to do."

"Then why were you arrested?"

"Sometimes, the people who make up the rules of the game change them on the fly depending on which asses need kissing, the political gestures that need to be made, and you know, all the usual bureaucratic bullshit. Well, maybe you don't know. At any rate, when the rules change and your bosses are caught playing by the old rules, well, that means shifting the blame downwind to someone else. A guy like me."

"What does that even mean?" she asked.

Ed had to laugh at the knots of confusion on her face, though he was pretty sure she thought he was laughing at her expense.

"The less I say, the better. Trust me. When the world returns to normal, people will be looking for me. They find out I was with you, they'll haul you in, ask you more questions than a week's worth of SATs, and make your life a living hell. The less you can honestly answer, and trust me when I say they can tell when you're lying, the better off you are."

Teagan stared at him for an uncomfortably long time as if she were still trying to figure out exactly what he was. She needed him to fit neatly into some preconceived notion of good or bad because that's the way light spilled against the prism of her sheltered adolescent worldview. Few layers of gray existed in her world of blacks and whites.

"So, how did it feel the first time you killed someone?"

Ed moved his eyes from the road, let up slightly on the gas, then looked to his right. To his relief, her expression wasn't that of a vulture searching the carcass for morbid details; it was the sparrow-like curiosity of an innocent child.

"What do *you* think it's like?"

"I can't even imagine it; it has to be awful."

"Yeah, it is that. It's also scary."

"You're scared?" she said, surprised. "But you shot those guys like you were picking up a carton of eggs and a gallon of milk."

"It's scariest the first time. But it's never *not scary*. You're always looking at two choices — run or act. With each choice comes a consequence. What happens if you run? Will those people continue to threaten you or those you're protecting? If so, then you really don't have a choice, do you? You must deal with it in the moment, unless you're outnumbered or have too many variables to deal with. And when you kill, you must always be prepared for the fallout. And you have less than a millisecond to make the right choice."

"Did you feel guilty about killing those men at the gas station? I mean, they might not even have meant us any harm. Maybe they were just like us; they had guns to protect themselves from the bad guys."

"Maybe," Ed said, "But I can't think about that. I can't cry into the rearview. If I ponder all the what-ifs, that leads to guilt and my instincts get dull. It makes it that much harder to act decisively the next time. Soon, I'm dead. Or worse, someone I'm protecting is dead."

"So how do you deal with those things?" she asked, slowly drifting from curiosity to full-blown psychological exam. "How do you just ... forget?"

"I disconnect from the situation. Remove all emotional residual, lingering doubts, and every ounce of guilt. I seal them all in a drum, fuse the lid, then drop it into the deepest ocean of my soul."

Ed could feel her staring.

"I don't believe you," she said, "I don't think you can just disconnect your humanity like that."

"You'd be surprised what you can do, *have to do*, when it's do or die."

"I'd rather die than lose my humanity," she said. It was her turn to stare out the window. Rain began to fall on the windows and roof of the SUV.

Ed flipped on the wipers. "That's a rather noble idea, really it is. But I guarantee you one thing — once your baby is born, you will go anywhere and do anything to protect it, and believe me, you have no idea what that means."

A sign ahead announced: *Cape Hope: 50 Miles.*

Ed hoped to find someone. He needed to lose the pregnant appendage. The sooner he was flying solo, the sooner he could quit the crap and get on with a solution to whatever happened last night.

"I know why you're not in a rush to get to your daughter," Teagan said, circling back to the original subject. "You're afraid of what you'll find, aren't you? You don't know what you'd do if she were gone?"

Ed kept driving.

* * * *

CHAPTER 7
MARY OLSON

Mary and Desmond crossed the parking lot, passed the attendant's booth at the far edge of the hotel, then stepped onto a narrow strip of State Street on their way to find Paola. Jimmy and John agreed to stay at the hotel, Jimmy downstairs with an eye peeled for Paola, while John swept the upper floors one more time for anything that might help them understand what happened to Mary's daughter, or the world.

The group agreed to meet back in the lobby of the Drury in one hour, whether they found anything or not. "You look like you actually know where you're going," Desmond said, a half-step behind Mary.

Mary couldn't smell Paola, not exactly. But she did know which direction to go. She was following a feeling more than a scent — her daughter's emotional bread crumbs. She'd first sensed them in the kitchen, and the trail seemed to be growing stronger with every step.

"Paola was here. She left the kitchen, crossed the parking lot, and then went that way." Mary pointed to a small, brick sandwich shop across the street on the corner of State and Trough."

"How do you know?"

"Because she went through the kitchen, I *felt* her there." Mary paused to see if Desmond's eyes gave question to her certainty or sanity, and was relieved to see they didn't. "Earlier, when we were searching the hotel, I thought maybe she'd come outside for some fresh air or something before heading back inside the hotel. But now I'm positive she left and walked this way. I'm just trying to understand *why* she left in the first place. I can't for the life of me see why she'd run off. That's not like her at all. Paola always thinks she's right and she loves to be the boss, but she's a perfectly sensible girl."

"Any chance she went off to find her dad?" Desmond asked.

"She wouldn't do that without me. But once we get to the base, I ought to at least see if he's still here, whether the rest of you want to go with me or not."

"I can't speak for the others, but I'll take you anywhere you want to go," Desmond said.

They crossed the street then turned onto Trough.

"Once we were back outside, I felt her immediately, like the wind was carrying her trace." She looked back at Desmond again. His eyes were still receptive to her weird ramblings. "And I swear it's getting stronger."

"Is it possible you're wrong?"

"Nope," Mary walked faster. "Well, of course it's *possible*. And I'm not claiming I can explain why, but I *know* she went this way."

"What do you mean? How can you *know*?" Desmond asked.

Even walking at a half sprint, Mary had time to love the way Desmond asked, not skeptical, just curious.

"I just do. It's like being hungry or remembering where you left your keys or getting turned on by a brush on your skin or a whisper in your ear. You *just know* — the feeling is there and as soon as it is, your body knows exactly how to respond and what to do next. Mostly animal, I suppose. Never noticed it before Paola, but I was so tuned into her patterns as an infant, I think I somehow learned to tune into the world around me. With Paola, tapping into the feelings and just *knowing* things has always been as easy as breathing. But now I find myself knowing other stuff, too, and with an almost terrible certainty. It's great when I'm lost without the GPS, terrible when it makes me *know* stuff like my husband is sleeping with Natalie Farmer."

"It's instinct. Everyone has it," Desmond said. "Sounds like you listen better than most, though."

An explanation so simple, Mary felt stupid. "Yeah," she nodded. "*Instinct*, that's exactly what it is. But it's more than that, too. Especially lately. For the last year or so, I feel like I'm picking up on Paola's *actual thoughts* every now and then, and before you call me crazy, I fully admit it *might be* my imagination. But I don't think it is. Sometimes I feel like I can *hear* her thinking. And she'll say stuff which confirms what I thought she was thinking."

Desmond nodded, still interested.

"Things have been different since the divorce, obviously, but I think it hit us harder than most families. I know that sounds arrogant. Divorce sucks for everyone. But we were happy. Ryan was a good husband and a great dad. We were married for 15 years and best friends for five before that. What he did was really, *really* stupid, and it made me hate him … no," Mary shook her head, " … not trust him, enough to end it, but that's the only thing I can put on his list. Otherwise, he was a great guy. He even left the seat down 95 percent of the time. I have one unbreakable rule, and he broke it. Since the divorce, things have been a lot rougher between Paola and me. She's gone from my sweet, little angel girl to my ultimate foe half the time. Her attitude is endless, and most days, I wake up and fall to sleep feeling like I'm fighting a losing battle. She knows what her father did to me and to us, but still blames me for breaking up a happy family. Half the time I think she's right."

"I'm sorry," Desmond said, not seeming to know what else to say. So he improved the subject without changing it. "I believe you about hearing Paola's thoughts if it makes you feel any better. Makes perfect sense. Other species communicate with one another through psychic transmission. Makes sense that we would, too. It's no different than instinct. I imagine we must have relied on something like that in earlier incarnations of our species. Before the Internet, before TV, before radio, hell, before the written word."

It was Desmond's turn to look at Mary. Mary suddenly turned her attention from Desmond to a tire depot on the next corner across the street and pointed.

"She's down that way."

Down that way was a narrow road that dipped below a billboard advertising: MAC - DADDY'S -- > *The BIGGEST Burgers In TOWN!!*

They walked faster, and Desmond continued. "Let's say brain waves left a signature? Who would know how to recognize and read Paola's signature better than you?"

A cold shock rattled inside Mary.

Ryan.

Suddenly she was certain that he did have something to do with this. The feeling was as strong as the others which led her this far. He was the only person, or thing, who could've possibly pulled Paola from the hotel. As certain as she felt, though, something was off.

No, it wasn't Ryan, but rather the thought of him.

Or a dream.

And then she remembered the dreams that Paola had of her dad, frequent ones she'd had since she was in preschool. Then Mary remembered one time when Paola was 6, and Mary couldn't find her anywhere in the house. Just as she was in full freakout mode, Paola came out of the closet, yawning. Asking what was wrong. She had sleepwalked in one of her hiding dreams.

Maybe she had done the same thing again. But out here, so far from home, there was no telling where she might be. Or what might find her if they didn't.

"Shit, Desmond. I'm scared." Mary's voice wound its way to a higher note.

"It's okay." Desmond took her hand, walked beneath the billboard, and onto McFadden, a narrow road of cracked concrete with a trail of sprouts leading to a small service station.

Mary tried to swallow her whimper, but it fell out anyway.

And then a horrible thought came into her head.

She's in pain. Terrible, terrible pain. And Ryan was there. He did this to her. Now she's on the concrete – cold, alone, stripped of memory, and dying.

Mary pointed to the gas station, and her heart sank into her gut. "She's there!"

Desmond squeezed her hand and pulled her across the street, running.

Paola lay on the ground, under flickering canopy lights cutting through the morning fog. She looked mostly dead. Mary lost herself in a primal cry, fell to her knees, and cradled Paola, holding her close to her chest. Her daughter looked like a corpse, white as a sheet and altogether hollow. Mary felt the girl's neck, and for a moment, couldn't feel a pulse.

No! No, no, no.

She moved her fingers around, desperately searching for movement. And finally, it came, and Mary closed her eyes, thanking God.

Paola's arms moved, twitched, like that creature on the side of the road and the one she left with a crumbling face just 20 minutes before on the third floor of the Drury Inn.

Desmond kneeled, cupped Mary's chin, and pulled her eyes toward him. "We've got this, okay. Everything will be fine, but we have to go right now."

Mary nodded.

Desmond tried two locked cars at the pumps before hitting a jackpot with the third parked behind the station. He was in the driver's seat for three minutes before whatever he was doing got the engine to turn. He pulled the car beside them, stepped from the car, opened the back door, kneeled down, scooped Paola's withered body into his arms, and placed her gingerly into the back seat.

"We're going to the Drury now. Everything will be fine."

Mary got in the back seat with Paola and placed her daughter's head in her lap.

"Everything will be okay," he repeated.

Mary echoed her vacant nod as she felt her world circling the drain. If Paola died, Mary would follow her into the darkness.

* * * *

CHAPTER 8
EDWARD KEENAN

Cape Hope was named in irony, at least the way Ed saw it.

The coastal community had seen better days, probably by at least a couple of decades, judging from the aged infrastructure, beaten homes, and general civic decay. Ed had seen hundreds of towns like this. Typically, they went one of two directions — slum, or a yuppie "renovation" that transformed the community into thriving strips of overpriced commerce and exclusive gated communities. Given its proximity to the ocean, Ed would've bet his every dollar on the latter.

"It used to be a nice place," Teagan said, as if reading his mind.

"Hard times all around," Ed said, noting that they wouldn't have long before the violet sky gave way to darkness. Fortunately, the clouds had parted, and the full moon hung fat in the sky, casting the world in a milky-blue haze.

"I'm in here," she said, pointing to the trailer park community yards from the beach.

"Well, location, location, location, location, right? You've got that," Ed said.

When Ed first found Teagan, he pictured her living in the suburbs somewhere, not a trailer park. Not that she looked like she came from money. But in his experience, kids who grew up in trailer parks looked tougher. They had to deal with a lot of shit from their peers blessed enough to live in nicer homes. But Teagan didn't have that raw exterior. She was soft, perhaps from a lifetime of paternal oppression. Despite her similarities to Jade, they could not be more different in this area.

As they climbed out of the SUV, Ed realized the trailer park wasn't nearly as bad as he initially guessed. The property was well-maintained, and the quality of the campers above average.

"That's mine," Teagan said, pointing to a sky-blue double wide with a vibrant flower bed around the porch. A small, tasteful cross was affixed to the door, just above a plain knocker.

She realized too late that she'd left the keys in her mom's purse in the SUV.

"I got it," Ed said. He pulled out the wallet he lifted from the home he'd broken into, retrieved a credit card, then slid it in between the door and the frame. "You coming?" He held the door open for Teagan and smiled.

"Wow, it's *that easy* to break into someone's home?"

"If you don't lock your top lock," he said. "Though I normally have tools for those."

Ed handed her one of his two lit flashlights as he held the door open for her.

"Hello? Mom? Dad?"

No answer.

Shit.

Ed stepped back outside, scanning the trailer park for signs of anybody else being home, but the place felt as empty as the rest of the world. He went back inside, looking around Teagan's home. It was small, but immaculately neat. Ed wondered what kind of taskmaster her father was, lording over his womenfolk to keep the place so tidy.

"I'm sorry they're not here," he said.

"I knew it, already," she said, "I saw them vanish."

"Yeah," Ed said, not sure what else to say, his mind trying to accept the new reality of caring full-time for another person. Maybe two people, if Jade were still alive.

Alive? Maybe everyone's gone, but that doesn't mean they're dead, does it?

Come on, Ed. What else would it mean?

"This is my room," Teagan said, opening the door to a pink bedroom that looked like it belonged to a girl far younger than her.

What kind of job did your dad do on you?

Ed checked himself, before allowing his judgmental side to run rampant. He'd not even met her father. And the man obviously had issues with his eldest daughter who killed herself, so a lot of things were in play other than him being a control freak and religious nut job.

Two other rooms were in the trailer. One was the master bedroom. The other, Ed assumed, was Teagan's sister's. The doorknob had been replaced by a deadbolt. Though he couldn't see the other side to determine if it had a thumb turn, he would bet money the deadbolt was a double cylinder.

What the hell?

Ed had to swallow hard to keep from asking Teagan about the deadbolt.

"Want a drink?" she asked, opening the door to a warm fridge.

"Thanks," he said, as she passed him a bottled water.

They both drank, neither saying a word about the elephant in the room — what to do with Teagan.

Though he'd been driving to North Carolina under the illusion he had a choice, truth was, he didn't. He was her guardian, like it or not.

"You can come with me; we'll drive to my daughter's."

"Are you sure?" she asked; a child afraid to piss off a parent.

He hid his disappointment behind a smile and casual wave of his hand. "Yeah, you two will get along great."

Neither highlighted the growing certainty that Jade would be gone, like everyone else. But still, if the two yokels at the gas station had survived, there had to be others. Maybe whatever happened hadn't affected Georgia or Florida.

"Go ahead and get whatever you want to bring and we'll head out in a few minutes."

Ed stood in the doorway, enjoying the sound of ocean waves and the smell of saltwater. It was the first time the world felt close to normal since the crash. He considered walking the path to the beach and sitting in the sand. It had been forever since he'd just sat on a beach and let the sound of waves, wind, and gulls set him at ease.

That's when he realized there weren't any gulls, or birds of any kind.

That's weird.

As he strained to hear over the waves, he picked up on the undeniable sound in the distance.

A helicopter.

They're coming for her baby.

* * * *

CHAPTER 9
BRENT FOSTER

Three quick knocks followed the first set as Luis and Brent traded glances.

"Do you think it's the aliens?" Luis whispered.

Brent shrugged his shoulders, uncertain what to do. If they didn't answer, the person, whoever it was, would leave. But was it a person, or something else?

Another knock, followed by a whisper, "Hello?"

A man's voice, familiar, but Brent couldn't quite place it.

"Hello?" Brent asked.

"Mr. Foster? Is that you?" a vaguely Jamaican-sounding voice asked.

"Yeah," Brent said, trying to match the voice to a face or name.

"It's Joe from maintenance."

Joe was the elder of the building's two maintenance men; a tall, thin man who had to be pushing 65, though he looked 10 years younger. He was always super-nice to

Ben, who called him Mr. Joe, whenever Joe came to the apartment to fix something.

Luis and Brent pulled the fridge away and unlocked the door.

Joe was in his red maintenance uniform, like always. But he looked 100 years older.

"Come in," Brent said, "This is Luis from across the street."

Joe smiled, and walked in, limping.

As Luis locked the door, Brent asked, "Are you okay?"

"Do you have any rice?"

"What?" Brent asked confused.

"Rice, I need some rice. Right away."

"You're hungry?" Brent asked, thinking Joe was injured and confused.

"No, not to eat, to keep them away."

"To keep *what* away?" Luis asked.

"The jumbees. Rice will preoccupy them. You pour it outside your door."

"What are jumbees?" Brent said.

"Do you have rice or not?" Joe asked, raising his voice, though it was edged with fear, not anger.

Brent grabbed a bag of white rice from the pantry and handed it to Joe, who asked Luis to open the door. Joe poured half the bag onto the ground just outside the door, then turned to Brent and said, "Do you have another bag?"

"Yeah," Brent said.

"Good," Joe said, pouring the rest of the first bag on the ground. He came back inside. "You can lock it now."

Luis did so.

"What are jumbees? And what's with the rice?" Brent asked as he ushered Joe to the couch to get off his injured foot.

"Jumbees are evil spirits. I used to think they were just old island folklore that my mother would go on and on about, but then I saw two of them tonight."

"What do they look like?" Luis asked.

"Jumbees can take different forms, but the things I saw on the street tonight, were dark, deformed, monstrous jumbees. They came after me, but I got away."

"You ran?" Brent asked, surprised Joe was able to get away.

"Yes. But they were also distracted. They saw someone else on the street and ... they ... " Joe looked down, like he might not finish the sentence. "They tore her up."

"*Her?*" Brent asked, fear stirring in his guts, "Who did they get? Did you know her?"

"No," Joe said, "A young Puerto Rican girl, maybe 20, I don't know. Nobody from this building, I don't think. They ripped her apart, though, limb from limb like some kind of wolves or something. Eating her."

Brent released the breath he'd been holding.

"How does the rice distract them?" Luis asked.

"The rice is supposed to slow them down. Jumbees are like kids passing a candy store. If they see a bunch of stuff spilled, they have to stop and count it. By the time they're done counting, daylight comes and they have to return to the spirit world."

Brent and Luis exchanged a *sounds-like-bullshit* glance.

"I don't think those things are jumbees," Luis said. "Because we saw some during the day. And they killed my friends in the apartment across the street earlier."

Whatever wind Joe had beneath his sails, evaporated. "So, if they *can* walk in the day, then the rice might not work."

All three men stared at the ground as if it were harboring answers.

"Have you seen anyone else?" Brent asked, "Gina or Ben?"

Joe's eyes widened, "You mean they're not here?"

"No, I woke up in the morning, and they were gone, just like everyone else."

"I'm so sorry," Joe said, his lips trembling, eyes red and glassy. "Other than the girl, I haven't seen anyone else. I went door to door. Nobody answered in your apartment earlier. I wasn't even gonna come back, but something told me to try again."

Joe turned to Luis, "You said you had some friends who were killed?"

"Yeah," Luis said, "Two friends."

"So there might be more people?" Joe asked.

Brent told him about the radio broadcast they heard earlier and that they'd be going to Black Island in the morning, once the streets were safer. They invited Joe to go with them. But first, they'd need to get some sleep.

Brent took the first shift, sitting in the recliner. Joe slept on the couch and Luis on the floor, which he swore he didn't mind at all.

As the men slept, Brent reached into his pocket and pulled out Stanley Train. Its big, goofy smile greeted him.

Brent prayed he'd be able to give the train back to its rightful owner soon.

**

In the morning, the men loaded supplies into duffel and grocery bags and prepared for the trip.

Brent wrote one last note to Gina, telling her where they were going. He doubted she'd ever see the letter, but it still pained him to write it. He imagined her showing up an hour after they left, stuck in the apartment with the jumbees, aliens, or whatever the hell the monsters were.

"We've gotta go," Luis said, likely sensing Brent's hesitancy as Brent took forever to tape the note to the phone on the wall.

They made their way downstairs, Brent and Luis carrying bags and weapons, while Joe walked behind them, a pistol in one hand, a bag of rice in the other. Joe had never used a gun, so Luis went over the basics with him, all three men hoping he'd never need to put his lesson to use.

As they reached the ground floor, Brent feared once they got outside that one of two things would be waiting — either a pack of creatures or a demolished car. But he kept the fear to himself.

The glass of the lobby doors was shattered. Luis readied his shotgun, pushing through to the street. He scanned the avenue, then waved for the other two men to follow.

The streets were still wrapped in the eerie fog, cutting visibility to 10 yards at most. The car was thankfully intact. Luis opened the trunk, loaded the supplies, then hit the button on his keychain to unlock the doors. The car's alarm beeped twice, then bounced across the empty hallways of the ghosted metropolis. Brent cringed, hoping the sound wouldn't attract the creatures' attention.

A shrieking sound from above crushed that hope.

They all looked up at once, unable to see anything other than fog.

"Get in the car!" Luis screamed.

The creature fell from the sky, landing between all three men.

It was at least a foot taller than Luis, its limbs impossibly long, just like its fingers. Its body was black, with lights under its wet skin. Its face was long, a giant maw of teeth for a mouth, and two almond-shaped eyes, ink-black. If it had a nose or ears, Brent couldn't see them.

It surveyed all three men, turning in half circles, body hunched as if ready to spring into action.

Luis took a shot as the creature leapt into the air, into the fog, and then came back down, landing on top of Joe. It stood up in one fluid motion, bringing Joe with it, one arm around Joe's chest and the other around his neck.

Joe dropped both his gun and the bag of rice — which didn't distract the creature a bit. It opened its mouth wider and made that god-awful *Click Click Click Click* sound, then held Joe up as a human shield.

"I can't get a shot!" Luis yelled.

Joe cried out, trying to squirm free from the creature's grip. As if in response, the creature's right hand moved up and gripped Joe's skull, its fingers covering his entire head and dripping half way down his face. Joe's entire body began to shake violently as the lights, or whatever it was beneath the creature's skin, pulsated brighter. Joe screamed as his body continued shaking as if being electrocuted.

"Shoot it!" Brent yelled, not confident in his ability to get a clear shot.

Luis screamed and ran toward the creature, gun raised. The monster threw Joe aside like a rag doll and brought its hands down to tackle Luis. Before Luis could take aim, Brent fired two shots — one hitting the monster's torso, the other striking its head.

The creature dropped immediately, and Luis descended, firing another shot and finishing it off.

Luis screamed, "Die, motherfucker!"

Brent, shaken, scanned around them for any sign of more creatures. Something moved in the fog above them, and Brent fired into the sky.

Luis raised his gun, "What? You see something?"

"I'm not sure," Brent said, heart pounding, eyes scanning the sky above as he circled his gun in all directions, praying nothing would pop up from a direction he wasn't looking. "I thought I did."

From the ground, Joe moaned.

"Shit!" Brent said, having forgotten that the old man was injured. He ran to Joe and noticed two things at once — the man's eyes were white and milky, the pupils barely visible. Dark, painful looking splotches stained his head where the thing had touched his scalp.

"Help," Joe moaned, his jaw shaking, drool streaming from the corners of his mouth.

Luis had the car's passenger door open, and they carried Joe and put him inside, Brent hopped into the back seat as Luis slammed shut the driver's door and stepped on the gas, putting the shotgun on the center console.

"Are you okay?" Brent asked Joe, who was moaning something incoherent.

Something was off about Joe's voice. It had lost the Jamaican accent and sounded lower, words slurred.

Luis stared at Joe, then shot a concerned look back at Brent.

"Mphrrr," Joe mumbled, his voice sounding even more different than before. Joe's head fell in a nod, chin on his chest, as he mumbled more.

No, he didn't look good at all. Brent put a hand on Joe's shoulder and was about to ask if he was okay, when the man's head shot up, turned back and looked at Brent with vacant white eyes, and said, "Daddy?"

But it wasn't Joe's voice.

It was Ben's.

* * * *

CHAPTER 10
CHARLIE WILKENS

"I like you, too," Callie said with a smile, seemingly oblivious to what Charlie was trying to say.

"No," he said, "I *like* like you."

"Oh," Callie said, her eyes widened in recognition. She paused, looking down to her hands. It was a longer pause than the one that usually comes before good news.

She finally met his eyes again, "Listen, Charlie ... "

Oh no.

"I like you too. You're a nice guy. But ... I'm not really looking for a relationship."

He looked down, and could feel tears welling up.

Don't you fucking cry!

"Oh," he said, not sure what else to say. "I'm sorry."

"Don't be," she said, reaching out across the chess board, putting a hand on his, "I'm flattered, I really am. But right now, with all this crazy shit that's going on, the last thing I want is complications."

He didn't say anything. Didn't know what to say, or do.

She went on, "You know how hard relationships are under normal circumstances, but this? This is zombies n' stuff. We need to be strong if we're gonna fight these things. And if things get weird, we lose whatever advantage we have. Besides, I wouldn't want to risk our friendship, you know? Does this make sense?"

Friend Zone, admission one.

"Yeah," he said, his eyes now watering.

Fucking baby!

He got up and left his room, embarrassed on too many levels.

"Charlie," she called, but he kept going. He didn't want to make a dramatic exit, but at the same time, he felt if she were to stop him, he would collapse into tears. He walked downstairs, past Bob, who was passed out on the sofa, and outside into the night.

Derek lived on a cul-de-sac with a dozen similar houses on the south end backing up to the Gulf of Mexico. He stared at the other houses, barely visible in the late hours. The house across the street was nice, also three stories. He ran to it, tried the front door, and was surprised to find it unlocked. He went inside, shut the door behind him, and locked it. He fell against the door and put his head in his hands and cried.

Big fucking baby! If Bob could see you now!

He hated himself for being so damned stupid.

Callie said she didn't want to risk his friendship, but he couldn't imagine how they could be friends with her knowing how he felt. It would be awkward as hell, and Bob would surely pick up on it and have a good ole laugh.

Charlie cried himself empty, then forced himself to stand, though he was unsure what he would do.

He took the stairs to the second floor and found himself in a spacious master bedroom that put Derek's to shame. Though the room was dark, Charlie could see it was beautifully decorated. The bed was huge, bigger than a King-sized bed, for sure. And though unmade, it looked inviting, far more than the uncomfortably sterile beds in Derek's guest rooms.

The bed was fluffy-looking, had a ton of pillows, and a giant, thick, white comforter, smooth and cool as a soft pillow. He slipped into the bed to see how it felt. He was asleep in minutes.

**

When Charlie woke, he wasn't alone.

A guy was standing in the corner, maybe in his early 30s. He had thick, dark hair, jeans, boots, and a black jacket. If Hollywood was casting for a bad ass to star in a movie, this would be the guy they called.

"That's some bruise you got there," the man said.

Charlie wanted to ask who the hell he was, but realized he was dreaming, and that the man wasn't a threat.

"Yeah," he said, "My asshole stepdad."

"My old man used to knock me around, too. Fuckin' cunt."

"Someone beat you up?"

"I wasn't always a tough guy. I used to be a scrawny kid. But once I learned what I needed to learn, I took control of my life."

"What did you do?" Charlie asked.

The man looked at him, eyes cold as steel. "You don't wanna know. Let's just say, nobody fucks with Boricio no more."

Boricio.

"Yeah, well, Bob's pretty scary," Charlie explained.

"They's all scary. But you know what ... they're all scared o' somethin' too. Everyone has a weakness. You just need to find it." He leaned forward. "When you find a pussy, you fuck it.

"Fuck it?" Charlie asked.

"Yeah, fuck it," Boricio said, then made a slitting motion across his neck.

**

Charlie woke in a sweat, fully expecting to see the man from the dream in the corner of the room.

The morning sun came in through the drapes, motes of dust floating on the rays. Charlie glanced at the alarm clock on the nightstand. It must've been battery operated, as it was still showing the time.

8:04 a.m.

Shit, they're probably looking for me.

He went to the curtains and looked across the road. The blinds were closed on all the rooms, so he couldn't see if they were awake, let alone looking for him. Maybe they were still sleeping.

He considered returning to the house, but he couldn't face Callie. Couldn't stand to look her in the eyes after running from the room, crying like a baby. Maybe he would stay in this house. It wasn't on the water, but it was nice. Better than he'd ever have done for himself, for sure. He'd stay here until the government, or whoever was in charge now, came around to put things back together.

Tell Bob to fuck himself. I got my own house. I live under my own roof. MY rules. And I'll grow my hair longer than Jesus.

He took a shower; the water was cold like at Derek's. Then he made breakfast — peanut butter on a bagel. He thumbed through some magazines, mostly old issues of *Popular Science* and *People*.

Charlie walked through the house, looking at the evidence of a life once lived, trying to imagine the family who called this place home until Saturday. A retired couple with a college-aged son, judging from photos. Lots of vacation pics, tropical islands, skiing, and all the other shit rich people did. From what he could tell, they lived pretty good lives.

Happy lives for a happy family.

He felt a pang of sadness, then started thinking of his mother and how cruelly he had judged her the past few years for being so subservient to Bob. Now that he'd been under Bob's spell a few days, he could see how chaotic life could be on your own. Especially when you were a heartbroken widow looking for someone to spend time with and maybe fill the void in your life. She'd been single a long time before opening her heart to another.

And how did Bob repay? By being an abusive fuck.

Everyone has a weakness. You just need to find it. When you find a pussy, you fuck it.

Oh, how he'd love to wipe that fucking smile from Bob's face. Take a bat and just smash his fucking skull in. But this wasn't a dream. This was the real world. And in the real world, the *real* Charlie Wilkens was neither a bad ass nor a hero. He didn't know dick about dick, and still needed Bob's skills if he was going to survive.

Asshole that Bob was, he knew how to fix things, hunt, and all the shit survivalist types know. Charlie was an ignorant child who couldn't last a day in the real world.

And like the pussy he was, he went home with his tail between his legs.

**

Charlie was crossing the street, wondering how worried Callie would be when she woke to see he wasn't there. Maybe Bob would be worried, too. Maybe he'd feel bad for being such a dick. Or maybe he would be mad that Charlie left and was gone all night. Who knew? The coin could land on either side with Bob.

But Callie, Charlie was sure, would be missing him. Maybe that would soothe the awkwardness between them a bit, he hoped.

The front door was unlocked just as he'd left it last night. He walked in, surprised that Bob wasn't still on the sofa sleeping off his drunk. He went to the kitchen, nobody there. He was about to go upstairs when he heard Bob laughing from out back.

Two large, tinted windows looking out onto the back patio. Bob and Callie were splashing in the pool.

Did they even notice that I was fucking gone?

Callie dunked Bob under and he grabbed her, pulling her down with him. When they came up, they were kissing. A long kiss, and Callie wasn't breaking away.

Charlie stared, not willing to believe what he was seeing. *How could she? Why? Why Bob?*

His heart pounded so loud, hard, and fast, he could feel it through his entire body. He wanted to run, wanted to scream, wanted to do anything other than stand there mute and paralyzed as he watched them kiss. Callie's arms locked around Bob, and he lifted her up slightly, and reached down.

He's fucking her right there in the pool!

Charlie could feel his nostrils flaring, rage coursing through his veins. An idea came to him, then spun him around and sent him to the living room where the shotgun lay propped against the sofa.

He picked it up. Bob had taught him how to load it and fire it. Charlie hoped he was good enough not to miss.

Charlie went to the kitchen, cocked the shotgun, and raised it, aiming at the couple in the pool. His finger curled around the trigger as his heart pounded louder, so loud, he could hear it in his ears, drowning out everything else.

He tightened his grip and leveled the gun. Callie opened her eyes, looking at the window. He didn't think she saw him, but he had seen her eyes. Her beautiful blue eyes that looked like she was looking past him into some distance he could not see. Charlie felt a tug at his heart which he couldn't ignore.

He closed his eyes, then turned away from the window, lowering the gun.

Charlie ran upstairs instead, grabbed one of his duffel bags, filled it with some food, some comics, a couple of pistols, some bullets, and kept the shotgun. Then he grabbed the keys to Derek's Toyota and drove as fast and far as he could, tears in his eyes.

**

As Charlie drove, he replayed the events in his head over and over again, wondering how long Callie had liked Bob. Wondering why she didn't tell him. Wondering if she was just using both of them, sticking with whichever one would provide a better chance of survival. If that were the case, Bob had Charlie beat by a long shot.

He wanted to be mad, *was mad*, but at the same time, he couldn't ignore biological imperatives. If the world really did flush all the people away, then it was survival of the fittest again. And a big ape like Bob was at the top of the food chain. He would get the best of everything, including the women. He'd get them despite the fact they were nothing more to him than things to fuck, use, and abuse.

The more things change, the more they seem the same.

**

Charlie was about an hour or so into Alabama, driving along the highway, jamming to a Tool CD. Neither Derek nor his lover seemed like the typical Tool fan, but who was Charlie to judge. People surprised him every day. At least this was a pleasant surprise.

He banged on the steering wheel to the throbbing drum tracks of *Forty Six and Two*, letting his rage out through music — the only therapy he believed in.

He wasn't sure where he was going, but would drive until he found something. He didn't know anyone outside of Florida, except his grandmother in New Jersey, senile and in a home. Well, she *had been* in a home. She was probably gone now, which was for the best. He didn't want to think about his grandma being eaten by zombies.

He liked the idea of just driving until something spoke to him.

More than that, he liked the idea of starting over.

Where nobody, assuming there was anybody left, knew him. Where he could reinvent himself as a stronger, cooler guy. The guy that got the girl. The guy who wasn't too pussy to go after what he wanted.

Someone other than Charlie Pussy-Ass Wilkens.

"My name is Boricio," he said into the mirror, rolling the 'r', even though the guy in his dream didn't seem Spanish.

If anyone asks, my name is Boricio. Heh, I kinda like the sound of that.

Charlie was speeding along the highway screaming out the lyrics to *Eulogy* when the car started acting weird, as if the engine had just been cut off.

He turned down the music as the car coasted to a stop. That's when he saw the red gas light on the dashboard.

Fuck me!

As the car died, he stared out his window along the long, rural stretch of road. Nothing as far as he could see ahead. And behind him, it had been at least a few miles since he'd passed any signs of what was left of civilization.

As if on cue, the sun was eclipsed almost all at once by dark, angry-looking clouds.

So, what you gonna do now, Charlie Boy? Only it wasn't his inner voice that mocked him. It was Bob's.

"Fuck you, Bob."

He thought about getting out of the car and walking back the way he came until he found a place to hole up for the rest of the day and night, or maybe find a new car. But as he was about to get out of the car, he was interrupted by the loudest thunder he'd ever heard. It sounded as if someone were tearing the roof from the top of the world. Lightning flashed not too far ahead.

Rain followed, hitting his windshield in fat, loud drops that sounded like rocks.

Charlie reached into the duffle bag, found a book, a collection of P.K. Dick stories, and eased his seat back. He was going to be in the car a while.

About an hour into this book, he saw headlights in his rearview mirror.

He pulled the seat back up and threw his book on the seat, then reached into the duffel bag for the Glock. He checked the ammo, and put the gun in his lap as the lights drew closer.

His first thought was that Bob and Callie had come after him. But as the vehicle got closer, he saw that it wasn't a car, but rather a van.

It parked right behind Charlie's car.

Oh shit.

Charlie sat, frozen, unsure what to do.

It was too dark and the rain falling too hard to see the driver of the van.

The van's lights flicked on and off twice.

He wants me to get out?

The lights flicked again as if in response.

Charlie put the gun in his waistband and stepped from the car, instantly drenched by the rain. He ran to the van's driver side, relieved as he got closer and saw that the driver was a woman. She looked a bit older, a little heavy, with long, dark-red hair.

She rolled down the window a bit, "You okay, honey?"

"Ran out of gas!" Charlie yelled over the howling wind.

"Get in," she said, pointing to the empty passenger seat.

"Okay, lemme get my bag," Charlie said, running back to the car, putting his book in the bag, along with the pistol from his waistband.

He eyed the shotgun sitting in the back seat, but would have to leave it. If he came running to the van with a shotgun, the lady would probably freak out and drive away.

He grabbed the Tool CD from the player and put it in the bag, then ran to the van and hopped into the passenger's seat.

"Where ya headed?" she asked as he got situated, putting the bag down between his feet. A black curtain separated the front of the van from the back.

"Wherever," he said. The van moved forward and that's when Charlie noticed that they weren't alone. The curtain parted and a man with red hair and a scruffy beard appeared, wearing all black, with something behind his back. As Charlie was trying to figure out what it was, the man quickly wrapped his arms around him and injected something into his neck before Charlie even had a chance to fight.

Seconds later, Charlie hit the dashboard and was out cold.

**

The first thing Charlie noticed when he came to was the shaking. And he couldn't see a thing, blindfolded and arms bound behind him. He was in the back of the van.

A woman was laughing in the front. Charlie's mind flashed on the woman who had lured him into the trap.

"You believe that shit?" a man said, also from the front.

Though he was bound, and in the back of a moving van, Charlie felt a strong impulse to squirm, kick, push, anything to break free.

Not now. Someone else is in the van.

"Shhh, you've been kidnapped," a voice said.

Only the voice wasn't coming from anyone in the van.

Instead, it was in his head.

Boricio?

"The one and only," the voice responded, "You just sit tight and let these people take you where they're gonna take you."

How are you talking to me?

"No time for questions, kid. Don't you worry 'bout a thing. You're about to meet the most awesome motherfucker you've ever laid eyes on."

You?

"Who else, kid? Just close your eyes, go back to sleep, and don't rock the boat until it's time for us to mutiny on these motherfuckers."

Charlie had never been one to believe in things like fate or things happening for a reason. But there was no mistaking that something was happening here. Something weird, fantastic, and terrifying all at once. He was on the verge of discovering his destiny in a man named Boricio.

* * * *

CHAPTER 11
BORICIO WOLFE

Now why can't he just shut the fuck up?

I've got Manny, Moe, and Jack to my right and only Moe has to be a fucking hard-on. Can't wait to shut your yap box, you whiney bitch. Gonna start things off with you, too. Should start with Manny, but fuck if you deserve to live an extra 16 seconds.

Boricio had been trying to brew banter with Adam for the better part of 15 minutes, but Moe kept butting into the conversation. If Adam were a chick, Moe was a Cock Blocker Extraordinaire. Adam knew something. *Something big.* Boricio needed to know what it was. That was enough to spare his life, but the kid had been smart enough to tip Boricio with another reason or two.

He could get answers out of Adam easy as shit, but only with rhythm, and that wasn't going to happen with Moe shoving his dick into the conversation every five minutes. Worthless piece of shit hadn't delivered a single fact Boricio could use, except maybe that the Jackson "Dead Guard Walking" fucker is a sadistic asshole, but Boricio didn't need a back bayou shaman to see that one. At least the other guys were mostly quiet.

"Hey, Jack, how'd you get caught?" Boricio asked, hoping if Jack spoke for a little bit, Moe might latch onto him and give Boricio some space to talk with Adam.

"Was the strangest shit. You'd never believe it if you didn't have all this other *no way, no how* to believe already. And it'd be funny even if it wasn't so goddamned terrifying, or maybe if I heard it from someone else. See, weird thing was, I was wide awake when it happened, least I had been just a ball hair before. I came home late, worked till 1:30 at the Ugly Tuna because Richie always stops showing up for his shifts whenever it's his first week with some new tail. And he ain't never gonna get fired because Nate's been married to his ma for the last two years. Anyways, I was out of there by 10 'til, and home by five after. Me and Nadine started fuckin' straight up at 2:12, because the clock is on her side, and we was both facing that way. So, I started getting my face on, you know, but right before I popped, I suddenly blacked out, except I wasn't gone nowhere unconscious. I was still fuckin' and feeling and all, but I was sorta suspended with animation, or whatever they call it. Couldn't move and couldn't see. Time just hung like that for a helluva spell until all of a sudden I was poppin' the weasel without a Nadine to catch it. She was totally gone, and the clock was blinking 2:16.

"So you only lasted four minutes?" asked Manny.

"I told you there was suspended animation."

"That's a crazy story, man," Boricio said, "You must have been out of your head! What did you do? How long until you found someone else? Where did you go?" Jack was sucking down his own story like a fat kid with cake, so Boricio obliged him with a new handful of questions.

"I left the house and saw the town was full of nothing but empty, then came back home for two days not knowing what to do. I finally got into Nadine's Honda; it had less gas in it, but got way more to the gallon than the Chevy, and I hit the road. I didn't see no one for a long while until I came on an old church my second day driving. The church looked Catholic, and all the lights were on, which seemed like a miracle in itself. Fool's gold, though. Before I hit the holy water no less than three guns were aimed at my face. Something hit me hard from behind and next thing I knew, I was in here."

A lot of shit seeped in the silences between people's sentences, finished and unfinished. That fucker Jack knew something about something, and wasn't saying shit about it. That wasn't gonna do Boricio one cunt hair of good. No, he'd get that fucker to kick a jumbo pot of beans before he ended him.

"That sounds so scary," Boricio said. "I bet it felt right good when you first saw those lights and thought you'd found some people." He seasoned his sentence with a sympathetic pause, then added, "Too bad it turned out like it did."

"Yeah, but at least I'm with other folks now. It was awful being in the middle of all that nothing ... "

There it was. Boricio heard it clear, even if everyone else was too stupid to hear the shit that wasn't being said. "What else did you see out there, man?"

Silence.

"It's okay, we've all seen some crazy stuff in the last few days. World's gone upside down. We'll believe you. Right, guys?"

A murmur of agreement rippled around the room, followed by a lingering silence. Boricio didn't press it. A long silence was exactly what Jack needed to be drawn into talking. Finally, he drew a deep breath and let it spill.

"Day before I hit the church I saw something moving off the side of the road. Crazy-looking and not quite right, a bit like road kill, but longer, more human. I slowed as I got closer, and sure as the shits at a chili cook off, it was wearing people clothes. I got out, real slow 'cuz it was just laying there, but laying there all wrong, if you know what I mean, though you probably don't. I was halfway to it before I thought to go back and grab the Winchester from the Honda. I tiptoed to the thing, and about lost it when I got up close. It was black and white, dirt and light. The grimiest, scariest, living scarecrow of a creature I ever saw, and I worked at a slaughterhouse for two years. The thing started making all sorts a unholy sounds, and then it tried to get up. I don't even know if it could have, but I emptied the rifle into it before I got the chance to find out. I put every bullet where its face should've been, just in case. Then I saw another creature just like it later that night. So the short of it is, I'm with the kid; maybe this place right here ain't so bad after all."

No one spoke, then Moe said, "Anyone else see these jitterbugs?"

A chorus of yeses followed, Boricio's included, though he added his last, and he was lying.

These Mexican bean jittery fuckers don't sound like no soldiers of any sort. They sound like some kind of accident, courtesy of whatever Armageddon dipshit let the fries burn in the first place.

"I seen worse," Adam said. "I seen a bunch of them things. First one was in my house. I swore the thing was coming for my old man. Would've sworn on a stack a Holy Bibles a foot high. I thought the Devil had come to bring him home, and I ran from the house as soon as I saw it. I ran straight for the gorge, since that's where I like to go when I don't want to be found, and I saw six or seven more on the way. When I got there, I couldn't believe what I saw — a couple dozen more of them things just quivering at the entrance. And just past them, that was the scariest shit I ever seen. There were bodies, dead people, hundreds, maybe even thousands. All of 'em stacked. Stacked so high you wouldn't believe. It looked like ... "

Eureka! Organized disposal! Hunters!

"What do you mean stacked?" interrupted Manny. "You mean the bodies were in a pile?"

"No, sir. Not a pile. A stack. The bodies were stacked in rows. Like pallets in a warehouse."

Boricio smelled something on Moe. Whatever the fuck had been brewing in that guy's ball sack earlier was boiling now. Something was off, and it had to do with the way Adam was telling his story.

There was a click, a whine, and a warm gust of air, followed by the unmistakable scent of that asshole, Jackson.

Looks like it might be game time. Don't know how much more I'm gonna dig from this crowd. I'm leaving with some intel and an ally. Might be ready to leave with a scalp or two, too. Maybe I'll let old Dead Guard Walking decide, give him a chance to live another small while just to be a good sport. But if he wants to live, he'll have to be a good puppy and show me.

"What's up, dipshit?" Another slap on the side of Boricio's ear.

"I'm sorry about earlier, Sir. Really I am." Boricio kept his hands behind his back, laying flat on the mat. "I meant no disrespect. I'm just awful scared. These last couple of days have been terrible hard, and I sure didn't expect to get thrown in here on top of it all."

"Aww, shucks, well ain't that a nice apology?" He'd become Dead Guard Walking the second he shoved food into Boricio's mouth, but he just sped up the sands in his hourglass with the condescending tone and a second slap to the ear. Boricio's ear stung loudly, but he didn't mind. It was fuel.

Boricio laughed.

"What're you laughing at? You need me to remind you about some of the rules before I show you firsthand who makes 'em?"

Boricio continued to laugh, harder and harder, forcing himself into the rhythm at first, until he lost himself to the insanity of the beat. He could feel Dead Guard Walking start to sweat. "Better tell me what you're laughing at, fucker, or I'll make you swallow your chuckles along with a few of your teeth." To punctuate his threat, Dead Guard Walking slammed a boot heel on Boricio's knee. He should've screamed, but Boricio only laughed harder.

"You've seen the *Star Wars movies*, right?" Boricio said, once he stopped laughing.

Dead Guard Walking was silent, but mostly because he didn't know what to say. Finally he said, "Course, everyone has."

"You know what a Tauntaun is? They're those furry snow camel kangaroo things from *Empire Strikes Back*. Remember when Han Solo has to keep Luke warm so he cuts open the belly of the Tauntaun to steal his heat? Well, I was just picturing doing that to you, except I'd be doing it just for fun, seeing as how I'm plenty warm as is. I got to laughing once I realized I couldn't truly picture it on account of me not knowing what you look like. So, I just pictured a big, old rusty sheriff's badge tacked to an asshole." Boricio erupted into an encore of raging laughter.

Dead Guard Walking leaned down and put his face just inches from Boricio. "What are you going to do with your hands behind your back, you fucking freak? Only thing you can do in the position you're in right now is suck my dick and thank me for the pleasure."

"I will thank you. I can't wait until your cock is in my mouth. Mmm, yummy," Boricio said, laughing. "I'll bite it off and swallow it without chewing, then I'll make sure I stick around long enough to make you gobble every bite of my shit, even if I have to drag you out of here half dead and screaming."

Dead Guard Walking took a big step back. Boricio laughed again. That type of fear was probably new for Jackson, but then again, so was Boricio's brand of crazy.

"You're jumping to the front of the line, asshole." Dead Guard Walking's final words were followed by a whine and the door shutting. Boricio figured he had maybe three minutes before Jackson was back, probably with Testosterone and Big Nippled Bitch in tow.

It was now or never.

Boricio gave up the pretense of being bound, and slowly reached up and took off his blindfold.

Well, fuck me.

He almost didn't believe what he saw.

::EPISODE 4::
(FOURTH EPISODE OF SEASON ONE)
"COME TOGETHER"

CHAPTER 1
BRENT FOSTER

Oct. 16
7:20 a.m.
New York City

"Daddy?" Ben's voice cried out through the old man's face.

"Ben?" Brent said, eyes wide, staring at Joe in a mixture of disbelief, horror, and ... relief. "Is that you?"

"Daddy?" His son again. Impossible as it was, it was without doubt his son's voice escaping from the maintenance man's throat.

"Can you hear me?" Brent asked.

Joe's lids closed on his milky-white eyes, then fell silent as his head dropped forward.

"Ben?!" Brent screamed, shaking Joe.

Joe was breathing, but he may as well have been dead.

Luis kept driving, navigating through the foggy streets of New York like a pro, though Brent was only slightly aware of anything beyond Joe.

"That was your son's voice?" Luis asked.

"Yes." Brent said.

"How is that even possible?"

"How is *any of this* possible?" Brent said. "Is Joe okay, do you think?"

Luis looked Joe up and down, "I dunno; what the hell is that splotchy shit on his head?"

Brent looked closer. Dark, web-like veins were running in scattered lines beneath Joe's skin, next to dark, mottled circles that looked like bruising.

"Looks like some sort of ... *infection* or something." Brent said. "Did you see his eyes?"

Luis nodded, "Do you think he's ... gonna turn into one of them? Like a zombie?"

The idea would have seemed insane a day earlier. Now, they were living in a world filled with insane.

"I don't know."

Luis said, "If he shows any signs, any signs at all, we need to shoot him before he infects us."

"We can't just shoot him."

"*We* don't have to; *I* will," Luis said.

Brent paused for a long time trying to think of the right way to frame his words without sounding even crazier than their theories of alien zombies taking over the city.

"What if he's connected to Ben somehow?"

"What?"

"You heard Ben, right? I mean, you don't know Ben's voice, but I do. And that was it. What if Joe is somehow channeling Ben from somewhere else? Maybe Ben is in trouble and somehow Joe, in a nearly comatose state, is able to pick up on the broadcast?"

"Sure, it may have *sounded like your son*, but all the old man said was 'Daddy,' not 'Daddy, come save me' or anything like that."

Brent stared in the rearview, but Luis didn't meet his gaze, his eyes fixed on the road.

"What are you saying?" Brent asked.

"I'm saying, and don't take this wrong, but maybe you're hearing what you want to hear. You want to believe your wife and son are alive and out there. Hell, I want the same thing for my little girl. But that don't make it so. I don't know why Joe sounded like your kid. It's freaky as shit, but I don't think it changes a thing. We still need to head to Black Island and get the hell outta here before more of those fuckers come at us."

Brent stared hard at the mirror, Luis' words seeping in, though it was hard to ignore a message from Ben, even if it wasn't the genuine thing. Even though he considered Luis' logic, which rang loud and rational in the practical side of Brent's brain, he still couldn't shake the sound of his baby boy's voice. It was as if Ben were there in the car, riding right beside them.

Brent stared at Joe, wishing the man would say something, anything else that might part the clouds on some answers. Or hell, even if it didn't, just hearing Ben speak once more would be enough to feed Brent's hope that his wife and son might still be out there somewhere.

He pulled Stanley Train from his pocket, stared at the smiling face, then clutched the train as if it were the last connection he had to Ben.

**

They'd made their way north to the Cross Bronx Expressway, still nearly three hours from East Hampton Docks, when Joe started to murmur again, head down and eyes still closed.

"This is ... " Joe said, in a man's voice Brent didn't recognize.

Luis and Brent waited for the rest of the sentence, but Joe spoke in a woman's voice instead. "We're here."

Luis looked in the rearview, his eyes asking Brent if he recognized the voice.

Brent shrugged his shoulders.

"Where are you?" Brent tried.

"Daddy?" Ben's voice again.

Brent's heart leapt into his chest.

"Is that you, Ben?"

"Daddy, I'm scared."

"Don't be," Brent said, tears filling his eyes at the sound of his son in fear. "Where are you?"

Joe murmured something else in a man's voice, in a language that Brent didn't understand. Another voice spoke over the first, in unison in what seemed like a Russian dialect.

Brent stared at Joe's mouth, open and moving, but out of sync with the voices, like a badly dubbed movie. Or ... *a radio.*

The two voices speaking impossibly at once sent a chill down Brent's spine even icier than the one he felt hearing his son's voice.

"Where are you?" Brent asked again.

"Square ... Times Square," Ben said.

Brent's eyes widened, his pulse quickened, "Times Square?"

"Square," another voice said, followed by three more, repeating the word.

Luis looked at Brent, shaking his head. "Don't even ask."

"Come on, man, we've got to turn around."

Luis bit his lip. "Do you *really* think they're there?"

"I don't know, but I have to find out. Whether you want to let me out right here, or what, I *have to go*, alien zombies or not."

Luis spun the car around, and headed back as Joe continued babbling the word "square" on repeat.

**

They reached the corner of West 59th Street and 7th Avenue when they ran into their first major obstacle on the roads.

Rows of cars blocked 7th Avenue southbound. More cars blocked 59th Street going east, packed so tight they formed a sea of cars you'd have to climb over to cross. The cars didn't appear to have been parked so much as *placed* to create a barrier. Luis spun the BMW around, but found both Broadway and 8th Avenue were every bit as barricaded.

"It's like someone deliberately blocked all street travel to Times Square," Brent said.

"So, what do you wanna do?" Luis said, frustrated and driving back to 7th Avenue. "Lookin' at a mile walk with God knows what out there."

"I don't have a choice," Brent said, "But you guys can wait here. I won't take offense."

"Bullshit," Luis said, "We're in this shit together, bro."

"What about him?" Brent asked, nodding toward Joe, passed out and silent.

"He's probably safer in the car. It is bulletproof after all," Luis said. "I'll just park it up next to these others here so it blends in and maybe nobody notices him."

Brent grabbed a pen and paper from his duffel bag, leaving a note for Joe in the air conditioning vent. The note said not to leave the car; they'd be back soon. Brent was going to write something telling Joe to take the car and leave if they weren't back by noon, but Luis only had a single set of keys and wasn't willing to leave them in the car with a half-comatose old man.

They stepped from the car and into the murky city, holding their gun-heavy bags.

**

Seventh Avenue seemed less like a street than a long hallway with a low ceiling of fog pushing down on them from 20 feet above. A long maze, with all the cars acting as obstacles. Visibility was limited to 20 feet in any direction, giving them little time to see any threats, especially if they came from above again. The only advantage they had, if any, was that the city was still impossibly silent, meaning they'd be able to hear the creatures even if they couldn't see them.

It also meant the creatures would *hear them* if they weren't quiet.

They climbed over the first row of cars, careful to make as little sound as possible, watching for anything that might be hiding inside, next to, or near the vehicles. They were vulnerable; at least Brent was as he climbed over each car, awkwardly holding his gun so he could still climb without putting it away, and still managing to hold his bag of guns. Brent's heart pounded in his chest, as he attempted to keep an eye on everything, in front of, behind, below, and above.

As they climbed over the eighth row of cars, Brent was out of breath and sweaty, wishing he'd been in better shape. He was relieved to see the barricade end. Though he couldn't see more than 20 feet, it seemed unlikely they'd run into a second wall of cars.

The walk, which should have taken 15 minutes or so under normal circumstances, would likely take an hour at the pace they were going, treading carefully along the right side of the road. Luis stayed in front, alternating his shotgun's aim straight ahead and above, depending on the sounds around him.

With the city so quiet, natural sounds seemed eerily amplified. Wind, birds in the distance — the first birds

Brent could remember hearing, now that he thought about it — and other unfamiliar sounds he tried unsuccessfully to recognize. Sounds were all sinister when you couldn't see their sources.

The duffel bag's strap dug into his shoulder blade, so Brent stopped to switch shoulders. Ahead, Luis said, "Fuck me."

Brent looked up — another wall of cars spanning the street's width.

Luis went first. Brent followed, hoisting himself on top of the trunk of an old Cadillac and stepping gingerly on the roof, hoping he'd not fall through. The metal dented under his weight. He jumped from the hood. Luis was ahead, climbing the roof of a Hummer. Brent followed, just as Luis hopped down and onto the hood of a red BMW.

A high pitched siren wailed the minute Luis's feet hit the metal. Startled, Brent raised his gun and fired into the fog above twice before realizing Luis had simply set off an alarm.

"Sorry," Brent said with a laugh.

Luis laughed, as the alarm continued to wail. "Dumb ass."

As Brent climbed on top of the Hummer and was about to jump down, he saw Luis' eyes widen, staring behind Brent.

The alarm! They heard it!

"Run!" Luis screamed, already hopping from car to car. Brent didn't want to turn back to see what Luis saw, but couldn't help himself. He glanced over his shoulder and nearly froze on the spot.

Dozens of the creatures came spilling from the wall of fog behind them: running, clicking, and shrieking.

* * * *

CHAPTER 2
CALLIE THOMPSON

Oct. 18
Mid-morning
Pensacola, Florida

    Callie woke up feeling as though she'd been kicked in the head by a team of horses.
    Dizzy and confused, she stared through the gauze of the faded white curtain blowing softly in the breeze thinking, for just a moment, that she was back home, the world hadn't vanished, and it had all been a bad dream.
    "Oh, you're up?" a familiar voice said next to her.
    She felt thin fabric brushing against her nipples and realized she was naked in bed. Naked and smelling of chlorine. She lifted all hundred pounds of her head, then slowly turned toward the voice. It was Bob, also naked.
    She wanted to jump up, run, vomit, anything as long as it was something far, far away. But her body refused to budge. Instead, she fell back on her pillow, trapped by inertia. She closed her eyes and swallowed, gathering her strength.

She sat up. "What the ... ?" she said, her voice as slurred as her mind felt.

She turned to Bob, who was strobing between full-on asshole and fuzzy blur. "You drugged me?" she asked, her voice somewhere between accusation and confusion.

The last thing she remembered was waking up, looking for Charlie, then drinking beer with Bob. After that, she had no memory at all. Given her state of undress, and sore vagina, she was sure she'd been raped. Rage, hurt, and fear flooded her system as she struggled to keep calm and avoid a full-blown panic attack.

She would have accused him; hell, she would have found something nice and blunt to bash Bob's fucking face in, but her head was a dumbbell's worth of hurt and she was far too dizzy (and defenseless) to risk provoking the savage animal he so clearly was.

She'd have to play it cool, bide her time, then escape.

"Drugged?" Bob said, laughing, "Girl, you were down with it. You *asked for it*. Not gonna say you were begging, but just between me and you, you kinda were."

It took everything she had, and then some, not to knock the smirk from his face.

"What did you give me?"

"I think the kids call it 'G,' it really fucks you up all sorts of good."

The date-rape drug?

"How ya feeling?" Bob asked, reaching over to cup her breast.

She pulled away, covering herself with the sheet.

"Oh, you're gonna play shy, now?" Bob asked. His voice was playful. He reached over again with one hand, the other playing *Jaws* beneath the sheet.

"Not now," she said, "I feel like I've got the worst hangover ever. My head is killing me."

"Want some water?" he asked, getting up from the bed, his cock pointing straight. She fought the urge to vomit.

"Yeah," she said, "JUST water."

Bob laughed.

Asshole.

Callie didn't wait for the water. She jumped out of bed, head spinning, and stumbled to the bathroom, then shut and locked the door and fell to the toilet and vomited. She took the longest shower of her life, not caring that the water was almost ice.

She sank to the floor of the shower, her bottom on the freezing tile and her head in her palms. She would have given anything if tears would finally fall, but they were trapped, burning her lids in horror and shame.

She hadn't cried once since the world went to hell.

She thought about everything that had happened since the world went away. Watching as her neighbor was torn to ribbons, missing her mother with a bottomless depth she didn't even know she could feel, and now getting raped at the hands of a creepy, white trash, old man. She should have been a broken mess. Water from the shower streamed down her face, her mouth opened in anguish, trying to open a spigot of tears that simply refused to flow.

She'd always been strong, had to grow up that way being a mixed girl in a lily-white neighborhood with fat pockets of deep-rooted, if slightly closeted, racism. But she wasn't heartless, far from it. She loved her mother more than life; so why wasn't she able to cry for her absence?

What kind of daughter am I?

She wished, not for the first time, that her mother was there for her. But at the same time, she was glad her mother had been spared whatever was happening. Monsters, rapists, and God knows what else. Maybe her mother was lucky, vanishing along with the rest of humanity.

A knock at the door. Bob.

"You want this water or what?"

"I'm good," she said.

He didn't respond, so she figured he'd gone off to start his daily boozing. She'd wait until he got good and drunk. That's when she'd leave. She'd look for Charlie, hope he wasn't too mad at her for rejecting him, and they'd take off together. She'd have to be careful, though. Bob was a ticking time bomb, and she wasn't sure how long she'd be able to bury her obvious disgust.

Maybe it was a good thing she hadn't been able to cry. It was as if someone unplugged the weakest part of her, so she could stay strong and do exactly what she needed to do to survive.

**

"That little fucker stole my shotgun!" Bob said from his spot on the couch, thumbing through porn magazines he'd picked up at a convenience store.

I hope he's not fueling up for me.

Other than briefly asking where Charlie had gone earlier in the morning, it was the first time Bob had even mentioned Charlie's absence. When Bob asked if she'd seen him, she was honest, saying Charlie was probably hiding because she'd rejected him. She felt horrible about telling Bob that, and even more awful when Bob couldn't stop laughing. But better to tell him that than give him more reasons to be mad at Charlie.

No wonder he ran off.

Her only wish was that Charlie had asked her to go with him. Though she rejected him, it wasn't because she didn't like him. She did, just not in the way he seemed to like her. He was a nice kid, maybe the nicest she'd ever known, but she wasn't attracted to him at all. He was too young, too green, and altogether not her type. Besides, love, lust, and sex, none of that was on her mind now. She was in survival mode, barely able to cope with her own feelings, let alone massage another's. She hadn't been lying when she said she wasn't looking for a relationship. The world had changed in a flash, and she had changed right along with it.

"When he gets back here, I'm gonna whip his ass," Bob said, cracking open another beer.

"Where do you think he went?" she asked, fishing for information. "Does he know anyone here?"

"I doubt it. Though who knows? The little freak sits in his room all day on the fucking Internet. Maybe he had a buncha other geeky computer friends all over the country just waiting to jerk him off. Joke's on him, though. Ain't nobody left to pull his pud. He'll come back when he realizes how bad he needs me."

Bob downed the beer and crushed the can against his head like some kind of frat boy asshole.

"You want another beer?" Callie asked, purposely making sure she was up when he finished.

"Yeah," he joked, "About time you make yourself useful."

She didn't respond.

"Aw, come on, I'm just messin' with you. Sheesh, women are so sensitive."

She went into the kitchen and found the plastic water bottle that was different from the others. For one, it was the only bottle in the fridge which had been opened and was only a quarter full. The bottle's label was also worn, indicating a lot of re-use. She didn't know if it was Derek's G, though she doubted it, or Bob's personal supply, which seemed all the more likely. She had no idea how much G you'd put in someone's drink, so she poured what seemed like twice the appropriate amount into Bob's open beer can.

She brought the can in and handed it to Bob with a smile. "I'm not feeling too good," she said, putting a hand over her stomach, "I think my friend is coming."

"Your friend?" Bob said, taking a swig, then realizing, "Oh, your menses. Hell, woman, you did *not* need to tell me that shit."

"I'm gonna take a nap," she said, "Call me if Charlie comes back."

"Don't worry, you'll hear the sound of him begging me to let him in."

Callie forced a laugh, then went upstairs.

**

She didn't know how long the drug took to work or even if it would knock Bob out completely. If it was his supply, maybe he had built up a resistance to it. Maybe it just made him delirious. She thought he'd said something about getting good and fucked up on it. She hoped it would at least impair him long enough for her to get out of the house without him noticing.

She waited 20 minutes, then got out of bed and snuck out of her room and down the hall to his. The door was open and the duffel bags of guns lay on the bed. She found the Glock she'd been practicing with. She grabbed it, along with a box of bullets and went back to her room.

She loaded the gun, grabbed a charcoal jacket from the closet, about three sizes too big, put the bullets in her pocket and headed out the window to get the hell away from Bob. She hoped she could find Charlie before Bob came looking for her.

**

Clouds hung low in the sky, as Callie stepped onto the street.

No sign of Charlie or the Toyota he'd taken from Derek's driveway. She hoped he'd not gone far. Though she didn't know him well enough to venture an educated guess, she thought he may have stayed relatively close, just to be on the safe side. Far away enough to make a point and hide from Bob, but close enough to run home if necessary.

She needed a car. She wasn't about to risk taking Bob's car, or the car in the garage. She went a few doors down on the opposite side of the street where a cute, purple VW bug sat in the driveway.

She knocked on the door on the off chance someone was home. The door was made mostly of etched glass framed in a deep redwood. Seeing no one inside, she tried the doorknob. Locked.

She glanced down, searching for a rock to break the window, then laughed out loud at the planter beside the walkway filled with small round rocks and one large square gray one, so out of place it may as well have had a label on it reading, "fake rock key holder."

She retrieved the key and let herself inside.

The house was warm, and the smell of cinnamon potpourri made her think of her mom's craft room. She went to the kitchen and combed the wall for a key rack and the counter for keys. Nothing. She headed back to the doorway to see if she'd missed an obvious spot where people might keep car keys. She found a mail sorter on a ledge, and a small box of random crap, but no keys.

Callie remembered seeing an anime decal on the VW's rear window, which made her think the car belonged to a teenager, so she went upstairs and found a door with purple letters spelling out "Meghan" on the door.

She went inside the room and into an explosion of purple. Light-lavender walls, dark-purple curtains and bedding, and dark-purple wood trim on the door, closets, and baseboards. It was a room Callie could definitely live in. Very cute. On the walls were some anime posters Callie wasn't familiar with. She was strictly a Marvel and DC girl. In the corner, a shiny, creamy-purple BC Rich electric guitar and Peavey amp.

"Cool!" Callie said, picking it up and strumming with a dark-purple pick that matched the strap. She wished the power were on so she could do a little shredding. She wasn't a great guitar player by any stretch, and didn't have the patience to learn other people's songs. Mostly, she played her own tunes. But she hadn't played anything in more than a year, since her band broke up due to excessive bitchiness of two of its members.

The strings felt good beneath her fingers. Felt right. She regretted not playing more.

She strummed a few chords, trying to remember a song she'd been working on. Just when she got it, and fell into a rhythm, she heard the door slam open downstairs.

Shit! Bob!

She sat the guitar on the bed, ran to the closet, and slid the door open. Despite the room's neatness, Meghan's closet was stuffed with boxes and mountains of clothes. Callie wedged herself inside, trying to keep quiet while also listening for sounds of footsteps coming up the stairs. It was a tight squeeze, but she managed to get in and slide the door shut, leaving the thinnest of cracks, still allowing her a thin sliver to peek outside. She wondered what she'd do if Bob came into the room. If she'd stayed where she was, she could have innocently claimed that she was just looking for Charlie.

But now that she'd hidden, her intentions were clear. She was on the run. And he would be pissed. And worse, if he realized she'd drugged him, he'd probably kill her. She grabbed the gun from her jacket pocket, and wondered if she could pull the trigger. This morning, when she realized Bob had raped her, she could easily have shot him. But now, a few hours later, her anger had been replaced with a steady drip of mounting fear.

The closet was an echo chamber for her rapid heartbeat and shallow breaths. She put her left hand over her mouth as if it could silence the sound of her breathing.

A crash sounded downstairs, something being knocked over.

Bob was pissed.

Then another crash.

And another.

Suddenly, Callie began to realize it probably wasn't Bob downstairs. As if the intruder sensed her realization, the creature made its horrible clicking.

And it wasn't alone.

* * * *

CHAPTER 3
BORICIO WOLFE

Oct. 18
Somewhere in Alabama

Boricio took off his blindfold.
Well, fuck me.
He almost didn't believe what he saw.
That pile of shit Moe wasn't wearing a blindfold, and he sure as hell didn't have a fucked up face. The other captives were as they said, knees on burlap and rags over their faces. And like he said, Adam looked just old enough to buy beer without getting carded. But Moe, that fucker was on his knees, and though his hands were behind his back and bound like everyone else's, he was in full custody of his eyesight. *For now.*

Moe drew a surprised breath the second Boricio leapt to his feet.

They stared at one another, neither speaking. The prisoners rustled beside them, sensing movement and tension, but could see nothing and prove even less.

Boricio slithered toward Moe, but Moe didn't flinch or move. At least not much. His lips were quivering, and his breath was scattered all over the place.

Boricio sniffed the room then put his hand at the back of Moe's curly mat of hair and yanked it by the root. Moe whimpered. Boricio leaned in and whispered low enough so only Moe could hear him, barely.

"*The itsy bitsy spider, crawled up the water spout ...* "

Boricio's fingers crept along the back of Moe's neck.

"*Down came the rain and washed the spider out. Out came the sun and it dried up all the rain ...* "

His fingers crawled over to the other side, the longest one making a circle inside Moe's ear. "*The itsy bitsy spider, went up the spout again.*"

"What ... what do you want from me?" Moe started to shake.

Boricio bit the edge of Moe's ear, right at the cartilage, just enough to hurt like a hard-on bent in half, but not enough to draw blood. He whispered again:

"*The itsy bitsy spider, crawled up the water spout. Down came the rain and washed the spider out. Out came the sun and it dried up all the rain ...* "

"You don't want to kill me, man." Moe said, more statement than plea.

"Don't I?" Boricio raised an eyebrow. The prisoners strained to listen. Boricio lowered himself to a squat. "What are you *really* afraid of? I'm unarmed and all you have to do is yell. Are you that big of a pussy, or is there a bigger, badder wolf out there than ole Boricio?"

A final whimper, then a vomit of words: "Look, we don't have time at all because any second now Jackson is going to come back in here and when he does, he'll be bringing Brock and Veronica with him and that's going to be big, bad news for all of us. I don't have the time to tell you everything, but I swear I can help. I can save your life, not just in here, but out there, too. I don't think you know what's out there. But it's not what you think … oh my God, I think I hear them outside … "

A rustling outside the door …

"Sit down, man, please." Begging from Manny.

"You're going to get us killed." Jack agreed.

"I think they're right, sir." Adam made three.

The rustling grew louder, then stopped.

"We're not finished," Boricio said, kissing Moe on the cheek and returning his blindfold, and laying back down on the ground with his hands beneath him.

A single set of footsteps preceded the sound of cloth scraping concrete followed by a squeaky hinge and burlap whipping air. A sixth mat was added to the floor, confirmed by the thud of a body.

A second later, Dead Guard Walking's bad breath was stinking up Boricio's personal air again. "Looks like I got shit to tend to on the immediate side," he said, "but you and me got unfinished business 'fore this day gets to being yesterday."

Boricio smiled. "You know, I was just thinking the same exact thing."

Another slap hit the side of Boricio's head, but Dead Guard Walking must've been in a hurry because Boricio barely felt it. A second later, the door whined shut, and the guard's scent fled the room.

Boricio was back on his feet and in Moe's face. "Alright, piggy, squeal. You got seconds, and I mean short ones, before I start creating new ways to fuck you up, starting with ones that hurt most, followed by the ones that just make me laugh."

Boricio introduced his heel to Moe's jaw, hard enough to prove he wasn't worried about getting caught, though he forced his fist in Moe's mouth to muffle his cry anyway.

"I ain't ready for them to get back in here quite yet," he said.

Boricio grabbed another thatch of hair and said, "Squeal, pig!" then started whistling the tune to *Gimme One Reason*.

Moe spoke in a whimper. "I *was* one of you. No different. Same thing happened to me when Veronica brought me here, just like all of you guys. Only difference was it happened to me on the first day. They told me I was gonna get spared so long as I played ball and told them what the prisoners was saying each time they was in here and so that's what I've been doing since. I just told you the thing about my cheek because I didn't want you to be suspicious. I'm not one of them, I'm just trying to stay alive."

Boricio stopped whistling. "Why don't you have a blindfold?"

"They want me to keep my eye on things. Let them know if I see anything weird. But I'm still locked up, no different." Moe tilted his head back to gesture at his bound wrists.

"That's the sorta *that's all there is* that makes a man stop breathing. I suggest you talk faster and actually start saying something, fucknut."

Moe swallowed, then continued to push words through a cry. "I think these people are survivalists, you know like the folks you hear about up holing away for the end of the world up in Montana. And this place is some sorta compound."

"Survivalists?"

"More than survivalists, though, I think they're a cult. I'd reckon every group has a leader, but these guys kept talking about a prophet or something."

"A prophet? Like Waco shit?" Boricio said.

"Exactly. No one's told me anything direct, but I heard a bit, including from some kid who disappeared the first day. Seems he was one of them until he had a change of heart up around 2:15 a.m. a few days ago. Guess it was family fun when it was all Kool-Aid and unicorns, but as soon as it was real, he wanted out. But there is no out, so Jackson was allowed to take care of things as he saw fit. I didn't see how fit that was, but I could hear some of it, and it sounded awful."

"Solid job," Boricio said, standing back up. "I'll give you a B-. 'Course, you'll need at least a B+ to keep breathing, so it's a good time to step it up. Tell me, what makes Señor Prophet so special, and what are they doing with the people they toss in here to trade bullshit with you? And don't give me none of that 'I don't know shit,' because the only thing that's gonna keep you from earning a big fat C is some solid info. Now."

"I can only guess about why they're bringing people in here. For sure they're looking for information. But it also seems like they're waiting for someone in particular to show up. They also seem keen to know everything they can about everything, but I've no idea how much they actually know. But they seem to have some big plans."

"What plans?"

"I don't know ... "

Boricio's nostrils flared.

"But everyone here does, and I know it's something bad. They're sorting things out; seems like they're gearing up to go after someone, but I don't know who. As far as what makes the Prophet so special, I think he dreamed about whatever happened before it actually happened. I can see how that would give a man a mighty lot of power. I know it ain't much, but it's the best I got, and it's honest to the word."

Well now, I don't think that's what I ordered at all. Dreams have been daffy as a diseased duck for days, which probably wouldn't mean shit if they weren't so goddamned Technicolor. And it's a sour gallon of fucking milk that I don't have a clue what they mean.

Boricio tried not to think about his own weird-ass dreams. Wasn't like Moe was gonna be much help figuring shit out. That fucker rode the short bus and licked the windows on the trip. "What else can you tell me about the grounds? How many guards?"

"Not sure how much more I can help," Moe said. "I've never been out of this room, except for about 15 minutes on the second day when they were cleaning this one, though it didn't look no different when we came back in. I guess I did see some stuff then."

"Like what?"

"There's a station just outside this main building, seems like a communication shack or something. And then there's a second cluster of buildings, looks like there's a farm with a silo, plus a big, long building, might've been stables."

"How many people you figure are in this place?"

"No idea, never even seen anyone from the other buildings. I seen maybe a dozen people total, but there could be 10 times that. Or more."

Moe didn't wait for his B+, just started begging instead. "I'm like you, man, just lucky enough to wind up here a few days earlier. I'll help you, I *want to* help you. These people scare the fuck outta me. And I'm the only one in the room who knows the way out of here, at least sort of. There's a garage by the communication shack. I'm sure there are cars in there. I'll take you there. If you don't waste time, you will survive. I want to get out of here, and I want to help you."

"Long as you're not one of them, it's fine with me," Boricio said. "Every number matters."

Yeah, we'll just see about that you Benedict Arnold motherfucker. Give me a reason to reach down your throat and pull your tongue out and gut you like a pig.

The newest prisoner stirred.

"I think our new friend is awake," Adam said.

Boricio couldn't have the new prisoner making noise and drawing anyone to the room; not before he was ready. He placed his hand over the prisoner's mouth, "Shhh," he said. "You've been kidnapped. But we're gonna get you outta here."

Uneasy recognition blended with the confusion on his face. "Boricio?" asked the prisoner, who looked to be around Adam's age.

Boricio paused, got down next to the kid, and clutched his throat. "How the fuck you know my name, kid?"

"Sorry," he said, "I'm... I'm not sure what I meant."

A controlled rage rumbled inside Boricio. "The fuck you talking about, boy? You said my name clear as fucking Windex. You wanna tell me why, or you want me to tear off your arm and beat you with the soggy end, you Kids-Eat-Free-On-Tuesday fuck? You don't use my name and not tell me why, unless you want it to be the last thing you do."

The prisoner swallowed. "I'm sorry, man. My name's Charlie Wilkens, and strange as this sounds, I met you in a dream. Last night. I fell asleep, and there you were, talking to me, just like you are right now. And then again, you were talking in my head when these people kidnapped me."

Boricio stared down at Charlie, curiosity creeping through him. "Oh yeah, what did I say?"

Charlie gulped again. "You said that your father was a fucking cunt and that nobody fucks with Boricio. You also said that the only thing to do when you find a pussy is to fuck it."

Icy shock wrapped around Boricio. The words were his alright. He vaguely remembered dreaming something along those lines, too, but the specifics were as lost as everything else in his recent memories.

Well that's about 14 inches of fuck me silly. Looks like Benedict Arnold might be onto something with this Waco motherfucker and the dream machine.

"No crazy talk," Boricio said, relaxing his grip on the kid's throat. "I don't have time for bullshit, or to figure out where we met before. Start with how you ended up here in the first place."

"I was with my stepdad, Bob. He also survived, which is unfortunate since he's such an asshole. We came across another survivor, a girl a little older than me. Once Bob decided not to crush her head with a crowbar, he went ahead and fucked her in the pool. Stole her away from me. So fuck him like the rest of the world." Charlie drew a quick breath, then added, "And fuck you, too."

The defiance on what was exposed of the kid's face was enough to make Boricio smile. It was obvious he never would've said what he had if given a second to think. And he sure as shit wouldn't have done it if the blindfold wasn't blocking the view of ole Boricio. Even now, the kid looked like he wished he could swallow his tongue, but he was still, unwilling to show fear. Even if his quivering chin betrayed him ever so. Still, Boricio had to give him credit for guts.

The room was silent. Manny, Jack, and Adam stayed quiet through the exchange with Moe, then the entire room had given him and Charlie the floor. Everyone was right where Boricio wanted — so terrified they could barely breathe, and ready to worship him as their new lord and savior if given the chance.

"So, who's up for busting out of here?" he asked.

Smiles and nods circled the room. Boricio reached into his boot and peeled back the sole, and retrieved his emergency razor blade, then moved in a line, freeing each of the prisoners from their restraints and blindfolds. When he got to Moe, he leaned in, blade to Moe's face, and said, "You give me one reason, and I'll kill you 'til you're a second from dying, then stop so these Kool-Aid-drinking motherfuckers can decide when you get your last two breaths, you dig?"

Moe nodded. Boricio turned to the room, slipped the razor back in its plastic case and slid it into his pocket.

"You're all untied. That means you're all invited to be valuable members of Team Boricio. Now if you're not on Team Boricio, then that means you're on Team Fucker. And let me assure you, every single person on Team Fucker is gonna die. So," Boricio gave the group his biggest grin, "who wants to be on Team Boricio?"

Everyone nodded.

"No one does a thing without my say and only when I give it. I don't know who these people are or why they want us here, but I can assure you, any fucker who walks through that door will be crawling out with a red smear behind them, if they're lucky enough to crawl at all."

Charlie laughed.

Boricio smiled. Kid had potential.

* * * *

CHAPTER 4
EDWARD KEENAN

Oct. 16, 2011
Early evening
Cape Hope, North Carolina

"What are we gonna do?" Teagan asked, as the helicopter grew from hum to thunder as it drew closer. "Where can we hide?"

"We can hide in here." Ed said. "But if they've got F.L.I.R., they'd still pick up the heat signature on the SUV's engine, exhaust, and brakes. If they've got ground troops, they'd come looking house to house."

"Are they looking for us?"

"Don't know," Ed said, "Maybe they're looking for survivors. Maybe they're here to help."

"You think?"

The pregnant teen stared at him, wanting to believe things might be okay. Ed didn't want to shatter her hopes.

He knew she was thinking of the dream where the men in helicopters came to take her baby. The more he considered it, the less credence he gave the supernatural nature of her dream. It was a first-time mother's fears of losing her child, that's all. Amplified in a young girl who found herself suddenly without parents, or anyone else to care for her.

Still, that quiet voice in the back of Ed's mind was there. Finely-tuned intuition: *It isn't just a dream; listen to the girl.* His intuition had always called bullshit on anything superstitious or psychic. But for some reason, its ears were perked now. Either she was sharper than he thought or he was growing dull.

"I dunno," Ed said. "I suggest we play it by ear. See what happens, prepare for the worst."

"The worst? What's that?"

"That they've come to harm us."

He ran to the car, grabbed the Remington 30-06 rifles and shells he'd taken from the men at the gas station, and came back inside to prepare. He wished he'd had the foresight to break into a gun shop and load up on more weapons. But he hadn't exactly expected to go toe-to-toe with helicopters.

That's when he realized: The men in the chopper were looking for him, not the girl. *Why didn't I think of that before?* Sure, he was probably presumed dead, and searches would be limited to the crash site and surrounding area unless evidence suggested he'd survived, but maybe someone had seen him and reported him to whatever authorities were still around. The rest of the world might be gone, but agents were roaches. Some survivors were a near certainty.

And now they are coming.

He couldn't take any chances. The men in the choppers *might* be there to help, but agents would say anything, show any face, to disarm you.

He'd have to act quickly, without question; fire the first chance he got. Like at the convenience store. And he'd have to prepare Teagan for what was going to happen.

"I need you to trust me on this," he said, meeting her frightened eyes. "If these guys are bad, or if I even *think* they're bad, I'm going to shoot, no questions. Understand?"

Teagan nodded.

Thunder grew louder.

Ed went to the window, peered through the curtain, and saw the chopper hovering above the trailer park, light sweeping the grounds. The chopper appeared to be a Black Hawk, which meant it wasn't likely scouring for people to save. There was room for maybe 11 troops in addition to two pilots and two crew chiefs, so even if they were flying with less troops, they couldn't be expecting to pick up too many people. Meaning they'd either specifically come for them, or to kill them. Of course, the chopper could be reporting to base or be flying in advance of a transport chopper, but Ed couldn't take the chance.

It's go time.

"Stay inside. Get whatever you need and get it now. Be ready to go in two minutes."

Ed stepped outside as the helicopter descended, raised his rifle and aimed at the cockpit. The pilots saw the threat, spun the chopper sideways, and a soldier stood at the machine gun, taking aim at Ed.

Ed had one shot before he'd be torn to shreds. While the top rotor made an easier target, it would likely require a few shots. A rear blade hit could bring the bird down quicker, but the shot was next to impossible. He steadied his aim on the rear rotor blades, held his breath, and took the shot. He managed two shots, both hitting the rear blade, causing the copter to spin violently out of control, nose pointed toward the tree tops as the pilot tried to wrestle the copter to a safe landing.

Ed loaded more shells into the rifle, then followed the chopper's descent to the beach as it crashed into the water. The top rotor blades, along with the tail of the chopper, split from the body like butter under blade and sent waves of debris flying toward the sand.

Ed waited for any sign of survivors, rifle ready. Two men emerged from the wreckage, dazed. Ed shot them both, one in the head and the other in the chest. Their bodies went limp then fell to the tide.

He waited two minutes' worth of nothing, as most of the chopper remained underwater.

He ran back to Teagan's house, yelling, "Let's go!"

Teagan was outside with two bags in four seconds, tossing them into the back of the SUV, as Ed pulled from the driveway and raced down the street.

"What happened?"

"They're gone."

Teagan's face was still. He could tell she was trying to work out whether to thank him or scold him for another round of murders. Guilt had a way of silencing criticism, so Teagan said nothing.

**

"Are we driving straight to Georgia?" Teagan said as the last of the sun dipped behind the horizon and the world fell into darkness again.

"Yeah, sooner we get to Georgia, the sooner we'll know if Jade is okay."

Teagan rubbed her belly, then looked up at Ed and said, "Thank you for saving us back there ... and at the gas station. You were right."

Ed nodded, uncomfortable getting accolades for being a good killer.

"Do you think we'll find anyone else? I mean, people who aren't trying to hurt us?"

"I'm sure there's good guys left," Ed lied, "If we're careful, maybe we'll find a few."

"What if we don't?" She asked, tears in her eyes. "What if everyone else is gone? How are we supposed to live?" Then, a hiccup from hysteria: "How am I supposed to raise a child? How am I even supposed to *have* a child with no doctors, or nurses, or hospitals?"

"We don't *know* if everyone is gone," Ed said in his calmest voice. "For all we know, this is localized to a few states."

"But what is it? What happened? Where did all the people go?"

"I dunno," Ed said, "I've been trying to figure that out since I realized they were gone. And every time I think I have an idea which might seem plausible, I turn down the path to see where it goes and slam into a dead end."

"Maybe God called everyone home?" she said.

Ed laughed.

"What?" she asked, offended.

"You really believe that?"

"Why not? It would explain why my parents went and I didn't," she said putting a hand on her unborn baby. "Maybe this is God's punishment for my sins."

Ed laughed harder, but stopped when he saw her pained look, ready for a fresh batch of tears.

"I'm not laughing at you," he said, "It's just that with all the evil shit going on in the world on a day-to-day basis, an unwed mother is the least of God's concerns, assuming there *is* a God. If you were denied entry into heaven because you're pregnant, the streets wouldn't be empty now. They'd be so full to the brim with sinners, you wouldn't be able to move six inches without bumping into another one. Believe me."

She looked like she wanted to argue, but didn't. Just stared out the window, like any other teenager who thinks the world, and God's judgment, revolved around her.

"Maybe we're not on Earth," she said after a few minutes of thought. "Maybe the reason there's not a ton of people around is because we're in purgatory. Not bad people, necessarily, but not good enough to get into heaven."

"I doubt it," Ed said, "I can't imagine a jury of angels debating whether or not *I* was a good person. If God had anything to do with this, I'd be in hell right now, trust me. And while we're in the Deep South, and some might argue otherwise, this is hardly hell."

Teagan laughed.

Ed was relieved when she closed her eyes. He didn't really want to explore their situation more than he'd already done a hundred times in his mind. He had no idea where everyone went. But there had to be a scientific explanation. Something that made sense. The problem with science was that it left so many things in the air. Despite millennia of theology and centuries of science, the world had expired before finding answers to life's biggest questions.

Maybe what happened wouldn't come with a pat answer. Maybe they'd just have to learn and adapt on the fly, like humans had always done.

Evolve or die.

* *

11:20 p.m.
Winding, Georgia

Jade lived in an apartment building that catered mostly to college students and young people in the town's thriving service industry. What it lacked in architectural style (a giant, dorm-style, five-story building), it made up for by being well-maintained and on the nicer side of town. Hers was one of four identical buildings surrounding a large parking lot, packed with cars, most of which had student parking decals and stickers of trendy bands slapped across their rear windows.

From outside, Ed didn't see any lights in the windows or sense anyone inside, deflating the small hope he'd reluctantly allowed to swell in his heart.

Teagan woke from her nap in the passenger seat, and said, "We're here?"

"Yeah," Ed parked the SUV behind a row of cars closest to Building B. "Looks deserted."

Ed grabbed his pistol, shoved it in his waistband, then opened the door. He grabbed a duffel bag from the back seat, filled with flashlights, food, and tools, including a crow bar, then headed toward the building's entrance. Teagan followed.

On the front double glass doors, was a sheet of white paper taped to the inside, facing out. On it, large letters written in royal blue marker.

Survivors - Meet Us In Room 410.

The handwriting looked like a woman's, though Ed couldn't be sure it was Jade's. A long time had passed since he'd seen her writing, 10 years, at least.

Ed handed a flashlight to Teagan, then took one for himself, and pushed through the doors. The hallway was dark except for a small red EXIT sign at the other end. He shined his light down the hall, and his heart nearly stopped.

Every door was open as if someone had gone into each of the rooms searching for something. *Looters?*

"Wait here," he whispered to Teagan, advancing down the hall with his gun drawn and flashlight scanning the darkness.

He held the gun and light as though a single instrument, one to banish the dark and the other to blast it to hell.

The rooms weren't looted, or in any way destroyed. Perhaps just the product of someone looking for others. Maybe Jade had opened the doors and was now in Room 410, he allowed himself to hope, though his cold, inner cynic warned him not to let his expectations carry him away. He searched four rooms before surrendering to his instincts, and the evidence at hand — no others were on this floor.

He found the stairwell at the end of the hall, beneath the EXIT sign, and called for Teagan to follow.

The second floor was the same as the first, open doors, including Jade's at 205.

He entered her apartment, gun down. Her walls were dark-red with giant prints of foreign movies. A black sectional with a pillow and blanket rumpled in the rough shape of a comma. He wondered if that's where Jade had fallen to sleep, watching TV before she vanished.

"Which room is hers?" Teagan asked, looking at two doors, both open.

"I dunno. I've never been here."

"Oh," Teagan said.

Ed went into the smaller of the two rooms. Slightly messy, lots of pillows on the unmade bed, and ... the blue unicorn they'd given her when she was a kid. He picked it up and brought it to his nose. He expected to smell her, flash back on some memories of them together, hugging her maybe. But the unicorn brought no memories. And it smelled different, not like her; unfamiliar perfume.

He glanced at Jade's nightstand, saw a framed photo from her 16th birthday party. He smiled, remembering the night, and the photo. One of the rare pictures he'd been in. However, he noticed he wasn't in the version on her nightstand. The photo had been blown up and reproduced, to edit him from the photo. A knot formed in his heart and throat, and he swallowed the bitter fact that his daughter didn't want reminders of him.

"Nice room," Teagan said from behind, snapping Ed from his thoughts.

He returned the unicorn to the top of her pillows.

"Let's go see who's in Room 410." Ed said.

They didn't bother checking the third floor. Ed opened the door to the fourth and came face to face with a young man with a baseball bat.

"Put the bat down!" Ed yelled, aiming his gun at the stick-thin, olive-skinned guy with thick, black-framed glasses and long, dark hair.

The guy was frozen, very likely the first time he'd ever had a gun pulled on him.

"I said fucking drop it," Ed said, voice sharp.

Dude dropped the bat and stepped back, "Sorry, man. I wasn't gonna hit you with it."

"Just wanted to play some ball, eh?"

"I didn't know if you'd be human."

"What?" Ed asked.

"I thought you might be *one of them*."

The man saw the look on Ed's face and said, "You haven't seen them, have you?"

"Seen what?" Ed was getting impatient with the clown.

The guy stammered, trying to find the right words, when the door to Apartment 410 opened behind him.

"Daddy?"

It was Jade.

* * * *

CHAPTER 5
BRENT FOSTER

Brent jumped down, ran over another car, then leapt again as he heard the creatures landing on the cars behind him, navigating the metal and plastic maze with ease. They wouldn't be able to outrun them, not when they were that fast and agile.

Brent's mind raced, keeping time with his heart, as he tried to think of something to do. He could barely keep up with Luis, now two rows ahead.

Just keep running.

A creature shrieked behind him, so loud it seemed like it was right over his shoulder, about to take him down.

Brent turned back and saw the black monstrosity. Distracted, Brent's foot slipped from under him, and he landed on the hood of an old Nissan, smacking his right cheek hard against the hood before he slid off, hitting the ground hard on his back. The bag of weapons slid beneath the car along with the gun he'd been holding.

The creature jumped over the thin space between the two cars as Brent rolled over, and reached for the pistol.

CLICK CLICK CLICK CLICK, the sound came from above, audible even over the incessant warbling of the triggered car alarm. The creature circled back, about to pounce as Brent got hold of the gun and rolled onto his back.

The creature landed on him, knocking the breath from Brent's lungs. It opened its large mouth and wailed an unearthly shriek as it straddled Brent's chest, swiping at Brent's face with its claws. Brent pushed against the creature's wet, fleshy chest with his left hand, trying desperately to hold it back.

"Fuck, fuck, fuck!" Brent screamed as he struggled to raise the pistol and steady his shaky aim. He fired twice. The bullets hit the creature's chest and head. The thing was still moving.

Brent emptied the clip into the creature and got a hot splatter of hot, black gore to the face for his effort.

"Fuck!" he yelled, trying to wipe the goop from his eyes and face as he pushed the twitching creature aside and got to his feet.

Before he was fully upright, something punched him in the ribs, sending him hard into another car. The gun fell from his clumsy hands again. Brent looked up just in time to see another creature coming at him, two eyes narrowed on him.

Two thunderous gunshots ripped through the air, knocking the creature back. Relieved, Brent turned to see Luis standing on the hood of a pickup truck. Luis fired another four shots at creatures Brent couldn't even see yet.

"Come on!" he screamed, though Brent wasn't sure if he were yelling at him or the monsters.

Brent ducked down, found the bag of weapons, grabbed two more pistols, fresh clips in each, and jumped onto the truck's roof beside Luis, who had opened fire with an Uzi.

Brent fired, too, missing more than he hit, but able to keep them away, and even take a few down.

"Die! Die! Die!" Luis screamed, emptying his clip into four creatures just below them.

As Luis changed his clip, something dark caught Brent's eye, moving in from behind, and coming right at Luis. Two creatures, in tandem, no, connected at the hip, were sailing over the cars behind them, barreling toward Luis faster than he could reload.

Brent fired six shots, the last two hitting the joined monstrosity and sending it to the ground.

Luis now had two Uzis loaded, and was firing them like a post-apocalyptic Rambo, still screaming.

Brent loaded fresh clips into his pistols, and stood to join in the firefight, only to find nothing left to shoot.

Nearly 40 creatures lay in scattered pieces around them. Luis called out, "Any more?!"

Nothing but silence.

After a long echo of the same nothing, Brent stared at Luis, somewhere in the middle of admiration and outright hero worship.

"You are a fuckin' bad ass!" Brent said laughing.

Luis's face, fat with rage just seconds before, melted to a warm smile, "Not a bad shot yourself. For a desk jockey. Come on, let's get outta here before more of them crawl out of the woodwork."

They raced over the last rows of cars and down the road, high with a confidence that could only come from living the action part of a popcorn flick while leaving a trail of dead monsters behind them.

As they approached Times Square, the silence was replaced by the sound of birds. Lots of birds. As if the entire city's avian populace had decided to flock to Times Square. Brent couldn't see the birds through the fog. Nor could he see the giant advertisements that usually greeted him at the world's most famous intersection. Without power, commerce was dead, and the giant LCD screens were just more objects barely visible in the fog. Even the solar and wind-powered Ricoh billboard was eerily dark and silent.

As they reached the corner of 7th Avenue and 42nd Street, the birds grew to a constant loud chorus of chirps, shrieks, and calls.

Luis, 10 feet ahead of Brent, stopped in his tracks.

As Brent picked up his pace, Luis turned, eyes wide, and said, "Go back."

"What?" Brent said, not listening, pushing past Luis. And then he saw for himself.

Thousands, if not hundreds of thousands of human corpses were lining the thoroughfare, in 10-foot-high mounds, piled like garbage.

Brent's throat ached, and his eyes welled. He stood, rooted to the spot, unable, *unwilling* to register what his eyes were clearly seeing.

"No," he cried, "No, no, no."

The bodies weren't rotting, burned, or emaciated, or in any way injured-looking to Brent, other than the torn eyes and flesh from the grazing birds. All were fully dressed, many in pajamas, as if plucked from bed and deposited right in the middle of the road. Dead.

Luis crouched on one knee, eyes bolted to the mass grave.

Brent raced forward and into the graveyard.

"Ben! Gina!" he screamed repeatedly, hoping they might be hiding somewhere among the dead.

His voice bounced off the buildings, bodies, and fog, sounding ever more desperate upon its mocking return.

He raced through the streets, among the bodies, screaming for his family until his throat was raw.

They have to be here. Ben spoke to me through Joe. He said Times Square!

Brent continued calling, running from pile to pile, searching for any signs of life among the rows of bodies. Not caring if he drew the attention of every fucking monster in the city.

"Ben!!" he screamed again, this time, crying more than screaming, as he fell to his knees.

"I'm sorry, man," Luis said, now crouching next to Brent and putting an arm on his shoulder.

"They can't be ... " Brent cried, his entire face hurting so much he thought it might crack open, "They can't be ... dead."

Brent's mind flashed on the moments he'd held his son tight, tucked him in, played with him, read to him, played peek-a-boo. Thought of Ben's happy face and bright-blue eyes. So full of life and innocence. He thought of the train in his pocket that his boy would never play with again.

They can't be gone.

Brent couldn't fathom a world where his son and wife were only memory.

Sudden recall hit Brent like a blade to the gut.

Last weekend, he was home, dead-ass tired, and just wanting to chill out and watch TV. Ben came in asking him to read him a book. *Stanley Train Goes To School.* Brent said, "Tomorrow, buddy, Daddy's tired."

Brent dismissed Ben's complaints at the time, a temporary disappointment that Ben would soon get over.

"Please, Daddy."

"Tomorrow," Brent said. Of course, the next night, Brent was working, along with every evening after that. Now, the look of sorrow on his 3-year-old's face would be frozen in Brent's brain forever.

"I'm so sorry," Brent said staring at the bodies around him. "Daddy's so sorry."

Luis dropped his guns and hugged Brent. Both men cried.

* * * *

CHAPTER 6
CALLIE THOMPSON

Callie held the gun against the back of the closet door, waiting for the creatures to make their way into the bedroom. She prayed there weren't more than two, three at most. She was confident she could take one of them out, *maybe* two. Any more than that, she was pretty sure they'd overwhelm her.

She heard the monsters stumble up the stairs, bumping between banister and wall the entire way. Her heart pounded so loudly in her chest, she was sure they'd hear. As one of them passed the bedroom door, Callie caught her breath and held it. The second creature didn't pass, though. It turned into the room, and it was all she could do to hold the breath in her lungs.

The creature was similar to the others: long, dark, black, and wet-looking with lights moving beneath its skin. Its face was an abomination of misshapen parts. It had just one eye, off to the side. Its nose was missing, with only two dark holes for nostrils. Its mouth was impossibly wide, almost so wide that if it chose to open it fully, the top of its head would probably fall back like a Pez dispenser. Rows of razor-sharp, rotted teeth filled the creature's mouth.

The gun shook in Callie's hands as the creature stopped in front of the closet, lifting its head up and sniffed.

Fuck, fuck, fuck.

The creature's face inched closer until it was maybe two feet from the closet opening. It sniffed again. Its eye widened as it stepped back, and pointed at the closet, letting loose with an ear piercing scream that sounded like an alarm.

Callie let out her breath and slid open the door so hard it nearly bounced back and hit her as she stuck her arms out and fired two rounds at the creature's head. The bullets sank into its skull like she were shooting a slab of beef. The first creature fell to the ground just as the second stormed into the room. She raised the gun to fire, but the creature's arm was too quick. It slammed hard into her hand and knocked the gun to the ground. The creature charged at Callie, mouth gnashing and open. Callie stumbled back into the closet, gripped the inside of the door and slammed it shut.

The creature shrieked and clicked as it hit the door with its body.

Callie cried out, the closet doors shaking in her hand. Another hit made the doors rock in their track. She wasn't sure how long she'd be able to hold the doors shut before the creature either ripped them open or pushed them off the tracks.

Another hit. And then more clicking and shrieking as one hit against the door was followed by another and another, and in such quick succession, Callie figured three of them had to be outside the closet working together.

Callie's inability to cry had found its cure. Tears streamed down her face as she pleaded, "Please, no! Don't kill me!"

She didn't even think about whether or not they'd understand her, let alone listen to her pleas. But those were the only words that would fall from her mouth between cries and gasps for air.

The closet door kept rocking in its frame as she desperately clutched them, trying to keep them together. The bullets in her pocket mocked her as the gun laid just outside the closet. No way would she be able to get to the gun before one, or all, the monsters got her.

Another hit.

She cried out.

Another hit and she heard something, a horrible, wrenching sound above as the doors broke loose from the track. The right door fell in and on top of her as a long, black arm reached in and swiped at her, its dark claws sinking into the meat of her forearm.

She screamed again, falling down and kicking out. Her foot found what seemed to be one of the creatures' knees, and it cracked with a sickly wet crunch, but the monster was unfazed, taking another swipe at her. Instead of hitting her, it lifted her last bit of protection, the door that was on top of her. Now it was just her and them. Her eyes darted around the room, but couldn't see the gun.

Three monsters surrounded her, each with a differently-misshapen, horrifying face, and all of them shrieking like banshee vultures ready to feed.

"I love you, Mommy," she said and closed her eyes.

A shot rang out. Callie's eyes opened just as one of the monster's chests exploded and hot black blood splashed onto her.

She spit out the rancid liquid, glanced up as the other two creatures looked back to the doorway, where Bob stood with a shotgun. He shot again, blasting another of the monsters, then dropped the shotgun, raised a pistol and fired four times until the last creature's head was gone and its body was left twitching on the ground.

Callie, still lying on the ground covered in black gore, stared in disbelief at Bob, who stared down at her with a look she couldn't quite comprehend.

Is he mad? Does he know I drugged him? He's going to shoot me, isn't he?

"You okay?" Bob said, reaching out to help her up.

"Thank you," she said, still stunned, and nervous. She hugged him, breaking down in tears. Real tears.

He didn't embrace her, which caused her to pull away. "What's wrong?" she asked.

"Why'd you leave?" he asked, a flash of anger ... or maybe confusion ... in his eyes.

"I wanted to find Charlie," she said. "I thought I saw someone peeking out the window here."

"Probably one of those fucking things," Bob said, picking up her pistol and handing it to her.

"Let's get the hell out of here. Charlie is on his own now. He chose to leave."

Bob started down the stairs, Callie following slowly behind.

"Did you want to go after him?" Bob said, "You're free to go if you want, but I'm not gonna be there next time some of these creepy crawlies come a calling."

She was trapped. He knew it. She knew it. The only thing in question was whether or not he knew she'd drugged him. Apparently, the drug didn't do much to dull his senses. Or perhaps, he never even finished the laced beer. She would give anything to know, but couldn't think of a way to ask if he'd drunk the beer without calling unwanted attention to what she'd done.

She'd have to play dumb, go home with Bob, and hope he didn't have a clue.

* * * *

CHAPTER 7
BORICIO WOLFE

Dead Guard Walking would be back in no time, so Boricio kept his stint as team captain short, telling the prisoners to keep still no matter what. Everyone needed to act like they were still bound, and stay that way until he made his move.

He finished just in time.

The door whined open, and Dead Guard Walking sauntered inside. He was alone, but his feet clopped on the concrete with the rhythm of a man looking forward to detonating a two-ton dirty bomb of downright nasty.

"Miss me, fucktard?" Dead Guard Walking was inches away, circling behind Boricio, trying to make him nervous. But Boricio was all calm with steady breath — in and out, in and out, in and out ...

"Where'd that smart mouth of yours run off to? I didn't beat it out of you yet, did I? Figure I'm not quite ready for you to quit." Boricio heard a dull thawp and peered between the narrow slit he'd made in his blindfold and saw the baseball bat Dead Guard Walking was smacking into his open palm.

Bullies hate to be ignored, so I'll just keep right on ignoring him, least until it's time to shove the fat side of that bat right up that fucker's bunghole. He ain't gonna be walking for long. He'll be a Dead Guard With Bleeding Anus Crawling in minutes.

"Well, truth of the matter is I don't much like tugging my pecker myself. Shit, that's the only reason I got married. And since you seem inclined to give me the ole frosty, how about we play a little game to loosen your juices? We'll call it Wheel of Misfortune," Boricio heard another thwap, then the sound of the bat dragged across concrete.

"Here's how we'll play: I'm gonna circle myself round the room like I'm playing Duck Duck Goose, 'cept when I get round to choosing a duck, I won't be patting no mop tops. What I'm gonna do instead is take this bat and make me a fresh batch of brain stew. See, me and this bat have been through some times together, what with me being a bouncer at the Cock Pit and all. Difference is, the Cock Pit had a lotta rules. My boss Jeff didn't want no lawsuits or police who weren't there to drink. So, Robin here," another thwap as the bat hit his palm, "well, he was just for show. Get it? A bat named Robin? Ha! Oh, yeah, you all can't see Robin, can ya? Well, now that Jeff's gone, Robin can finally come out to play. Because I'm the boss *and* the motherfucking law."

Robin dragged across the concrete. Dead Guard Walking started speaking in a delighted whisper. "Duck ... duck ... duck ... duck ... duck ... duck ... duck ... "

He circled the room, lingering behind Boricio a bit longer each time, but never doing more than giving him a gentle tap on the head. Boricio was glad the asshole was too knee deep in being a dick to pay attention to the prisoners, at least anything below their heads, otherwise he'd have noticed their lack of restraints.

"Looks like you might make a good goose," the voice came from a few feet away, though he wasn't sure if Dead

Guard Walking was referring to Adam or the new kid, Charlie.

"I didn't like this game in kindergarten," Charlie said, "And I *hate* it right now. If you're gonna kill me, go ahead and do it. Or tell me how I can help you. I'm happy to do that, too, but I can't do it if I'm scared."

Boricio bit his lip to keep from laughing. *Holy shit, the kid has balls.* Boricio wondered if the little fucker knew he had leverage because he was the freshest in the box, or whether the end of the world had just put an inch on his prick.

"Well how about that, ladies and gentleman," Dead Guard Walking said. "We have today's first contestant on Wheel of Misfortune."

Boricio actually heard Charlie swallow.

"Do what you need to," Charlie said. "But I'm done being afraid and wondering what's the worst that can happen to me. If this is it, well alright then. Looks like there's not much else going on out there anyway."

A long pause followed: probably Dead Guard Walking figuring how he could punish the rule breaker without actually killing him. Boricio tensed. The reel wasn't supposed to roll just yet, but if the movie was gonna play, well fuck it if Boricio wasn't ready to be the star of the show.

"Ha, I like the way you play, kid," Dead Guard Walking said. "How about I give you a wild card?"

Charlie said nothing.

"What? You don't want a wild card? Well, that's probably 'cuz you don't know what a wild card is! A wild card means you get to pass *your turn* to another player. I'm happy to let you live, seeing as how you're the only one who seems to possess both balls *and brains*. Now you can take the wild card I so generously gave you and pass your turn to someone else." Dead Guard Walking's voice dropped an octave. "That means you can pass your brain stew to whoever you want. Course, you get to choose, it being your wild card and all, but I'd suggest this pussy licker over here with the mouth big enough to drive a gangbang's worth of cocks inside."

Boricio felt the end of the sentence with a hard kick to his knee. Pain radiated through his body, but it was nothing compared to what he would soon deliver. *Keep adding fuel, buddy.*

Adam said, "Why don't you just leave everyone alone?" *Shit!*

Fucking kid. You're 'bout to get yourself straight dead. You can question a bully, but you can't tell 'em to stop. Charlie rode the edge without falling. You're tumbling into nothing fast.

"Ding ding ding, we have us a winner!"

Boricio stiffened at the sound of glee in Dead Guard Walking's voice. Things were about to get retard ugly for Adam if Boricio didn't do something.

"So, here's what's gonna happen, just so there aren't any surprises." Robin scraped the concrete then landed with another thwap in Dead Guard Walking's palm. "This here's about to get loud. Not the brain bashing, though I ain't never had the pleasure of actually making a pot of brain stew, if I'm being honest. I *imagine* it ain't that loud, least not as loud as the shrieks that are gonna be leaking from this fucker over here in another few seconds."

The blindfold was off, and Boricio was on his feet. Dead Guard Walking didn't have time to tighten his grip before Boricio grabbed the bat and threw it to the ground. Boricio grabbed Dead Guard Walking's shoulders with both hands and drove his knee into the guard's chest. Air fled his body, and he doubled over just as Boricio's right elbow landed square in the small of his back.

Dead Guard Walking lay face down on the floor. But that wouldn't do for Boricio. He wanted to see the fucker's pupils dilate. So, he kicked him in the ribs to roll him over. The guard tried to cover his face, but Boricio kicked his hands away, then put every one of his 200 pounds behind the heel he smashed into the fucker's face.

Dead Guard Walking was still trying to catch his breath from the knee to the gut, so he couldn't scream. It didn't help that he was choking on three teeth, not including the one he spit. Boricio casually walked to the baseball bat, picked it up, then swung it in wide, playful arcs.

"You all can take your blindfolds off now, and watch, as the game is about to begin. Hey batter, batter, swiiiing ... Hey batter, batter, swiiiing ... " Boricio looked around the room to see just what his little army was made of. Manny, Moe and Jack all wore morbid curiosity. Charlie was smiling. Adam was covering his eyes.

"I do wish we had more time together," Boricio cooed to the guard. "Unfortunately, we're going to end our rendezvous early, because I'm about to fuck you like you was paying for it."

Boricio raised the bat high above his head.

Dead Guard Walking cried out, "Wait!"

"What's that?" Boricio said, lowering the bat and leaning on it like he was the Monopoly Man slouching on his cane.

"Please," Dead Guard Walking said through tears, "Don't kill me."

Boricio laughed. "Wow, what happened to the high-octane bad ass? Mr. 'I am the motherfuckin' law?' Did he have to go potty?"

The man whimpered something as Boricio picked up the bat and shoved the ball end into the back of the man's neck, hard.

"Just as I thought, all fuckin' talk, you Try Hard wannabe. I could smell your counterfeit cock in cunt's clothing, fake-ass macho shit the minute you walked in."

"Please, I'll do anything," the guy said. "I'll help you escape."

"Anything?" Boricio asked, ignoring the offer of escape. "Hmmm, how about sucking my dick?"

Boricio smiled at the defeat in the man's eyes. It was like the opposite of a glimmer of hope in someone's eyes. Boricio often thought of it as a *glimmer of nope*.

"Open your mouth," Boricio said.

Dead Guard Walking stared.

"You deaf *and* dumb? I said open your fucking mouth!" Boricio raised the bat.

Dead Guard Walking opened his mouth.

"Now close your eyes and don't make me ask you twice."

Dead Guard Walking closed his eyes, bitch-ass tears running down his face. Boricio took the narrow end of the bat and shoved it in the man's mouth. Dead Guard Walking gagged, lurching back, trying not to vomit. He didn't try hard enough.

"What's that?" Boricio said, digging the bat deeper, forcing Dead Guard Walking to gag and swallow his own vomit.

Boricio laughed, squatting, pulling the bat just slightly out of the man's mouth, chunks of vomit on the handle.

"Say it," Boricio whispered into the man's ear.

"What?"

"Say you'll be my bitch."

Dead Guard Walking squirmed, and for a moment, seemed like he might try to fight. Boricio shoved the bat in deeper, causing the man to gag again, dry heaves this time.

"Say it, bitch," Boricio said.

"I'll be your bitch!" he cried.

Boricio smiled. This asshole had been too easy to break. He'd love to have an hour alone with him, to really show him what Boricio was capable of when properly motivated and inspired. So rare that his victims actually earned what was coming to them, so moments like these were special, and Boricio hated wasting them.

He pulled the bat from Dead Guard Walking's mouth. The man collapsed, wiping his mouth with the back of his hand, too ashamed to look up.

"Yoo hoo," Boricio whispered to get the man's attention as he raised the bat high above his head. The guard looked up as Boricio brought the bat down fast and hard. A dull thwap echoed through the tiny room. Not quite brain stew, but Dead Guard Walking had finally earned his name. Well, except for the walking part.

Boricio dropped the bat and turned to take a bow. The room was still, except for the sound of the bat rolling across the floor, but the men were on their feet, ready.

"What's next, boss?" Moe said.

No hesitation. Boricio walked up to Moe, threw a flat palm beneath his chin, then kicked his feet from under him. His arms were around Moe's neck in a second. Boricio twisted his head and snapped his spinal cord. Moe's body dropped to the floor like an empty sack.

"He was a traitor, and we can't be running with none like that," Boricio said. "I ended him for all of us."

He looked through the room; sure as shit they all agreed.

"So, we have to wait, but we have the advantage. Them fuckers out there don't know what happened in here, and whoever walks through that door is gonna have to face all five players of Team Fucking Boricio."

Boricio gestured around the empty room. "As you can see, not counting Robin there, we don't have any weapons other than these," he held up his fists, "so that means we're gonna have to make a decision, and we should do that before that door bitches open again. We can get the fuck out of here, or we can fight this shit out, stick around and get some goddamned answers. Seems like these cumdingers might know a thing or two. So who's for fighting and who's for staying?"

Charlie said, "I want to fight."

"Me, too." Adam was nodding his head.

Everyone else was silent.

Just as he figured, the two kids wanted to brawl while the old fuckers wanted to tuck it between their legs and bitch their way out of the blue.

Fine by me. Three's company, anyway.

They spent six minutes standing: Boricio in front, bat in hand, Manny and Jack in the middle, Charlie and Adam in back.

The door whined open, and Boricio smiled.

* * * *

CHAPTER 8
MARY OLSON

Oct. 16
Evening
Belle Springs, Missouri

 Mary did nothing but helplessly stare as her daughter vacillated between writhing uncomfortably on the couch beneath thick layers of guttural moaning, and falling into long silences where she lay so still Mary had to check her breathing. It had been nearly 12 hours, maybe more since they'd found Paola. Mary had stopped paying attention to time as it seemed to slow to a crawl as her daughter lay on the verge of death.
 Moaning occasionally turned to murmurs, but never clear enough to inform Mary of what Paola was trying to say or what she might be dreaming. The murmurs were just enough to give Mary an icy chill — her daughter was in danger, and she was powerless to do anything about it.
 Her dreams must have been vivid the way Paola was thrashing about. Her eyes had darted open, not once but

twice, as if to protest the atrocities happening behind drawn lids.

Mary felt helpless, unable to do anything to help her. She couldn't latch on to her daughter's thoughts as she had been able to do increasingly over the years. Specific thoughts would be nice, the kind she occasionally *overheard* and would have done anything to hold on to now, but Mary would have gladly settled for the psychological equivalent of a pulse.

She'd read about amputees who could feel a tingling where their limbs once were. Doctors called it phantom limb syndrome. Made perfect sense to her. Why shouldn't you feel the ghost of something that had been a part of you forever? Mary should be able to feel Paola, but her daughter wasn't even a phantom.

That was bad.

Worse was outside.

When she and Desmond returned to the hotel with Paola, another of the creatures had been milling about the parking lot. Desmond opened fire, but missed the shot, shattering the glass lobby doors behind it. His second shot tore through the creature's torso. A large chunk of its midsection fell in wet chunks to the ground before the rest of the creature followed.

At least the creatures were easy to kill. Or so they thought.

They went into the hotel, got Paola bundled in a bed, then barricaded the front door, leaving a space large enough to look out of, and shoot out of. Six hours passed until they saw another creature. After that, they started multiplying, more and more showing up every hour. Maybe a couple dozen were there when they went to sleep. At least twice that by morning. The number gained weight all day.

Mary stayed by Paola's side while Jimmy, John, and Desmond took turns with two-man guard duty. The creatures were congregating at the far edges of the parking lot, as though an invisible retaining wall were holding them at bay. The wall seemed to work just fine until early twilight when a trio of the beasts were suddenly standing just outside the lobby doors.

John was first to notice, and act, running outside and emptying his gun into the creatures. Jimmy and Desmond joined the volley, and the three of them managed to hold off the threat. And while nobody mentioned it, they all must have realized it had taken more bullets than before to bring down the creatures. Especially since the creatures seemed to be multiplying in numbers as the hours ticked by.

If Paola was better, it'd be different. At least then they'd have a chance to run. The creatures didn't seem terribly fast.

Yet as long as Paola was in this state, they couldn't leave. Though Mary couldn't hear or even feel any of her daughter's thoughts, she felt like Paola was ... waiting for something. Perhaps it was Mary's imagination, wishful thinking, or just trying to hold onto anything and afraid to do anything wrong, but the sensation was strong. Paola was waiting ... for something.

Desmond was suddenly behind her. "How you doing?"

She looked up, happy he was checking on her again.

Her smile was weak, but stronger than she felt. "Worried about Paola. What did you find out?"

"There's a bunch of bleakers ... "

"Bleakers?" Mary asked.

"Yeah, that's what Jimmy's callin' them, and the name kinda stuck. Anyway, there's a bunch still huddled around the Suburban and the cargo van, maybe 10 total. I've been watching them. Odd as it sounds, I think they're getting stronger, faster, maybe even smarter. I'm thinking we take them out, back the cargo van into the hotel, to hell with the front doors and the body of the van, throw a mattress in back for Paola, then hit the road in a hurry. We leave first thing in the morning."

"Okay," Mary wasn't thrilled but didn't want to explain that she wanted to wait, because she felt silly. Besides, Desmond seemed so full of hope as he laid out his plan.

"Desmond?"

"Yeah?"

"What do you think happened?"

He sighed, then sat next to Mary on the couch. "You're starting to make me feel bad every time you ask me. I wish I had a different answer, but I just don't."

"That scares me more than anything. You have a cargo van and guns, but you're not the survivalist type. You're the sharpest guy I know, and I'm sure you *at least* have a theory. Why are you so scared to tell me what it is?"

"I'm not scared; I just don't want to speculate. Information is everything. When you give the wrong information, even once, people trust you less."

"Sorry, Desmond, but your business is dead. If you have a theory, I want to hear. Come on, don't be stingy. Maybe whatever you say will be good enough to make me feel fine throwing my comatose child in the back of a cargo van while 'bleakers' wait outside to kill us."

"Well how can I argue with that?" Desmond stood. "Mind if I pour us an evening glass? I promise I'll drink just enough for good theory, but not enough to dull my rather awesome bleaker-killing abilities."

It felt good to laugh, so Mary was glad when she didn't hold it in.

"Yes, please. Make it two."

Desmond was back a moment later with two full glasses of Pinot noir.

"Here ya go."

He made her wait behind a long sip, then said, "Okay, now remember, I have no idea here, so I don't even count this as theory since that implies a hypothesis that would require an educated guess at least. This is me talking entirely out of my ass. Unmitigated bullshit. I love theory; I just don't like talking about it. At least not before I can link theory to facts. Before then, it's just popcorn. Yummy, but no nutritional value."

"Not everything has to have nutritional value," Mary said. "Sometimes, popcorn is great just because that's the best way to watch *Amelie*."

"True," Desmond smiled, raised his glass, took another long sip of wine, then continued. "What if this is the planet's way of starting over? Maybe Mother Nature is sending us back to dusty roads and wooden wheels, and it's all for a reason."

Mary took a sip of wine and looked curiously at Desmond.

"The technological achievements of the last decade are staggering. We may not have jet packs and moving sidewalks like *The Jetsons* promised, but we have video conferencing and a ton of stuff Hanna Barbara couldn't imagine. Yet, the more people get, the more they want. And the less happy they are with what they already have."

Desmond paused, took another sip, then set his glass on the end table beside him. "Do you know about Moore's Law?"

"Is that the one about technology doubling every five years, or something like that?"

"Sort of. I'm gonna get geeky, okay? Moore's Law states that the number of transistors you can place on an integrated circuit doubles every two years or so, each time at a reduced cost. And so far this has held true, for more than 50 years. This means the power of everything is exponentially climbing: processing speed, memory capacity, the number of pixels in your Canon."

Interest colored Mary's face. Desmond's story gathered speed. "So, the big question has always been, what happens *after* Moore's Law hits a wall? Best-guess experts place that possibility around 2020, or soon after when suddenly we hit a technological singularity."

Mary's face must've given away how crazy she thought Desmond was being. He laughed, sending a stream of Pinot into the air. "I'm sorry," he said, still laughing. "I realize I'm being ridiculous and confusing. The whole idea of this conversation is just ... ludicrous ... I mean, I think about this stuff in my head all the time, but never out loud to my neighbors and never because it might have value outside my own brain. Not to mention I'm probably not making a whole lot of sense."

Mary took her second sip of wine. "I'm completely following," she said with a smile, "and loving every word. Go on."

"Okay. Thanks." A final laugh, then, "You've seen *The Terminator* movies; *The Matrix*; *I, Robot*; *Battlestar Galactica*; all the end-of-the-world, robots-win-and-we-all-lose type movies, right?"

"Of course."

"That's the technological singularity in action. Technology gets smarter and faster until it's smarter and faster than us. The created become the creators. Fascinating concept. So, what if that's in play here? Maybe we created something without realizing it, or maybe nature created something to fight back against something we did? I don't know the who or why, and really, I couldn't even guess, but something about this seems almost ... *organized*."

Mary shuddered at the thought of the bodies at the river. She leaned forward in her chair, but before she could open her mouth a horrible clang came from outside, too loud to be an accident.

Desmond sprang from the couch, gun in hand by his third step. John and Jimmy were on guard duty, each stationed on the far end of the lobby. They had moved to the middle and were standing side by side in front of the doors. Jimmy pointed, "It's that one."

He meant the bleaker in front, but three more were directly behind, four of them moving like an arrow flying toward them in slow motion.

"Alright guys, we have time. Aim before you fire. And go for the forehead. Don't aim anywhere else and don't pull the trigger until you think you can make it. I've got the leader."

Desmond stepped outside, Jimmy and John followed. All three found their targets then held their aim. John shot first — over the head of his target and into a tree trunk. Desmond's was next with a bullet that whizzed by the leader's cheek. Jimmy shot last. No telling where his bullet went, but it wasn't anywhere close.

Mary stood behind the three men, still inside the lobby.

John and Jimmy's second shots rang in unison, then disappeared together.

Desmond's second bullet sailed straight through the leader's face, which crumbled to the ground even as its body raced forward before falling after three headless steps.

The remaining creatures regrouped, suddenly single file, but still moving slowly. Desmond got another shot off, and the front creature dropped. Almost as if on cue, the two creatures behind, split up, charging the front of the hotel at full speed, forcing the men to split their attention, and increasing the odds that one of them wouldn't hit their target and the creature would break through.

"Take the one on the left," Desmond shouted. Three guns emptied themselves in the creature, and it joined its brothers on the pavement.

The final bleaker was on them in seconds. Jimmy kept clicking his empty gun toward it, panicked. John put his arms around Jimmy's waist and pulled him back inside the hotel. Desmond charged toward the bleaker with a swift kick to its midsection, then circled behind it, pulled a second gun from a shoulder strap, and shot the creature dead.

Desmond glared at the parking lot where the rest of the creatures shrank back behind a pair of vans. He then went back into the hotel, out of breath.

"That was close." he said.

"We have to go!" John said, panicked almost to the point of shrieking. "They're moving in packs now! We can't sit this out the night. We need to get Paola in the van and move out now."

"We can't do that," Mary said. "She's waiting for something."

"What?"

"I know it sounds crazy, but she is. She's waiting for something in her sleep. I don't know what it is, and I can't feel her at all. But I *know* she's waiting. And I'm not leaving here until she's ready."

"This is crazy," John said turning away from Mary and talking directly to Desmond. "You can't possibly agree with this?"

"Not exactly," Desmond said. "But I don't disagree. Mary, you sure?"

"Yes," Mary said, somewhat offended that Desmond didn't say more to support her.

Suddenly, a scream from Paola. Mary spun around, dropping next to her daughter's side.

"See — something is happening inside her right now. We, or at least I, have to see it through. If nothing happens by morning, we can leave, no argument from me. I'll even load her in the van myself."

"Happy?" Desmond asked John.

"No. But I'm not *unhappy*."

John walked away, and Desmond followed, leaving Mary alone with her daughter.

**

Paola lay still throughout the night. Mary found sleep impossible for more than a minute or two at a time during the night. By morning, she was exhausted, and barely able to keep her eyes open.

John agreed to wait until the afternoon since little was happening outside and the creatures' numbers no longer appeared to be growing. That gave Mary a chance to catch some sleep while Desmond watched over them both.

"I think something's happening," Desmond said, waking Mary with a start.

She sat up, looked at Paola. Her skin was warm, and color returned to her face. Her mouth opened and she murmured something — a handful of not-quite-connected syllables that sounded mostly happy. Like she was talking in her sleep.

"Something's happening," Mary called to the entire lobby.

"Over here, too!" Jimmy was pointing outside, causing Mary's heart to speed up. She couldn't handle another rush of monsters. Not now.

But the deafening sound outside wasn't from monsters, but rather a helicopter.

"W-T-F?" Jimmy said.

"Did you just *say* 'WTF?'" Desmond shook his head and rolled his eyes.

Mary looked toward the doors, though she couldn't see the hole in the barrier from where she was. She looked back down at her daughter." She squeezed Paola's hand and whispered, "I'll be back."

She went to the door and looked outside, beads of sweat nesting on her forehead as a chill ran down her body. Walking toward them was an old man, tall and thin, next to a small boy who couldn't have been more than 8.

The boy.

That's who they were waiting for. She knew it. Praise be to whoever sent him, even if it was the same, horrible god who had up and ended the world.

* * * *

CHAPTER 9
LUCA HARDING

    Luca and Will flew through the sky in the helicopter they'd just grabbed from the local airport. This helicopter wasn't like the first one. It was old and beat up. It reminded Luca of the "weekend car" Mr. Roberson kept in his garage under a big, gray blanket. They had to trade the plane, which made Luca a little sad because it wasn't nearly as noisy as the helicopter and felt a lot, lot safer, but it was okay because Will said there wouldn't be enough runway for takeoffs or landings, so they needed something that was easier to move around with while they looked for the people.
    Will said they were going to some place called the "Drury Inn." Luca asked him about 100 million times how he knew where the people were and even though Will tried to explain it repeatedly, it didn't make sense to Luca. Will said, "Instinct is the nose of the brain, and as long as you're willing to listen, it usually tells you everything you need to know before your brain has a chance to figure it out."
    Luca was only 8, but he knew when grown-ups were keeping part of their stories a secret. There was something about Will's dreams he didn't want Luca to know.

Four *Drury Inns* were in the area where Will said the people might be, but Will had a feeling that they'd be in the one they were now flying to.

"I still don't understand how I can help her." Luca said. He didn't believe he could do anything to help the girl from their dreams, but Will kept insisting that Luca would just know exactly what to do when the time was right.

"I'll tell you how it works if you promise not to think I'm crazy?" Will offered.

Luca thought about it for a minute, then said, "But what if I think you're crazy anyway? Will you be mad at me?"

Will laughed, "Of course not. Think we should give it a shot?"

"Okay."

"I think, in fact I'm sure, you have something called The Touch. People, everything really, are packed full of energy. That energy blends with their environment. Most energy stays in the body, you know, the thing that lets you carry your brain with you everywhere you go." Will tapped Luca's noggin then gave him a wink.

"Am I making sense so far?"

"Only kind of," Luca said. Then added, "Well, not really."

Will laughed. "It's simple. Because living things are always exchanging energy, someone with the *Touch* can clear the channels needed for healing." Will was quiet for a moment, then said, "Do you know how often your mom used to get her hair cut?"

Luca thought, then said, "Yes. She goes on the same Tuesdays when she brings the bread home from the bakery that has the fruits that taste like candy. That's one time every month."

"Does her hair ever look much different?"

Luca shook his head. "No, it always looks the same."

"Why do you think she paid for a haircut every month if her hair never looked any different?"

"Because she likes to look pretty."

"Good answer," Will said. "If your mom stopped getting her hair cut, her ends would split. Hair doesn't grow well while the ends are split. People with the *Touch*, people like you, Luca, know how to make cells grow again, kind of like a hairdresser gives your mother a fresh haircut and makes her hair all thick and shiny."

That's probably why whenever Mommy was sad, I only had to hug her to make the smiles come back. Maybe it's why Daddy calls me Liquid Sunshine.

Will's attention was suddenly out the window. He slapped his knee, then pointed out the window and said, "There it is!" He swung the helicopter in a wide arc, heading left as he lowered them toward the hotel parking lot.

Luca saw the *Drury*, and it made something inside his stomach twist and tingle as the frames of reality and dreams started to overlap.

Will pointed below at the clusters of creatures that carpeted the concrete. They were a lot like the ones Luca saw laying in the empty corners in his dreams, except these ones were standing and moving around.

"What *are* they?"

"Not sure," Will shook his head. "That's the first time I've seen them outside my sleep, at least since the first day."

"You've seen them before?"

"Yeah, two in fact. These look stronger, and they're standing. Ones I saw could barely move. I don't know what they are."

"Are you scared?"

"Not yet," Will said. "Besides, we've got our guard dog."

Dog Vader barked, which made Luca laugh and pet the dog behind his thick, furry ears.

Will set the helicopter at the edge of the parking lot, then hopped from the cockpit and held his hand out for Luca. Luca's eyes were wide with fear, but he took Will's hand and jumped to the concrete.

"Don't let go, okay," Will turned to Luca and squeezed his hand. "Trust me."

Will pointed to the lobby doors. "We need to get through those doors. Don't take your eyes off the glass, and don't let go of my hand. We'll walk slowly. And we'll get there in less than a minute, safe and sound. I promise. Okay?"

"Okay, Will."

Dog Vader leaped from the cockpit, and the three of them walked side by side toward the front doors of the *Drury*. The dog's lip was curled, and his teeth were bared, growling at the scary monsters that surrounded them.

To Luca's surprise, the monsters kept their distance, as if he, Will, and Dog Vader were the scary ones, not them.

When they reached the front doors, three men came out to greet them.

"We're here," Will whispered patting Luca on the back. "You did perfectly."

Will released Luca's hand then walked to the man standing in front of the other two. The people in front of the boarded-up doors were the people from the dream, including the teenager and the woman standing behind them. She was the little girl's mother.

Luca couldn't see the girl, but he could feel her close by.

"I'm Desmond," the man said, offering his hand to Will.

Will shook Desmond's hand and introduced himself to the group, then cleared his throat. "I don't know how else to say this, so I guess I'll just pour the words from my mouth and see how they fall."

He faced the woman. "Ma'am," he said, "I believe your daughter needs some help, and I'm quite sure that's why we're here."

The woman gasped, then nodded, and burst into tears. She gestured for Will and Luca to come inside the lobby. Desmond, the leader, put his hand on her arm and whispered in her ear. She nodded, then kept walking toward the makeshift bed where her daughter was sleeping.

Will and Luca stood side by side in front of the girl. "What's her name?" Luca asked.

"It's Paola." Her mom said, brushing the girl's cheek.

Paola.

"Are you ready?" Will asked Luca.

Luca said nothing, just looked at Will and nodded, then took a step toward Paola.

It's just like when Mommy gets her haircut. The girl needs to be pretty so her energy will start working and make her better again. I know how to do it if I just do what I know, like when I don't think about anything but hugging Mommy and then her sad spiders go away. She said I'm the best at that, and not just because I'm her little boy.

Luca placed his palms on Paola's forehead and squeezed his eyes shut.

* * * *

CHAPTER 10
PAOLA OLSON

Paola had no idea how long she had been trying to figure out where she was, but it felt like forever. Time had definitely gotten weird. So had everything else.

The world was familiar, but ... soupy.

It was Daddy at the gas station, but something awful happened and he suddenly wasn't Daddy. He did something bad to me ... something to my thoughts ... then he went away and left me ... here.

She was lying on the ground of the gas station for a while, until her mom and Desmond came to get her. They drove her back to the hotel.

Why can't they hear me? They just keep looking at me, worried.

She didn't feel like a ghost, or like she imagined being a ghost would feel like. It felt more like she was standing on the other side of the looking glass in a Lewis Carroll book. She could see her body, her mom, and Desmond in the vehicle, as if she were watching through a giant window that only she could see through. Paola pushed her hands hard against the world in front of her until the web of reality pushed back, seeping between her splayed fingers.

She gasped and fell a step back.

She looked around her again.

At the far end of the lobby was a giant, oak door. It hadn't been there before, and couldn't have been real since it was too tall to fit the lobby, with a small moat circling the front. A moat full of dead people.

That's where the kitchen used to be.

The door turned into a drawbridge, and the moat multiplied 20 times in size. Paola started walking toward it. That dark thing that had pretended to be Daddy had promised her answers. It was probably inside.

She stepped through the large, oak door where the kitchen used to be, but no kitchen counters were on the other side. Just a black hallway with a small square of light at the center.

The hallway wasn't long, but when Paola reached the far end and stepped into the light on the other side, she was obviously on some sort of neverending road. And while it wasn't yellow, it was made of brick. The walls around her had fallen away, replaced with flowing fields of grass as far as she could see in every direction.

Above her was the clearest, bluest sky she'd ever seen — an endless canopy hanging over miles of neatly bricked road that wound through a meadow, across a flower-carpeted ground, then up into rolling knolls of emerald grass, where it vanished at the horizon.

The road was a thing of fairytales, but something about it was scary. False like the thing that had pretended to be her daddy. She turned back around, but her opportunity to return to the hotel vanished, along with the door and the entire hotel. Nothing but grass. And the road.

She took a step forward, and then another.

Paola kept walking for what felt like years, in that way that time seemed to sometimes stretch in dreams. She desperately wanted to run into the thick, tall forests that had cropped up on either side of the meadow and see everything she could not see.

It was wonderful where she could not go; she just knew it. That's where the Fantasy lived, all the make-believe her mind had ever made, frolicking free, away from the memories and hard textures of truth.

But I have to stay on the path. It would be terrible to get lost ... here.

If she didn't keep walking she would never get to the end of the road. And that's where the answers were; her dream logic told her.

Without warning, the scenery changed, instantly shifting from rich, warm colors to a sea of grays. From Oz back to Kansas.

Flat landscape gave way to a tapestry of small, gray hills at the front, larger ones in back, growing in size until they crashed into charcoal- smeared mountains that stretched high and into churning, gray clouds overhead.

Paola was walking for hours, or perhaps seconds, when she realized what the mountains were made of. At first, they seemed like nothing more than ash-colored wedges of dull pulp, but as they grew in size, they sharpened in detail.

Piles and heaps and rivers of refuse were there; herculean hallways of nothing but garbage: cracked plastic, shredded paper, twisted metal.

The piles, along with the rising landscape getting closer to the clouds above, sent Paola into a cold claustrophobia. Paola saw a figure in the distance standing on the right side of the road, its shoulders slouched and its back to Paola. It looked like it was holding something close to its body as it swayed from side to side.

She inched toward the figure, and brushed against a gnarled root coming out of the ground. Only it wasn't a root, but rather, more garbage. As she touched it, her mind flashed back to when she was 6 years old.

They'd been looking everywhere for her kitten, Doodles. But the cat had gotten out when Paola had accidentally left the front door open. Someone was at the front door. Their neighbor, Mr. Jerry. He said he'd found the kitten in the road. It had been hit by a car. He held it in his hands, its rear legs crushed. Paola cried both as a child, and now as she relived the memory.

That's when she realized that each piece of the garbage was, in fact, made from her memories. She wasn't sure how she knew it, but she was suddenly certain that the memories were painful and could swallow her whole, if given the chance. As if the memories were stripped of nutrients and only the bad stuff was left.

The stuff that made you cry or feel lonely; hide or want to die.

Paola gasped when she realized the person on the side of the road was her father. He was pushing a broom and clearing the road of any stray or dangerous memories. He turned to Paola. "Not quite safe to pass yet," he shook his head. "Been going as fast as I can, but they just keep piling up."

"What happened?"

"Something upset the apple cart. Plowed right through, fast as it could. Looks like it took everything with it." Paola's dad pointed off the trail toward a black, bricked spire rising from the ground and pointing toward the sky. "See that, that's where *he* is."

"Who?"

"You know who," he said. "Same one who sent you inside here."

"Why is he inside me? I can feel him in me."

"He's not whole. Most of him already left, but a part of him broke off. Like a snake."

"Do I have to go inside?" Paola asked, looking up at the black castle, and the dark memories surrounding her suddenly seemed less scary by comparison.

"No, sure don't," he shook his head. You could wake right now if you want to. Everyone will see you, and you'll see them. But you won't know who they are, no matter how hard you try. You won't even know who *you are*, not ever again. Because all this," he waved his hand at the mountain of memories. "Every bit of it's gonna be gone."

"What's inside the castle?" Paola asked.

"I don't know anything you don't," he said, "but I can tell you what you'd probably guess anyway if you think it will help."

Paola smiled. The man who was only sort of a memory of her father had said that exactly like her real daddy would have.

"Okay," she said. "Then tell me that."

"That castle is the middle of you. It's your soul. Inside, there's something to fight or face, or team up with or tell off. I don't think you can know until you get there, but you can expect it to get rough. Just make it through and never forget what's on the other side of the spire."

"What's on the other side?"

"Me, your mom, the rest of your life, of course. But you can't have it without this." He snapped his fingers, and the warm colors of Oz flashed across the sky before going dim a second later.

"Are you still alive?" she asked.

"What do you think?"

Paola didn't know how to answer the question.

"It's time for me to go," he said. "Time for both of us to go."

Paola went to hug her father, but he disappeared just as she drew close. So did everything else, except the black castle, barely visible in the darkness. Paola couldn't even see the ground, her feet vanishing in the clouds which flowed like thick, fast-moving fog blanketing the world.

Every step Paola took toward the castle caused it to move two steps farther away. She was walking a few minutes before deciding to try a step back. She was rewarded with the castle moving two steps closer toward her. Cold, wet wind whipped her and lashed at her hair, as she wrapped her arms around herself for warmth.

Paola continued to walk slowly backward, a foot at a time, careful not to fall over the edge of a narrow road, which was now high in the air with nothing but endless empty on either side.

Each step sent her back into another awful memory.

Small memories seemed massive, each one an attacker in the dark at her most unarmed. She longed to turn, run toward the barren land behind her, then keep running until her dying breath. It would be better than this.

But she couldn't.

The blackness swam over her face, threatening to swallow her.

She was going to die.

The dark memories were in her mind, her lungs, her body.

Every step back was another cool blade warmed by her blood, but she kept pushing forward, knowing that the icy black of a starless universe was better than the hollow void of a doused existence.

I'm supposed to be in bed, but Mom and Dad are asleep. And the movie I'm not supposed to be watching has horrible monsters and terrible screaming. And fires. Lots and lots of fires. When a mouse scurries across the floor, my screams bring my parents running into the room.

I'm 8, saying Bloody Mary into the bathroom mirror. I know it's just my mind playing tricks, and not something staring back at me with red eyes through the glass, but my heart feels like it's going to explode and no one can hear me scream.

I'm in Grandma's room, just after she died. I've fallen asleep on the bed facing the mirror. I wake up slowly and can hear Grandma's whisper behind me. Her image shimmers in the glass, and I'm sure there is more than one reality.

No more.

Paola peeled the black from her body, yanked it from her throat, then stepped outside her memories, letting terror drop to the road like an empty wetsuit. Paola found herself standing in front of the open castle door. A dim-red light bathed the walls inside the castle, making it seem almost warm. While she was so cold.

A booming voice thundered through the black.

"Very good," it said. "You're almost here. Just a few more steps."

Paola crossed the bridge then stepped into a huge room with massive ceilings that she couldn't see through the clouds. The floor was carpeted in plush black, with threads so deep and thick they looked like colonies of crawling worms.

Across the room was another open door. Paola stepped inside. It was a small room with nothing in it. She expected a throne room with evil claiming his castle seat, but fear and evil often thrived in whisper.

"What do you want from me?" she asked the empty room.

Except the room wasn't empty. The voice was everywhere. And when it spoke, its waves rolled through Paola.

"Nothing," it said. "I've taken everything I need already. The only thing I want now is to give something back to you."

"You don't want to give me anything."

"Oh, that's not true," the voice soothed, flowing through her and making her feel almost ... *good*. "I've taken so much, now I long to ease your pain."

"By taking my memories until there's nothing left of me?" Paola shook her head. "No thanks. Tell me how to get my memories back and how to leave. You're inside me, that means I know what you do, and you have to tell me."

Something screeched inside the walls.

"You can leave whenever you want," it hissed. "I'm not holding you here."

"Yes, you are."

The door where she'd entered disappeared, and a new one opened on the other side of the room, slowly widening to Oz-colored meadows. "See," the voice said. "What are you waiting for?"

Paola looked out the window then shook her head.

The voice started to rumble as the walls began to shake and the red light within them grew brighter, hotter.

She closed her eyes and started slowly rocking back and forth, chanting to herself to keep the voice's long strings of nasty words away.

"LEAVE!" the voice thundered.

Thick smoke smoldered through the room. It was what was left of the creature.

Paola smiled. Its anger was making her stronger.

The Oz-colored meadows outside flickered with ash, then turned warm again.

"Looks like your lie is wearing off," she said.

The voice bellowed. "I'll kill everyone left in the world, starting with your mother." The black smoke swirled through the room, then added, "Then I will find your father."

Something collapsed inside Paola. The evil had found her single biggest, creeping fear. She tried to keep the whimper inside, but lost it anyway.

The voice went still, and every inch of her world was quickly turning to black, the red walls of the castle now cold and dark. Wind howled through the room, wet and *so cold*.

She squeezed her eyes shut, bit her lip, and started murmuring.

You're not here. You left because you're an empty disease, and I was too good for you. You can't hurt my mother, and you can't hurt my father. You want me to leave because then you can take over.

"But I won't let you," she said, standing up and opening her eyes as the smoke swirled, gathering strength from the wind, growing thicker, and louder.

"Goooooooooooooooo!" it shouted, its voice an almost mechanical echo.

"You go!" she yelled, "YOU GO!"

The clouds above met the swirling smoke around her, spiraling into a funnel cloud of chaos that picked her up and lifted her toward the unseen ceiling. Scraps of memories slammed into her from all sides, coming and going so fast they blurred into one another, causing her to cry, fear, panic, rage, and scream all at once.

I won't go.

She lifted higher, her body now spinning in the outer band of the swirling cloud, like Dorothy caught in the tornado.

She closed her eyes and thought of her parents, struggling to hold onto good memories as bad ones continued to assail her from all sides. Each time they hit her, they ripped into her body, piercing it like knives.

I won't go.

Something slammed into her, and she felt her body fly higher and higher, fear coursing through her, certain she was going to hit the ceiling. But she kept flying upward, caught in the tide.

I won't go.

And then, like that, she was in free fall through the clouds, the dark smoke gone. She closed her eyes, praying she wouldn't plummet to the Earth, only to die. Before she fell, though, she passed out.

When she woke, she was back in Oz, under blue skies and a warm sun. She was still in the dream, but reality seemed closer than ever. She ran as fast as she could through the daisy-covered meadow to find a boy her age, or slightly older, swinging on a swing set in the middle of a clearing.

He slowed to a stop. "Would you like to swing with me?" he said pointing to the empty seat next to him. "I've been saving this one for you."

* * * *

CHAPTER 11
LUCA HARDING

This doesn't feel like I thought it would. It's like swimming, except it's air and not water, and everything is clear instead of blurry. It's like swimming through the sky with special goggles.

Everything faded to white, and Luca found himself walking through a large meadow with a tall, wooden swing a hundred or so feet in front of him. Two empty seats were there. Luca chose the one on the left and started to swing, saving the other for Paola.

He could see her not too far off, stuck in the shadows with that thing that hid in the *terrible scary* and made all the good dreams go bad.

Once she knows I'm out here she'll want to come and join me.

Luca knew it with certainty, so he wasn't at all surprised when Paola managed to make the bad disappear, then stepped outside and into their shared sun. She saw Luca, then crossed the meadow, and stood beside the empty swing as he slowed to a stop.

"Would you like to swing with me?" he said. "I've been saving this one for you."

She said yes, then sat and started to pump her legs back and forth.

Up and down ... up and down ... up and down.

Luca swung, too.

Up and down ... up and down ... up and down.

They were quiet for a while until Paola finally broke the silence.

"Thank you."

"For what?"

"Coming to help me."

"I'm not really sure what I did."

"Me either, but everything looks so pretty now."

Back and forth ... back and forth ... back and forth.

Back and forth ... back and forth ... back and forth.

"Do you know what happened?"

Luca shook his head. "Even Will doesn't know."

"Who is Will?"

"My friend. He's the one who brought me here. He's been dreaming about you and your mom, just like me."

"Do you know what's supposed to happen now?"

Luca shook his head again.

"Do you know how we get home?"

"I'm not sure, but I think we can probably go whenever we really want to."

"Do you want to?"

"Not yet," Luca said.

"Me neither. I miss my mom, but everything here is so ... calm."

"Yeah."

Back and forth ... back and forth ... back and forth.

Back and forth ... back and forth ... back and forth.

The Indian was leaning against a tall Jacaranda tree, like the kind across the street from Luca's house in Las Orillas. The fallen blossoms painted purple on the ground around him as the Indian looked into the sky and smoked his giant, plastic pipe.

"Do you see the Indian over there?" Paola asked.

Luca laughed, "Yes, he's my friend. He's actually my dog."

Paola didn't seem surprised. "What's his name?" she asked. "The dog, not the Indian."

"I call him Dog Vader, but he doesn't really like that very much. So I call him Kick, but only out loud. And most time, I forget, and call him Dog Vader."

Paola laughed, and Luca joined her, then they fell into quiet together.

They swung in silence. They had no way to count minutes in a place that didn't have any hours, but they swung back and forth and up and down until Paola finally flew from the top of her swing and landed with both feet in the soft, flowing grass.

"Okay," she said. "I'm ready."

Luca slowed to a stop, then joined Paola. He took her hand, because it seemed like the right thing to do, then they walked toward the rainbow together.

The rainbow was both near and far. They took only a few steps then the colors scattered into darkness. They found themselves blinking awake beneath the dim light of the hotel lobby.

"Mom!" Paola yelled.

Her mom was sobbing. "I'm so glad you're okay!"

Everyone seemed happy, but Luca felt another feeling in the room as well.

They're staring at me, and they're scared. They're looking at me, but their thoughts are the same as if they were looking into the terrible scary.

Luca noticed that his clothes were all torn, including his shoes.

Will's hand was on Luca's shoulder. He dropped to his knee and whispered, "Come with me," then led Luca across the room to a pair of full-length mirrors on the other side.

Luca stared at his reflection.

He was him, but not like he remembered.

He was now slightly taller than Paola, with a full head of hair that fell just past his shoulders. The face staring back at him was at least a good five years older, and looked remarkably like his father's.

* * * *

CHAPTER 12
TEAGAN MCLACHLAN

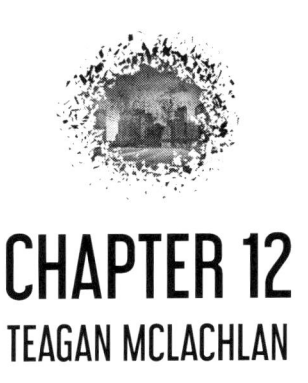

Teagan stayed hidden in the stairwell as Ed negotiated with the emo-looking guy with the bat. When the guy swore that he didn't mean any harm, Teagan cringed, praying Ed wouldn't shoot first and ask questions later as he'd been doing since they met.

When she heard the bat hit the ground, relief washed over her. She was fairly sure Ed wouldn't shoot an unarmed guy. If he had, she might have lost it right there and taken off, as far and as fast as she could.

She was grateful to Ed for helping her and possibly saving her life twice, but that nagging part in her brain was still reminding her that not once had he waited to find out if the people he killed were friend or foe. Shoot first, ask questions later. Except when people were dead, there wasn't a lot they could answer to.

Had the men in the gas station posed an *actual threat* to them? Maybe they were just people looking for answers, like them. And who was to say the helicopter wasn't from the government looking to help?

When Ed started talking rather than shooting, Teagan found her breath again. Perhaps they'd found someone else after all. Someone they could work with to figure out what was going on, or maybe find others who were still here.

When Teagan heard Jade, she emerged from the stairwell.

Ed's daughter looked like she was in her early 20s, with auburn hair and green eyes like her. If Jade's hair had been long instead of a short pixie cut, she could have easily passed for Teagan's slightly older sister. Their resemblance was uncanny, which made Ed finding Teagan, a girl who looked so much like his daughter, after the rest of the world vanished, a most odd coincidence.

Yet, there they were, all breathing just a few feet apart.

Jade ran to her father and threw her arms around him. Ed held tight like he'd not seen her in forever, and maybe never would again. As the two embraced, Teagan felt a longing for her own father. Not the man she'd come to know, but the one who'd once been a kind, doting daddy, not yet reduced to shreds by life's slings and arrows. He hadn't been that man in a long time, so Teagan was only missing a ghost of a ghost. A good feeling, once remembered.

As the two hugged, Jade's eyes opened, then found Teagan, making her feel like the biggest third wheel ever in the history of ever.

Jade looked confused. She pulled away from her dad, and walked toward Teagan with a smile, "Hi, my name is Jade," she said with a confidence that surprised Teagan, though it shouldn't have, given how direct and confident Ed was.

"I'm Teagan," she said, shaking the girl's hand.

"I ran into her on the road. Her parents vanished right in front of her while they were driving home," Ed said, almost apologetically. "She didn't have anyone else."

It was then Jade noticed Teagan's swollen belly.

"Oh," Jade said, "How far along are you?"

"Five months," she said, her hands instinctively massaging her baby's home.

"Do you know the sex yet?"

"I didn't want to know. Wanted it to be a surprise. Didn't expect this sorta surprise, though," she said, shrugging her shoulders at the missing world.

"This is Ken," she said, introducing the guy with the bat, who looked like a college student, too. A good-looking, emo-artsy-coffee house type.

"Hi," she said, shaking Ken's hand.

"Did you hear from your mother?" Ed asked.

"No, I called when the phones were still working. But no answer. I was gonna go to her house, but then we saw the things."

"What things?" Ed asked.

"Whatever they are," Ken said, "They're nothing like I've ever seen."

Ken looked frightened, as if he'd seen a ghost, monster, or something else unimaginable. Ed looked like he was about to make a joke, but then swallowed it, perhaps not knowing the relationship between Jade and Ken.

"Come here," Ken said, "I'll show you what I'm talking about. Do you mind?" he asked, pointing to his bat.

Ed's foot found the handle, pushed against it, propped it up, grabbed the business end, then handed it to Ken in one quick movement. Teagan wasn't sure if that was Ed showing his alpha dog status as dads tended to do with guys who dared to date their daughters, or if it was just Ed being the all-business, all-bad ass, all the time that he was. Teagan was surprised to find herself laughing inside.

Pity the poor guy who wants to date Jade.

They went into Apartment 410, which technically didn't belong to Ken. He had been staying with a friend the night everyone vanished. When Ken said *friend*, and mentioned the friend was a guy, with a look in his eye and a momentary pause, Teagan figured maybe Ed had nothing to worry about concerning Ken and Jade.

Room 410 crackled with a blast of static coming from a battery-operated baby monitor.

"The other one's downstairs," Ken said. "That's how we knew you were downstairs. We heard you in the hallway, and I waited with the bat, just in case."

"In case what?" Teagan asked, surprising herself with the question.

"You were one of the monsters."

Ed laughed.

"You didn't see any when you were driving up? They've been outside since yesterday," Ken asked.

"Monsters?" Ed said, "No, I can't say we saw any *'monsters'* on the way in."

"No, I'm serious," Ken said, "Take a look."

Ken led them to the window, then pulled the shades aside three inches, raised a pair of binoculars to his eyes, looked outside, then handed the binoculars to Ed.

"There, in front of the building across the street."

Ed took the binoculars, adjusted the focus on top, then froze.

It took him a while to find his voice. When he did, he said, "What the hell *are those?*"

"Monsters," Jade said. "They killed a girl who left the complex last night."

Teagan couldn't believe what she was hearing. "You're saying *monsters* killed someone?"

"Tore her to shreds," Ken said, eyes dead serious.

"Lemme see," Teagan said, joining Ed at the window.

Ed ignored her at first, not wanting to take his eyes off whatever was in his sights.

"Lemme see," Teagan pleaded.

Ed turned to her, then shook his head, "I don't think you should see this."

She grabbed the binoculars from his hands and raised them to her eyes, focused, and saw the walking nightmares for herself. She was suddenly confused, and dizzy, as if the world were sliding out from under her.

The air gained weight and pushed her to the floor.

**

When she came to, Teagan was in a bed, daylight bleeding through thick, black curtains.

"Where am I?" she asked, head pounding. Her hands found her baby, and for a terrifying moment, she thought she couldn't feel anything inside her. Then it kicked, as if to answer her fears, and Teagan found herself crying, then cursing herself for being so emotional.

"You okay?" a voice beside her said.

Jade was lying next to her. "You fainted. But Dad said you'd be okay. I said I'd stay with you."

Jade handed her a bottle of water.

Teagan was surprisingly thirsty. And hungry. "Thank you," she said, gulping half the bottle. "Where is everyone?"

"Dad and Ken went to search the other rooms for more weapons, though I'm not sure if they'll find any."

"Why are they getting weapons?" Teagan asked.

"My dad said we're gonna need all the weapons we can find to protect ourselves."

"Yeah, that sounds like your dad," Teagan said smiling.

"What do you mean?" Jade asked, face suddenly serious.

"Well, you know how your dad is, all that secret agent stuff." Teagan said, waiting for Jade's muscles to relax. Instead, her cheeks tightened.

"What did my dad *tell you?*"

Teagan was afraid she'd said too much.

What if Ed is so secret an agent that not even his own family knows what he does for a living?

Teagan was sure Ed said that his family knew what he did. *Right?* No, she wasn't certain. But she was mortified that she might have dropped a ball that would destroy an already fractured relationship between Ed and his daughter.

"He didn't tell me much, just that he worked for the government." Teagan considered saying he was also an ace with a gun and had taken down two men and a helicopter, but decided to keep her big mouth shut.

"Listen," Jade said, "I don't know what my dad told you, or what you *think* you know about him, but he's not some government agent, a spy, or cop, or whatever crazy thing he told you."

"What do you mean?" Teagan said, "He told me you two never saw each other because he was always on the road working for the government."

"On 'the road,'" Jade said, with a bitter laugh, "That's cute. I guess that's what he's calling it when he's on the run from the law, 'on the road.' My dad isn't what he says he is, or who you think he is. He's been on the run for four years for murder. The reason we didn't see each other was because he was locked in a mental institution until he broke out a few months ago."

Teagan felt dizzy again.

* * * *

::EPISODE 5::
(FIFTH EPISODE OF SEASON ONE)
"WELCOME DARKNESS"

CHAPTER 1
LUIS TORRES

Oct. 16
Early morning
New York City

"I have to find them." Brent said, staring at the thousands of bodies piled in Times Square. "I have to see for myself."

"There's too many." Luis said, "Even if your wife and son *are* in there, and we have no reason to think they are, we'd be here all day searching. And then we'll miss the ferry to Black Island. Plus, we've still got Comatose Joe waiting in the car."

"Go without me," Brent said, walking through rows of stacked corpses, searching for any sign of his family. "I'm staying here."

"You can't stay here, those creatures are gonna come back."

"I don't care!" Brent said, fighting tears. "Let them. I need to know."

Luis shook his head, letting out a long sigh and scanning the fog for signs of more creatures.

But it was just them and the dead ... for now. Staring at the bodies, he found it curious none seemed to have suffered injury. Whoever or whatever killed these people, it probably wasn't the monsters he and Brent had encountered. For one, the creatures would have left the corpses in pieces. And he doubted the bodies would be so neatly stacked.

Whoever did the stacking, Luis was guessing it was humans. And the only people organized and with manpower enough to dispose of bodies in such an orderly manner would be the government. And if it were the government, Luis had to wonder how deeply they were involved in whatever happened. How much did they know?

If he and his group had known of the event before it happened, odds are, someone else did, too. Someone on the inside. Someone prepared. He doubted the government had anything to do with whatever caused the deaths and disappearances of so many people. Even though he knew his government was capable of atrocities over the years, he doubted it would actually kill so many of its own people. Which meant they likely knew *something* was going to happen, maybe even *what*, but had no actual part in it. Nor could they prevent it.

So, they did what they could, collected the dead, and organized.

Even though Luis had dreamed of this event and had known many would die, it did nothing to prepare him for the reality or the pain of seeing so many bodies. Staring at the faces of so many dead men, women, and children, many with wide-open and vacant eyes, pierced a part of his heart he'd worked most of his life to harden. Watching Brent move from stack to stack, searching for his family, dug the blade deeper.

"What are you gonna do when we don't find them?" Luis asked. "These bodies are stacked! Are we gonna start moving people, peeling them off the piles like we're looking for the TV remote in a pile of clothes in our bedroom?"

"You don't have to do anything!" Brent snapped, "Just go. I'll look."

"And what then?" Luis asked, "What will you do if you *do* find them? It won't bring them back, you know."

Brent stopped his search, and glared at Luis.

"Don't you want to know?" Brent asked, stepping toward Luis, eyes red. "Don't you want to know if your daughter is dead or just missing? I mean, if she's missing, then there's still hope we can find her, right? Or did you just write her off as gone and you're ready to move on?"

"I didn't write her off," Luis said calmly, letting the accusation slide beneath Brent's grief.

Brent stepped even closer to Luis, a bit too close, puzzled.

"Really? Then why haven't we been looking for her? I can't think of anything besides finding my family, yet you seem like you don't even want to look for yours."

Any other person, any other time, Luis would've knocked a clown out for talking like that to him. He could feel his nostrils flaring and heart starting to race. He slowed his breathing to counter the growing rage. But it wasn't enough to calm him completely. Finally, he gave in to his need to snap back.

"Maybe I'm not all tore up because I don't feel guilty. Because I didn't ignore my family for years, only to be filled with regret the moment they're gone. I spent time with them knowing that nothing is forever. Whether it's cancer or the end of the world, I knew someday the clock would run out. And I lived and loved like my family actually mattered to me."

Brent's eyes narrowed, and he took a swing at Luis.

Luis could have easily dodged the punch completely, but moved just far enough that Brent's punch landed harmlessly on Luis's right shoulder rather than his jaw. Luis figured it was probably the first time Brent had ever thrown a punch.

"Feel better?" Luis asked, voice still somewhat calm.

Brent stared, face flush with guilt, and turned away.

"Listen, bro," Luis said, "I know you need resolution, one way or another. I get it. But at the same time, there's *no way* you can search through all these bodies before another pack of those uglies comes hunting you down. I would stay and help if I thought it would do any good, but there's too many for us to take on by ourselves, even if we had a week."

"I have to know," Brent said, meeting Luis's eyes. "If I leave now, I'll never know for certain."

"Whether they're dead or just vanished, the fact is, they're gone for right now," Luis said. "Maybe you'll see them again on this side, or maybe in heaven, but the only thing we have for sure is right now. And right now, there's nothing we can do to bring them back."

"Aren't you even curious to know if your little girl is here?" Brent asked.

"I've known for years this day would come. I knew I'd have to let go. It doesn't make it easier, and I wish like hell it didn't happen, but I'm not still clinging to straws either. I'm not saying I moved on, but at the same time, I can't hope for something I know won't happen. In my dreams, she was gone. And I can't question the dreams."

Brent scanned the rows of bodies again, likely adding them in his head. While Manhattan was home to more than two million people, no more than a few thousand bodies could have been stacked in the Square, maybe as many as 100,000. But that left plenty still unaccounted for. For all Luis knew, more bodies were on the next block, or the one after that, or hell, stuffed in buildings and heaped ceiling high in Madison Square Garden, but they couldn't search all of Manhattan. Not with those monsters scouring the city. Brent was probably realizing what Luis already knew: Their best shot was to find whoever was broadcasting from Black Island and hope others had made it to safety.

"Okay," Brent said, shoulders hunched in defeat, "Let's go."

"It's gonna be okay," Luis said, even though he didn't believe it.

**

They arrived at the car to find Joe in worse shape than when they left.

Black veins covered his face, and his skin was slick with something slightly thick and wet. His breathing was labored, and eyes still closed. Luis considered feeling for a pulse, but the dark splotches on the guy's face looked infectious. The only thing that kept Luis from putting the old man on the side of the street and leaving him there was the concern in Brent's eyes. This wasn't just Brent's maintenance man, it was the last person he knew in the world. His only connection to his past, and given how shaken Brent already was, Luis didn't want to risk pushing him over the edge by severing it.

"You okay, Joe?" Brent asked, as he climbed into the back seat.

No response from Joe.

"We need to get him help," Luis said as he got in the front seat and keyed the ignition, wanting to get to the ferry as fast as possible so Joe wouldn't puke, bleed, or die in his car. "Hopefully, they'll have someone at Black Island."

"Daddy?" Ben's voice said, again from Joe's mouth.

Luis glanced in the rearview and saw Brent's torment.

"I'm so ... " Ben's voice said again, voice so weak it seemed as if Joe could hardly form a breath much less a word.

"What?" Brent asked leaning forward in his seat to better hear Joe's murmurs.

Joe's head rose, but his eyes were still closed. "I'm so ... hrmph ... " the voice said again, though this time it sounded like a mixture of Ben's voice and Joe's.

"*What's* he saying?" Brent asked.

"Beats the hell outta me," Luis said, confused and just wanting the old man out of his car.

Brent leaned closer, and Joe inched forward with great effort, eyes still closed, as if he were unconscious.

"I'm so ... hungry," Joe said, his voice growing.

"Hungry?" Brent asked.

Luis looked over just as Joe's eyes shot open, no longer white, but pitch-black. Joe's mouth opened impossibly wide, the flesh at the corners of his mouth ripped and bled black down his chin. Joe, suddenly alive and energized, thrust forward, grabbing Brent's head and trying to bring it closer to bite.

Luis slammed on the brakes, causing Joe and Brent, neither of them wearing seat belts, to lurch forward. Brent hit the back of Luis's seat and snapped back into the back seat. Joe sailed forward, head smacking the front window hard and leaving a red splotch on the bullet-resistant glass.

Joe screamed, an unearthly banshee cry, somewhere between man and monster, then turned to Luis, leaping onto him. Luis's guns were out of reach, in the back seat. The shotgun on the center console had slid forward and fallen on the floor in front of Joe when Luis hit the brakes. Luis tried to push Joe back against the passenger door. With one hand on Joe's thin chest, he kept his right hand tightened around Joe's forehead, struggling to keep Joe's open mouth from biting him.

"Gimme a gun!" Luis shouted back at Brent, who he could not see in the backseat.

Suddenly, something cracked in Joe's neck, and he swiveled his head sideways and bit down hard on Luis's arm.

"Fuck!" Luis screamed, reaching back frantically with his left hand and finding the door handle, pulling it open, then unclicking his seatbelt, and falling backward to give himself enough room to kick at Joe, awkwardly at first, then finally with enough force to push the fucker off him. Hanging half out of the car, Luis kicked hard, pressing both feet into Joe's chest, trapping him against the passenger door as Brent scrambled in the back seat.

"Gun!" Luis screamed.

Joe's head shook violently back and forth so fast it was nearly a blur, screaming and clicking the entire time, black spittle flying from it and landing all over Luis and his car. Joe reached down and grabbed hold tight of Luis' leg, clenching down impossibly hard for an old man.

Luis screamed, sure the thing that was once Joe would rip right through his flesh. With renewed fear and anger, he kicked both his legs up with all the force he could muster, found Joe's jaw, and kicked it straight back. He kicked again, repeatedly, as hard and fast as he could, bashing Joe's skull into the window until it was a bloody pulp and his body stopped twitching.

Luis hopped from the car, screaming, adrenaline coursing through him, air stinging his lungs as he gulped deep mouthfuls. Brent climbed from the back seat, gun in hand. Luis grabbed it from him, ran around to the passenger side, opened the door, and yanked Joe's body out, then threw it to the road, and fired four shots into the corpse.

"Fuuuuuuck!" Luis screamed, wiping at his stinging, bloody arm. The injury was worse than he'd thought, a mouth-sized chunk of flesh torn from his right forearm.

Brent ran to him, "What the hell happened?"

"He was infected," Luis said. "He was turning into one of those things."

"Holy shit," Brent said, staring at Joe's body, eyes wide in disbelief. It took a moment, but Brent's eyes soon found Luis's injury. "What ... ?"

"It bit me," Luis said, feeling fear for his own life for the first time in decades.

* * * *

CHAPTER 2
BORICIO WOLFE

Oct. 18
Somewhere in Alabama

The door whined open, and Boricio smiled.

Testosterone must not have been expecting trouble because he sauntered in like he owned half the South. Two guards were behind him, neither one holding the guns in their holsters.

Stupid shits.

"Now!" Boricio growled.

The door was open just three seconds when the flat of Boricio's bat was beating the air straight from Testosterone's lungs. He hit the floor with a throttled wail and both hands curled around his gut. Boricio left him writhing, then turned his gnashing teeth to the other two guards.

Killing the delicate was like popping a zit, and the two flowers in the doorway were just a few seconds from wilting.

The two guards reached for their guns. Boricio swung the bat and broke the knuckles of the first guard before he'd even unfastened his holster. Boricio dropped the bat, grabbed the man by his neck, spun him around, and reached into his holster. Boricio pulled out the guard's Colt, and shot him once in the chest, followed by a second shot to his head on the way down.

A geyser of blood rained onto Testosterone, who was still thrashing around on the ground, though quickly catching his breath. He opened his mouth as if about to scream for help, and Boricio pressed the Colt hard against his cheekbone.

"Gimme one reason," Boricio said, shoving the gun so hard into the man's face it would leave a bruise.

It was one-on-four on the other side of the room. The remaining guard had his gun drawn. "Stand down!" he screamed, waving the gun back and forth at Team Boricio, who surrounded him. Adam and Charlie stood behind the guard while Manny and Jack stood in front of him.

He obviously wasn't the one who signed the checks, but he might also have been given orders to keep the prisoners alive, since despite his boss licking the concrete and his comrade already growing cold, the guard just stood there with a shaking gun and hollow eyes.

Stupid fucking asshole. That right there is the last dumb-ass decision of your wasted life. Pull the trigger five times and BAM! Ashes to ashes, we all fall down. Maybe you'd manage to get us all, maybe you wouldn't. But if you don't pull that trigger in the next two seconds, you're dead no matter what you get around to doing.

"Stand down!" the guard barked again.

"Shoot him ... " Testosterone finally found his voice long enough to issue a command. Boricio smacked Testosterone in the head with the butt of the pistol, then stood up.

Boricio flashed the gunman his most winning smile and raised his hands in the air. "Not so fast," he said. "I can do the math, I surrender." He kept inching forward. "My hands are up. You got me."

"Stand down or I will shoot you in the face!"

Boricio stopped, 10 feet from the guard. Would've been plenty close if the flunky wasn't waving a .45, but it was a few feet farther up shit creek than Boricio would've liked considering Team Boricio was unarmed and G.I. Joe was just seconds from gathering another round of breath to order them all dead.

"Chill out, man. I said I surrender. Need me to start speaking French so's I can prove it?" Boricio kneeled, laid the gun on the floor, barrel first, then stood with his hands in the air.

He kicked the gun across the room just past the guard and between Adam and Charlie. "See," he said, raising his eyebrows. "I'm surrendered, just like I told ya."

The prisoners were all too scared to move.

Boricio heard Testosterone's heavy breath rising from the floor behind him.

Team Boricio is made up of flash-frozen idiots. If I was standing over there, that fucker's gun would already be in his mouth. They may as well be playing pocket pool. If you're on Team Boricio, you best be useful.

Boricio charged toward a surprised Manny, tackling and then spinning him around until Boricio's eyes were bolted on the flunky with Manny between them.

Boricio hurled Manny into the guard then dove to the ground.

Testosterone was back on his feet, but Boricio had already hit the floor, sweeping the guard's feet from under him. The guard's head landed with a loud crack on the concrete. Boricio lifted him by the hair, then sent his head back to the floor with a fatal aftershock, coating the floor in the man's blood.

"The fuck man!" Manny screamed.

"Tell me I've been naughty later," Boricio growled and blew a kiss, then turned to face Testosterone.

"Not so fast," Testosterone said, aiming his gun behind Boricio. Predator's guess said it was at one of the prisoners trying to retrieve a weapon.

"Why don't you kick that over here instead?" Testosterone said.

The gun slid across the concrete and through Testosterone's splayed legs, landing just behind him, a few feet from the wall. He smiled and turned his gun to Boricio. "You know," he said, "We were just on our way in here to deal with you. We were gonna take our sweet, sweet time, have ourselves a little fun."

Pile of shit wants to motherfucking monologue. Tell me how big and bad he is, and how he's gonna make me pay. But no shots have been fired, so if they were really planning on taking their sweet, sweet time, and I expect they were, no one else is coming in for a while. I get that gun, it's game over.

Boricio said, "Easy to be the Grim Reaper's right hand when you're waving a loaded gun. And the way you probably toss off all the lonely boys around here, your trigger finger's probably even faster than that tiny pecker of yours."

Testosterone laughed, then crossed the floor to the baseball bat, keeping his aim on Boricio. He kneeled, picked up the bat, then slipped his gun back in its holster.

"Bullets wouldn't be much fun," he said. "I'd rather beat the loud right out of your mouth. Maybe I'll celebrate with a shot or two to the kneecap once I'm through. Or maybe ... "

He didn't wait to finish his sentence — tried to catch Boricio by surprise instead with a wide swing somewhere around the word "or." But Boricio saw the bat coming. He dodged the blow, and the bat whistled by him.

Boricio charged Testosterone, throwing both hands around the bat. Testosterone saw him coming and tightened his grip as Boricio latched on. They stumbled across the room, each trying to gain control of the bat as Team Boricio stood on the sidelines like fucking spectators or cheerleaders, nobody going for the other gun in the room.

In a battle of brute strength, Testosterone had the edge. He pulled the bat free, sent Boricio sailing to the floor with a swift kick to his chest, then landed the first blow to Boricio's ribs before he was halfway up.

Boricio fell back to the floor, just as the tip of Testosterone's boot clipped him beneath his chin. Another half inch or so and the fucker would've broken his jaw.

"You're gonna wanna stop right there." Charlie said.

Well how about that? Janie got a gun. Looks like someone just made the highlight reel on SportsCenter.

"Shoot him!" Boricio yelled.

"No, no, no," Testosterone shook his head and wagged his finger back and forth. "I'm the only thing that can keep you alive right now, believe you me. You all are dead the minute you step out this door. But you shoot this fucker here," he gestured toward Boricio, "then you and everyone in this room gets to see the only future there is left."

"Why'd you bring us here to start with?" Charlie asked.

"No, I'm not answering your questions until you put a bullet in this grease ball," Testosterone said, "This is your one chance to join us. Or join the dead. Your choice, kid."

Boricio turned to Charlie. "Now I know you're too smart to believe a single word this fucktard is saying. He brought us here to kill us, all of us, and that's what he's gonna do. He's the cunt hair who ordered you tied up; I'm the one who set you free."

Charlie closed his left eye and steadied his aim toward Testosterone.

"Stop," Manny said, "Think about what you're doing, man. This guy is a monster." He looked at Boricio. "Think about what you've seen and heard since you've been in here. I mean, the guy just used me as a human shield. It's only a matter of time before he turns on any or all of us. We're only here to help him get from point A to B. He won't care what happens to us at all once we're out of this place."

Boricio laughed. "Awesome job, Captain Obvious." He turned to the rest of the Team Boricio. "Every word he says is true. I am one gen-u-ine fucker of a Frankenstein. And yeah, I do need all of you to help me escape, and I really don't see us all playing house once we get outta here. But true as that all is, it's even truer that none of you is leaving here without a fair hand of help. And yours truly is a whole Hands Across America right now. I won't kill you, because you're all on my team. I killed that fucker earlier because he was a turncoat. Anyone else wants to be a free agent; I'll kill them, too. Because that's what it takes to protect the team."

He turned to Manny. "And no disrespect intended. I assessed as best I could. You were the only thing gonna keep the five of us alive in the seconds I had. Just good math is all."

Manny glared at Boricio.

I'll have to end him anyway. He don't wanna be on Team Boricio, and I don't need no cancer creeping through the group.

Two shots rang through the room, and Testosterone dropped to the floor. Charlie stood there, shaking.

"I had to shoot him," Charlie said. "He was reaching for his gun."

"Good boy!" Boricio hollered. He walked over to the Colt on the ground, picked it up, handed it to Adam, then turned to the group. "We ready to roll?"

Manny grabbed the gun from Testosterone's holster. Boricio went to the door, looked into the narrow hallway outside, then said, "We're clear," motioning the gang through the threshold. Manny was last to pass. Soon as he did, he felt the barrel of Boricio's bat pressed against his skull.

"Gonna need your gun," Boricio said.

Boricio held his hand out, and Manny filled it without argument. Boricio handed the gun to Jack, then turned to Manny.

"Despite that little bullshit back there, I've every intention of letting you live. However, I sure as hell don't want my biggest critic holding a gun and walking behind me. We get more weapons, maybe you get to earn yours back. Besides," Boricio patted his bat. "If I can go without one, you can, too. Now, chop chop." Boricio waved his hand toward the hallway.

They stepped into a short hallway without any doors or windows. On the far side was a set of six steps leading to an angled, wooden door.

They'd been held in a basement.

Whatever ugly the end of the world hadn't managed to kill was waiting right on the other side of the cellar door.

* * * *

CHAPTER 3
TEAGAN MCLACHLAN

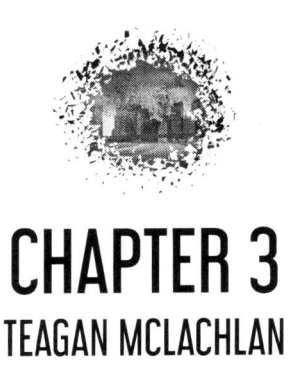

Oct. 17
Morning
Winding, Georgia

"What do you mean your father murdered someone?" Teagan asked. Jade was sitting on the bed next to her, cross-legged. "You mean he's *not* a cop or government agent or something?"

Jade shook her head. "He was a mid-level manager at an investment firm. He was a workaholic, burned out, barely present at home most of the time. Then one day out of nowhere, he started talking about people following him. He said he was worried about us, and that we needed to be careful. Said there were 'agents' watching him and if anyone came around asking questions or asking us to go with them, to say nothing, and escape the second we got the chance. One day he was at the office, and went totally ape shit. Didn't just shoot one person, but four."

Teagan's tongue wouldn't work while her brain tried to make sense of what Jade was revealing.

"It was all over the evening news. On a Friday afternoon, right there in the parking garage, he killed four people. He told my mom they were secret agents, but that part wasn't reported. His lawyer claimed it was a psychological collapse caused by Post Traumatic Stress Disorder from when he was in Iraq. It never went to trial. He copped an insanity plea and was placed in an institution."

Teagan found herself suddenly staring at her recent life through a new filter — had the men in the store been a genuine threat? What about the helicopter and the people aboard it? She'd had a hard enough time accepting that Ed had killed so many people to protect them from possible threats. But what if none of the people was really a threat to begin with? What if all the people he'd killed were innocent? All the people he'd killed *for her*? Her headache went from dull throb to roaring thunder as she sifted through what Jade was saying.

"Oh my God. I don't even know what to say ... Did you and your mom visit him?"

"We did at first, but then he ... "

The bedroom door opened, it was Ed and Ken, severing Jade's words mid-sentence.

"We're back," Ken said. "We found a few guns, but not a whole lot of ammo."

Ed said nothing, eyes on Teagan, as if he sensed they'd been discussing him, that maybe his daughter gave him up.

"So, what's the plan?" Jade asked.

"I'll go out there," Ed said, "See if I can get to the SUV, and bring it as close to the front door as I can get. If they come at me, we'll see how strong they are and adjust our defenses accordingly."

"What if they kill you?" Jade asked. "I don't think you should go out there."

"We can't wait here and see what they'll do," Ed said. "Better to act than react."

"It's too dangerous, Dad."

"I'll go," Ken offered.

"You ever fire a gun?" Ed asked.

"Well, um ... no," Ken said.

"Then you're not going anywhere. That bat won't be enough." Ed said matter-of-factly, no insult intended, though the kid's face went crimson all the same.

"I haven't seen you in three years and you're just gonna run out and get yourself killed?" Jade said, voice going from serious young woman to scared young girl.

"I'm not gonna get killed. I can handle myself just fine."

"You don't even know what those things are; how can you say something like that?!" Jade turned, pouting.

To Teagan, Ed looked like a beaten man, too tired to muscle through the motions of an old and weary fight reminiscent of ones he'd had too many times in the past, if not with Jade then surely her mother. Teagan wondered why he didn't go to his daughter and give her the hug she so clearly craved. For all his so-called talent at reading people, he sucked at reading women. Or perhaps Iraq had rendered him incapable of showing emotion outside machismo.

"Trust me," Ed said, "I can handle anything that comes my way."

Jade shook her head, and Ed left the bedroom.

Jade stared at her lap, trying not to cry, slowly failing. Teagan felt uncomfortable, but forced herself to lean over and hug the girl.

"I'm sorry," Teagan said.

"He's so fucking stubborn," Jade said, surrendering into Teagan's embrace. Ken, also uncomfortable, left the room, closing the door softly behind him.

Jade pulled away, "He always does shit like this."

"What do you mean?"

"He takes unnecessary chances, puts himself at risk to be the big fucking hero."

Teagan was confused, "What do you mean?"

"Even though he wasn't a cop or agent or whatever the hell he told you he was, he was always stepping in whenever someone was in danger or if someone had done something bad. Like when I was 9 and we all went out to eat in New York City. We were walking back to our hotel when some guy snatched a woman's purse right in front of us. The guy took off running while everyone on the street just stood around. Well, everyone except my dad, who, without a word to my mom or me, took off running, chased the guy down the block, caught him, and then beat the hell out of him. He came jogging back a few minutes later with the woman's purse and handed it to her."

"And that's a *bad thing?*" Teagan asked.

"Well, at first, I thought it was kinda of cool. Like he was my dad, the super hero or something. But he started doing this shit all the time. And then it got worse. He would start acting if he *thought someone* was gonna do something. He'd jump them or scare them off. And when we asked why, he just said he knew the person was *gonna do something.* He *felt it*, he'd say, like he's some kinda psychic or something! It got to the point that we never knew what he was gonna do, and we were scared to even go out with him. Even more scared when he was out by himself. Because then he'd be out late, and my mom and I would be worried that he'd done something stupid and gotten hurt, or worse. And then, a few years ago, when he started talking about the agents and stuff, we should have known it had gotten worse, whatever *it* was. But I don't think there's any way we could have known he'd go that far."

"What happened to him in Iraq?" Teagan asked, afraid she might be prying, but too curious not to ask.

"He won't say. I asked him once, and he said he doesn't like to talk about that stuff. I don't know if he's ever told anyone."

Teagan was quiet for several minutes, sorting through all that had happened, when Jade asked her about herself. Teagan gave the condensed version, then when Jade asked her how she had met her dad, Teagan filled her in on everything, including how Ed had saved her.

"He shot down a helicopter?" Jade said, eyes wide and hurt. "Oh my God."

"He thought they were coming for me," Teagan said, "for my baby."

"Why the hell would he think that?"

Teagan felt her face flush, "We stopped at a hotel after he picked me up, and when I slept, I had a nightmare about people in helicopters coming for my baby."

Jade stared at her. She didn't come out and say, "Oh, you're crazy, too, just like my dad," but her eyes managed for her.

"I feel terrible," Teagan said, "He killed them for me. I told him it was a nightmare, and it was probably nothing, but he … "

"He probably would've done it, anyway. My dad would've found his own reason if you didn't have one. You just gave a little shape to the nebulous conspiracy theories already spinning in his head."

"Does *he know* that he's not really an agent?" Teagan asked. "Does he know that *you know* he's not one? What if he asks me if you told me anything?"

Jade thought for a moment. "Oh, he fully believes he is some kind of secret agent. As far as my mom and I are concerned, he thinks we think he's crazy. Or that he was so deep undercover that we don't know and now we don't believe him. As far as you're concerned, we never had this conversation. I don't think he'd hurt me or you, but there's no way to know for sure how far he's messed up or how deep his paranoia runs."

Teagan just stared at Jade, not sure what to say.

"I shouldn't have said anything." Jade said. "I don't want it to be all weird between you two now."

A knock at the door. "Come in," Jade said.

It was Ken. "Your dad just went outside to get the SUV."

"He did WHAT?!" Jade said, jumping from the bed and running into the living room. "He didn't even say goodbye?"

* * * *

CHAPTER 4
LUCA HARDING

Oct. 17
Late afternoon
Belle Springs, Missouri

Luca stared at his reflection. He'd gone from an 8-year-old to a teenager in the span of minutes.

He was himself, but not like he remembered.

He was now slightly taller than Paola, with a full head of hair that fell just past his shoulders. The face staring back at him was at least a good five years older, and looked remarkably like his father's.

His clothes were torn, as if he'd grown right through them. Like the Incredible Hulk, except Luca wasn't green or full of muscles.

"It's gonna be okay," Will said, throwing a robe around Luca. "Come on; let's find you some new clothes."

He could feel all the frightened feelings sitting inside of the people. Even the leader man, Desmond, looked at Luca like he was scared in the places he didn't like to talk about. It made Luca's sad spiders start to crawl.

He couldn't explain what had happened to his face, or his body, but he knew it wasn't his fault, and hated to feel like the room was looking at him like was he part of the *terrible scary.*

Especially Paola's mom, Mary.

She smiled at him because she knew he had helped her daughter, but Luca could see behind the smile, and her thinking didn't trust him.

She thinks I could hurt Paola if I wanted to and that maybe when I helped her it was only by accident. She wants me to stay away, but feels bad for feeling that way. Like when Daddy has work to do.

Mary cradled Paola. "I was so, so worried. Thank God you're safe."

Will and Luca went into one of the hotel rooms that had a bunch of suitcases laid out and open. "I'll wait out here," Will said, leaving Luca alone in the room. "You find some clothes that fit you, okay?"

Luca didn't bother to ask whose clothes these were. People who had disappeared. *Like his family.*

He found a pair of blue jeans, a red T-shirt, and some underwear, socks, and sneakers that were a close enough match to his new size. As he got undressed, he saw hair in places he'd not had hair before. Though he was curious about his new body, he was also embarrassed, as if he were looking at someone else, so he got dressed quickly, so he didn't have to see so much of himself.

He wanted to talk to Will alone, but when he came back out of the room, Will was already in the lobby. Luca joined the group, feeling more self-aware and shyer than normal. Though the people weren't staring at him, he could feel them looking when he was turned away, like they were trying to figure out how he did what he did.

Everyone could tell Mary and Paola wanted to be alone, so Jimmy and Will went to the bar. John and Desmond went to guard their areas. Luca was left to wander the lobby, looking at his feet and keeping away from the mirrors. He wondered where Dog Vader was. Then he spotted the dog curled up near the front door, sleeping. Probably tired from all the adventuring and walking the past few days, Luca figured.

I sure could use a friend right now.

He thought about his best friends back home. Scott, Omar, and Billy. He'd been missing his parents so much, he'd hardly thought about his friends at all. He wondered if they were missing, too. Or if maybe they were looking for their parents, too. He hoped they were okay. Luca laughed when he thought of how Omar might react if he saw Luca now looking so much older. Omar was the oldest of the bunch, by six months, and he never let anyone forget it, often acting like he was way older, and therefore more experienced at things than the others. Sometimes the other kids would get in fights with Omar because of the way he was, but Luca never minded. Omar was just being Omar, and Omar was his friend, no matter what.

Luca stopped in front of a wooden shelf with lots of pockets, all stuffed with brochures, then began pulling them out one by one, starting at the top left corner and moving row by row, and skipping the duplicates, until he pulled the 23rd brochure from the bottom right.

Luca took his pile of brochures, then sat in a chair to read the sad spiders away.

He read about the "bird's eye view from the Gateway Arch," the "thrills and spills at Six Flags St. Louis" and the "exciting dioramas on display" at the Lewis & Clark Boat House and Nature Center.

They all sounded like fun adventures, and the pictures looked nice, especially the roller coasters at Six Flags. But none of the 23 brochures helped the sad spiders go away. He still missed his mom and dad and Anna, and couldn't keep from thinking about how he was making everyone afraid.

I wish I knew if everyone was really thinking the stuff I think they're thinking, but I can't tell where my thoughts stop and theirs get started. Hearing their thoughts seems un-possible. Even if Will thinks it isn't.

He was wondering if sad spiders filled the entire hotel when he heard Jimmy's voice behind him. "Hey, little man, how you doing?"

"I'm okay," Luca said.

"No, you aren't," Jimmy shook his head. "Tell me what's wrong."

"I was only trying to help, but I think I might have made things worse."

"Don't be silly." Jimmy threw himself into one of the oversized chairs next to Luca. "It's just that we're all getting used to seeing all sorts of strange shh ... stuff we're not used to seeing. And you gotta admit, that was pretty weird back there." Jimmy leaned toward Luca. "Any idea how that happened?"

Luca shook his head.

"Well, it's not like it matters anyway," Jimmy said. "Hey, wanna play a game?"

"Sure! What kind of games do you have? Does this place have a Wii?"

Jimmy laughed. "Ha, I wish! I'd love a PS3 and some *Uncharted 2* right now, but I'd definitely settle for a Wii. Hell, I'd settle for a DS! I found a PSP, but the batteries went dead the first day. Least I thought it was the batteries, but all the other batteries I tried went dead, too. So I figure it had to be the PSP is busted. So, no video games. But I *did find* a deck of Uno cards; wanna play that?"

Luca loved Uno. "Yes, please!"

"Be right back." Jimmy said.

Jimmy returned two minutes later with the fattest deck of Uno cards Luca had ever seen.

"Why are there so many?" Luca asked.

"I found four decks in the hotel. Guess Uno keeps the kids quiet. I put all the decks together and made a super deck. More fun that way."

Luca agreed.

"Okay, now I haven't played in a long time," Jimmy said, "So, you promise to go easy on me?"

Luca laughed, "I promise."

Jimmy laid out two piles of seven cards as he glanced around the lobby. Will, John, and Desmond were still up front, and Mary was sitting at the bar. Paola walked toward the card game.

"Hi," she said to Luca. "I'm Paola."

"Nice to meet you," Luca said.

Paola shook Luca's hand then sat in a chair across from him, next to Jimmy.

"Can I play?"

"'Course you can play," Jimmy nodded, flicking seven cards into a third pile.

"Why so many cards?" She pointed at the top-heavy deck.

"It's my super deck. Way more fun."

Jimmy and Luca traded a smile.

The first game lasted just three and a half minutes. Paola had two Draw Fours, three Draw Twos and a Skip. No one stood a chance.

"This isn't a hand, it's a foot!" Jimmy said, looking at his cards.

Paola laughed. "You're right; the super deck *is* more fun."

She blew raspberries at Jimmy. He gathered the played cards, shuffled, slipped them into the super deck, then counted three fresh piles from the top.

"How are you feeling?" Jimmy asked Paola.

"Good," she nodded. "A little weird."

"You mean beyond going missing then comatose?" Jimmy smiled, then fanned his cards in front of his face with a satisfied nod. "You start," he said to Paola.

She put a red 4 on top of the red 1. "I don't remember anything that happened, even though I feel like I should. I know it was something important, and it's like the memory is at the edge of my brain but I can't quite touch it."

"BAM!" Jimmy said, laying down a red Draw Two.

Luca drew two cards and said, "You don't remember *anything?*"

Paola dropped a green Draw Two on top of Jimmy's red one, then stuck her tongue out and turned to Luca. "No, not really. I sort of remember waking up the other night and walking toward the kitchen. But there's nothing else until I woke up."

"You were moaning like crazy in your sleep." Jimmy drew two cards.

Luca played a green 6. "Do you remember me?"

The color drained from Paola's face, then returned a moment later in a deeper flush. She nodded. "I do," she said. "We were swinging. But you were younger."

Luca nodded.

"You helped me, didn't you?"

Luca nodded again. "I think so, but I don't know *how.*"

Jimmy looked from Luca to Paola, shaking his head. "It's like *Inception* in 4-D," he said.

"I think that's why everyone's scared of me," Luca said.

"They're not scared of you!" Paola said, surprised. She looked at Jimmy. "*Are they?*"

"Well, I don't know that anyone's gonna be Luca for Halloween, but yeah, you missed some crazy stuff. We got a real magic show from junior grandpa here."

Luca wished everyone would just play and stop talking about what happened.

"Yeah, when Boy Wonder walked in a half hour ago, he looked about the same age as the Wilson kid."

"You mean the one with all the freckles?"

"I was gonna say the one whose face looks like it caught fire and someone tried to put it out with a fork, but yeah, same difference."

"That's mean, Jimmy." Paola turned to Luca, then back to Jimmy. "The Wilson kid is 7."

"I'm 8," Luca said.

Paola shook her head and played her green 3. "That's not possible. You're taller than I am."

"I'm telling you," Jimmy said, throwing a green Skip on top of the pile, "a half hour ago he was a munchkin."

"Uno!" Luca said, putting the red 3 on top of the green 1. "Can we talk about something else now?"

"Man, you can't let it get to you," Jimmy said. "We may not understand what happened, but whatever went down, you can obviously do cooler shit than any of us can. Seriously, I'd love to have someone make me five years older."

"Jimmy! Don't swear."

"Call me Jim and I won't," he winked at Paola, then turned to Luca. "Anyway, embarrassing stuff happens to everyone. That's where confidence comes from. It's how you deal with it. And given the current world population, you might just have a chance at being the most confident kid in the world. Now," he dropped a red Draw Two, "would you like to hear about a time I was embarrassed? I've got about a billion."

Luca drew two cards and said, "Okay."

Paola played a red Skip, Luca played a red 7. Jimmy started talking.

"So this happened in eighth-grade math. I had to go to the bathroom *reaaaaal bad*. And it wasn't just draining pipe; I actually had to drop the boys at the pool, which I NEVER do at school if I can help it. My teacher, Mr. Mellakar, was a real jerk, partly because I gave him attitude, but mostly because he was born that way. Sometimes, he gave me detention for breathing, but whatever; I figured if I really had to go, I really had to go. So, I raised my hand and asked, but he just shook his head and told me I could wait until lunch. But that wasn't gonna fly because the turtle was already poking out of its shell."

"Ewww!" Paola made a face, and Luca giggled. Everyone kept dropping cards and drawing new ones while Jimmy went on.

"So, he finished drawing a chalk cylinder on the board, then asked us to figure the area and when he went to his desk, I got up and quietly asked him again. I told him I *had to* release the hounds and that it wasn't gonna wait until lunch."

"Did you actually say you had to *release the hounds?*" Paola asked.

Jimmy laughed. "No, I think I probably said Number Two. Anyways, he finally said okay, but he was sort of a jerk about it and told me I'd better hurry. Like I can control how long a shi … um, poop takes. So, I ran to the bathroom, but both stalls were taken. I had to do the crap dance for another five or six minutes, which felt like an hour. Finally, the stall opens, and I run inside. I sat down and bombed the oval office, but it was coming out so fast, it was like I was making batter. Took a whole roll of toilet paper to clean myself, too."

"This is way, *way* too much information," Paola said making an ill face. She put a green 9 on top of the red 1.

Luca couldn't stop giggling. He liked the way Jimmy talked, super-fast and excited. Dog Vader padded his way into the room and barked. Luca wasn't sure if Vader liked, or didn't like, the poop story.

Jimmy thought he played a yellow 6, but Paola said it was a 9, so he put down a green 7 instead. Luca put down a green 4.

Jimmy continued. "So, I get back to class, but it's like 20 minutes later. Soon as I walk in, Mr. Mellakar says, 'So you're FINALLY back!' then asks me what took me so long. I mumbled that I had to go Number Two and he said, 'I can't hear you,' then kept making me repeat it until everyone in class was laughing, including Amy Ensile, who I really, really wanted to ask to the end-of-the-year dance. But I couldn't even look her in the eye after that."

"Why?" Paola said. "Everyone poops." She played a blue 4.

"Yeah," Jimmy said, "but not everyone gets laughed at in front of the entire class. I got called Lava Cake for the rest of that year and all summer. Only thing that saved me was high school, and doing some other stupid thing which earned me another nickname." He put down a blue 2.

"What name was that?" Paola asked.

"Um, probably not a story for the kiddos."

Luca put down a Draw Four, then said, "Uno!"

Paola grumbled from behind her smile, then drew four cards and gestured toward her mom, deep in discussion with Will, sitting at the bar. "What do you think they're talking about?"

Jimmy looked at Luca's face and the single card waving just below his mouth. Jimmy's hand hovered over the deck, then returned to his own cards, where he pulled another blue 2 and set it on top.

"Not sure," Jimmy said. "Probably how we're going to get out of here, and where we're gonna go next. You know, the stuff we don't get to have an opinion about. What do you think?"

Paola studied her mom, then Will. "I think they're talking about me. I think Will knows something, and I don't think my mom wants to believe it."

Luca played his final card and smiled. They couldn't see his sad spiders, and had no idea that Paola was kind of right. Luca knew what Will knew, that something bad was still gonna happen. Only difference was, Luca didn't know what the bad thing would be. He suspected that Will *did*, though.

* * * *

CHAPTER 5
MARY OLSON

Any plans they had on leaving the Drury Inn were nixed when the creatures began multiplying outside. On the advice of Will, the group decided to wait. For what, though, nobody knew. Will said they should wait until the next morning. When asked why, he couldn't elaborate beyond a feeling. John insisted that things wouldn't get any better and they ought to leave immediately, as planned. Desmond, however, said that since Will and Luca were driven by dreams to fly from California to there to save a girl they didn't even know, Will was obviously tapped into something that none of the Warson Woods group understood.

John wasn't happy about it, but since everyone else agreed, he kept his grumbling to a minimum ... so far.

Though the bleakers had let Will and Luca pass into the hotel unharmed, nobody was willing to take the chance that they'd allow them to leave with such ease. For one, the creatures sounded as if they'd grown angrier. Their shrieks grew louder, their clicking more incessant. And in some cases, when one of the group passed by a window or the front doors, the creatures hissed at them.

Since they weren't going anywhere, Mary and the group decided to kill some time while getting to know their new guests.

Mary sat in the bar sipping a soda as she watched Paola playing cards with the boys, a smile on the girl's face, almost as if she'd managed to temporarily shed the horror of the last few days. Laughter rolled in a circle, from Jimmy to Luca to Paola and back to Jimmy. It was impossible to tell her daughter had been at the edge of death a few hours before.

Paola hadn't died. But *something* had happened.

Paola didn't remember much, though. She remembered her father calling her out of the hotel in her sleep. But the man wasn't really her father. She thought she'd been dreaming, but also knew she wasn't. Something visited her. Paola knew it. And Mary sensed it. Something had invaded her child's soul. And while Luca had somehow saved her, Mary couldn't be certain that whatever happened wouldn't happen again. Or that the danger was gone.

Once your child is threatened, especially by something so mysterious, Mary figured, you never really feel completely safe again.

Paola's laughter rang through the room; beautiful music Mary had been longing to hear. She was happy to see her smiling, covering her mouth as Jimmy flaunted his loud personality. Jimmy was such a talker, but the last several days had worn on his voice. It was nice to see him stepping into his natural rhythm again. The group could certainly use the humor.

Mary wished she wasn't so suspicious of Luca. But she felt hot, and the guilt was a parka wrapped around her. He had dropped from the heavens and rescued her daughter with barely a word. She *should* feel nothing but grateful.

And she was, but grateful didn't soothe the *knowing* inside her. The knowing that said something was horribly off about the boy. And not just the aging. Sure, that was weirder than Koontz, but she could almost accept that. Life didn't come with free lunches, and perhaps the price of saving Paola was paid in age. It was amazing the boy had been willing to pay it. That should have been enough for Mary.

But it wasn't.

Her instincts said something was wrong. *Really wrong.*

"Mind if I sit?" Will said, taking a seat next to her.

"Of course not."

Will smiled then sat. "Long morning?"

"You could say that." Mary couldn't help but smile. Something was undeniably warm about the old man. Wild, but sweet. Her instincts said *shelter*.

"Looking forward to leaving, I imagine," Will said.

"Yeah, I don't even care what happens. I just don't want it to happen here."

"Where's home for you?"

"Here, Missouri. You?"

"Everywhere, anywhere where there's interesting people. I never stay long enough to get bored, though."

Mary changed the subject to the one she'd been wanting to ask about since he had arrived with Luca. "You said you had dreams about us. What happened in the dreams? How did you know to trust them?"

Will looked shy. "I can't really say what happened. Long story short, whenever I tell people what happens in my dreams, it never turns out good. It's best if I can just do what I can to try and help as much as possible."

"But you can tell me what you saw with Paola, what already happened, right?"

"I wish I could. But in her case, the details were vague. It's not even a matter of me not wanting to tell you, I'm really unable beyond a feeling."

"What was the feeling?" Mary asked, leaning so far on the edge of her seat, she might fall at the slightest jolt.

"There was something bad in her." Will said, "Something that's bigger than all this stuff going on. But I also knew that Luca could help her."

Mary stared at Will, then over at Luca, not sure what to say.

"He's a good kid, Mary. The best. He gave his soul a beating for Paola, and it left him with a temporary scar. You're not sure how to feel about this, are you?"

Mary looked down, ashamed. "I don't know why, but I feel like something's *wrong* with the whole thing, and hate that I do." She looked up, a tear sliding to her chin. "I know what he did for her, and for me, but something feels so *ugly*."

"Look at it like this." Will leaned forward. "Whatever happened between Luca and Paola helped her, right?"

Mary nodded.

"So, if there was something terrible inside Paola and now there isn't, that means Luca took it away. So where do you think the terrible thing went?"

Mary gasped. "Into him? That's terrible."

"I think that's why you're sensing something bad in him. But he's gonna be fine. Trust me. He'll process it. If he weren't able to, we wouldn't be here right now. He'll be good as new in no time. Then you'll see what I see, and I'll get to hear you tell me I was right."

Will winked, and Mary smiled.

"It's all just so hard to believe," Mary said. "I mean, how do you even *know* any of this? How did you know to trust your dreams and come here?"

"I don't, but I tend to see things a lot of people don't." Will said, "Most people see things from their own limited viewpoint. And that makes it hard to accept things like what we've got going on here. But when you consider possibilities, the things we don't know, and keep an open mind, weird things like this, oddly enough, are a bit easier to grasp. Are common dreams really harder to believe than any of this?" He waved his hands toward the parking lot and its lurking monstrosities.

"No. Not at all. Much easier, actually." She sat quietly, then asked, "Any theories on the aging?"

Will scratched his head. "Sure, I got *theories*. Which one you want? I got the one you won't like, the one you'll like even less, and the one that probably won't bother you at all, which also happens to be the one I'd say is most likely anyhow."

"Let's go with that one," Mary smiled uncomfortably then shifted in her seat.

"You ever heard of rapid aging diseases in children?"

"Not really." Mary shook her head. "I mean, I think I saw something on *Oprah*, but I'm going to sound like an idiot if I try to tell you what I know."

"There's a disorder called Progeria. It's a genetic mutation, hereditary but just barely. Kids who get Progeria rarely live past their mid-teens or early 20s. And most of the minutes spent between birth and death are misery. The disorder's rare, but indiscriminate, hitting both sexes and every ethnic group. There are other accelerated aging diseases, but what makes Progeria different is that while other diseases are caused by DNA damage in the body's cells, Progeria is caused by a gene mutation. With me so far?"

Mary nodded.

"Kids with Progeria show symptoms around a year and a half to 2 years old. These are the kids you've seen on TV:

hair loss, crinkly skin, brittle bones. Even their teeth are mangled, either barely there or missing entirely. Sound like our boy to you?"

Mary shook her head. "No, not at all."

"If Progeria is a gene mutation and the other disorders are DNA-related, and none fit with what's happened to Luca, where would you guess the problem lies?"

Before Mary could answer, John was three feet away, clearing his throat. "It's getting worse out there," he said. "Desmond's been watching the bleakers, and it's looking bad. Their numbers are growing, and they seem to be moving faster and getting smarter. They're opening unlocked car doors and climbing inside. Desmond's getting worried about the cargo van, but still thinks we should wait until morning to leave. I'm not so sure."

He turned to Will. "I was thinking we could use the helicopter and shuttle out to the airport. You could fly us in turns. Maybe we could get a plane. What do you think?"

"Not gonna work. I don't think we should split up." Will said with a pleasant keeping-the-peace sort of smile. "I think that when we're ready to leave, we should all leave together. And besides, it's not as easy as grabbing a plane and getting it in the air. You've no idea how hard it is to find the right one, fuel up, make sure everything is working. It isn't like we have a ground crew. Took me a helluva lot of prep to get us here in the first place. Plus, we have a lot more weight to handle now. Of course, we can find plenty of transportation at the airport, guaranteed, but it might be smarter to stay on the ground, at least until we know where we're going. Altogether, I'm not so sure the airport is the best idea. But," Will shrugged, "if that's where we elect to go, I'll get us there safe."

"You don't seem too concerned," John said, a hint of accusation in his voice which annoyed Mary, but seemed to bounce off Will. "You still operating on this hunch of yours?"

"For now, that's all I've got," Will said. "And as for my concern, well, no, I'm not, really. Don't get me wrong." he gestured outside. "There's a nightmare waiting, but it's not meandering around the parking lot of a Drury Inn, least not yet."

John stared at Will, as if he weren't sure whether he was dealing with idiocy or dementia. "What on Earth are you talking about?"

"Those things outside? They're more scared of you than you are of them."

"Bullshit," John said.

Mary wondered how long Will would stay polite to John's growing bitchiness.

Will shrugged again. "You see it from whatever angle you like. But those 'bleakers,' as you call them, are just children. They'll grow up and get mean like most of us do, but right now, we need to let them be and get out of here precisely one second after it makes sense to do so. It's not like they're storming in here or organizing an effort to attack, right?"

"We're in danger every minute we're here, and it seems like common sense went the same place as the rest of the planet's pulse." John turned on a heel and headed back to his station by the front. Dog Vader barked from the other side of the bar.

"See," Will said with a wink to Mary, "even Dog Vader agrees."

"Your dog's name is Dog Vader?" Mary asked.

"Luca's dog, Luca's name for him."

"Ah," she said, "So where were we? I think you were trying to bore me with talk about DNA and gene mutation, right before you told me that none of it mattered."

Will laughed. "Right. Well, it doesn't, really. But rapid aging exists in science, and I wanted to illustrate what science already knew, so I could paint an accurate picture of what it doesn't. I don't believe Luca's age has a thing to do with his DNA, and I don't think he's suffered a mutation. I think it's all up here." Will tapped the side of his temple.

"What do you mean?"

"You've heard the urban legend that if you die in your sleep, you'll die in real life, right?"

"Yeah, I've heard that. But it's not true. *Right?*"

"No, not true at all. But the legend makes sense since the mind is the mother of everything. If you believe something strongly enough, you can sometimes will it to happen. Like sometimes you won't want to get sick before a big event or something, and sure enough, a day or two before it's set to occur, you've got the sniffles. You willed yourself to sickness, even though it wasn't intentional, and the last thing you wanted to do. You created the conditions to make it happen though, activated parts of your body, shut others down, and a bunch of stuff we don't even know we're doing. Now this doesn't mean you can get money to rain from the sky like those quacks from *The Secret* would swear, but the brain *is* amazingly complex and powerful. And as advanced as science is, in many ways, brain research is still in the Dark Ages. And I hate to say it, but it looks like research just slowed by a century or so."

"So, are you saying Luca just *made* himself older?"

"Ha, if you want to reduce my theory to a simplified sentence, sure. Our bodies are capable of so much we don't even know. Unfortunately, we usually find out through accidental discovery like when people's skin turns to bone and the rapid aging stuff. I'm just saying our bodies contain all sorts of buttons and features we haven't even seen. Maybe whatever got inside your daughter and Luca hit a switch."

Desmond walked up, heavy breath and sweat on his brow.

"Am I interrupting anything?"

"No, just playing a round of 'What The Hell Is Going On Here?'" Mary exchanged a smile with Will. "What's up?"

"Well, the bleakers are definitely more ... *confident*, and it seems the later it gets, the more of them show up and the more energized they are." Desmond gestured nervously toward the front door. "John's edgy and wants to leave right now. I can see why; it's getting grim out there. But I'm inclined to think we should stay. What about you, Will? What's your gut tell you?"

"I'm still thinking morning. I won't argue if everyone else votes to leave now, but I don't think those gruesome uglies pose much of a threat."

Desmond raised his eyebrows. "Really?"

"I think they *will* get dangerous, and soon, but I don't think they're there yet. And if their numbers are thinner and speed slower in the morning, as you all said they were, that seems like the ideal time to split. One more night in a comfortable bed won't make much of a difference, and might end up being what keeps us all alive."

"What makes you so sure?" Desmond asked. Mary noted that, as usual, curiosity, not confrontation, edged his question.

"I never claimed certainty, but it's what I feel inside." He turned to Mary. "Mary knows what I mean."

"Great, now there's two of them." Desmond raised his hands over his head in mock frustration. "I suggest we hunker down early and get as much sleep as possible tonight. We'll head out as early as we can in the morning. Sound good?"

"Sounds great," Mary said.

Will nodded.

Desmond saluted, then turned and went back to John.

"How many more interruptions you think we'll have?" Mary asked.

"Twelve." Will smiled.

"So, if Luca could make himself five years older, does that mean he can make himself five years younger, too?"

"I don't think so. I mean, growing is a natural occurrence. His just sped it up. Growing backwards, though, not natural. I won't say it's impossible, but I think it highly unlikely."

Mary sank into the weight of what Will was saying, then changed the subject, pointing toward the trio of Uno players. "Think they're having fun?"

"You ever seen anyone *not* having fun with a deck of Uno?"

Mary rolled her eyes. "Obviously, you don't have children. Kids these days can look like they're not having fun while playing PS3 on the floor of a candy factory."

"Ah," Will said. "The old *too much and not enough* syndrome."

"Yeah, that's about right." She was still studying the group. "They look so … happy."

"That's a good thing, isn't it?"

"Of course," Mary said. "Just seems … *unnatural*. How can they laugh and smile with everything that's going on?"

"That's ridiculous, Mary, and you know it. Don't try and tell me you haven't found reason to laugh or smile or hope in the last few days, because I know full well you have. And I don't have to be in your dreams to see it, or to watch you light up every time Desmond Do-Right over there opens his mouth."

"Not true," Mary said, barely hiding a smile.

"Okay, whatever you say. But that's the beauty of the human condition; we're always able to see the spring on the other side of winter, so long as we're willing to try."

Will slid back in his chair. Mary sank into hers.

She allowed the old man's warmth to blanket her. Maybe he was right about Luca; maybe she had nothing to fear. But a new *knowing* was inside her, one that was only now starting to surface; seeds germinating in the silences of all that Will *wasn't saying.*

But a small part of her could hear it, and that part sensed how terrible it was.

* * * *

CHAPTER 6
BRENT FOSTER

Oct. 16
2:14 p.m.
East Hampton Docks
East Hampton, New York

 They spent nearly five hours getting to the docks, after first stopping at a clinic and bandaging Luis' arm, then grabbing some medicine and first aid supplies for the road. They ran into a wall of stalled cars blocking passage to the bridge, so Brent had to get out of the BMW and move nearly a dozen cars. They all had keys dangling from ignitions, but the majority were either out of gas or dead as the world, and needed to be pushed aside.
 Fortunately, they'd not seen any other aliens along the way.
 Unfortunately, the fog had grown so thick and dark, their visibility was even worse on the coast than in the city. And the coast was just as much a ghost town, if not more, due to its lack of skyscrapers. While Brent half expected to

find a bunch of people waiting at the docks for the ferry, or cars left by people who'd taken it across already, they found neither.

Instead, they saw a large, yellow cardboard sign with big black letters, reading:

FERRY WILL RESUME TOMORROW at 8 A.M.

"What the hell? I thought they were supposed to run until nighttime," Luis said. "Now we're gonna have to find somewhere to stay."

They had no shortage of homes to choose from, and most were quite nice. They grabbed the duffel bags from the car and headed across a field toward a two-story house, which probably cost more than Brent would have made throughout his entire career.

"Anyone home?" Luis said, knocking on the front door. No answer, so he tried the doorknob. It was locked. But the front window wasn't, so they slipped inside like burglars.

The house, while nice on the outside, was a letdown inside. The owners were an older couple, judging by the photos, and it looked like they hadn't redecorated since the Clinton administration, maybe even the first Bush. The only new item in sight, standing bold amid the dated furniture and faded paint, was a large, flat-screen TV.

"Mind if I stay in this one?" Luis asked, glancing out the window. They had a decent view of the docks from where they were, probably the best view on the block given the thickness of the fog.

"We can stay here," Brent said.

"No," Luis corrected him, "What I'm saying is do you mind if I stay here. You should find another house, preferably one I don't know where you are."

"What are you talking about?" Brent asked.

"That thing bit me. It's only a matter of time before I turn, just like Joe did."

"You don't know that. That thing didn't *bite* Joe, it ... I dunno, dug its fingers into Joe's skull. It left marks. You didn't have any marks on you, other than the bite."

"I might now, though," Luis said, holding up his bandaged forearm. "For all we know, it could be a whole mess of nasty under here. I'm thinking we should split up, just in case I go full zombie and shit."

"No," Brent said, "I'm not leaving you. Remember? We're in this shit together. You said so yourself. Don't fight me on it, either, or I'll have to unleash my Fists of Journalistic Fury on you again."

Brent smiled, waving his fists like an old time boxer from silent movies, and Luis broke into a laugh.

**

As the day surrendered to darkness, Brent and Luis sat in the living room tossing back warm beers as the sound of ocean waves and salty breeze washed through the Colonial-style front windows, which they left open. Brent had never been much of a beachfront guy, seemed like a lot of expense for not much return. But as the music of the lapping ocean waves relaxed him, he could see the appeal.

Brent sat in an ugly, but comfortable recliner, while Luis lounged on an even uglier, if it were possible, checkered, beige sofa. They didn't want to risk using flashlights any more than necessary and potentially alerting any creatures that might be lurking outside along the coastline, so they ate and drank by the bright moonlight, which bathed the living room in blue.

The conversation had moved from why the Mets sucked, to whether the Jets had a shot this year, to what kinds of dads they had growing up. Luis had a strict Catholic father who died when he was young, so he was mostly raised by his mother, forced to be the man of the house and look out for his long-deceased younger brother, Ricky.

Brent cracked another beer and said, "My dad was a tough blue-collar guy who worked at a steel mill. He hated every fucking minute of it; I could tell, but he never let us know how much the job was busting his ass. I was too stupid to appreciate how hard he worked at the time. I was more concerned with having fun, buying shit we didn't need, and stuff. We were in the suburbs, and I'd been hanging out with the preppy crowd."

"No shit, you?" Luis said, laughing.

"Yeah. I had these grand schemes that I'd be this famous writer; I'd make my first million by the time I was 22. I wasn't gonna bust my ass for some job that would dry up when the company shipped all the jobs overseas. I wasn't willing to be anyone's schmuck. I'd make my own living, thank you very much."

"So how did your dad feel about your career plans?"

"Actually, he *didn't* want me to follow in his footsteps. He had a hard job because that's all he could get at the time. He wanted me to have the opportunities he didn't have. He wanted me to go to college and make something of myself. But when I was in high school, college was the last thing on my mind. I wanted to goof off and have fun, you know. In my junior year, I was on the verge of being held back. Then one day, I was waiting for my mom to pick me up from school. I was hanging out in the front of the school with these girls who were way out of my league. I was doing my best to impress them, and being pretty damned charming, if I do say so myself. Anyway, here I am, about to win over this girl I'd been lusting after for two years, when all of a sudden, my dad shows up."

"So?" Luis asked, "That a bad thing?"

"Oh yeah. You see, my mom had the 'good car.' While my dad had this beater car, biggest piece of shit to ever roll off a factory floor. I was mortified. I couldn't let these girls know I was poor and that my old man drove the Shitmobile 3000. And God forbid he got out of the car looking all dirty and shit. I would have died right there on the spot. Fortunately, he hadn't seen me, because we were standing in this alcove near one of the doorways. The minute I saw him, I told the girls I had to go to the bathroom, then ran to the other end of the school, out the side doors, and started walking home on the road where I knew he would pass me."

"Oh shit," Luis said.

"Yeah, so I was walking for about 10 minutes when my dad pulled up beside me, and opened the door. I got in, and he asked me why I was walking. I told him some lie about how I didn't think anyone was gonna pick me up because it had been late, so I figured I'd walk. He told me that my mom's car was broken down and that he had to take time off work to come get me, which meant he'd have to make up the hours on the weekend. He wasn't complaining, or anything, just telling it like it was. He seemed more concerned that I'd had to walk. He reminded me it was dangerous to be walking alone on the road. Man, I felt like such a shit heel. How the hell could I be embarrassed by my own dad like that? So, as we were driving home, I found myself watching him, seeing him for the first time like the real man he was — a guy who took care of his family and always did the right thing. And I started to see how insignificant I was, and how lazy, and I vowed right there not to waste any more time and to work as hard as I could to get ahead."

"Wow," Luis said. "That's some heavy shit. So, was he proud of you when you got your first job?"

"Yeah. I got a job at this small paper in our hometown. A shit paper with 20,000 readers, maybe, and I was writing obits and cats-in-tree stories for the first year, but whenever I saw him, he'd comment on whatever story I wrote no matter how insignificant. He was connecting with me through stories I was writing about other people. It was weird and completely cool at the same time."

"That's awesome," Luis said. "What did he think when you had a kid?"

"He died of lung cancer, even though he never touched a cigarette, a month before Ben was born," Brent said, starting to tear up. "I know he was looking forward to having a grandchild more than anything, though. He kept going to the store, even when he was sick, and buying stuff for Ben. He bought him this, actually," Brent said as he pulled the blue train out of his pocket and held it up so the moonlight captured the train's big smile. "Stanley Train, Ben's favorite toy ever."

"What about your mom?" Luis asked.

"My mom got to see Ben. She loved him and doted on him like a good grandma does. But she died a year to the day my dad did; a stroke."

"Jesus," Luis said.

Brent stared at Stanley's smiling face, and told himself he wasn't going to cry even as he felt his chin quiver.

"So, that's why you worked so hard and never saw your family?" Luis asked, "To prove to yourself that you were the man your dad was? To be a good dad like him?"

"Ironic, eh?"

"No doubt," Luis said.

They passed the next several minutes in silence until Brent fell asleep in his chair.

He woke in the darkness to the sound of a car outside.

* * * *

CHAPTER 7
LUIS TORRES

Oct. 16
5:40 a.m.
East Hampton, New York

Luis woke about five minutes before Brent, having heard the car stop across the street at the docks, where it had sat since, two spots from his own, with the lights on. Luis grabbed a chair and his shotgun, then sat in the darkness, watching and waiting.

Though he could only vaguely see the taillights through the dark and fog, the car looked like a Toyota.

"What's it doing?" Brent whispered, yawning as he took a seat next to Luis.

"Maybe waiting for the ferry, too." Luis said.

"Another survivor? Well, shit, they ought to turn off the lights and not call so much attention to themselves!" Brent said.

"Maybe they haven't seen the aliens or monsters, or whatever the hell those things are," Luis said.

"Think we should go out there?" Brent said. "Let 'em know there's at least two more people and tell them to turn out the lights?"

"I dunno. Shit could go south real quick if we approach the car in the dark, even if they're friendlies. We'll wait. Besides, we don't know if they've attracted any unwanted attention. So, we stay put until we need to move."

"So, we use 'em as alien bait?" Brent asked.

"Well, not intentionally, but it's a good way to see if there are any out there before we go out."

"We'll step in to help if we need to, right?" Brent said.

"As long as I don't see Red Sox bumper stickers on the car," Luis said with a smirk. "Otherwise, they're on their own."

"What time is it?" Brent asked, yawning.

Luis glanced at his watch, and through a yawn said, "Five forty. Got another hour or so before the sun is up."

"Mind if I take a shower?" Brent asked.

"Go ahead, but take your gun. You'll hear me shooting if I need you."

Brent paused before he started up the stairs, "How's the arm?"

"Stings like a bitch," Luis said. "I'll check it out when I shower."

"You're not feeling weird or anything?"

"If you're asking am I gonna turn into a zombie, I'm not getting a craving for brains or anything ... yet."

Brent laughed, if a bit nervously, then went upstairs with a flashlight in one hand, his gun in the other.

Luis turned his attention back to the car, wondering if he should take a chance and head outside. He didn't like having unknown variables in play. And not knowing who was in the car when they needed to get to the docks shortly was a pretty big variable as far as he was concerned.

"Why don't you turn your damned lights off?" he whispered before getting up and heading toward the kitchen. He was famished and craving junk food, something he rarely allowed himself back before the world flushed its people. He found a box of granola bars in the pantry. Chocolate chip peanut butter. Close enough to junk, he supposed. He ripped the foil from the bar and took a bite.

Wow, this is like the best granola bar ever!

He downed it in seconds, then gobbled another. He went to the fridge and grabbed a bottle of water from the more than 20 that filled the bottom crisper bin. He wasn't sure how long before the plumbing stopped working in a world without people to power the water plants, but figured they probably had enough bottled water to last a few hundred years. He never saw sense in paying for bottled water, but was glad enough people had been frivolous enough with their cash to create a demand that might supply survivors for a century.

Of course, he hoped it wouldn't come to that, hoped Black Island would offer hope, to let them know this event, whatever it was, was localized. That the rest of the world was alive and kicking, thank you very much, and the prophetic dreams Luis had been having, along with the other 215ers, were just a weird ass coincidence.

He also hoped his daughter and Brent's family were still out there, too. And while he was feeling hopeful, he went ahead and hoped Joe's bite wouldn't turn him into one of those fucking creatures.

But Luis knew better than to get his hopes up.

He had a bad feeling. And as the hours ticked, the certainty something horrible was going to happen grew even stronger in his gut. He grabbed a third granola bar, then returned to his post at the window.

The car's lights were off.

He put the granola bar down, picked up the shotgun, and scanned the distance between the house and parking lot. He saw nothing but darkness. Perhaps the driver had finally decided he or she didn't need the lights on and would simply sit and wait for morning. Luis would sit, too, and wait for the sun to come up so he could get a better idea of what he was dealing with.

**

Brent came down, dressed in black sweat pants and a grey T-shirt, two or three sizes too large with a picture of a golf ball on the front, as big as a target. Luis laughed. "Damn, bro. That is hideous."

"Wish I'd thought to pack some clothes," Brent said. "Don't worry, I saved all the cool clothes for you."

"Can't wait to see what passes for cool in this house," Luis said, looking at his bloodied jeans and tee shirt. "But I'm good, I've got some clothes in one of the bags."

"You fucker," Brent said with a laugh. "You'll be dressed like usual, while I'm wearing Oldy McOlderson's tacky workout gear."

"I don't know," Luis said with a grin. "I think you make it work."

"Fuck you, sir. So, what's happening with the car?"

"Lights went out while I was in the kitchen, but I haven't seen anyone, so I'm thinking they're just waiting until morning when the ferry rolls in. Once the sun's out, we can check it out, if you want."

"Alright," Brent said, searching for something to eat in the kitchen. "Oh, man, you ate the last of the granola bars?"

"Sorry," Luis said, laughing. "Didn't see your name on 'em."

"That's okay," Brent said a minute later. "I found some Pop-Tarts. I haven't had these in forever. Of course, it's the damned unfrosted cherry ones."

"And without power, we don't have a toaster," Luis reminded him.

"Oh well," Brent said, returning to the window with a Pop-Tart and a bottle of water. "You gonna shower? I'll stand guard down here."

"Alright, if anyone gets out of the car, come get me. Don't go out there, or answer the door if they come knocking."

"Okay," Brent said, sitting down.

"And keep your gun ready," Luis said, as he headed up the stairs with his bag, flashlight, shotgun, and one of the first aid kits he'd grabbed earlier.

**

The flashlight stood on the sink, its light bouncing off the mirror and ceiling of the bathroom giving Luis just enough light to bathe by. He stood under the shower, allowing the cold water to wash the blood and dirt from his body. Would've been better if the water were piping hot, but Luis didn't care. After recent events, any water felt good. *Cleansing.* He leaned forward, allowing the pulsating jets to massage his shoulder blades. He glanced at his right arm. The bandages were soaked and sure to fall off soon if he didn't do anything.

He remembered how Joe's face had changed after he'd been infected. The black veins and splotches on his skin right before he *turned.*

He continued staring at the bandage, wanting to change the dressing, but not wanting to see what laid beneath. If he *was* infected, he was as good as dead. He knew it like he knew the sun would rise. What he didn't know, was how quickly the infection would spread. Would he even know it was happening? He remembered the look in Joe's eyes — at first white, then all black, almost alien-like in the way they seemed to bore into Luis. Nothing was left of Joe in those eyes; it was all alien, monster, whatever the fuck the infection had put into him.

Luis leaned against the shower wall and began to claw at the bandage with an immediate need to see.

The wet bandage fell to the shower floor with a plop. Luis stared at his arm, not believing the dim light's certain lie. He reached from the shower and grabbed the flashlight, and trained it on his arm.

The bite was gone, completely healed, though the burning and pain were still present.

What the fuck?

He put the light under his chin, and began to rub his other hand along the wound. The skin was smooth, as if never broken. He brought his arm closer for a better look, when something moved beneath his skin.

"Fu ... " he shouted, the light slipped, bounced around the shower floor with a loud echo, before coming to a stop. Luis grabbed it, focused the beam back on his arm, waiting for movement.

Maybe I'm just seeing things.

Something moved again, and this time he was *certain* he'd seen it. And not just one thing moving, but several worm-like shapes, just beneath the surface of his skin.

Luis stared in horror. Eyes wide, unable to look away.

Infected.

No, I'm not going out like that.

Luis yanked the shower curtain aside, threw the light into the sink where it rolled before pointing at the mirror, and grabbed the shotgun. He sank to the floor of the shower, water pouring over him, blinding him, as he wrapped his lips around the barrel of the shotgun.

He prayed that suicides didn't go to hell, and he would see his wife and daughter again in the great beyond.

* * * *

CHAPTER 8
JOHN LARSON

Oct. 17
Early evening
Belle Springs, Missouri

The afternoon was long. Despite creeping danger outside and mounting evidence that they should leave, Desmond wouldn't budge. A weird kid, a crazy old man, and the Olson Twins had made sure of that.

At least they had finally managed to fortify the hotel. Four entrances were there, but before they effectively blocked them all, the party was vulnerable. And leaving in the morning or not, that wasn't going to fly, which is why he, Desmond, Mary, and Will spent the afternoon moving furniture and shoving it against the windows and doors.

Desmond even walked two blocks to where he'd seen an oversized 4 x 4, then brought it back and parked it flush against the rear door of the hotel farthest from them and therefore most susceptible to attack.

That made John feel better, but not much. No, much didn't come around until his third, maybe fourth, shot of scotch.

He would have been content to drink the day to memory, sleep off the stupidity of everyone around him, then wake in the morning and get the hell out and onto the road. But he preferred to drink alone, and no one would let him. Everyone kept dropping by the bar to check on him and make sure he was okay. First Will, then Mary and Desmond together, and now Jimmy, who wasn't old enough to drink (though that didn't stop him from getting high), so he just sat beside John on the barstool with a stupid grin, a glass of soda, and his endless reserve of verbal vomit.

"Come on," Jimmy said, "Isn't there *any* part of you that sees this as an adventure?"

John stared at Jimmy, poured himself another shot, then lifted it to his lips, tilted his head and drained it with a grimace.

"You don't know me well enough to realize that ignoring me just makes me more eager to break down your defenses," Jimmy said.

John stayed silent.

Jimmy said, "It really, really sucks about Jenny. I'm sorry about that, believe me. But there's nothing you can do to change it, and every minute you spend thinking about it now is a minute you're not spending living the only life you have left."

John poured himself another shot, then set the bottle on the bar and turned to Jimmy. "You have no idea what you're talking about. You're a kid. You don't know the first thing about love or loss or sacrifice, and you don't know what it feels like to lose the one thing in your life that matters most."

"Fuck you, man." Jimmy shook his head. "I don't mean any disrespect, but that's bullshit. You think I woke up with my family and friends gone without feeling a thing? No, I woke up just as scared as anyone, and I've stayed just as scared, but I'm not letting those feelings live my life, or stink up the air of everyone around me. We're all in the same boat. You don't have a monopoly on sorrow, dude. We've *all* lost people we love. And we're *all* trying to survive and make the most of this."

"Well," John said, "looks like one of us is just more honest than the other." He drained his shot and poured another.

"Hope the end of the world heightened your tolerance to alcohol, because you're on your way to the floor. Again." Jimmy slid from the barstool, gave John a mock salute then sauntered off.

Punk-ass kid was way too full of himself. Of course, he missed his family, but that wasn't the same. You were born into your family, you didn't choose them, and they didn't choose you. Losing the one person who knew you inside out and upside down, the one who could soothe your wounds and make sure you're loved, well that was something else. The loss had left John with a hunger that all the grain in the world had no hope of sating.

He felt a hand on his shoulder. Desmond, again. *Fuck.* For a guy who acted like the role of leader bore the weight of a cross, he sure wore his duty with a smile.

"Anything I can do for you, boss?" John said.

"No need for that," Desmond said, then sat on Jimmy's empty barstool and reached across the bar for an empty glass. He studied the row of bottles, then grabbed a short, stout flagon of Tres Campañeros and poured himself a shot. "Any chance there's something I can do to help *you*, or even better, a chance you'll *let me?*"

"Any chance you can turn back time, bring back the dead, or hell, recover your common sense long enough to stop listening to an old hippie and lead us out of this deathtrap?"

Desmond sighed. "We're doing the right thing by waiting until tomorrow," he said. "I know this is hard on you, and I know it's hard to stop thinking about Jenny. I didn't lose anyone, not like that at least, and I'm not so callous as to say everything will be fine. But I can offer the cliché 'It's better to have loved and lost than to have never loved at all,' because I believe it. Everyone in here is suffering, John. Jimmy lost his family, Paola lost her father, hell, Mary almost lost Paola. Your grief doesn't run deeper than theirs, and you need to help us all out by letting your best self surface. You're one of the nicest, most caring people I've met. Please," he added, "we need you."

Desmond swallowed his shot.

John's body started to quiver. "It's not that easy, and believe me, you don't understand."

"Then help me understand. I'm here for you. Whatever you need."

John suddenly shattered. Through cracked sobs he started spewing: "Jenny and I never fought. And I mean *never*. Twice in seven years. The fight we had the other night was only our third one, but it was the worst one of all."

John wiped his eyes, caught his breath, then completely unraveled.

"We never argue, never even raise our voices in anger. We talk about everything, so we never have any pent-up bullshit that sabotages most people. We're lucky; most couples don't manage to get what we had in a lifetime." John started to choke, and for a moment, he felt like he was going to lose his liquor in chunks.

He drew a deep breath then said, "But that night, everything went to hell."

"What happened?"

"It started small. Jenny had a God-awful day at work. Her boss was riding her ass all afternoon, her assistant didn't show because morning sickness turned into all-day sickness, and Jenny dropped the ball on some big report she'd been working on for two weeks. She hated her job, and a lot of this was the same old shit, so it would've been fine, but she got a flat on the way home and that just amplified everything."

John took a moment to breathe, then continued. "She called Auto Club, but it turns out that somehow, I'd let our membership lapse. She tried to call me, but my cell phone was off, so she ended up stuck in the rain for over an hour."

John wiped his eyes.

"Soon as I walked through the door, she launched right in, yelling at me for the first time since she saw me answer my ex-girlfriend back on my Facebook wall two years ago, which was Fight Number Two, in case you're keeping score. So, I asked her why she was so hysterical. She said I didn't pay the Auto Club bill and that I obviously didn't care about her safety. I told her that was ridiculous and she said not to call her ridiculous. I told her I wasn't calling *her ridiculous*, but that saying I didn't care about her safety *was* ridiculous. I asked her what happened, and she told me about the flat tire. So I asked her how long it had been since she took the car in for service. Definitely the wrong thing to say."

The tears had stopped, and John found control of his voice. "Things went from bad to worse. For some stupid reason, I told her she was acting just like her mother, even called her Mrs. Rasmussen. She was standing behind the kitchen bar when I said it, and she threw a bottle of ketchup. It sailed behind me and skidded across the floor. It was plastic, so it didn't break, and I laughed, but that just seemed to make her madder."

John took another drink, then continued. "We spent the next two hours fighting, saying some horrible, horrible things. Things we'd never said before. She told me that

I wasn't a *real man* because I didn't know how to do the things that real men knew how to do. And as the Man of the House, I should've looked after the car and made sure it was always serviced and the Auto Club dues paid." John swallowed. "So, I told her maybe she ought to service her man a bit more often, but it didn't really matter anyway, because she fucked like a corpse."

"Ouch," Desmond said, taking another shot for himself.

Though he was no longer crying, John felt utterly defeated. "And that was pretty much that. She left the room, and I made myself comfortable on the couch. When I woke the next morning, she was gone. So was everyone else."

"I'm so sorry," Desmond said. He remained still, waiting to see if John was through.

"No, *I'm* sorry," John said. "I shouldn't be putting this on everyone else. I should have buried it already. You've been right from the beginning — I'm not serving anyone, including myself."

"We understand," Desmond said putting a hand on John's shoulder.

Though John would've shrugged off Desmond's friendly touch just moments ago, now that they'd had this moment, John found Desmond comforting. He could see why Desmond had become the de facto leader of the group.

"You're grieving," Desmond said, "and your circumstances are making mourning that much harder. Go to bed; sleep it off. You'll feel like a new man in the morning, and if not, I'm here for you. Anytime."

John smiled back. "Thanks, Desmond, for everything. I'll pull myself together, I promise."

They shook hands, then John turned and headed toward his room, both comforted and embarrassed that Desmond had seen him so vulnerable.

* * * *

CHAPTER 9
BORICIO WOLFE

Oct. 18
Evening
Somewhere in Alabama

Boricio opened the cellar door to the cool dark of a late Alabama evening. *Free, at last.*

Like Moe said, the compound had a farm and silo, and what looked like a communications building, and a large hangar. The cellar they'd been in was beneath a large, three-story home, smack in the middle of two others that looked just like it. And another building Moe hadn't mentioned was there — long, shotgun style, beside the three houses. Additionally, a high brick wall neatly circled the compound.

"This way." Boricio motioned toward the steady roar of a generator rumbling from behind the house. Team Boricio followed.

The escapees huddled in the shadows behind the house. Between night's shadows and the loud hum from the generator, they were almost invisible.

"What do we do now?" Adam whispered.

Boricio hadn't a fucking clue, and that made him want to break teeth. Too many things he didn't know; too many things could go wrong.

"I'm thinking that house over there's our best bet," he said, pointing toward the one at the far end of the row, near the front gate, which was the only house with its windows lit. "I'm guessing that's where the rabble sleeps," he said, nodding toward the longer building. "That means whatever's in these houses is mucho importanté. The lights are all on over yonder at 1313 Mockingbird Lane, so I'm guessing that's where the king is probably holding court."

"All the windows are barred." That was either Manny or Jack whispering. Boricio couldn't tell over the generator, and wouldn't have cared anyway.

"So we get close and wait," Boricio said. "We'll see something. And when we see something worth seeing, we'll do what needs doing. We assume this place is a Rambo factory, you can be sure as a Friday night fuck in the ass, these shit heels'll be shooting to kill. But that doesn't mean you can go popping off and thinking you're gonna see sunrise. Shoot when you know it's right, maybe a second before. But never pull the trigger just to pull it, and always use your nose. And don't think too much."

"What do I do?" Manny asked. "Shoot 'em with my dick?"

"I'm sure that's a miniature fucking weapon," Boricio laughed. "If you hadn't been such a throbbing cock, I wouldn't have had to put you on time out. Just stay out of the way and if you can get a gun from one of the guards, take it and use it ... but not on me."

Boricio called clear, and they crept to the house at the end, then into another tangle of shadows until they hit the brick wall flush with hiding places in bushes that lined the inside of the wall.

"Stay here," Boricio whispered. "I'm gonna check out a few things."

"Wait!" Adam said.

Boricio turned.

"Take this." Adam handed Boricio his Colt.

"Thanks, kid," Boricio said, handing Adam the bat. He put the .45 in his pants, then dropped to the dirt and slithered along the wall so he could get a better look at the main house.

The house wasn't ornate, but was far nicer then Boricio would have expected. Wood was new, the paint fresh, and the fixtures weren't from the local hardware store. Iron bars secured the windows.

Boricio couldn't see inside since most of the windows were dark or the curtains were drawn tight. But he had a perfect view of the front porch about 15 yards off, just behind a wall of underbrush. The three men talking on the steps put the odds of Boricio escaping via the main gate, which was closed and about 40 yards away, highly unlikely.

Just past the three men, through the only open and lit window of the front of the house, Boricio saw the big-nippled bitch sitting down. It appeared as if she were furiously scribbling something at a desk.

Everywhere else was dark.

The men on the porch would be easy to kill, but it was impossible to know how many more were inside, or how quickly they could sound the alarm. Might be better to say *fuck it* and slowly head for the exit.

Boricio crawled back to the side of the house to get Team Boricio, but stopped short a few feet away.

His men were standing, hands in the air, as one of the survivalist fucks pointed an assault rifle at them.

Boricio stayed low and inched forward, shrouded behind the drapes of evening black. He could hear commotion coming from the rear of the house, faint but growing louder.

They found the bodies.
Shit, meet fan.

A loud bark from the mouth behind the rifle: "Where's the other one?"

Boricio inched forward, his footfalls disguised by the generator's racket.

"We have no idea," Charlie said. "He left us behind. He's a no good son of a bitch, and we're glad he's gone."

Good kid.

Boricio shot from the dark and into the survivalist fuck's chest, pulling the rifle from his grip then shattering his jaw with its butt in a single fluid motion. Once the survivalist fuck started screaming, Boricio figured the pussy was already out of the bag, so he relieved the rifle of a few of its bullets, then tossed the .45 back to Adam. "Alright cowboy, let's go kill us some injuns," he said.

Adam handed his bat to Manny.

Just then the trio of survivalist fucks who'd been milling on the porch rounded the corner, guns drawn.

Boricio yelled, "Duck!" as the first gunman fired a shot. Adam didn't need the warning. He was on the ground and firing at the soldier, though every one of his shots found nothing but air.

Only thing keeping us alive is night. This place gets lit, and we're deader than the fucking radio star. Need to get close. If we can't smell the battle, we're losing it.

Boricio roared, then flew at the trio.

He knocked the rifle from the lead man's hands, kicked it behind him, then spun to his backside. Boricio put the Colt to the top of the survivalist's head and pulled the trigger.

One down. Two to go.

The two remaining survivalists had moved past Boricio, chasing down his men and emptying their guns into the dark, too scattered to realize they were one man down.

Boricio pointed at the second survivalist fuck, about 10 feet away, and pulled the trigger. Like most hunters, Boricio's night vision was second to none. The fucker fell 10 feet from his buddy in the dirt. Boricio took out the third man with two shots.

As his team raced forward, a shot rang out and Boricio saw Jack's head burst like a melon. "Let's go!" Boricio shouted at the three remaining members of Team Boricio. "NOW!"

Another two survivalist fucks rounded the corner from the rear of the house, and Boricio fired a pair of shots. One sank right into the first man's forehead, and he went down. The other went into his buddy's shoulder. Would've been cool as a $100 cream pie if Team Boricio could help him with the slack. But 10 bullets left three guns, and only two found their mark. Fortunately, one landed square in the injured guard's face.

A spotlight lit the top of the first house, dressing a sniper in light. Boricio swiveled to the side as a hollow crack flew through the air, followed by a splatter of dirt beside him.

"Follow me!" Boricio crouched and ran, behind the building and out of sight, but not out of the sniper's range. Adam and Charlie followed close. Manny, too, but not close enough. Another hollow crack thundered in the air, and Manny fell to the ground. Adam grabbed his bat, and ran to Boricio, out of breath, sweaty and panicked, just like Charlie.

FUCK! We're surrounded and about to get a bullet bukkake straight to the face. Least it looks like I still got the two best apples in the barrel, for what that's worth.

"Alright, listen up," Boricio said as they ducked behind the brush against the wall. The spotlight swept overhead, then back, searching for them as men shouted at one another from the front yard. "Them assholes are dead because they were supposed to be. You're supposed to stay alive. All three of us. Now we need to get from here to there." Boricio pointed at the hangar about 50 yards away, in the back of the compound. "We can do it, but we have to keep going and can't stop for nothing. Got it?"

They nodded.

"These fuckers are multiplying by the minute and if we're not out of here yesterday, we're gonna be the meat in the middle of a dead fucker sandwich. So just keep running. Night's on our side. They'll shine that light on you, but you zig and zag every time they do. Do NOT run in a straight line. Run like you're the craziest Forest Gump mother fucker to ever put on a pair of Nikes. Don't stop for nothing and wait for my lead."

Another dozen footsteps slapped the dirt from the rear of the house. A few seconds, and they'd be surrounded. Boricio peeked out at the three survivalist fucks who must've lost all common sense when everything else in the world went adios since they had their guns drawn but were standing right out in the open, facing the front yard instead of the back.

"Cover my back!" Boricio yelled, then flew into the open, splitting five bullets between three survivalists and dropping them all.

Boricio was about to tell the boys to go, but something grabbed his attention like a punch to the balls.

A fluttering curtain parted from an open window on the second floor on the side of the house. And time froze for Boricio.

It felt like someone was pouring iced reality down Boricio's throat then making him piss it right back out.

That dumb bitch from New Orleans — the one from the world's last night alive, the one whose body had disappeared and blood turned to bleach stains — she was staring at him from the window, with secrets in her eyes and a broken promise on her lips.

She put her pointer finger to her mouth, shook her head, then closed the curtain.

Boricio gritted his teeth and snarled. It took everything inside him not to rush the house and figure out exactly what in the beer-battered bullshit was going on.

"What are you waiting for Mr. Boricio?" Charlie asked.

FUCK!

A second spotlight doused the black from the sky and more survivalist fucks were spilling from the front of the house. Shit was about to get ugly as a nun with a goiter.

Boricio looked up at the window again. He could see her silhouette, the same silhouette he'd stared at for months. The one he'd been saving for Christmas.

Charlie again: "Should we go?"

FUCK!

Boricio growled, "Just waiting for the perfect minute. Keep your guns down and ankles moving. I'm gonna need you on the other side." He looked back, nodded and said, "NOW!"

They tore into the night, and sure enough, a trio of gunmen was waiting just around the corner of the rear of the house. Boricio charged at full speed, ending their lives as he passed.

No one looked behind as their world exploded: whistling bullets, flying dirt, and shouted orders. They veered across empty space like the worst football team ever, somehow crossing the distance — zigging, zagging, and clinging to every molecule of available darkness.

Bullets hit the hangar with a clang. Boricio opened the door, rushed inside, and closed the doors just as his team scrambled inside, leaving just enough light to see several cars and trucks.

"I'm gonna need you to shoot any fuckers who try and get in here," Boricio said to the two kids. "I'll look for keys and if I can't find any, I'll hot-wire. Either way, I'm gonna need a few minutes."

Charlie and Adam nodded, then split, each one taking an opposite side of the hangar. Bullets smashed against the hangar's corrugated metal walls, some bouncing off, some ripping through, as Boricio searched through four trucks and found exactly dick. He circled back to the first truck, and tore the large, plastic panels from the top and bottom of the steering column and pulled the wiring from inside. He looked up just in time to see a survivalist fuck appear from nowhere, grabbing Charlie in a headlock and putting a gun to his head.

"Outta the truck!" the fucker yelled at Boricio.

Boricio didn't even need his thinking cap. Adam slipped behind the toady and bashed the fucker's skull in with the bat.

Team Boricio is getting better and better.

"Great job, boys!" Boricio hollered through the open window of the truck, slapping his hand on the roof. "One more minute and we'll be outta this bitch!"

Boricio dug his nail across the top of the wire's coating until the metal was exposed, then twisted the ends together. The dashboard lights came on, and Boricio howled again.

Charlie opened the hangar doors, as Adam fired shots outside. Boricio revved the engine and drove up to the doors. "Get in!" he yelled, and Charlie and Adam each jumped in on opposite sides. Boricio floored the gas, and the truck roared from the hangar.

Several dozen survivalist fucks were lined up near the front gate, waiting with rifles aimed and empty shells flying from the side as bullets tore through the night. At least another two dozen soldiers were spread throughout the compound and the entire place was lit like gay Christmas.

Boricio mowed through any survivalists stupid enough to stand in the way, keeping his head low as bullets kissed the metal in a symphony of deafening dings. Bullets that found the windshields hardly left a scratch.

"Woo-hoo!" Boricio hollered. "Nice of them fuckers to armor the truck for us, eh boys?" He turned to the back seat. Adam was quiet but smiling. Charlie's grin took up half the back seat.

Boricio spun the truck and aimed for the gate, which didn't stand a chance when Boricio barreled through it going 40 MPH six seconds later.

The truck flew up and over the small lip at the edge of the gate, caught air, then landed on the street, fishtailing a bit before Boricio got control of the wheel. Damn, it felt good to hit concrete.

Boricio glanced in the rearview and saw another truck, surprisingly close behind.

"Ha!" Boricio laughed. "That all them redneck fuckers got? You boys ain't worried, are you?" He turned to the back seat.

Adam looked behind him at the truck, then back up at Boricio and shook his head.

Charlie leaned forward. "Anyone know how to use this thing?" He had a grenade in the palm of his hand. "I lifted it from the soldier in the garage after Adam shot him."

Boricio laughed then pounded the dashboard.

"Holy shit, you little fucker! Look who just stepped up to claim MVP!" Boricio grinned at Charlie through the rearview. "Now I ain't no expert, but I say you just lean out the window, pull the pin, release the spoon, then chuck that fucker behind you. Just make sure you throw it *outside* the window or we're gonna be on the worst episode ever of *Funniest Home Videos*."

Charlie nodded, then rolled down the window, grinning ear to ear. "Die, FUCKERS!" he yelled, pulling the pin and dropping the grenade onto the highway.

For a moment, it seemed as if nothing would happen. The truck was too close, and it looked like Charlie dropped too early. But just as Boricio was starting to think he'd have to outdrive the fuckers, the grenade did its job, taking out the back of the gunmen's truck, causing the truck's headlights to swerve out of sight in the rearview.

"Woo-hoo!" Boricio yelled. "If Moses saw the look on your two faces, he would've had to add an extra commandment!"

They roared into the night, kings of the fucking road.

* * * *

CHAPTER 10
BRENT FOSTER

Brent had eaten both Pop-Tarts in the foil wrapper and was still hungry. He returned to the kitchen, grabbed a Twinkie, then sank back into his chair.

He laughed at the cliché of eating a Twinkie at the end of the world. Truth was, he could think of far worse foods to be stuck with into an eternity. Like those cans of weird meat that looked like flesh from another planet. That would suck if that's all there was left. He hoped more Twinkies than cans of meat were sitting on store shelves.

As he swallowed the last of the cake, Brent found himself wondering if Ben had ever tried one of the famous Hostess treats. He and Gina were strict about only giving him healthy food, except the occasional cookie. But even those were homemade oatmeal raisin, not some hydrogenated sugary wad of fat. The more Brent thought about it, the more certain he was that his 3-year-old had never tasted a Twinkie, which made him sad. Every child should have a Twinkie at least once.

Brent started thinking of all the other firsts his son would never have — first day of school, first love, first heartbreak, first job, the first time he realized what he wanted to do with his life, followed by a dozen or so changes of mind. Brent had tried not to dwell on his family. Tried not to imagine their dead eyes staring back at him from nowhere. Tried to imagine they were somewhere, anywhere, other than that rotting high-rise of death in Times Square.

Trying wasn't succeeding, though.

He was no longer certain they were alive. A hell of an admission, even if only to himself. It was surrender, and a father wasn't supposed to quit on his family.

He closed his eyes, tried to think of anything else, and saw Joe's dead eyes looking at him just before he attacked. Luis was right. Joe *had been* infected by those creatures. How or why, he had no idea. It seemed like a parasitic infection, like an alien in a movie infecting someone before taking control of their body.

He wondered if Luis had taken the bandage off yet. The shower was still running upstairs. As if in response to his question, something thumped and rolled above him. Luis had dropped something in the shower — the flashlight, Brent figured, unless Luis showered with the shotgun. He waited for another sound, but only heard the hum and patter of the shower. He thought about checking on Luis, going to the door and asking if everything was okay, but something outside caught his attention.

A light on in the car.

Between the fog, and the frosted windows of the car, the light was mostly a blur, but it captured and held Brent's attention. Shadows moved against the window, slow at first, then fast.

Something was happening in the car. And then he heard the unmistakable shrieks and clicking of the monsters.

The hairs on the back of Brent's neck stood on end. He gripped the pistol and searched the darkness.

Suddenly, the car's taillights came on, and the car reversed, quickly, straight toward the house. The parking lot was nearly 70 yards away, but the car was in full speed. As the car drew closer, Brent saw two of creatures on top, riding the car from the roof as it barreled straight at the front windows.

"Luis!" Brent screamed, clearing the stairs two at a time, and pounding on the door. Before he could say a word, a loud crash shook the house as the car crashed, in reverse, straight into the living room.

Luis burst out of the door, naked, shotgun in hand, eyes wild and confused, like he'd been snapped from a daze.

"What the hell?" Luis said, pushing his way past Brent. One of the creatures was at the bottom of the stairs, stunned, getting to its feet.

Luis blew its head off in one shot, then kicked it out of the way as he ran naked into the living room, aiming at the second creature on the hood, which was still screeching at whoever was in the car.

"Fuck you!" Luis screamed, unleashing another shot, hitting it in the chest. The creature flew back, and out the hole in front of the house. Luis gave chase, firing into the darkness.

Brent scanned the living room with his gun, making sure no other creatures were in the house, then turned to see a dark-haired woman passed out, face against the deployed air bag, and a young Asian girl, about 6, in the front seat. Her mouth was wide and face red, crying, "Mommy," over and over while struggling to push the airbag from herself and her mother.

Luis came back inside, and looked inside the car. "She okay?" he said, running to the driver's side, and opening the door. Brent opened the passenger side, and the girl screamed, backing up toward her mother as if Brent were going to harm her.

"It's okay," he said, "The monsters are gone."

Luis, on the other side, felt for a pulse on the girl's mother.

"She's alive," he said, glancing up at Brent, before racing upstairs. He returned with the first aid kit, wearing a pair of black jeans, his body still wet.

The woman raised her head, then murmured something unintelligible through her groggy haze.

"You're okay," Luis said, rushing to the woman's side. "You crashed into the house."

"I'm s ... sorry," she said, as her daughter clung to her. The woman embraced her daughter, though she was too weak to do anything other than lightly place her arm on the girl's back.

Luis helped the mother from the car, the little girl clinging to her the entire time, then ushered her to the love seat that had just missed getting hit by the car, instead of the couch, which was thoroughly destroyed.

Luis approached Brent. "She's got a small head wound, nothing too bad. I need you to clean it and put a bandage on, okay?"

Brent wondered why Luis would ask him, when Luis was closer. "I'm infected," Luis said, sensing Brent's confusion.

Brent stared, trying to process the news, as Luis hopped in the woman's car, drove it from the house, and parked it diagonally to block as much of the house's gaping wound as he could.

Brent grabbed the first aid kit, and went to help the woman, but couldn't stop thinking about what Luis had said.

**

"What are those things?" the woman asked, sipping from a water bottle, hands shaking.

The girl sat next to her mom, wiping tears from her eyes, traumatized.

"We don't know," Brent said, "I'm guessing aliens, but definitely can't say for sure. We ran into a bunch of them in the city this morning. Where are you all coming from?"

"Jersey, near Clifton," the woman said.

They exchanged vanishing stories, though Brent and Luis left out the Times Square bodies and Joe getting infected parts, and definitely left out the part about maybe Luis now being infected, too. They wanted to comfort the mom and her child, not scare the hell out of them.

The woman, Jane, a 30-year-old stay-at-home mom, was woken at 3 in the morning by her 6-year-old, Emily, saying she'd had a bad dream that monsters came to take them away. The girl then asked, "Where's daddy?" Jane found that her husband, Michael, was missing. So was their cat, Cinnamon. Jane tried to call her husband's cell, but the power went out. She went door to door in the middle of the night, before realizing the entire block had also vanished.

They went back home, Emily crying the entire time, and turned on the battery-operated radio to see if an emergency broadcast message or something was broadcasting. But all they got was static until they picked up the message regarding Black Island. They waited for a while to see if Michael would come back. When he didn't, they decided to take a chance and drive to the docks.

"I know they said not to drive at night, but I couldn't wait any longer," Jane said. "I had no idea there were these … aliens out there. What do you think happened?"

Luis told her about the dreams he'd been having, not that it offered much explanation for reality.

Outside, the morning sun had risen on the horizon, though it was only a blur lost in the low-hanging fog.

"So, what do we do now?" Jane asked, hugging Emily.

"We wait for the ferry and hope no more of those aliens show up," Luis said, staring out where the window had been, lost in thought.

"I want my daddy," Emily cried, leaning against her mother.

Brent felt his heart break while staring at the small girl, so delicate and shaken. He wanted to tell her everything was going to be okay, that she'd see her dad again, and maybe even her cat, Cinnamon. But he'd never been a very convincing liar.

"I know, baby," Jane said, kissing her daughter's head, "I miss Daddy, too."

Though the girl was 6, she wasn't much taller than Ben. Brent thought about giving her the Stanley Train in the pocket of his sweat pants, but truth was, he didn't want to let it go, even if it might bring joy to another child. Letting it go meant he might never be able to give it to Ben. Instead, he went to the kitchen, and brought them some Pop-Tarts. Jane thanked him and opened the package, handing one of the pastries to Emily.

"Thank you, Mr. Brent," Emily said, reaching out for the Pop-Tart with her tiny hands and taking a tiny bite.

**

As Jane and Emily sat on the couch, Brent and Luis were in the kitchen, packing the duffle bags with food and supplies. Brent noticed Luis wasn't wearing a bandage. In fact, his arm looked as if it had never been bitten.

"Where's the bite?" Brent asked, keeping his voice low enough that it didn't travel to the living room.

"Gone," Luis said, continuing to pack, clearly not wanting to discuss the subject.

"Lemme see," Brent said.

"Nothing to see," Luis said. "The bite healed itself."

"But you just said you were infected. It looks okay to me."

"It's not okay," Luis said. He stopped packing and met Brent's eyes. "There's something in me."

"What?"

"Look," he said, holding up his right forearm.

And then Brent saw the shapes swimming beneath his skin.

"What the … ?"

"I don't know, but I've gotta get outta here. I can't be around you all when I turn."

"No," Brent said, "I'm not leaving your side, especially when we're so close to being rescued."

"Listen dude, I appreciate it. Really, I do. But those two out there, they didn't sign up for this shit. I can't put you all at risk."

"We'll get you help from Black Island," Brent said. "Maybe they know what those things are. Maybe they can cure you?"

"Yeah, and maybe they'll lock me up to run experiments on me, too. I'm not gonna be some lab rat with doctors poking me and shit. I'm fine with dying. Hell, I didn't expect to wake up on Oct. 16. So, I'm already living bonus time, extra lives, and all that shit. I'm just gonna go off and see how things happen, far away from where I can do anyone harm."

"Wait a second," Brent said. "What if what you said is true? What if they *do* run experiments on you and stuff? Maybe they can find a cure. Maybe you can help others who are infected? I don't wanna sound all new-agey, especially when I don't believe that shit, but what if you were infected for a reason. Maybe that's why you're still here, to be cured, to help others get cured?"

Luis stared at him, silent for a full minute.

"I hate when you make sense," Luis said. "Okay, I'll stay, and get on that ferry, but you've gotta promise that if I show the slightest sign of changing, you will shoot me in the head."

"Jesus, that's some promise."

"Just promise."

"Okay," Brent said, "I promise."

"Don't say it unless you mean it."

"Okay, I promise, if you turn into a zombie-alien, I'll shoot you in the head."

"Thank you," Luis said.

In the living room, Jane called out, "I hear the ferry!"

* * * *

CHAPTER 11
EDWARD KEENAN

Ed descended the stairs, pistol in each hand, trying to clear Jade from his mind.

He couldn't afford to think about her being mad at him or take time to ease whatever fears she was harboring. He had to act quickly and without emotional baggage weighing him down.

It was bad enough he'd taken on the girl, Teagan. Now he had to worry about his daughter — his flesh and blood, which meant all his decisions were compromised. He couldn't think logically. Jade, and Teagan, would inform his decisions. In short, he could no longer trust his instincts if he gave emotion free reign. He must be a machine, divorced from feelings that could impede necessary action.

He pushed through the double doors on the ground floor and headed to the SUV. Across the parking lot, in front of one of the other three apartment buildings that formed a square around the giant parking lot, stood four creatures. They were long and black, with shiny skin. He couldn't tell if they were aliens or the results of a government lab experiment gone awry. But even at a distance, he was certain of one thing — they were predators. He would have just seconds to act once they saw him.

He was 15 yards from the SUV when two of the creatures broke from the pack and began loping toward him, running on both hands and feet. Fast.

He sprinted towards the SUV, heart hammering in his chest. He reached the driver's door, yanked it open, and keyed the ignition. As he threw the truck in reverse, the windshield filled with a creature and its dark, soulless eyes, clawed hands, and jagged teeth.

"What the fuck are you?" Ed yelled as the creature jumped onto his hood, bashing its hands into the windshield and causing it to crack. The second hit spread a web across the window, which quickly collapsed and rained chunks into the cabin.

Left hand on the wheel, Ed raised his pistol, fired twice — once at the thing's chest, another at its face. Both shots met their target, and the creature fell and Ed ran it over. Just then, the SUV was rocked as something landed on the roof. Above him, the creature screamed something unlike any animal Ed had ever heard. The sound reached into the recesses of Ed's brain and turned his insides to frost as the creature scraped its talons on the roof, trying to either hang on … or claw its way into the truck.

Ed spun the wheel and floored the gas pedal, racing back and towards the other two creatures. The truck hit at least one. Ed stepped on the brakes, causing the SUV to screech to a stop. The creature on the roof flew backwards and tumbled to the ground. Ed jumped from the SUV, turned back and fired a shot at the head of the creature he'd hit but not killed. Its head popped into a mist of black goo. He turned and fired at the monster that had been riding his roof.

Both shots went flying by as the creature bounded toward him, closing in fast. He steadied his aim with the second pistol as death raced toward him. Twenty yards, 15, 10, and getting closer.

Every instinct said *run, get back in the car, drive*. But his battle-tested training overrode his natural instincts. As the creature sprung into the air toward Ed, arms outstretched, he found the inner calm he needed to hit his target directly in the face, causing it to explode in a mad gush of black gore.

Ed fell to the ground, ducking out of the way, as the creature sailed over him and onto the asphalt behind.

As Ed stood, he spun around, searching for the last of the missing beasties. It wasn't behind the truck, nor inside, as he approached with guns drawn. His heart was pounding, and his breathing was fast as he turned in full circle, scanning the parking lot.

Nothing. It was gone.

Except he knew it wasn't truly *gone*.

No, it was *hiding*.

He glanced down at the dead creatures on the ground, trying to figure out what they were. But nothing in his personal history gave a clue as to what he was looking at. It might have once been human, or started out as human, or was maybe a hybrid mix of human and something else. *Something alien*. While the creatures shared many similarities with one another, subtle differences were noticeable. One had clawed hands, while another had no fingers, just stumps. And though the clawed one was tall and lanky, the other was shorter, sturdier. Their skin was black as night, coated with something wet. Beneath the skin, Ed could see what seemed to be fading light, like a freaky translucent deep sea creature he'd once seen on TV.

Ed hopped into the SUV, then drove to the front doors of Jade's apartment complex. He parked horizontally, so the driver's side door and cargo door were as close to the front of the building as possible, then scanned his surroundings once more before leaving the relative safety of the SUV and entering the apartment building.

**

When he returned to Apartment 410, Jade ran to greet him, embracing him hard. Tears covered her face. "I thought you were dead!"

Ed realized the three of them had been watching from the window, and had seen the whole battle unfold.

"I'm okay," Ed said into Jade's ear.

Having his daughter in his arms felt so good. After years of frosty silence, hugging her was somewhat awkward, like he wasn't hugging his little girl, but rather a woman he barely knew any longer, a woman with a new perfumed scent. Yet, somewhere deep inside the hug, was that bond that could never be broken between parent and child. And it was there he found himself getting lost in the memories of his prior life as a father. Before his life as an agent had spiraled out of control.

He wanted to hold her forever, but couldn't allow himself to get tangled in emotion. A part of him would have collapsed into tears, begged for forgiveness from his baby girl, if they had the time and luxury of a safe world where they could repair past damages. But this was not that time. And with the introduction of monsters into this new world disorder, he was afraid their wounds could go forever unhealed.

Now was the time for strength, not healing.

He kissed his daughter on the head, then broke the embrace.

"We've got to get out of here. Find a safe place."

"What were those things?" Teagan's eyes were wide with fear.

"I don't know. I've never seen anything like it. As crazy as it sounds, my guess would be aliens of some sort."

"Do you think that's what's behind all the people vanishing? Aliens came and took everyone?" Ken asked.

"Could be," Ed said. "This is the first we've run into them all the way from Ohio, so I'm hoping they're just here. Either way, we need to get out of here right now and find somewhere safer. Pack whatever you need. I've got the truck ready to go downstairs."

"Where are we gonna go?" Teagan asked, hands on her pregnant belly. "Is *anywhere* safe? We've got government agents in helicopters, hillbillies with guns, and now aliens! Where are we supposed to go?"

"I've got a place in Florida all set up," Ed said. "It's solar powered, has a well for fresh water, and a safe room to protect us in case the shit hits the fan. Well, if any more shit hits the proverbial fan."

"You were *prepared* for this?" Ken asked, with a huge grin.

"Not *this*; just prepared," Ed said. Both Jade and Teagan were looking at him suspiciously.

"What kinda job did you have?"

Ed wasn't sure if the kid knew and was just fucking with him or if Jade really had kept quiet.

"You didn't tell him?" Ed asked, turning to Jade.

"Your name didn't come up much," she said, a look in her eyes he didn't want to see.

"The less you know, the better, Ken," he said. "Let's just say it was my job to be prepared for any eventuality. And I was good at my job."

Ken smiled nervously before breaking eye contact. Ed didn't think the kid was sleeping with his daughter. He seemed effeminate and looked like he'd fold like a lawn chair at the first sign of opposition. Not the kind of guy he'd want dating his Jade. But then again, girls tended to go out with exactly the kind of guys most likely to disappoint their absent fathers. And being an absent father, there wasn't a whole damned lot you could do about it.

As Ed watched Ken scramble to fill a grocery bag with items, he felt like someone was watching him. He turned to see Jade and Teagan both staring. Unlike Ken, Jade kept eye contact.

"I'll be right back," Ken said, "I need to get *something* from next door."

The way Ken said the word *something* and exchanged glances with Jade, Ed figured it was some kind of drug. Hopefully it was only weed and not meth, cocaine, or any of the really dangerous shit. Otherwise, he'd have to play Strict Dad, a role he never felt comfortable in, especially given how little he was present in Jade's life. However, that didn't mean he would stand idly by if he thought she was endangering herself. Being a parent meant sometimes you had to be the Bad Guy — a role Ed was all too familiar with.

"So, this place of yours in Florida," Jade began, "How long have you had it? How do you know it's still there?"

Ed, confused by the line of questioning. "It's still there. Trust me."

Suddenly, a scream came from the next apartment. Ken, followed by an unholy shriek and clicking, then the crash of furniture and someone hitting the wall.

Well, there's the missing alien.

Ed grabbed his guns, raced into the hall and into the next apartment. Ken was on the ground balled up and screaming as the creature stood over him, swiping down. Fortunately, it was one of the aliens with stumps instead of clawed hands.

Ed raised his pistols, surprise on his side, and went for the shot. Something hammered Ed in the back, knocking the wind out of his lungs and sending him sprawling forward into a circular dining room table. He landed on top, and went tumbling over it, taking the table with him, as his head slammed into a chair and the gun in his right hand bounced away.

To his right, the first creature, atop Ken, turned, eyes dialing in on a motionless Ed, who was lying on his back, the back of his head splitting in pain.

The alien who had hit him from behind — and Ed was almost positive it was an alien now — stood fully and opened its mouth wide, releasing a shrill screech and clicking sound which bore deep into Ed's skull. The one that had attacked him from behind, which *did* have claws, joined in the clicking. As both creatures approached, Ed fought to maintain consciousness, vision blurring at the edges as pain threatened to shut him down.

Must fight it ... Pain is an illusion. It's how you respond to it that matters ... Push it down, drive it down deep.

He fought the pain, raising his left arm at the clawed creature, trying to aim for its head. But his vision was too blurred. He felt like he was looking through sheer wet cloth. He closed his eyes, then opened them again, as the creature screamed louder and lifted its arms.

Gunshots thundered through the apartment as the first creature, to his right, fell to the ground. In his blurred vision, Ed made out Ken, standing, holding the gun Ed had dropped. Ken turned to fire at the second creature as Ed unloaded his clip.

"Die, you fucker!" Ken screamed as he fired shot after shot until the creature dropped. The gun went empty, but Ken's arm kept shaking as his finger kept squeezing the trigger.

"You got 'em," Ed said, standing. "Thank you."

He reached out and took the gun from Ken, who was in shock and crying.

"It's okay," Ed said. "They're gone."

That's when Ed saw Ken's shoulder, bloodied beneath his shirt. "Are you hurt badly?"

"It bit me," Ken said, his voice shaking, "It fucking bit me! It was gonna eat me."

"You're safe now," Ed said, "Come on, let's get back to the girls and get the hell out of here."

Ed retrieved fresh clips from his back pockets and loaded them into the guns. He would need more ammo soon, especially if they were going to run into more aliens.

When they returned to 410, Jade and Teagan were terrified, "Oh my God, what happened?" Jade said, running to Ken.

"He got bit," Ed said, "We need to get out of here. Now."

"Are you okay?" Jade asked them both.

"Yeah," Ed said, "Ken really saved my ass back there." May as well throw in a good word for the kid, Ed thought. Maybe Ken wasn't as weak as he seemed. Ed wasn't sure if the kid were gay, but if he wasn't, he just proved himself worthy of Jade's attention. "We need to leave right now, though. God only knows how many more of those things are lurking outside."

Ed went to the window to see if any more aliens were in the parking lot.

That's when he saw them. Not monsters, but two black vans in the parking lot that hadn't been there before.

The window in front of him shattered and something stung him in the chest. He glanced down to see he'd been hit with some sort of dart. Jade, Teagan, and even Ken screamed as a second dart crashed through the window. Ed turned to see them looking at him, horror in their eyes.

Then he fell.

* * * *

CHAPTER 12
JOHN LARSON

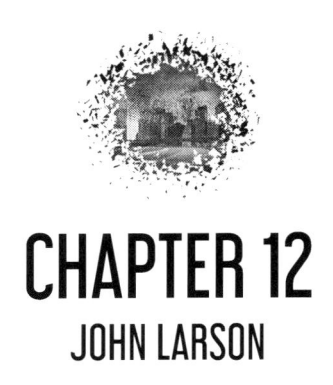

After he got good and drunk and spilled his secrets to Desmond, a guy he didn't even particularly like, John slinked off to his hotel room. What alcohol didn't help, he hoped sleep would.

He was snoring in seconds, and stayed that way until he shot straight up in bed, wide awake and ravenously hungry. The room was dark, save for a soft white glow coming through his frosted window.

John swung his feet to the carpet and rubbed his eyes.

What time is it?

Hard to tell since the world was quiet and a working clock wasn't in the room.

The air felt liquid, like a dream. Or maybe he was still heavily intoxicated.

He was drawn to the window. The parking lot and trees looked beautiful in the moon's luminescence, reminding him of an illustration from a childhood book his mother used to read him. He couldn't remember the name of the book, but he remembered the picture, a house underneath a smiling moon. And the sky was a beautiful shade of dark violet he'd never seen in nature ... until now. He remembered staring at the picture as a child and thinking how cozy the house looked, how safe, cool, and inviting. Countless times, he wished he could have jumped into the pages of the book.

And that's just how the world outside the hotel now looked. Safe, cool, and inviting.

The bleakers were lined up, standing in a wide arc. The one at the front was motioning for him to come outside. The creature's movement was so slow John felt as if he were watching time lapse photography.

What's the harm, it's not like the creatures can hurt me in a dream.

He opened his window and jumped, landing three feet from the head bleaker. It took a step back, as did the bleakers behind it, parting as though John were a king walking a red carpet. Their eyes, so big and black seemed not scary as they had before, but rather curious.

"John!" called Jenny's voice in the distance.

Jenny?!

His heart sped up as he searched the night for her.

He stepped past the head bleaker and the rest crowded the empty space behind him, as though sending him off and wishing him well.

"John!" Same voice, more urgent.

He crossed the edge of the parking lot, jogged across the street, then broke into a full run on the other side, heading into the nearby woods. Though he knew he was dreaming, a large part of him didn't care. He might never see her again in the waking world. But, if he could see her in his dreams, that would at least be something. The worst thing he could imagine would be to forget her completely. The sound of her voice, the look in her eyes when she looked at him, the way her nose crinkled when she smiled.

"John!"

He saw Jenny, standing beside a slender tree, wearing the matte silver dress he loved, the one that made her look like an Ann Taylor princess.

He approached his wife, tears filling his eyes. "I'm so sorry," he said.

Jenny was silent.

"Please, please, please forgive me," he said. "I never meant to hurt you."

Her lips didn't move.

Her silence pained him. Though John knew it was a dream, cold indifference was a coffin of discomfort.

"Please," he begged, "Answer me."

John reached out to touch her face, but recoiled in terror as it started to shift, starting with her eyes, which went hollow. Her face reshaped itself into a breathing image of agony. His wife was gone, and in her place was the burned hide of a corpse. Its cracked skin was crimson and black, its eyes ebony and large and almost circular in shape, like a snake's. The bones beneath the thin flesh of its face rolled like ocean waves beneath the surface as it tried the faces of people from John's neighborhood, starting with Mary, and then Paola, Desmond, and Jimmy, moving on to everyone from the Franklin kid to the old man who spent his evenings calling out for his dog, Miley.

John took a step back, confused. How did it know how to make all those faces? It was as if the monster was running through John's mental Rolodex.

The beast's face softened, then relaxed into the familiar creamy cheeks with a rosy glow John had loved since the second he first saw her.

Perhaps, John thought, all that darkness was simply his feeling about their fight manifesting in some monstrous shape.

Jenny smiled at him.

She was back.

"I'm sorry," he said.

"It's okay," she said in that familiar voice that greeted him every morning, holding her arms open. "Everything will be okay."

John's heart melted and broke all at the same time. Happy that she'd found the heart to forgive him, but then sad in the realization that this was surely just a dream. And when he woke, the world would continue to decay without her.

"You don't have to go back," she said.

"What?"

"You can wake up now. And be with me."

"What do you mean?" John asked. "If I wake up, I'll be back in the hotel."

"No," Jenny said, "*That* is the dream. This is a dream. But in reality, I'm at home, in bed, waiting for you to wake up. Right now."

John's head was pounding in confusion, trying to make sense of what she was saying. It didn't seem right. Everything that had happened the past few days, that was reality... he thought. But the more he considered events, the less sense that world made. A world where everyone vanished, where bodies floated down rivers, and monsters attacked you. A world where a little boy comes and saves the day but ages in the process. Maybe *that* was the dream world.

"How do I wake up?" he asked.

"Just let me in."

"What?"

"Just open your mind. Open your heart, and let me in."

"How do I do that?" he asked, now crying and more confused than ever. His head felt like it was in a vice, being squeezed tighter and tighter. He was so afraid to make the wrong choice and risk losing her forever.

"That headache you're feeling right now... that's your dream self trying to stay in the dream." Jenny said. "Don't let your fear keep you from waking. Reality is waiting. You just need to let go. Come to me, John."

She held her arms open.

Tears streamed down his face. But they weren't just tears of love or joy at being reunited with Jenny. Something else was there which he couldn't quite place.

"Just let go," she whispered as he fell into her embrace and kissed his cheek.

She brought her lips to his, then reached her hands up his back, and found the back of his head. Her fingers swept through his hair in that way he loved, swirling and massaging, and then ... tightening.

What the ... ?

Her fingers began to dig into his skull, feeling like several bits drilling through his flesh and bone. He tried to scream, but couldn't. Nor could he move.

And that's when he recognized the true source of his tears — the realization that he was about to die.

* * * *

CHAPTER 13
MARY OLSON

Oct. 18
Dawn
Belle Springs, Missouri

Mary woke feeling happy.

She couldn't wait to smell the fresh air of the open road. She was sick of the hotel and sick of the waiting. It wasn't that she didn't understand John's urgency; she wanted to leave every bit as much as he did. But she wasn't willing to put her daughter in danger or leave before everyone was ready. And she trusted Desmond's judgment completely, Will's, too, even though she met him just the day before.

The last few days had been long, but the sun was breaking, and in an hour they would be on the road to whatever was next. Desmond had stayed up all night on guard and finalizing plans with Will. Desmond had to be exhausted, but he kept going like he thrived on exhaustion.

"I was just thinking of you," she said as Desmond approached.

"Have you seen John?" he asked, minus his characteristic smile.

Mary shook her head. "No, why?"

"Because I can't find him anywhere, and he was in bad shape last night. I'm trying not to worry, but I'd be a liar if I said I wasn't."

"I imagine you've checked his room?"

"Yeah, I went through all the rooms on the first floor, but didn't see a thing. Mind helping? I don't want to tell the others because I don't want anyone to worry."

"Of course, what can I do?"

"I'm hoping he crashed in one of the upper rooms, trying to get as far away from the rest of us as possible. I'll start on the top floor if you start on the second. We can meet in the middle. Sound good?"

Mary nodded. Desmond handed her a gun.

"Do you know how to use this?"

"I think so," she said.

"Good," Desmond said, "Just shoot or scream, and I'll come running."

She took the stairs to the second floor, stepped off, then started opening doors. The first three rooms were empty, but Mary opened the door of the fourth and saw John lying motionless in bed.

Her heart nearly stopped when she saw him.

He was face down, motionless, his bare feet caked with dirt, as were the ankles of his jeans.

"John," she said tentatively. For a sick moment, she was certain he was dead.

Then John rolled over, sat up, and opened his eyes.

They stared at one another for 10 full seconds of silence, and Mary felt a vacuum of recognition as if he had no idea who she was. Goosebumps prickled her skin.

"Are you okay?" she asked.

"Never been better." he smiled, all teeth. "Today's the first day of the rest of my life."

* * * *

::EPISODE 6::
(SIXTH EPISODE OF SEASON ONE)
"LIKE DOMINOES IN A ROW"

CHAPTER 1
JOHN

John saw from behind a thick stew of growing fascination and utter disgust.

Who are these foul, repugnant creatures, and why are they so ... unstable?

Their minds were all so disparate, yet each seemed to ignore their true selves so they could fade into the background of collective humanity. Empty echoes of obsolete originals, mocking distinction by granting themselves individual names, and walking through life as if they had free will; like they were snowflakes rather than seeds.

It stared at Mary, one of the humans and the mother of the girl Paola, whose mind and body had been too immature to occupy. The exploration was entertaining, but she wasn't a suitable host: too soft where it mattered. Of course, the human called John was also soft mentally, still swimming in the primordial ooze of self-discovery.

It didn't concern itself with such self exploration. Not when so much was out there to ingest, absorb, and assimilate. *It* found its purpose, and first suitable shell. This shell was good enough, with access to everything *It* needed to grow: the dark light of the planet's spreading disease, and the collective memory from her most repellent species.

It would be *John*, at least until its strength expanded enough to make titles pointless.

John rubbed its temples. The shell's memories were occasionally painful. It was different with the girl; she hadn't been carrying nearly as many, and the ones she had, were wrapped in a sort of delicate innocence. The shell's memories were different. Even the best of them bled with a darker edge, as though the simple act of living had marred all purity and sewed misery into even the most joyous memories. And while the girl's feelings were sweet, they were too sweet. Sickly sweet. *John* preferred the dusk of depression. The shell's emotions were murky and though it pretended to be strong, it was weak. Weaker than the child had been. That weakness coupled with a desire to cling to his own darkness is what made it so easy for *It* to summon John out of the hotel and to infiltrate.

"John, it's time to go."

It was the woman, Mary, still standing in the doorway after waking him. She was eager to leave, and was hurrying everyone along, even though it had been she who caused them all to stay behind in the first place, at least according to the sharp memory in the shell's bank. But that was the thing about these human's memories: constant prejudice made them impossible to trust.

The rat dog snarled.

Growl ... Growl ... Growl ...

John looked at the filthy, four-legged rat with two narrowed slits of brewing hate, then turned his attention to the woman.

"You sure everything's okay?" she repeated.

"Yes," *John* nodded. "I'm ready to go, too. It's been a long few days."

He got out of bed and followed Mary downstairs and into the lobby where all the others were standing around. John sorted through the memories he'd collected from both John and Paola, so he could relate to each of the humans in an appropriate manner.

The dangerous one, Desmond, was speaking with the man-child, Jimmy. Both wore the loathsome look of concern, making them look even more like the weak, pathetic creatures they were. They were discussing him, or at least the shell that was once the man John, their conversation a miserable blend of worry and disquiet. *John* wished his shell wasn't so limited. It could not hear thoughts, nor could it even hear the wide spectrum of sounds that *It* could normally hear in its native form. *John* wondered how humans had gotten as far as they had with such limitations.

The dangerous one nodded, slapped the man-child on the shoulder, then headed toward the lobby doors. The man-child headed toward *John.*

John's shell was suddenly hot. Scorching. *It* looked at the shell's limbs but they weren't burning, weren't even red, even though they felt like they were on fire. *It* wondered if this was a normal condition humans all shared or if it was some sort of limitation to inhabiting their shells. Whatever the case, *John* was not pleased with yet another limitation. But *It* would have to continue inhabiting this shell, or another, if it were going to fulfill its destiny.

"Sorry about last night," the man-child said to *John.* "I was out of line."

John filed through a sliding bank of the shell's possible responses.

Fuck you, and the horse you rode in on.

You're just a kid; you don't know anything.

It's fine, Jimmy. Let's just get going. You were only trying to help.

Thanks, Jimmy. Everyone needs me. Thanks a lot for helping me see that.

Though John was all but evicted from his mind, *It* could still access how John would respond to stimulus. *It* was intrigued that John would have probably throttled his instincts, choosing what he *should* say, rather than what he wanted to.

How weak, pathetic, and temporary. Thoughts built from bent willow could barely stand against a breathing wind. This species deserved its departure.

"Thanks, Jimmy. Everyone needs me. Thanks a lot for helping me see that."

John smiled, keeping his nature buried, though he could tell that the man-child felt a bristle at the base of his neck.

"Thanks for saying that, man. Really. I appreciate it," Jimmy said with a nervous grin. "You know I've nothing but respect; I just want us all to get along. And it kills me to see you throwing down shots like you were last night. Reminds me of my Uncle Micky, and believe me, you start drinking like Uncle Micky, nothing ends well."

John stared at the man-boy, transfixed. He should have been filing through verbal records so he could fill the air with blather, but he had wandered down an unexpected memory.

The shell is just a boy. His father is drinking. His eyes are red and hair a mess. The woman beside him, the shell's mother, is holding her nose.

The atmosphere is lead. The sorrow thick. Air sour.

"Hey Jimmy," Desmond said, approaching from behind. "I need you on the second floor while we start moving out. Eyes out the window, okay."

Growl ... BarkBarkBarkBark ... Growl ... The dog was barking.

The dog could see that John was not himself. Fortunately, the people didn't understand the dog's warnings.

"Thanks, Jimmy." Desmond turned to John. "Everything okay?"

Get the fuck out of my face, Desmond.

Sure thing, boss. Just taking a minute to mourn, if that's okay with you.

I'm great, thanks.

Yes, of course. Why wouldn't it be?

"Yes, of course. Why wouldn't it be?"

"Well, you had a pretty rough night last night, and you seem ... I don't know, *off* this morning. I'm sure it's a massive migraine on an empty stomach, but I've not seen you eat anything. Like I said last night, I just want to help. You think of a way I can do that, let me know, and it's half-done already, okay?"

What's your endgame, boss? What's in it for YOU?

You could pay more attention to getting us out of here than you do to Mother Mary.

Thanks, Desmond. I'm good.

I appreciate your concern and will work harder to be one of the team from now on.

"I appreciate your concern and will work harder to be one of the team from now on."

The dangerous one took a step back, wrestling his expression.

Being a human required more than words and motions. *John* had yet to absorb the subtleties. What he was trying to say wasn't getting the reactions he expected.

"How about we get you something to eat? An empty stomach can't be helping." Desmond said.

Is that why I'm burning? Because the shell is famished? How useless — a mind dependent on a bottomless shell for survival.

The dangerous one disappeared, then returned a few minutes later with a banana, crackers, and a bottle of water. "Here you go," he said, handing them to *John*. "Sorry about the banana. Nothing we can do about fruit getting old, except maybe get out of here and start growing our own." He smiled awkwardly. "Alright, be ready to leave in 10 minutes, okay?"

You can kiss my ass in 10 minutes.

Thanks for the banana. I'll never be hungry again.

Sounds good.

Thanks for everything, I feel much better now. Ready to go when you are.

"Sounds good."

The man-boy ran into the lobby. "You guys are gonna want to see this," he said. He turned, ran back toward the stairs, then sprinted a flight to the window on the other side of the second floor door. The dangerous one, the old man, the mother and daughter, the boy-child and the dog all followed, with *John* close behind.

Why am I burning. It shouldn't be this HOT.

"Christ on a cross," the dangerous one said. "When did this happen?"

"I've no idea," the man-child shook his head. "They've more than quadrupled in the past half hour."

Everyone stared as what the humans had called "bleakers" had packed the parking lot hundreds strong.

John smiled. His legion was growing stronger by the second.

They know; that's why they're coming. To help usher in the change.

But he wasn't ready, not yet.

The dog: *Growl ... BarkBarkBarkBark ... Growl ...*

Furious shrieks were followed by a low growl of uncurling hatred.

Will said, "Looks like Lord Vader doesn't like them bleakers at all!"

But the rat wasn't looking out the window, its snarl was curled at *John*; teeth bared, saliva pouring from the open side.

"Luca," Will said, "would you mind taking the dog downstairs so we can figure out what to do?"

"Okay," the boy buried his fingers in the dog's coat and led it toward the stairs. The daughter followed.

"So, what do you think?" The old man, the one who sometimes *saw things*, was looking at the dangerous one as though he was the only one in the room. The shell's disdain for Desmond tainted *Its* perception of Desmond, also. An unsettling realization for *John*, that the human's feelings could affect *Its* perceptions. *How limiting, to be so easily swayed by perceptions. Maybe I can use that to my advantage in dealing with these creatures.*

The dangerous one shook his head. "I don't know. Seems like it's too risky to leave now. But if they're growing that fast and have us in their sights, maybe it's a bigger risk to stay." Desmond looked out the window again, then tilted his neck and peered as far as he could in the other direction. "Christ, I can't even see where they end."

BARK ... RUFF RUFF ... BARK ... RUFF RUFF

John could still hear the dog barking a floor below. He wondered why the dog had not just attacked him the moment it noticed the ruse. *Do dogs also throttle their desires?*

The room rained with flames only *John* could feel. His head was in pain and he felt like the contents of his stomach might spill out at any moment.

The man-boy spoke. "It's not just me. You guys all feel that, right? Like something really, really bad's about to happen."

Mary turned to the old man. "Still think the bleakers aren't much of a threat?"

The old man shook his head. "My theory just expired."

"What changed?" The dangerous one's mouth was open, but the man-boy made the words first.

"I don't have a foggy," Will answered. "But something definitely has. Their power is growing, and so are their numbers. We all feel it. What I don't like is the tone."

Perhaps the humans aren't as deaf to such things as they seemed.

"The tone?" Desmond said.

"Yeah," the old man nodded, "the tone. It's different. I always felt like they were waiting, but now I feel like they know what they're waiting *for*. Like they were lost. But now they're found."

"Amazing grace," Desmond said with a sigh.

"Will's right," Mary said. "I feel it, too."

The dangerous one looked helpless. He turned to *John*. "What do you think?"

Thanks for giving a shit about my opinion when there's no right answer.

It never mattered before. Why bother to ask now?

I think we should stay a little longer and see what happens. Please excuse me; I need to use the restroom.

You know best. We should probably stay, but if you think we should go, I'm right there behind you.

"I think we should stay a little longer and see what happens. Please excuse me; I need to use the restroom."

Everyone stared at *John*, mouths open as he turned and headed for *his* room.

John went into the room, closed the door, then into the bathroom where he plugged the tub and filled it with water.

He peeled the clothes from the shell then stepped into the bath, letting water flood the shell's face as *John* went underwater.

Finally.

The water was cool against its skin. The shell was overheating. *John* was over-taxing its available memory. The water soothed *John*, cooled the body several degrees, clearing *his* mind long enough to let *him* see his next move with clarity. *John* sat up in the tub.

It would stay, and foster *its* growing strength as long as possible. After all, they were coming for *him*, and if *It* lingered long enough, *It* would have the planet to command.

Cancers were born from a single putrid cell, but soon enough, they seeped into every crevice of the system. *John* smiled. It would be fun, doing what *It* had been born to do.

* * * *

CHAPTER 2
TEAGAN MCLACHLAN

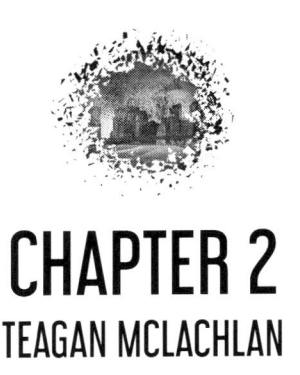

Oct. 17
Morning
Winding, Georgia

Teagan screamed as Ed fell to the ground, clutching at the darts still loosely dangling from his flesh.

"What the hell?" Jade screamed.

Ed moaned, trying to crawl toward the group.

Another dart flew through the window and hit the wall. Ken shouted, "Get down!"

He dropped to the floor, crawled to Ed, who was now motionless, and felt for a pulse. "He's alive," Ken said, clutching a rag over the bloody wound on his left shoulder where he'd been bit.

Jade ran hunched to the table where Ed had set his pistols, then took one for herself and slid the other to Ken.

"You know how to use one of these?" Jade asked Teagan, who shook her head. Jade crawled to her father, pulled the darts from his chest, then threw them to the ground.

"I shot two of those alien-looking things, not bad for a beginner." Ken said in a loud whisper as he crawled beside Jade and tried to peer outside without getting shot through the window.

"Who's shooting at us?" Teagan asked, hands over her suddenly kicking baby.

"Well, not the aliens," Ken said.

Teagan thought of the dream — the men in the helicopter coming for her baby. Maybe this was them. Her heart raced as she mentally scoured the room for a hiding place. But the room was too small with nowhere to hide.

"Come out with your hands up," a loudspeaker's voice blurted outside.

Ken, Jade, and Teagan exchanged confused glances.

"This has to be because of my dad," Jade said to the others. "Who's out there?!" she shouted out the window.

A firm voice: "We won't ask again. Come out now, hands in the air. Or we will move in with force."

Ken strained to peer out the window then ducked back down, "Men in black uniforms, black vans. They look official."

Jade and Teagan exchanged glances then looked down at Ed, still out cold.

"This has to be men looking for him," Jade said "Let's just do what they say."

"What if they're not the good guys?" Teagan asked, scared.

Jade crawled to Teagan, put her hands on her shoulders, then looked her in the eyes. "Look, I know you had that dream and stuff, but these men are only here to take my dad in. They're not looking for your baby."

"How do you know that?" Teagan asked, unable to cease her quivering mouth or the tears stinging her cheeks.

"Because that's what makes the most sense," Jade said. "And in my world, the things that make the most sense are usually the answer. Not wild conspiracy theories and secret agents. We've got a fugitive in here. They've come to get him. And given the hell outside, I'd rather go with them, answer a few questions, and maybe be safe, than end up getting eaten by monsters."

"What do you mean fugitive?" Ken asked. "Your dad's a fugitive?"

"Not now, Ken." Jade said annoyed, then turned back to Teagan. "There's no one coming to get your baby. It doesn't make any sense and my dad should never have let you believe that."

"But we don't know," Teagan said, feeling whiney, but not caring. This was her baby they were talking about. They'd get no do-overs if they made the wrong choice.

"Even if they *have* come for your baby, or all of us for that matter, there's nothing we can do. We have two guns, and I'm a shit shot. If they want to get to us, they will, and there's nothing we can do to stop them. So we've got to run with logic over fear."

Teagan cried out, and Jade hugged her.

"They're not coming for you, I swear."

"On the count of 10," the loudspeaker voice called before initiating countdown.

"We're coming!" Jade yelled, annoyed, putting her gun on the ground. Ken did the same.

"Wait," Teagan said, "Maybe we should keep a gun in case we run into more of those things in the hallway."

"Good point," Ken said, picking up a pistol and slipping it into the waistband at the small of his back.

Jade knelt, kissed Ed on the cheek, then whispered something Teagan couldn't hear. Teagan looked back at the man who may, or may not have, saved her life twice. For all that had happened, she didn't want to see him come to any harm. She felt a connection to him, however tenuous, that she wasn't ready to see severed.

They stepped into the hallway. Jade shined a flashlight as they entered the stairwell and started their descent. At the ground floor, Ken paused before opening the door to the lobby, pulled the gun from his waistband, and put it in the corner of the stairwell. "Don't wanna get shot," he said.

They pushed through the door with their arms raised and were met by two men in white space-age looking Hazmat suits, complete with enclosed helmets and breathing tanks. With them was a third man, in a black outfit, like a SWAT team would wear. He wore something on his face that looked like a gas mask and had his rifle aimed right at them.

"How many more are with you?" he said, voice muffled by the mask.

"Just my dad," Jade said, "You guys shot him with darts, and he's passed out upstairs."

One of the two Hazmat-suited men shined a light on the three of them, then trained it on Ken's injury. "What happened to you?"

"I was bit," Ken said, "By one of those alien-looking things."

"We've got an infected," one of the Hazmat men said into a microphone. Suddenly, two more SWAT team men ran in with rifles aimed at Ken, Jade, and Teagan.

One of them yelled, "Outside, now!"

Teagan felt hands on her, pushing as they were rushed out into the parking lot, three guns at the back of their heads.

"Please, don't shoot us," she cried.

"Shut up," one of the SWAT men said, "Keep moving."

Outside, they were met by two other SWAT men in masks along with a woman in a Hazmat suit.

"What's going on?" Jade asked.

"No questions," one of the SWAT men said. He walked up to Ken, "How long ago were you bit?"

"About 10 minutes ago," Ken said. "Why?"

"Were any of the rest of you bitten?" the woman in the Hazmat suit asked, waving some sort of light wand over them.

"No," Jade said, "just Ken. What's going on? What *are* those things?"

"How about the man upstairs? Was he bit?" one of the SWAT men asked.

"I don't think so, was he Ken?" Jade asked.

"No, just me," Ken said. "What's going on? What did you all mean *infected*? Am I infected?"

"Get these two in the van," one of the SWAT men said to the woman.

"Yes, Sergeant," she said, and turned to Teagan and Jade, "I need you to come with me, please."

"Wait a second," Jade said. "What are you gonna do with Ken? With my dad?"

"Please," the woman said, her voice kind, but firm, "just come with me. We can't stay here long."

"What's going on?" Ken said, pushing past one of the SWAT team and trying to join Jade and Teagan. "You're not taking them anywhere."

"On your knees!" one of the SWAT team yelled at Ken, rifle aimed.

Ken's eyes were wide, face panicked, as he stepped back, "Please, just tell me what's going on! Where are you taking them?"

"On your knees!" the same SWAT man yelled out.

"Fuck you!" Ken spit out.

The man fired the rifle once, straight into Ken's head, and he dropped like a rag doll.

Teagan and Jade screamed as the woman pushed them toward the open doors of the waiting van. To see Ken shot right in front of them like that was nothing short of surreal. That they would kill someone so easily meant that now anything was possible. Including government soldiers who kidnap you for your baby.

"Fuckers!" Jade cried, trying to break free, and run to Ken.

Another SWAT man swung a nightstick into the small of Jade's back, and she fell to the ground in a heap. Teagan's head was spinning in indecision. She wanted to help Jade, but hands were on her, pushing her, and she couldn't risk the baby. Everything was happening so fast.

Jade struggled to get up, and the SWAT man hit her again, this time in the ribs, and she screamed. Teagan was being pulled farther away, toward the open back of a separate black van. The world spun as Teagan's feet threatened to betray her and cause her to stumble to the ground; she reached out for support, someone to hold.

She fell into the woman in the Hazmat suit, looked up at the woman's face, cold, sterile behind the glass dome.

"Please, don't hurt my baby," she said, before passing out.

* * * *

CHAPTER 3
BORICIO WOLFE

Oct. 19
3:15 a.m.
Somewhere in Alabama

"So, either of you scrawny fuckers get your dicks wet yet?"

Boricio tore down the darkened dead highway in the armored truck, trying not to notice the nothing seeping in from everywhere while doing his best to keep himself entertained. Entertaining himself wasn't easy with two passengers who had yet to unzip their flies and give life a decent pounding.

Silence from the back seat.

"What, no stories? Don't tell me I'm trying to make an almighty pyramid of tip-top fuckers with two bitches at the bottom. I don't give a fat fuck with fairy wings if you went dipping your fingers into Mayonnaise Mary every other Monday, or the best you ever had was emptying your pecker into your sister's dirty panties; I want a story. Now," he said, turning to the boys in the back, "who wants to go first?"

Before either could answer, Boricio said. "Never mind. Fuck you both. I'll go first. You two think of your stories, then conjure ways to make 'em not suck while I tell mine."

Boricio turned his eyes back to the road and began telling his tale.

"I was 13, and no, I ain't embarrassed to admit it took me that long before I was moving out of Palmdale." Boricio cackled and slapped the wheel. "I was at my cousin Charlie's for a kegger. And yeah," Boricio caught Charlie's eyes in the rearview, "his name was Charlie, too, except he wasn't no faggot. He liked pussy, and loved to talk about it. He was my mom's oldest brother's kid, a real asshole and about as sharp as a fucking marble, but he hated my old man and looked out for me, which was plenty more than just about anyone else did or wanted to do at that point in my life. So, I was with him one weekend, like I was a few times a year, and he was having one of his Big Gulp-sized soirees at the apartment. It was packed with people. To this day I don't know what they were smoking in there; I was only allowed a little because Chuck said it was expensive. But one hit was all I needed to Fuck. Me. Up. BAM! I was out like unpaid electric."

Boricio turned to the backseat. "Y'all listening back there? I'm dishing some primetime entertainment; it'd be nice to see ya' on the edges of your seats."

Adam and Charlie laughed, then they both slid forward in their seats.

"Much better!" Boricio slapped the empty passenger seat. "So, I woke up who knows how in the fuck much longer later, with a mountain of empty cups all around me and a bag of hammers pounding in my head, and the speakers Chuck ripped off from City of Strings blaring full blast and making it worse. They were playing ... ah, what's that song, what's that song ... " Boricio snapped his fingers then looked to the back seat. "Ah, like you'd fucking know. This was way before your mamas were trying to decide whether they should swallow you or take you in their honeypot." He slammed his hand on the steering wheel. "*Groove Is in the Heart!*" he said.

He turned to the back seat. "You ever hear that one?"

Both boys shook their heads.

"Well, believe you me," Boricio said, "it's a ripe fucking oldie. Anyway," he went on, "the inside of my head was practically bleeding, and for some reason I didn't have no shirt on. Whatever I smoked had fucked up my vision because I couldn't see shit in front of me. I stumbled into the bathroom and puked up everything I had in me. Soon as I was empty, I stumbled back into the bedroom and fell asleep. When I woke up, it felt like just a few minutes later, and I could hear the sound of my zipper coming down. I tried to look up, but couldn't because my head was swimming. Before I knew it, some bitch's mouth was all on me. I don't know how many times I'd put mayo on my own knuckle sandwich before that, but there it was, shit happening to me in 3-D. I had an angle on my dangle in no time. I took off her shirt and started kissing her like I saw people do in the movies. She tasted like ash or asshole, but I didn't care — I was about to FUCK."

"So, what happened?" Charlie was practically in the front seat, eyes lit up like a kid on Christmas. Adam's mouth was open and eyes wide.

"Well, she went down and put my entire meatsicle in her mouth. I couldn't believe that shit neither; figured I'd wake up any second with my sheets all wet, but sure enough, she just kept on painting the fence, while I lay on the bed squealing like a piglet. Finally she said, 'You wanna cum inside me?' I said, 'Hell yeah!', then she sat on me. But that was that; I was barely inside before the baby batter was leaking back out."

"That was it?" Adam said.

"Yeah ... except the round of applause. Turned out, Chuck and all his fucking ape friends were in the room watching, maybe 10 of them, and I never even noticed."

Charlie and Adam started laughing.

"Did I tell you it was some fuckin' story, or what? Okay, Adam, your turn." Boricio turned to Adam. "When's the first time you chopped down the cherry tree?"

Adam looked embarrassed, but knew there was no getting out of the story. "I was 16, and it happened at the park. I've never been allowed to have people over to the house, but there was a girl I really liked named Rebecca, and we were in the same group for our sophomore-year history project. I can't really call her my girlfriend because we never really went out or anything, but I knew she liked me and I liked her. One day school let out early, and my parents didn't know, so we went to the park to work on our project together. She asked if I wanted to 'do it,' but I didn't think it was the best idea because I always felt like my dad was right behind me even when he was nowhere around. But as soon as she said it, I was hard as a rock. Then she started blowing in my ear and rubbing my pants. Even though I was scared, I finally stammered, 'Okay,' and we went across the street and climbed into the back of her old Corolla. It only lasted a few minutes. And it was definitely better than all the 'practice' I'd done at home, but not at all like I thought it would feel. She told me I'd done great. I didn't want to go home, so we sat in the backseat talking for a couple of hours. I ended up getting home later than usual, and my dad walloped the shit out of me."

"Least you pounded some pussy before your dad pounded you!" Boricio said.

"Yeah," Adam nodded, though he looked far away.

"So?" Boricio said, "You bang her again?"

Adam shook his head. "No. The only other time we were alone outside of class, we were standing in front of the school, both waiting for a ride. My dad picked me up. When I got in the car he called her a whore and said anyone who'd let me fuck them had to be a bigger loser than me."

Boricio shook his head, then looked in the mirror at Charlie. "How about you, Charlie Brown? When's the first time you got to bumpin' uglies?"

"I'm still a virgin," Charlie said, slightly red-faced. "I used to really like this one girl named Josie, but ever since she started hanging out with Shayanne and the rest of the Bitch Clique, she started giving me the ugly eye. But fuck her, anyway. Like Adam, my stepdad rarely let me leave the house without a detailed explanation, so I didn't have much of an opportunity."

Boricio erupted into laughter. "Yeah," he said, "that's it. Couldn't be 'cuz you're gangly as a fucking Gomer and it looks like you wash your face in fried chicken!" Boricio tilted the rearview and met Charlie's eyes. "You know I'm just fucking with you, right? This is how Team Boricio bonds, bitch! Now, since you ain't gonna tell any tall tales about twat, why don't you spin us a story or two about what a fucker your old man is."

"Nah," Charlie said. "Nobody wants to hear that."

"Yeah, we do," Adam said, probably wanting to change the conversation to something less embarrassing for both of them.

"Bob wasn't nearly as bad as Adam's dad; mostly he just liked to humiliate me as often as he could. Called me Nancy, Mary, even Melinda — any girl's name he could think of, really. Anything he could do to bring me down a peg while elevating himself. When he wasn't calling me a girl, he'd call me gay, faggot, and other shit like that."

"And your mom let him talk like that to you?" Boricio asked.

"No, he usually wore his nicest face around my mom. She knew he gave me a hard time, but not the extent of it. And to make matters worse, he'd convinced her it was for my own good. Like he was doing me some kind of fucking favor! And though he didn't really smack me around, except for a few occasions, there was this one time he scared the shit out of me. My mom was out with her girlfriend Colleen, all day for a *mid-life makeover* as Colleen called it, and Bob told me that if I didn't scrub the trash cans inside-out, which he'd promised my mom he would do while she was gone, he would take me out to the woods and do what he should have done the day he met my mom. He said 'ain't nobody gonna hear you scream out there,' so yeah, he never put my hand in a garbage disposal or nothing, but he was a Grade-A fucker for sure."

Charlie collapsed to the back of his seat.

"Funny thing is, I think I would've been able to tolerate Bob if he hadn't been such an asshole to my mom. But he treated her like total shit, always tearing her down and making her feel small. She used to be fun, before Bob. You can call me a pussy, but she was probably my best friend before she met him. And over time, he sucked her dry, took her joy and turned it into fear and emotional slavery."

The truck was quiet for nearly a full minute, when Boricio glanced in the rearview and said, "Pussy."

Charlie closed his eyes and then burst into laughter. Adam joined, and the three of them laughed for about half a mile. Ahead, was a gas station. Lights out, nobody home. Boricio parked, then turned back to Charlie and Adam.

"Most of the world's fuckers are dead," he said. "But, Charlie, it looks like you got yourself a raw deal with your personal fucker making it through the apocalypse and then taking your bitch on top of it. How would you feel about the three of us gentlemen paying a friendly visit to dear Ole Bob?"

* * * *

CHAPTER 4
LUIS TORRES

Oct. 17
6:40 a.m.
East Hampton, New York

Brent, Jane, and Emily stared out the window as the ferry's lights sliced through the morning fog. The ferry wasn't supposed to resume until 8 a.m. but the clock read 6:40 a.m.

"It's time to go," Brent said, turning to Luis.

"I dunno," he said, "Something's weird. Ferry wasn't supposed to show until 8."

"Maybe they're early," Brent said, "Or maybe 8 is the departure time, but they board early."

No, something was wrong. Luis felt it in his gut.

"I dunno," Luis said. "I say we wait a bit."

"What are you talking about?" Brent said. "You think aliens commandeered a ferry?"

"No, it's not that," Luis said, now literally feeling something in his gut. Sharp pain pierced his stomach, causing him to double over. He felt like he had the worst case of food poisoning ever.

"You okay?" Brent asked.

He shook his head, no he was not alright.

He raced up the stairs to the dark, windowless bathroom, then fell to his knees, just making it as his insides flew up and out his throat, then exploded into the toilet. He slammed the door, then reached out and grabbed the flashlight from the sink. He clicked it on, then set it back on the sink, light pointed at the ceiling.

He wiped his mouth with the back of his hand, hoping that was all he had in him. The invisible blades twisted in his stomach another time. He cried out then let loose another explosion into the toilet. The liquid came out thick, like black ropes. He grabbed the flashlight and pointed it into the toilet bowl to see what he'd evacuated. The vomit actually looked like rope. *No, not rope.* It was moving.

Like worms.

He slammed down the metal toilet handle to flush the mess, then glanced at his arm again. The worms beneath his skin had multiplied. On a whim, he looked at his left arm, which hadn't been bitten. Worms were racing under his skin there, too. It was spreading throughout his entire body. *Infected!*

What the hell is in me?!

Outside, Brent knocked on the bathroom door. "Are you okay?"

"Go away!" Luis snapped, reaching out and locking the door.

He puked again, then stood, and swung open the mirrored medicine cabinet so hard the mirror shattered.

He scanned the shelves until he found what he was looking for — an old-fashioned razor blade.

Brent banged on the door. "You okay?"

Jesus, this guy is annoying.

"I'll be out in a bit," Luis growled, "Go away."

He grabbed the razor, looked back down at his arm, at the *damned fucking worms*, and ran the blade across his right forearm.

He clenched through the pain, as blood poured into the sink. His blood was dark amber, almost the color of liquid rust. He set the blade down, and dug two fingers into the open wound, fished for two of the bastard worms, wet and white with streaks of blood, and circled his fingers around them, and pulled. Rather than breaking apart as he feared they would, the worms held as he pulled them like slick noodles from his arm. He pulled six inches, 12, and finally a full 15 inches in length until he'd pulled two entire worms from his body.

He held them up, inspected the heads: a tiny, open mouth, with several needle-like teeth. The worms slithered in his hand, slippery and coated in a mix of blood and black liquid.

Jesus Christ.

He threw the worms into the sink in disgust. They smacked the sink like wet spaghetti, then darted toward the open drain and vanished down into the plumbing.

His mind was in full panic mode, wanting, no, *needing* to yank every last one of the fuckers from his body. He was about to dig back into his arm when he noticed the wound had begun to heal itself.

Panic receded, replaced by awe as he watched his skin stitch itself together, leaving the wound a memory.

What the fuck am I?

He stared into the mirror, and saw something moving beneath the skin just under his left eye. He closed his lids and leaned forward, letting the top of his head press against the cold mirror.

A knock at the door. Again.

He unlocked the door, yanked it open, and saw Brent.

"What?!" he yelled.

Brent stepped back, eyes wide. Luis realized he was losing his temper, something he rarely did. He prided himself on remaining calm under any stress. But this was something else. Stress, anger, and fear were dueling for control of his mind ... likely along with whatever had invaded his body.

"I'm sorry," he said. He wasn't feeling sorry, but knew what he was supposed say. In reality, he felt a sudden urge to hit Brent. *Hard.* He swallowed it.

Brent said, "We've gotta get going. I don't wanna take a chance that the ferry will leave without us."

"I'm not going," Luis said.

"Why not?" Brent's eyes scanned the bathroom; broken glass, blood, black liquid, and a razor blade. No fooling this reporter. "Oh my God, what happened?"

"Just go; get on the ferry with the girls, and leave."

"I'm not going without you," Brent said. "Come on, these people at Black Island can help you."

"Really? And how do you know that, Mr. Reporter Guy? Is that something your fucking paper wrote about?"

Even though Luis knew he was completely overreacting, he couldn't help himself. He was getting increasingly pissed each time Brent opened his mouth and didn't just leave him be. He shouldn't have to explain himself.

"We need to get you help," Brent said, eyes meeting Luis's.

The rage subsided, as quickly as it came, replaced by fear, regret for what he'd said, and a new, bottomless sorrow. Whatever was inside him was fucking with his emotions big time.

"You need to go without me," Luis said. "Something's happening. And I don't want to hurt anyone." He was on the verge of tears.

"I told you, I'm not leaving you, man. We're gonna get through this. We're gonna find our families."

Luis smiled, unable to meet Brent's eyes. "That dream, again?" The smile dissolved to tears as he pictured his daughter's sweet smile. He thought again of their final day together. So many kids these days seemed to be almost born jaded, yet Gracie was still innocent, loving him with a sincerity and openness that melted the walls he'd so carefully built around his heart ... just as her mother had done.

He swallowed hard, tears stinging his eyes.

"Do you think she's still alive?" Luis asked.

"I do," Brent said, putting a hand on Luis's shoulder. "I really do."

"Goddamn, you hopeful bastard," Luis said, trying to manage a smile.

"And you think the people on the island can help me?"

"Yes," Brent said.

"How do you know, though?" Luis asked, entirely aware he sounded like a scared child, but unable to keep his emotions from riding off the rails.

"I feel it, just like you all felt your visions of Oct. 15 were real."

Fair enough.

Downstairs, Jane called, "Come on, I think the ferry is about to leave."

"Leave?" Brent shouted, "It's not even close to 8!"

Luis closed his eyes, fighting back the tears. He wanted to believe Brent. Wanted to have faith. Wanted to take a chance and believe he wasn't going to become a monster like Joe had. That he might see his little girl again.

Stranger things had happened.

He stood.

"Okay, let's go."

* * * *

CHAPTER 5
CALLIE THOMPSON

Oct. 18
Pensacola, Florida

Callie spent much of the day alone after Bob saved her and brought her back "home."

She couldn't tell for certain if he knew that she'd drugged him or not. He was acting weird, telling her he needed time to "think about shit and stuff." Which was fine by her. She went up to her room and decided to pass time. Without power, though, she didn't have much to do. So she went to Charlie's room hoping he'd left behind some books or comics, anything to read, really, other than the business books which made up most of the home's library.

She was disappointed to find that he'd taken the duffel bag which had the good books and graphic novels. She was about to leave the room when she saw a smaller blue duffel bag in the corner. She put the bag on the bed and unzipped it. Inside were a dozen or so spiral notebooks, most of which were well-worn, outsides filled with doodles and sketches of monsters, shapes, and alien landscapes. Charlie was a pretty decent artist.

She pulled out the top notebook with a green cover. The pages were filled with math problems interspersed with more doodling. The next few notebooks were also filled with schoolwork, though some pages had better drawings. One of them was an ink sketch of a girl sitting at a desk, which he'd obviously drawn during class. The way he'd drawn the girl with such detail, features soft while his other images were rough and unfinished, seemed to indicate a crush on the subject. It was like peeking into the mind of a teenage boy, something she'd never had such open access to.

She was somewhat surprised that his drawings were not all pornographic in nature. She imagined most boys who had the talent to draw, would draw all sorts of lurid stuff, both real and imagined.

Charlie was a nice kid. Callie smiled.

She heard Bob downstairs making something in the kitchen. She stuffed Charlie's notebooks back in the bag, rushed to her room, and shoved the bag under her bed. The thought of Bob catching her looking at the spirals made her stomach turn. No doubt he'd want to check them out and likely have a good, old laugh at Charlie's expense.

Callie had known a lot of guys like Bob in school. Insecure, usually jock types, who seemed to thrive on bullying those weaker than them. Different than them. She never understood why so many girls went for such assholes. Then again, girls acted the same way, viciously going after anyone who didn't fit into their tightly-formed cliques. Callie had run-ins with such people until she learned to stand up for herself.

When she was in eighth grade, this girl, Brianna, decided to make it her personal mission to make Callie's life miserable. She started spreading rumors, intentionally bumping into her, laughing, and name calling. Callie never let the bitch see her sweat, though. She did her best to ignore the girl. But at night, she often cried to her mom. Her mom always told her she was doing the right thing to ignore the abuse. Eventually, her mom said, Brianna would find someone else to pick on.

That hardly seemed like an answer to Callie, though. Even if the girl had moved on to someone else, she was still being a bully. And that her mom thought it was okay so long as Brianna wasn't picking on her, bothered Callie.

After four months, it was apparent that Brianna *wasn't* going to find a new target, though.

One day after gym, Callie went to her locker to change out of her sweaty gym clothes, and was shocked to see that someone had opened her locker and doused her clothes, her purse, and books in vinegar. They also wrote NIGGER DYKE in big, red marker across the inside of the locker.

"Geez, Callie, douche much?" Brianna said, cackling with her catty clique.

Callie wanted to cry. But she wouldn't let Brianna have that satisfaction. She closed her locker, and began to walk away, intending to tell the gym teacher, Mrs. Parker.

And then something hit the back of her head.

She turned around to see a wad of paper on the ground.

And that was it.

Callie lost it. She ran straight at Brianna, screaming like a maniac, and shoved the girl backwards into the locker.

Brianna's eyes were wide in disbelief.

She never expected someone to hit her, least of all, Callie. Brianna might have backed down right there, if not for the girls all gathering around them, chanting, "fight, fight, fight," like a mob demanding blood. Callie had little doubt whose blood they wanted to see. People only rooted for the underdog in movies, not in middle school.

While part of her wanted to turn and run away, and take back the last minute of her life, another part told her she had to own the moment and do what needed to be done.

She cocked her arm back and punched Brianna in the face as hard as she could. And again, as Brianna scrambled sideways and fell to the ground.

Callie fell on top of her, swinging, fists pounding into Brianna's face, head, and chest, screaming the whole time — in part because she was enraged, but also to scare anyone else from even thinking about jumping in to help Brianna. No way could she take on a whole mob of girls.

Finally, someone did step in. Arms closed around her and pulled her off of Brianna. Callie screamed, and was going to turn around and strike out until a voice in her ear said, "Calm down!"

It was Mrs. Parker, who'd always been super-nice to Callie. She wrapped her arms around Callie until she calmed down, while the rest of the girls gathered around Brianna, who was still on the ground.

"She's not getting up," one of the girls said.

Another coach, Mrs. Timmons, rushed over and picked up Brianna, "We've gotta get her to the school nurse."

As Mrs. Timmons carried Brianna out of the locker room, Callie realized how badly she'd hurt Brianna. The girl's face was covered in blood as if she'd been attacked by a dog or something. And as the door closed and Callie sat transfixed by the moment, she realized everyone in the locker room was staring at her. Staring at her with a mix of fear and something else, which Callie would soon recognize as respect.

At first, Callie was afraid she'd hurt Brianna so badly that the girl might die. When she didn't die, Callie was worried that Brianna was so embarrassed by the event that she'd spend months plotting revenge, which would lead to an ever-escalating war that would end up with someone dead. However, that didn't happen, either. Brianna had to be on her best behavior as her parents were busy trying to sue the school and even Callie's mom, painting Brianna as the golden child who was roughed up by a thug. There were even accusations that it was a hate crime, with Callie being the perpetrator. But too many girls had come forward and told what Brianna had written on Callie's locker.

Nothing came of the threats, thankfully. And Brianna's dad got a new job, so the family moved at the end of the school year.

That was the last time anyone had fucked with her like that. Sure, some petty shit happened, but no outright bullying.

Once Callie heard Bob go back to his "thinking room," she grabbed another spiral notebook from Charlie's bag, and settled into the bed. This spiral was black, no drawings on the outside, and in neater condition than the others. She opened it and her eyes widened at what she'd found — Charlie's diary.

She closed it at first, her gut telling her not to read what she had no business reading. However, curiosity led to an inner debate over whether any real harm could come from sneaking a peek. Perhaps, she reasoned, she might gain a better understanding of him, which might help her find him. That seemed like a good reason to read, she decided.

She wasn't being nosy, just caring.

She found herself back in the pages which were dated a year ago.

Dear Dad,
I don't know how much longer I can take this.
Nothing is the same.

If you could see Mom now, you wouldn't even recognize her. She used to be so vibrant and happy. She liked to do things. She liked to do things with me. But now, Bob sucks up her time and energy like some sort of black hole.

He's a freaking vampire, sucking joy and happiness instead of blood. It's like the lives we lived before he came along don't exist. It's like YOU never existed.

Sometimes, I'll mention you at the table, and mom will get all uncomfortable like it bothers Bob, so I ought not to do it.

What the hell? She's betraying you for BOB?!

God, Dad, if you could see him you would just laugh. He's nothing like you. If someone looked up the antonym of you in a thesaurus, they'd see this smiling cancer of a human.

I don't know why Mom had to marry him.

I mean, I could maybe understand if he had lots of money or something.

I like to think sometimes you can read these letters I write to you. That sometimes you can see our lives from wherever you are. But times like this, I think it's better that you can't see us. You can't see what's become of Mom.

Or how I've let it happen.

Love,

Charlie

Callie's eyes filled with tears.

She stared at the window, drapes drawn tight, and wondered where Charlie was. Even though she barely got a chance to know him, she found herself missing him more as she poured through his thoughts on the pages.

She fell asleep thinking about him, and how she had to get away from Bob as soon as possible, monsters be damned.

**

Oct. 19
Morning
Pensacola, Florida

She woke in the morning, Bob knocking on her door and barging right in. Confused, she looked up at him, realizing too late that she'd left Charlie's diary open on the bed. If Bob noticed, he didn't say anything. Instead, he was looking out her window. She slid the spiral under the blanket seconds before he turned back to her.

"Pack your shit; we're getting out of here."

"What?" she asked, surprised.

"I'm not waiting around for those fucking things to come back. I saw two more last night, and I'm thinking we need to find somewhere new to go before more show up."

"But what about Charlie? What if he comes back? How will he find us?"

"Fuck Charlie," Bob said. "He made his coffin; let him lie in it."

"But he's your stepson; you can't just leave him out there to die!"

Bob glared at her, "Listen, sister, I didn't leave him; he left *us*. He chose to walk out the door. The boy never thinks about anyone but himself. I'm tired of everyone actin' like I'm the fucking bad guy here and going 'poor Charlie' this and 'poor Charlie' that. Fuck that shit. His mom is gone. I don't need to hear that shit from another bitch."

"Excuse me?" Callie said, now glaring back at him. She no longer cared to play along with his games. Let the cards fall where they may. "What did you say?"

Bob's eyes met hers, and for a moment, she was certain he'd take a swing at her. But like the bully he was, he shrunk back from a strong response.

Instead, he smiled that bullshit smile that seemed to fool so many people for some reason, allowing him to skate through life getting away with shit no human should get away with. It was some sort of reptilian charm which seemed to work especially well with women. But not her.

"Hey, I wasn't calling *you* a bitch, I was just generalizing. Didn't realize you were so damned sensitive. Shit."

She stared at him, not saying a word, as she tried to think what to do next. She couldn't leave, not while Charlie was still out there. She had to find him.

"I'm not going anywhere," she said. "I'm waiting for Charlie."

"Hah," Bob laughed. "You got a thing for the little geek or something?"

"It's not like that," she said, annoyed.

"I didn't think so, seeing as how he's just a boy. You need a man."

"Like you?" she said with a sneer before she could bite her tongue.

"You didn't seem to mind having my manhood in you."

That was it. She was done playing nice. She got in his face.

"Make no mistakes; you fucking raped me. And if you think I forgot that little fact, think again, you pig fuck."

Bob's eyes flashed, anger clouding them, and flushing his face. He was frozen for a second before he swung the back of his hand and hit her square in the jaw. The pain shot through Callie like fire, and she fell to the ground.

Fuck, get up.

She rolled over as Bob circled her, "You fucking cunt."

She spat at him and missed. He kicked her hard in her left ribcage.

"Fuck!" she screamed out.

"Bitch, you ain't even seen rape yet. That was foreplay," he said grabbing his cock through his jeans.

He kicked at her again, in the leg, and she balled up, trying to present as small a target as possible until she could get the advantage.

Then he was on her, arms pushing her hands above her head as he used his legs to push hers apart and roll her onto her back.

She screamed out, spitting at his face, this time connecting.

He let go of an arm and smacked her hard across her left cheek. The pain was intense, and she began to feel sick to her stomach like she was going to pass out.

"It's time I teach you a thing or two, bitch," Bob spat out as he grabbed at her sweatpants and started to rip at them.

Suddenly another voice in the room spoke.

They turned to the doorway to see two strangers standing there. The older of the two men was holding a baseball bat. And he spoke.

"No, I think it's you who'll be doing the learnin' and luckily for you, Boricio is one fuck of a teacher, Bobby."

Then a third person entered the room ... Charlie.

* * * *

CHAPTER 6
EDWARD KEENAN

Ed woke in handcuffs, for the second time this week.

He was in a chair, arms bound behind him, staring at his reflection in a streaked mirror. The harsh neon lights mocked every line of his nearly 40 years. Behind him was a gray door, reminding Ed of a police "interview" room. Or, to use a more appropriate name, the interrogation room.

They'd caught him, which meant the world hadn't come to a grinding halt, after all. The powers that be were still in power. And he was still important enough to capture and silence. His head was pounding. The last thing he remembered was staring out the window. And then looking up to see the girls.

Shit.

Jade! Teagan! Ken! Where are they?

He struggled in his chair, but knew that even if he managed to break free, someone would be in the room in seconds. He was being watched. He could feel eyes on the other side of the mirror.

"Where are they?!" he shouted, flaunting his anger. "What did you do with them?!"

No answer.

He closed his eyes and tried to piece together where he might be. But without knowing how long he'd been out or what time it was, he was lost. All he knew was the place had electricity — and interrogation rooms, which meant either a police station, or perhaps one of the agency's government compounds, one of the secret locales scattered across the country where agents could snatch whoever they wanted, then interrogate, or torture them, if necessary, to extract information. He'd been on the other side of the mirror too many times to count. Hell, he could've been in this very room before and not recognize it now.

"You've got me. You win. Just tell me where they are and I'll play nice and go sit in a cell and rot."

Still no answer.

They were trying to push him. Let his fear mount, so their leverage would be greater when agents eventually came into the room. They were waiting for him to crack, to show signs of weakness they could exploit. Under normal circumstances, he wouldn't give in to what they wanted. But they had Jade, Teagan, and Ken. And he was tired of fighting.

He was ready to surrender, to give them whatever they wanted. He considered breaking down and crying, but if they knew him, if they *really* knew him, they'd know he'd not break that quickly. They'd see it as the ruse it was, and he'd probably be stuck waiting even longer for someone to come.

So he went with reality and stared straight ahead, through the mirror, at whoever stood unseen on the other side.

"I know you're in there," he said with a straight face and even, if somewhat tired, tone. "You caught me. Yes, I ran when the plane went down, but I had nothing to do with the crash. Shit, I thought *you guys* engineered it to take me out, or hell, even extract me to use as deep cover or something. So, I've got to ask — what do you want from me? Just tell me and it's yours. Want me to go along with your little story, make a public plea that I'm crazy as hell, and sure, I'd shoot more people if given a chance? Get a camera and start rolling. Whatever you want, I'll do it, say it, cop to it, whatever. Just please, let my daughter and the other two kids go."

He swallowed, still staring at himself. A long time had passed since he saw beyond his appearance in the mirror and was forced to contemplate the man beneath the skin — the father who'd lost so much, if not everything. He closed his eyes to keep self-pity from taking root in his mind.

"Do you have kids?" he asked his invisible captors.

"I've gotta tell you, they can be a real pain in the ass sometimes. My wife and I weren't planning on having any. Well, *I wasn't*. And she said she wasn't, but who knows what goes on in the deepest parts of a woman's mind? They're hardwired to want kids. So, even when they say they don't, there's still some biological part deep inside that says, 'Oh yeah you do.' Maybe men are hardwired, too; I don't know. I didn't think I wanted a kid, but when Jade came into our lives, I changed my mind."

Eyes still closed, Ed continued.

"Funny thing about kids, you have this idea about who you are. What you want in life. What you want to do, be, and all that hubris. Your plans can be cast in concrete, and you can carry an unshakable belief that you were meant to do one thing and one thing only. But the minute your child looks at you in that way, wide-eyed and full of trust and love and all the things you feel you don't deserve … the minute they look at you like that, you question everything. You begin to think you were meant for something better. To be someone your child can look up to. To make a difference in their world. Some people go their whole lives and never get that message, that call to be something greater than themselves. They never experience that moment. But I did."

He opened his eyes, looking at the mirror again.

"And I went against it. I chose the agency over what my heart was telling me. I did what *you* wanted me to do. I ignored that call to be a better person, father, and husband. I kept following *your* instructions because *you* all said the world would be better, safer, blah-blah-blah. Take a look outside. Tell me, for all the shit we've done, all the lives we've taken, all we've sacrificed, did it make us any safer? Is the world any better off? Could we prevent whatever the hell happened?"

Ed swallowed hard, glanced at the floor, then returned his gaze to the mirror.

"Was *this* worth selling *your* soul?" he asked not just the men behind the mirror, but also himself.

The lights above him flicked off, casting the room into darkness — and a terrible silence.

**

Ed woke with a jolt to the sound of a chair scraping across the floor.

A man in a blue dress shirt, charcoal slacks, and thin, wire-frame glasses sat in front of him. He wore short-cropped brown hair above the fat cheeks of a baby face, despite otherwise appearing in his mid-30s.

"Hello," the man said, his voice low, face professional.

"Who are you?" Ed asked.

"You first," the man said, pulling a pack of Marlboros from his pocket and offering it to Ed. "Want one?"

"No, thank you."

"Don't mind if I do?"

"Go ahead," Ed said.

The man flicked open his lighter and lit a cigarette.

Ed spoke again, "You don't know who I am?"

"Should I?" the man asked, taking a deep drag on his cigarette.

Ed grinned, "I'd be surprised if you didn't."

"Well, prepare to be surprised," the man said, "Because we don't."

"Who's *we?*" Ed asked, the man's smoke spiraling around him. Ed hated cigarette smoke, but didn't give the man the pleasure of seeing his annoyance.

"You handled yourself pretty well in the parking lot," the man said, "like you were trained."

"Maybe because I was."

"And yet when I ran your face and fingerprints, you didn't show in our system."

"Weird," Ed said, not buying the guy's bit for a second. Though the guy was obviously trained to counter the telltale physical signs of deception, he couldn't pull the wool over Ed's instincts.

"So, where'd you learn to use a gun like that?"

"You'd be surprised what you can learn on YouTube," Ed said, grinning.

His smile wasn't returned. "What's this *agency* you were talking about earlier?"

"Let's cut the shit, guy. Just tell me what you want from me, and I'll do it. Want me to go on the 6 o' clock news and tell everyone I'm a psycho gunman and not at all an agent of the government, fine. I'll do it. Just, please, I want to see them."

"Who do you want to see?"

"Jade, Teagan, and the guy, Ken. I assume you picked them up when you grabbed me."

"Well, we've got two of them."

"What do you mean, two of them?"

"One of them didn't make it."

Ed swallowed, not sure if the guy was pushing his buttons. He kept calm. "Who?"

"The man, Ken. He was infected so we had to purge him."

Ed stared at the guy, trying to gauge his honesty. If he was lying, Ed couldn't tell. "What do you mean infected?"

"He was bitten. We can't risk bringing the infection here."

"So, he's dead?"

"He would've died, anyway. Or become one of them."

"What are they?" Ed asked.

"You've yet to tell me your name."

"Edward Keenan."

The man paused for a moment. Ed wasn't sure if it was deliberate or Ed saying his name had thrown him for some kind of loop. *Do they really not know who I am?*

"Well, hello, Mr. Edward Keenan. A pleasure to make your acquaintance. My name is Sullivan. Now, tell me, Mr. Keenan, what is it that you do?"

"Are you fucking with me? You really don't know? Who the hell are you that you don't know who I am? If you were a legal authority worth a damn, you'd know my name, even if you didn't know who I really worked for. So, if you really *don't* know that information, I'm sure as hell not at liberty to tell you."

Sullivan smiled. "I'm gonna tell you what I think, Mr. Keenan. I think you think you're something you're not. Because trust me when I say, if you were anybody worth knowing, I would know who you are, and we wouldn't be having this conversation. So, why don't we start over and tell me who you really are and what it is that you do?"

Ed closed his eyes, then opened them, "I'm not telling you shit until I see my daughter and Teagan. After that, I'll sing whatever song you like."

Sullivan stared for a moment. "I can bring you Jade, but Teagan had to be moved elsewhere."

"What the hell are you talking about?"

"Sorry, Mr. Keenan, I'm not at liberty to tell you."

* * * *

CHAPTER 7
MARY OLSON

Oct. 18
Morning
Belle Springs, Missouri

In the last week, Mary had been forced to face an entire world gone missing, her only child thrown into unimaginable danger, and a lingering imprisonment in a godforsaken *Dreary* Inn. Yet seeing the brooding despair colonizing the children's faces on the other side of the bar was an altogether different sort of torture.

"It's going to be okay," she said in her best sitcom mom voice. "Desmond will have a plan in a few minutes. Then we'll either be on our way, or camping out here for another day. Either way, we're safe. I promise." She dropped a maraschino cherry and straw into each of the two Shirley Temples, then slid them across the bar to Paola and Luca.

"How do you *know* everything will be okay, Mom?" Paola said.

"I just do," Mary answered, even though she didn't.

"Outside," Luca said, "it's more of the *terrible scary*."

Paola and Mary traded a glance. It was weird seeing the boy aged. Weirder still, when he still used language like an 8-year-old, rather than the young teen he appeared to be.

Paola said, "What's the terrible scary?"

"The black stuff that wasn't there before the bad stuff happened."

"What do you mean?"

"Do you ever get sad spiders?" Luca asked Mary.

She couldn't help but smile. "Sure, I think everyone probably gets sad spiders sometimes."

"Well, the *terrible scary* is filled with sad spiders. I think it might even make them. And the *terrible scary* gets bigger and bigger until it's everywhere, so if the *terrible scary* outside is like the terrible scary I saw on the way to the lobster tacos, we have to go right now."

Paola said, "What happens if we don't?"

"I don't know," Luca said, shaking his head, "but I think we might become part of the *terrible scary*, too."

A cold chill flooded Mary's back. She poured herself a glass of water, wishing it were something harder, and drank it all in one gulp, then said, "I'll be right back."

"Where are you going?" Paola looked at her mom, quietly pleading, *don't leave!*

Mary answered with apologetic eyes, but said, "I'll be quick. I have to talk with Will and Desmond. We have to sort this out. Need a refill before I go?"

Paola nodded. Mary topped off her daughter's drink with a quick squirt and two more cherries.

"You?" she turned to Luca.

"I'm good."

Mary smiled, then left the bar. A minute later, she was between Will and Desmond, arms crossed, demanding answers.

"I don't understand," she said, shaking her head at Desmond. "You've been five steps ahead since this all started. We need you right now. What's our plan? If we have to stay then we have to stay. But we can't just stay because we're not going."

Mary felt herself teetering at the edge of hysteria.

"It's okay," Desmond said. "I'm sorry I'm indecisive, but I honestly don't know what to do and am having a hard time sorting through my thoughts. I usually listen to instinct, but right now, I don't know what else to say other than my Spidey sense is tingling, and the solutions aren't showing themselves to me like they usually do."

He found her eyes. "What do *you* think we should do, Mary?"

She shook her head. "I don't know, and I really don't care. I just want to do something and I want to know what that something is. I don't want to be scared; I'm sick of it. Impossible starts the second you let fear get bigger than faith."

"At the risk of everyone here thinking I'm just some old hippie," Will interrupted, "I need to go off and do a bit of my best thinking. That requires herbal supplementation, so I'm off to find Jimmy. If you still trust my instincts after this morning's monster roll-call, I promise I'll be back with a plan in less than half an hour. If not, well I really can't blame you. I am an old man, after all, who's about to go off and get stoned in our hour of need." Will smiled, then walked off.

Desmond turned to Mary. "I'm sorry," he said. "I feel like I'm letting you down."

"No, you're not letting me down. I guess I've just grown over-reliant on your awesome leadership. And this is all a bit ... much."

"Do you trust Will's advice?" Desmond asked.

"If I knew how I felt about that," Mary said, "I'd feel a million times better. But right now, I don't know which way is up."

"I know what you mean. I'm not used to my instincts waffling around like this, and I've never felt like so many lives were dependent on me. Plus," he looked past Mary for a second, then swallowed the sentence.

"What?" Mary prodded. "Say it."

"There's something about John," he lowered his voice, "that's making me uncomfortable. He woke up all weird. I mean, we had this heart-to-heart last night and he was way drunk, so maybe he's feeling ashamed to have opened up to me or something. But it feels like there's something more."

"I felt the same way when I woke him up," Mary said, though with everything that was going on since then, she couldn't remember what it was that made her feel that way. She tried to think back to the moment she went into his room, but it was like a word on the tip of her tongue that she couldn't quite recall.

Dog Vader started to bark again, staring at them from across the bar.

They stared at one another, neither saying a word. Mary wondered what the dog knew that they didn't.

When Desmond spoke he ignored the subject of John, returning to Will. "If you didn't trust Will, and you had to put your finger on *why*, what would you say?"

"That's the thing," she said. "I don't think there's been a single dishonest word to leave his lips, but I get the feeling there's a lot he's *not saying*."

"Like what?"

"No idea, really, but I think it might have something to do with Luca."

"I don't know," Desmond said with a sigh. "I think the way they showed up and he walked through the door and pulled your daughter from the brink, then went all Rip Van

Winkle is just so out-there weird that anything they say or do is gonna seem weird to us."

"Do you think Will knows something more about Luca?"

"I think he knows a lot about Luca," Desmond said, "and a lot more than you get from idle conversation."

The room was thick with everything Desmond wasn't saying.

"Tell me, Desmond," Mary said, "please."

Desmond's brow relaxed. "Something bothered me about Will the second I saw him. At first I couldn't figure it out, no matter how hard I wracked my brain. But it finally came to me last night."

"What is it?"

"Will reminds me of someone I researched about 18 months back, a scientist studying quantum entanglement. Will even said something that was nearly identical to something the scientist said."

"What's quantum entanglement?"

"Not now," Desmond laughed. "In simple terms, let's say everything in the universe was once one atom. You know, before the Big Bang spread us in a zillion directions all across creation. Even though we're all separate now, we're still connected on some level. Everything means you, me, and everyone. We're all *entangled*. And somehow, those two are perceiving things that we can't. They knew we were here and in trouble."

"I can see how that makes sense," Mary said. "But it still doesn't explain the bleakers or whatever happened to Paola."

"No," Desmond said, "maybe not just yet. But it's something that makes Will and Luca a little less frightening, right?"

"I suppose so," Mary said.

Dog Vader whined again.

"So, does any of this help us figure out what to do next?"

"It's a piece of the puzzle," Desmond said. "I just need some time alone to try and figure it all out and make sense of it. Believe me, we're going to leave here. One way or another."

Mary didn't want to consider what Desmond meant by *another*.

* * * *

CHAPTER 8
DESMOND ARMSTRONG

Desmond sat in a small cubicle at the far end of the temporary offices once offered to business travelers in need of 15 minutes of Internet and quiet while staying at the Drury Inn. The monitors were black, as blank as they would be for the rest of forever, and a fair reflection of the answers in Desmond's mind.

He stared at the scribbles and sketches that blackened the three sheets of paper spread on the desk. He had no easy way out. Just two choices: frying pan or fire. And if he chose poorly, he'd end up marching everyone over the edge and into an unknown abyss.

If he could pull the edges of his mind together, perhaps he could get the colors of the Rubik's cube to click into place. Unfortunately, his mind was frayed and splitting; each time he came close to threading a feasible answer, the seams of logic would split and tear his theory in two.

Desmond typically solved life's problems with a simple formula:

Replicate, isolate, fix.

A mechanic couldn't be expected to fix a problem until he saw or heard it, which is why you couldn't just describe the sound your engine was making; you had to reproduce the rattle to isolate the problem.

Whether you were dealing with a rattling engine, some bad lines of source code, or a looming economic catastrophe, effective problem solving meant you must dive deep, narrow your focus, and thin your variables. Only then could you get to the best part — fixing it.

Desmond loved to fix things, and had shown natural aptitude since he was a child. It's what made him successful in life and business. But every solution started with the variables; they paved the path for the predictors that allowed him to assess the situation and arrive at the next best steps. Yet, when the laws he once knew had softened to gelatin, even seasoned estimation was little more than guessing.

Start with what you know.

Desmond went back to the beginning.

If the entire world, or at least the few hundred miles they'd traversed, had disappeared, how were a small cluster of survivors from Warson Woods, all living next to and across the street from one another, able to survive?

There had to be a reason, and it couldn't be geography, not with Will and the boy crossing the country from the west coast. They were the anomaly, at least from the Drury Inn side of the equation. And Will had already told him that they'd not seen another soul along the way.

They'd had plenty of unexplained drama in Missouri, but nothing compared to what the pair of travelers brought, with supernatural connections and rapid aging, not to mention a dash of dream sharing, which apparently sent them across the map to help the Warson Woods gang in their hour of need.

It almost seemed like a ... *plan.*

But if it was a plan, someone had to be the planner.

Desmond snapped one of the hotel's complimentary pencils, then flicked it to the edge of the desk and ran his hands through his hair.

He'd give anything for access to his hard drive and a working network. After all his team's research on Quantum Entanglement, he couldn't help but feel something was obvious, some connection, something that could help him, help all of them see the other side of a solution.

Desmond swept the trio of sheets into the trashcan, then turned his notebook to a fresh page. He drew a giant circle, then sketched smaller circles around it to mimic the hive like clusters forming outside.

A *hive!*

That was it — *the bleakers are a hive.*

If they were a hive, they had a queen.

And if they had a queen, she had to be somewhere close, or drawing closer.

The bleakers were exploding in numbers. It made sense that something was pulling them in, like ore to magnet.

Desmond groaned, then stood and stretched. He reached down, tore the sheet from his notebook, then crumpled it into a ball and tossed it in the wastebasket.

He left the cubicle, crossed the hotel lobby and pool area, and went into the small gym at the far side of the inn. He hopped on an exercise bike, one of the kind that didn't need electricity to provide resistance.

Ideas arrived faster in motion.

Desmond rode for three minutes, then dialed the resistance to 4, the highest setting before riding turned to racing, then moved his legs for a few more minutes, skating along the edge of several ideas, but unable to grab a single one, and knowing they were all wrong before he even tried.

He was glossing over something obvious, something that would illuminate truth and steer them clear of danger. Something he already knew had to be useful, something in his memory banks, already discovered then filed away like any of life's impressions that are irrelevant at the time imprint.

Desmond dialed the bike to 6 and pedaled faster.

Sweat painted his face as the fingers of his mind finally wrapped around the frayed edges of an answer. He hadn't pushed himself this hard on a bike in months. That old familiar "runner's high" was kicking into gear. While endorphins stimulated pleasure receptors in the brain, they also had a secondary effect on Desmond, stimulating his creative process. He'd had many of his best business ideas during, or shortly after, a good run or bike ride.

If he could just push himself a little bit harder, a little bit faster, he would find the answers he needed now ... or die trying.

* * * *

CHAPTER 9
DOG VADER

Earlier that morning ...

Dog Vader paced in a circle.
Where are Luca and Will?
This wasn't how things were supposed to happen. It wasn't how it was in his dreams.
It is here. This is bad.
Mary should have been able to understand him, but she couldn't. He was just a dog to her. But he had to let her know that the soft man was an impostor; the dark one, the thing that made everything black.
"John, it's time to go."
Growl ... Growl ... Growl ...
The impostor looked at him with eyes full of hate, then turned to Mary.
A sea of rot hung like a thick fog in the room, putrescence dripped from the impostor. She should have smelled him. But humans didn't smell things like dogs did.

He had to get Luca to sleep. That was the only time they could talk, or at least it was the only time Dog Vader could say what needed saying and be sure Luca would understand. They had managed alright outside of sleep, at least the first two days, but that was before they found Will.

Of course, they were supposed to meet Will, just not so early. And not like they had.

Jimmy and Desmond joined Mary and the impostor, but Will and Luca were still nowhere. Luca was probably with Paola. Vader wondered if Will was off smoking somewhere.

Jimmy headed toward the stairs, leaving the impostor and Desmond alone.

Growl ... BarkBarkBarkBark ... Growl ...

Dog Vader's barks bounced across the nearly empty hotel. He trotted toward the offices. The problem with humans was answers were usually everywhere and solutions often obvious, yet they rarely opened their minds wide enough to grab them.

Luca came out from the hallway and Dog Vader galloped toward him, nuzzling his knee and rubbing up against his leg.

"I'm happy to see you, too," Luca said.

Jimmy ran into the room. "You guys are gonna want to look at this!"

He blasted back through the stairwell door. Everyone followed. Luca led Dog Vader by the scruff of the neck, through the door and up to the second floor.

"Christ on a cross," Desmond said. "When did this happen?"

Dog Vader looked out the window.

The tide was rising. Fast. Too fast. Definitely ahead of schedule.

Dog Vader could feel the impostor soaking in his mounting power.

BARK ... BARK ... BARK ... BARK ...

YOU DON'T KNOW WHAT YOU'RE DOING.
THIS MAN ISN'T THE SOFT ONE, JOHN; HE'S AN IMPOSTOR.
A PLAGUE OF NEVERENDING PESTILENCE.
A STARLESS NIGHT, DROWNING EVERY DROP OF THE PLANET'S LIGHT.
BARK ... BARK. .. BARK ... BARK ...
"Luca," Will said, "would you mind taking the dog downstairs so we can figure out what to do?"

Luca nodded, then led him by the neck back downstairs.
BARK ... RUFF RUFF ... BARK ... RUFF RUFF

"I'm sorry Lord Vader, but I can't help you if you don't stop and tell me what's wrong." Luca tried to listen, but had already forgotten how.

BARK ... RUFF ... RUFF ... BARK ... RUFF ... RUFF
THE SOFT MAN IS AN IMPOSTOR. THIS WASN'T SUPPOSED TO HAPPEN!

BARK ... RUFF ... RUFF ... BARK ... RUFF ... RUFF

Luca looked at him with kind eyes, then sat cross-legged on the floor and petted his hair. It was strange, the way the boy's cheeks had thinned in minutes. Vader had to talk to Luca. If he could only get him to sleep, everything would be okay. But the boy wouldn't sleep until night. And given how much was going on, he might not shut his eyes until later in the night.

Vader didn't know if they'd have that long before the bad man did something horrible.

"You're a good boy, Vader, er, I mean Kick."

Paola opened the stairwell door.

"Hey," Luca said.

"Hey," she said. "Wanna play Blokus?"

"No," Luca said, shaking his head, "I don't like playing it with just two people. Besides, Blokus makes me miss home most."

Dog Vader whined.

"How about Monopoly?"

"I'm not really very good at that game," Luca said as he looked down. "I'm okay, but sometimes it's hard when the numbers get big. How about Battleship?"

"Okay," she agreed, "but only four games. Then we're playing two games of Sorry and three of Konexi."

"Why do you get an extra game?"

"It's called interest," Paola said, then laughed. "Now come on!"

Dog Vader whined.

"I'll be back, okay, Vader?"

He whined again.

"You can come, but you won't have fun," Luca said. "I can't pet you when I'm trying to concentrate."

More whining but Luca wasn't getting the message.

"Okay, you can sit with us. But don't expect any attention!"

Vader trotted behind Luca and Paola, then sat beside the boy as they unboxed their game of Battleship.

Dog Vader could feel that he was in grave danger. The impostor would end him the second he had the chance. He wouldn't be reckless, or do anything in front of anyone else. For the moment, Vader was safe, but that moment would fade and time wasn't smiling.

If he was going to die, so be it, but he had to go knowing his work was done. If he could warn the boy, at least it would be something. Not many like him were left, breathing bridges between what had happened and what was about to.

He had to get the boy alone and snoring, which usually wasn't hard in the middle of the afternoon. But too much commotion was present with the other kids.

BARK ... RUFF RUFF ... BARK ... RUFF RUFF

"Stop it, Lord Vader!"

BARK ... RUFF RUFF ... BARK ... RUFF RUFF

"I mean it! If you don't stop barking you can't play with us anymore."

Growl ... Growl ... Growl ...

Dog Vader trotted toward Desmond, standing at the front of the lobby. The black things were outside, but had moved back a bit, making the people less afraid that the things would storm the hotel. Dog Vader watched the things, then watched Desmond watching the things. He didn't want to interrupt Desmond. He could tell that the man was figuring out something. Desmond could smell stuff better than the rest of them, even Will, at least in his own way. They both stood there for nearly 10 minutes. He could sense that Desmond was close to discovering what Vader already knew.

He wondered if Desmond could understand him. He was the most intuitive of the group, other than Luca.

If Desmond could understand him, then Dog Vader would be willing to tell him everything he needed to know. He couldn't wait any longer; he had to get Desmond's attention.

BARK... RUFF RUFF ... BARK ... RUFF RUFF

"Not now, boy," Desmond said.

BARK... RUFF RUFF ... BARK ... RUFF RUFF

Desmond moved his gaze from the window to the dog, then dropped to one knee. "What is it?" he said. "What do you know?"

BARK ... RUFF RUFF ... BARK ... RUFF RUFF ... THE SOFT MAN IS AN IMPOSTOR, A PLAGUE THAT WILL RUIN EVERYTHING. HE IS A STARLESS NIGHT THAT WILL SLOWLY FADE UNTIL THE SKY IS AS BLACK AS HIS INSIDES! ... BARK ... RUFF RUFF ... BARK ... RUFF RUFF

"You smell something," he said, then stood and shook his head. "Me, too."

"Lunch!" Mary called.

Desmond walked toward the bar and Dog Vader followed. They were halfway there when the impostor and Jimmy entered the lobby.

BARK ... RUFF RUFF ... BARK ... RUFF RUFF RUFF

"Maybe we should put the dog in one of the rooms," the impostor said.

"No, he's okay, right, boy?" Luca tried to soothe him.

BARK ... RUFF RUFF ... BARK ... RUFF RUFF ... RUFF

Desmond said, "Maybe John's right. Just for lunch. Okay, buddy?"

"Okay" The boy looked down, then over at Dog Vader. "Come on," he said.

The impostor turned to the group, "I'm going to keep watch on the second floor if you don't mind. I'm a bit worried about what's happening outside, and not too hungry."

"Sure thing, John," Desmond said.

Luca led Vader to the far side of the kitchen, opened the door, gently ushered him inside, patted him on the head and said, "See you soon!" then closed the door behind him.

This couldn't be it.

This couldn't be the end.

Vader barked, hoping Luca would come back.

The impostor would be coming soon. Dog Vader had to stay alive, at least long enough to get to the boy's dreams, where everything would be okay and he could finally tell him everything; finally finish what he'd been brought along to do.

Vader pawed at the outside door.

Maybe he could get everyone's attention if he could get outside and circle back to the front of the hotel. He never should have let Luca lock him inside the kitchen. It was only a matter of time before...

The doorknob turned and the door swung wide.

He smelled the air, but nothing was there.

No … something was there: faded … tired … dehydrated … *rotten*.

The impostor entered the kitchen and leaped at Dog Vader, before he'd even had a chance to growl.

Dog Vader's world went dark.

* * * *

CHAPTER 10
CHARLIE WILKENS

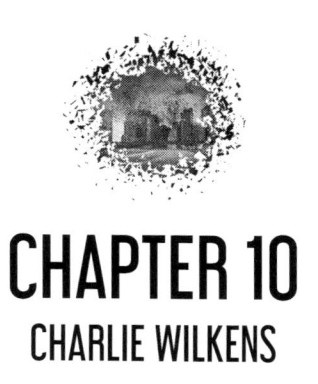

Oct. 19
Morning
Pensacola, Florida

"Who the fuck are you?" Bob said, rising from the floor, buttoning his jeans.

"Boy, you ain't a good listener; I already told you my name was Boricio. I know class was in session, so that must mean you were staring out the window. I sure hope you don't get held back, but rules is rules, and your attention span might not leave Mr. Boricio with much of a choice."

Charlie stared at Callie, on the ground, sobbing. Bob had tried to rape her, which made Charlie wonder if he saw what he'd thought he saw in the pool. Perhaps Callie wasn't a willing participant, after all. It wasn't like he hung around long enough to get a good look. He'd been so disgusted by the thought of a girl he liked being with Bob, he ran. Now, as he looked down and saw the look in her eyes, he felt horrible. If Bob was raping her then Charlie could, no *should*, have done something. Instead, he fled like a pussy.

"What the hell is going on here, Charlie?" Bob said, face red and eyes aflame.

"Why don't you tell me?" Charlie said, his voice a third as confident as he wanted to sound. He imagined returning to slap Bob into place, armed with the barrel of motivational speeches Boricio delivered over several hundred miles.

"The only way to get power," Boricio had said on the ride to Florida, "is to step to the fuckin' plate and swing your bat in its fat fuck of a face. That's how shit's done on Team Boricio. Fuckers who don't like it get squashed."

Charlie agreed. He'd been scared of bullies his entire life. Now was his chance, to take control of his life, courtesy of Boricio. He felt like he could do it, felt brave all the way to the house, through the front door, and even up the stairs. But now, seeing Bob again, some part of him fell into the familiar role — where Bob was the man of the house, and Charlie, the bitch. A familiar, and Charlie realized with some sickness, comfortable role. After all, if someone else were responsible for keeping you down, you couldn't blame yourself when life was shit.

"Take your little friends and get the fuck outta here," Bob said in an annoyed voice, pointing at Charlie, and completely ignoring Boricio.

"I'm not leaving without Callie," Charlie said.

Bob laughed.

"Ha! You think she likes you? The minute you were out the door, she was on my cock like a dirty whore."

"That's not true!" Callie cried, "He drugged me."

"Drugged you?" Boricio said, mock indignation on his face, "Bob, Bob, Bob, I'm shocked. A big stud like you needs to drug a lady?"

Bob said nothing, probably hoping he could will Boricio from existence.

"Come on, Callie, we're getting out of here," Charlie said, holding out his hand.

"She's staying," Bob stepped between them.

Callie stepped around him, then rushed toward Charlie. Bob reached out, grabbed her by her hair and yanked her back. She screamed out as she fell to the ground, still in Bob's grip like a dog on a leash.

"Let go of her," Charlie said, stepping forward meeting Bob's enraged eyes. He wished Boricio had let him bring a weapon, but he said he had his reasons, and it wasn't like Charlie could argue.

"Or what? You're gonna have your goons beat me up? I've got a better idea; why don't you and your little butt buddies go back to whatever queer, little fuck fest you got going on?"

Boricio laughed, "Goons? Hey, pardner, I resent being called a goon. I'm fucking captain of this team. Besides, I'm pretty sure Charlie can take care of you just fine. Us boys are just here to watch. You know, though if you're interested in some butt buddy shit, I'm sure we can accommodate you, handsome."

Boricio winked playfully at Bob.

"Don't make me tell you again," Charlie said, trying on a bravery that felt five sizes too big. "Let go of her."

Bob stared, then glanced at Boricio and Adam, who hadn't budged. "Fuck you, kid. She's not going anywhere."

Callie pulled away, this time successfully, stood up, and ran to Charlie. "Fuck you!" she screamed.

Bob came at Charlie.

Charlie, recognizing Bob's intent too late, dodged, but not quickly enough.

Bob's fist slammed into Charlie's forehead, sending a bolt of thunder between his temples, though Charlie was sure it would have hurt far worse if knuckles had landed on his nose.

Bob fell forward with the momentum of his swing. He regained his balance then scurried out the door and toward his bedroom. Charlie raced after him, seeing Bob's target a moment later: a pistol on the dresser.

No!

Panic ignited the fuel in Charlie's veins. If Bob got the pistol, Charlie was done for. He could hear Boricio and Adam following behind him, but he was the only person who could stop Bob in time.

He reached out, grabbed the collar of Bob's shirt and yanked back, causing them both to roll to the floor.

Bob cried out as he hit his head on the dresser. His eyes met Charlie's, full of a fiery hate Charlie had only glimpsed before now. If any doubt had been in his mind that Bob wanted to murder him, it evaporated that second.

Bob kicked out, hitting Charlie in the chest, clearing his lungs of air and sending him reeling back into the bed.

Bob stood quickly, grabbed the gun and took aim at Charlie, who closed his eyes and waited for death. But instead of a gunshot, he heard a thunk followed by a scream.

Charlie opened his eyes.

Bob had dropped the gun.

Boricio's bat was on the floor beneath him.

Boricio had thrown the bat at the gun. "Okay," Boricio said, looking down at Bob, "I lied. I helped him just this once. Now you're on your own, Charlie. Take that fucker out."

Bob's eyes narrowed on Charlie as he bent over to grab the gun.

Charlie dove to the floor, grabbed the bat, and without thought, swung at Bob's knees. Hard.

Bob fell to the ground in agony, but still held the gun in his quivering hand.

Charlie rolled over and swung again. Harder. As the bat connected with Bob's right wrist, a sickening crunch preceded the gun's descent to the floor. Bob cried out, left hand now cradling his broken right one.

"You fucker!" he wailed, threads of saliva stretching across his wide-open mouth.

Callie, who had just entered the room, ran past them, then grabbed the gun and aimed it at Bob, who sat, hunched over, crying, "I'm gonna fucking kill you, you little brat."

Charlie looked back at Boricio and his giant grin. Adam was staring next to him in the doorway, in wide-eyed disbelief.

"You hear me? I'm gonna hunt you down and fucking kill you!" Bob cried out, head down, staring at his broken hand.

"You're not killing anyone!" Callie said, as she marched forward and put the gun to the top of his head.

Bob looked up, stared at her, his eyes equaling the hate he held for Charlie. A sick smile spread across his face. He turned. "Gonna let a girl do your job for you, *Charlene?*"

Why the hell is he goading us? Shut up, Bob. Goddammit!

Charlie couldn't understand why Bob was pushing his buttons. Didn't he realize what was happening? How much the odds were stacked against him? He was backing Charlie into a corner, forcing him to respond. Though Charlie had come here seeking revenge for all the shit Bob had ever done, now that he was staring down at the crippled version of a pathetic man, his hunger for vengeance had soured.

If Bob would just shut his mouth, Charlie would be happy to leave with Callie, even if it meant disappointing Boricio.

Callie looked at Charlie, as if waiting for approval. He shook his head no. "Let's go."

"You're not gonna finish the job?" Boricio said. "Goddamn, kid, you're a better man than me."

"I just want to leave," he said, taking the gun from Callie and hugging her. It felt so good to have her in his arms, even if they were just friends. "He's not worth it."

"But this fucker raped her," Boricio said, "And he ruined your mother's life. You said it yourself! You're just gonna let that go?"

Boricio's eyes looked like those of a child who'd just been told on the night before Christmas that Santa wouldn't be making the rounds this year.

Charlie felt pangs of guilt. They'd driven all this way with Charlie all pumped up to take care of Bob once and for all, and now he was letting the team down. And though he barely knew Boricio and Adam, their bonds were forged in fire at the compound.

"He ruined your mother's life," Boricio pleaded, working Charlie's guilt.

Boricio was the first man since Charlie's father to show him respect. But when it came right down to it, Charlie wasn't a murderer. While he'd fantasized many times of shooting every bully in school, he'd never *actually plotted* to do it. Despite his bravado and his darkest fantasies, Charlie didn't think he could snuff out someone's life unless he was defending himself or someone he loved.

He handed the gun to Boricio and started toward the bedroom door with Callie behind him.

"He said I ruined his mother's life?" Bob said, laughing.

Why won't he just shut the fuck up?

"I was the best thing that ever happened to that bitch. She was a goddamn mental case when I met her! Always whining about her dead fucking husband and shit. What guy wants to hear that kinda crap?"

Something shifted in Charlie. His blood ran cold, and his skin started to tingle. Tears glossed his eyes with everything he'd been holding back for too many years.

He turned to Bob, jaw quivering, "You shut your fucking mouth."

"About your bitch mom or your dead bitch daddy?"

"Whoa!" Boricio said sounding like Al Pacino. "You did NOT just say that about the boy's daddy!"

Charlie swung the bat and hit Bob in the left knee. It popped, and Bob screamed.

"You aren't even a 10th of the man my dad was, you piece of fucking shit!" Charlie screamed, spit flying from his mouth at Bob.

"You sucked the life out of my mother like a fucking vampire! She didn't love you. She was *scared* of you, you piece of shit!"

Bob laughed.

"Stop laughing!" Charlie screamed, tears streaming down his face.

Bob looked up at him, eyes wild, manic, chest heaving in mocking laughter.

"Stop fucking laughing!" Charlie said, swinging the bat again, this time hitting Bob's left arm above the elbow.

Bob screamed out, but still forced a laugh from his lips, meeting Charlie's eyes. Daring him to strike again.

"Let's just go," Callie said from behind, putting a warm hand on Charlie's shoulder. "He's not worth it."

Charlie glanced back at Boricio, who smiled and nodded approvingly. Adam's eyes were wide, scared. Callie's were sympathetic, sorry for Charlie.

But he didn't want sympathy.

As Bob's laughter grew, it dug into Charlie's core, pulling a plug on a bucket of memories. As the self-denial and selective amnesia flowed down the drain, Charlie was forced to remember all the shit Bob had ever done. All the little insults, orders, exploitation, and the many ways he slowly murdered his mother — a woman who had been so sweet and full of life. Charlie remembered a time before

Bob, when he was putting on a puppet show for his mom. She laughed so hard. Smiled at him. Yeah, she missed her husband, and Charlie missed his daddy. But they had each other. And that was enough.

Until Bob.

Bob's laughter mocked everything that was pure and good in Charlie's mother. Mocked his father's memory.

Charlie turned to Boricio, Adam, and Callie, and said, "Get out."

"What?" Callie said, trying to meet his eyes. But he couldn't look at her.

"Go out there and wait for me. Bob and I have some shit to work out."

Boricio smiled the widest smile Charlie had ever seen, as he put his hands on Adam and Callie and led them from the room. "Come on, team; let's give our boy some privacy."

"You don't have to do this," Callie said, looking back.

Charlie turned away. "Please. Leave."

Boricio led them out and shut the door softly behind him.

Charlie turned to Bob. They were alone.

And only one would leave the room.

* * * *

CHAPTER 11
LUCA HARDING

"Boy, your dog was really getting worked up," Paola said.

"He didn't mean any harm. He's a good dog," Luca said, arranging his battleships on the board.

"He's cute." Paola said. Luca looked up to see her smiling. She had a pretty smile.

"What was school like where you were from?" Luca asked Paola, trying to make small talk and avoid any more conversations about scary stuff.

"Sort of boring," she said. "I just started middle school. I sort of liked it better because we changed classes and teachers, plus the school was bigger so there were more friends to talk to and play with at recess, but it's still pretty boring."

"Why is it boring?" Luca asked. "Didn't you get to learn neat stuff? I was already in division for my Rocket Math. I was almost on Q."

"No, not really," she said. "I mean, I guess you're supposed to learn stuff. But most of what we learned at my new school I already knew when I got there."

"How come?"

"Because I used to go to this school called Oak Hill, kindergarten through fourth grade. It was really good, but I stopped going two years ago."

"How come?" Luca asked.

"Because my dad said that only rich people went to that school, and he didn't want me to be a spoiled brat like most of the girls who went there. But that wasn't the *real reason*. Almost all of the girls at Oak Hill were actually really, really nice. I think my dad didn't want me to go there because he couldn't afford it, which meant my mom had to pay for it. I don't think he liked that, even though he wouldn't admit it."

"You liked your old school?" Luca asked.

"Actually, I really like my school. The people are nice and I have, or had, a lot of cool friends. It was just boring. I couldn't learn anything there that I couldn't learn from reading books, and I've been reading everything I could ever since I knew how." She looked at Luca. "Do you like to read?"

"Yeah, I just started reading chapter books this year," he said.

"Oh yeah? What's your favorite?"

"I started reading *Harry Potter*, but I didn't like it very much."

"You don't like *Harry Potter*? Something is definitely wrong with you! What are you reading now?"

"*How to Eat Fried Worms*. Have you read it?" Luca said.

"No, but I saw the movie. Is the book any good?"

Luca nodded. "Yeah, I liked the book better than the movie."

Luca felt Paola trying not to stare, could feel her thinking how odd it was that they looked the same age.

"Don't be embarrassed," she said, as though reading his mind. "I know it's strange, but whatever happened to you only happened because you helped me. That makes it a good thing, right?"

Luca nodded, but felt like he was going to cry.

"It's okay!" Paola laughed and gave him a playful slap on the knee. "Everything will be fine." She changed the subject. "What do you think Dog Vader was so upset about?"

"I'm not sure, but I'll be able to find out as soon as I fall to sleep."

"What do you mean?"

"Oh," Luca said. "You didn't know? Dog Vader isn't *really* a dog."

"What?!"

"Well, I guess he *is* a dog, but he's not *just* a dog. He's also an Indian."

Paola looked at Luca cross-eyed. "An Indian?"

"Yes," Luca said, "but only when I'm sleeping."

"If you're not messing with me, then you'll have to tell me everything, starting from the beginning."

"Dog Vader is a dog *and* an Indian. Not the kind from the other country, but the ones you're not supposed to call Indians, Native Americans. He's the one who led me to Will."

"And he *talks to you* in your sleep? Like you and Will talk ... and like you talked to me?"

Luca nodded, staring at his shoes, still embarrassed, though not quite sure why.

"How do you know you're not just dreaming something that isn't really true?" Paola asked.

"Because he's always right."

"Oh," Paola said. "So he's a psychic dog/Indian?"

"Lunch!" Paola's mom called from the bar.

"What do you think we're having?" Luca asked.

"Not sure, but I'm guessing something from a can." Paola gave Luca a weak smile, then said, "Ready?"

"Yes." Luca slid from the chair and started walking toward the bar beside Paola, when John and Jimmy entered the lobby from the hallway.

Dog Vader started barking again.

BARK ... RUFF ... BARK ... RUFF RUFF

Luca pet Dog Vader. "It's okay, boy" he said. "Everything's okay."

"Maybe we should put the dog in one of the rooms," John said.

"No, he's okay, right, boy?"

BARK ... RUFF RUFF ... BARK ... RUFF RUFF

Desmond said, "Maybe John's right. Just for lunch. Okay, buddy?"

"Okay," Luca looked down, then over at Dog Vader. "Come on," he said, leading him away by the scruff of his neck.

John said, "I'm going to keep watch on the second floor if you don't mind. I'm a bit worried about what's happening outside, and not too hungry."

"Sure thing, John," Desmond nodded.

Luca led Vader to the kitchen, opened the door, gave him a final pat on the head, then said, "See you soon!" and closed the door behind him.

Luca returned to the bar and picked at his food. It would have been good if he was hungry, but he couldn't stop thinking about Dog Vader, or tease his appetite long enough to swallow.

"Food's probably going to be a problem, isn't it Mom?" Paola said.

Mary said, "Maybe, but I think we'll be able to manage. We have a ton of stuff in cans, and as long as the population is as small as we think it might be, grocery stores will have plenty. We'll just need to stock up when we can."

"Are you worried?"

Mary smiled at Paola. "Yes, of course, but I also think we're going to get through this." She shook her head. "No, I *know* we're going to get through this." She stopped spreading peanut butter and set the knife on the bar, then reached across the counter top and kissed Paola on her forehead. "I promise, everything will be fine and I'll always make everything taste as yummy as I can."

"That's not what I'm worried about, Mom! You could make anything taste good, even if we have to start eating squirrel!"

"I don't think we'll be eating squirrel any time soon, at least I hope not!" Mary looked at Luca's plate. "You're not eating anything, sweetheart," she said. "Just tell me what you want. I'll make you anything I can."

She leaned across the bar but Luca only shook his head and said nothing.

Mary's voice dropped to a whisper and she put her hands over Luca's. "It's okay," she said in a nice mom voice. "Everything will be fine. Are you worried about your dog?"

Luca nodded.

Mary smiled. "How about I make a delicious meal for Dog Vader and something else for you? I'll put his food in a doggie bag and yours on a tray, then you all can eat in the kitchen with him. Or," her voice dropped even lower, "if he's stopped barking, you can bring him out here and he can eat next to you on the bar. Sound good?"

Luca smiled and said okay, then made small talk with Paola while Mary gathered food for the boy and his dog. Cocktail wieners and canned ham for Dog Vader, mac 'n' cheese and chips for Luca.

"Thanks, Mom. That was really cool of you," Paola said.

"Thanks, Mrs. Mary." Luca said.

"Just Mary," she said, pushing the lunches across the counter.

"Do you want to come with me to get Dog Vader?"

"Of course!" Paola said.

They crossed the lobby and entered the kitchen, but Dog Vader wasn't inside.

"Lord Vader!" Luca called.

Nothing.

"Where do you think he went?" Paola asked.

Luca looked around the room. Dog Vader wasn't sleeping, and he wasn't hiding. The freezer door was sealed, but the door leading outside looked like it was open a crack.

"Look!" Luca pointed at the door.

"I see it," Paola said, her tone making his sad spiders start to crawl.

They heard noises from the other side of the door.

No barking, no growling and no whines. Only the sounds of tearing, like reams of paper being pulled apart, punctuated by splashes from something thick and wet, and ... *chewing.*

"Do you want me to go get Desmond?"

Luca shook his head and started walking toward the door.

"Are you sure?" Paola repeated.

Luca didn't answer, just kept inching toward the door a half step at a time until he stepped outside to find his dog.

Outside, Luca didn't cry. He couldn't; the horror was too much to react in any way other than stare.

Dog Vader was in a dozen pieces, with everything from his head to paws getting torn, chewed and mangled, before being cast to the concrete in bits of meat and bloody fur. Two of the monsters were fighting over what looked like Lord Vader's front leg, while another was crouched on its knees, dipping its face into the dog's guts.

Pools of blood ran from Vader to Luca's feet.

The monster that was eating Dog Vader's stomach, stopped, then looked at Luca and smiled, revealing dozens of sharp, blackened, blood stained teeth. It suddenly shot up to a standing position. It was at least 7 feet tall.

Paola screamed. "Come on, Luca, we have to go *now!*"

Luca stood frozen.

Paola wrapped both arms around him, pulled him into the kitchen, then slammed the door behind them and slid the lock closed.

"Mommy!" she screamed.

Luca sank to the floor and cried.

* * * *

CHAPTER 12
EDWARD KEENAN

Ed opened his eyes to a new visitor.

Two people were in his room, Sullivan and someone new. The new man was short, older, with graying, curly hair and dark, brooding eyes beneath thick, dark glasses. He wore a long-sleeved, light-blue shirt with gray slacks.

Scientist. Name is Williams.

Wait, how the fuck do I know that?

"Hello Mr. Keenan," said Sullivan. "How are you feeling today?"

Today? A day has passed?

"This is Mr. Williams. He'd like to ask you some questions."

"Great, my favorite game," Ed said, as he pondered how he knew the man's name. "And I'm still waiting for answers. Where is my daughter? Where is ... "

Shit, what is her name?

Ed's head was fuzzy. The pregnant girl's name was on the tip of his tongue.

Tongue ... Tuh ... Teagan!

"Where's Teagan?"

"I'm afraid we had to move her somewhere ... safer." Williams said in a slight British accent. "As for your daughter, she's nearby. Don't worry; we're taking great care of her. We told her you were receiving a few medical tests and some treatment, so she isn't too worried."

"How thoughtful of you," Ed said. "Where are we? Where's Teagan? What's the danger here?"

"In due time, Mr. Keenan. It is Mr. Keenan, correct?" Williams said, peering down at his clipboard and flipping to the next page.

"Yes, Edward Keenan."

"And you're certain of that?"

"Of course," Ed said, annoyed, rubbing his temples raw.

"Are you okay?" Williams asked.

"Just a headache, it'll pass."

"Do you get headaches a lot?" Williams asked.

"What are you, some kind of doctor?"

"Actually, yes," Williams said, "you can say that. Now, about those headaches. Do you get them a lot? How long have you been getting them?"

"I dunno, on and off most of my life. Migraines, a doc told me. Used to be worse when I was younger."

"Do you have any other symptoms?"

"Is this a fucking physical?" Ed asked, agitation growing. "I told you my name. Said I'll cop to whatever you want. Toss me in lockup; throw away the key. I don't give a shit anymore. Let's get on with it already."

"Why would we want to lock you up?" Williams asked.

Ed stared, confused. His head felt like it was going to crack from the growing pressure. His vision blurred and for a moment, Williams had become two rather than one. Ed squeezed his eyes shut, shook his head, then opened them back to minor blurring.

"Are you serious?" Ed said. "You don't have any idea who I am or what I've done?"

"No. Why don't you tell us."

"Everything, from the beginning," Sullivan added.

"My name is Edward Keenan, I work for The Agency. Well, I did, until something happened."

"The Agency?" Sullivan asked, "You mean the CIA?"

"Yes. Well, a division within it, which you probably never heard of. If you want to know more than that, you'll need to speak to my superiors. Assuming any are left out there. By the way, while we're in the Q & A section of this game, mind telling me what the hell happened out there to everyone?"

The two men stared at each other for an uncomfortably long moment.

"What do *you* think happened?" Williams asked.

"Jesus Christ, can't you people answer anything?" Ed sighed, rolling his head back.

"I was on a plane," he said, trying to remember exact details, but his thoughts grew fuzzier as the pain in his head intensified. It sounded like bees were buzzing behind his ears.

"When?" asked Williams.

"When what?" Ed asked, confused.

"When were you on the plane?"

"I don't know, a few nights ago. Late Friday, early Saturday morning."

Williams flipped some papers on his clipboard, then said, "On the 15th?"

"Yeah, I guess." Ed said, thoughts slurred like he was drunk or something.

The two men exchanged another glance. Though his head was pounding and the men who grabbed him were with the government in some capacity, Ed no longer thought they were Agency. At least not his division. Their confusion seemed suddenly sincere. Knowing that made it easier to comply and answer their annoying questions.

"I fell asleep. When I woke, the plane had crashed, and I somehow survived. When I went to see if anyone else had made it, there was no one. No bodies, no survivors. It was like I was the only one on the plane when it crashed."

"Then what?" Sullivan said.

"The world was a ghost town, no matter where I went. I grabbed a truck and started to drive. That's when I ran into the girl, Teagan. She said she was in the back seat while her parents were driving home from vacation. Something happened, she said, this black cloud or something in the car, and the next thing she knew, her mom and dad vanished."

"Vanished? Can you elaborate?" Williams asked.

For a moment, Ed was drawing a blank, as if someone had deleted the memory from his head. And then, the next moment, it was back, in full clarity.

Ed continued, "One second there, and when the cloud disappeared, so did they. Anything more, you've got to ask her. Like I said, I wasn't there. And I didn't see anyone on the plane vanish, though I assume they did, because I was sleeping."

"What else can you tell us about yourself, Mr. Keenan? Are you married?"

"Yes."

"And your wife's name?"

Ed paused for a moment, not sure why it was important. But the intel wasn't classified, and their split was public record in the Agency. "Julie. We split a few years ago."

"And Jade is your daughter?"

"Yes."

The two men looked at each other again, and finally Ed ran out of patience.

"Okay, I told you everything you've asked me. Now, it's your turn to answer some questions."

"Fair enough, Mr. Keenan," Williams said, "But we're not at liberty to say much more than we have."

"Fuck that," Ed said, "Then find me someone who *can* answer questions."

"We've arranged that," Williams said, "Someone will be in to speak with you shortly, and they'll answer all your questions. In the meantime, I'd like to thank you for your cooperation."

"Can you at least tell me where the hell we are?" Ed asked.

Williams looked at Sullivan, who nodded.

Williams said, "You're at Black Island Research Facility."

* * * *

CHAPTER 13
BRENT FOSTER

Brent had never been happier to see a ferry.

They raced to the docks, duffels in hand, loaded with supplies and the smaller weapons Luis had on hand. They weren't carrying weapons on their person for fear of being mistaken for threats in what would likely be a clamped-down ferry ride to Black Island.

They were met by four armed men in black uniforms with unfamiliar emblems on their shoulders, standing guard at the end of the dock where the ferry was tied. The men were wearing some sort of masks. They seemed like military to Brent, which was a good sign because they could likely handle the aliens, if any more showed up.

But something about the soldiers caused an uneasy feeling to creep through Brent's insides.

"Please put your bags down and stand with your arms in the air," one of the men said through his mask.

All four rifles were on them.

"We're just here for the ride to Black Island. We heard the radio broadcast," Brent explained.

As they set their bags down, one of the soldiers stepped forward, rifle no longer aimed at them, but at the ready.

"Have any of you been bitten?" the soldier asked.

Jane and Emily shook their heads and said "No." Brent did the same. Luis had no response.

What? Why is he saying no?

"Sir, please respond; were any of you bitten?"

Luis glanced at Brent, then shook his head no.

Why are you lying?

Brent's uneasiness escalated.

"I need you all to remove your clothing, all of it, and step forward, to this man right here," the soldier said, pointing to a fifth man in black, who was standing at the dock entrance. The man had no gun, but instead, some sort of high-tech looking flashlight. "Step forward one at a time, as I call you," the man said.

"Our clothing?" Jane asked, "Why?"

"Just do it," one of the men snapped, in a voice unwilling to compromise or coddle.

Jane undressed Emily, who asked, "Why are we getting naked?"

"It's okay," Jane said. "It's okay, baby."

Luis glanced at Brent, shaking his head, almost in accusation that Brent should have let him leave.

They undressed, each of them stripped not only of their clothing, but their dignity at the hands of the soldiers. Brent's guts were turning as he exchanged another glance with Luis, trying to apologize with mere expression.

A soldier came and collected their clothing, throwing it into a large, thick, black plastic bag. "You'll get assigned new clothing on the ferry," a soldier said.

Assigned? Like prisoners?

"The kid." A soldier barked. "Send her forward."

Emily took a hesitant step forward, and Jane attempted to follow.

"Just the girl," the main guy snapped, aiming his rifle at Jane.

"Mommy, I'm scared," Emily called out, not wanting to move.

"Go!" the soldier snapped, pointing for Emily to step forward.

"It's okay," Jane said, clutching her arms across her chest. "Mommy's right here."

Emily approached the man with the weird light device. He turned it on. It seemed like a black light, except the light was a deeper, truer, brighter blue. He waved the wand over Emily's entire body, head to toe.

"She's clear," the light-wand guy said. One of the armed soldiers put a black gloved hand on Emily's shoulder and led her to a spot right at the steps. The man handed the girl a black blanket to wrap around herself.

"You," the guy in charge said, pointing at Jane.

She stepped up, then closed her eyes. As the wand went over her chest, something buzzed, and a light on the device went red.

The gunmen immediately turned to Jane, rifles aimed at her.

Emily cried out, sensing the danger, and tried to run toward her mom. The soldier next to her grabbed her, dropped to a knee to lower himself, and held back the child.

"What's wrong?" Jane cried.

That's when Brent noticed the scar running down the center of her chest; Brent figured from heart surgery.

The soldier with the light turned some dials on the device, then ran the light over her again, slowing when he reached her chest. The red lights didn't go off this time.

"Okay," he said, "clear. Please move forward."

Jane joined her daughter, face red with either anger or embarrassment. Jane took Emily from the soldier's arms and picked her up, holding her tight. She was also given a blanket to wrap herself in.

Luis stood in front of Brent, next in line. Brent looked over Luis, trying to see any signs of the things Luis had seen under his skin. Luis's left arm spasmed, twice. Luis stared straight ahead, either not noticing or trying to hide the spasms.

Brent's heart pounded hard as he glanced around at the gunmen, each of their rifles aimed at him and Luis. If something went down, they couldn't do a thing. No Rambo-like theatrics or last stands in Times Square. They'd be shot down like prisoners in old war footage Brent had seen years ago.

"Okay, you're next," the man in charge said, using his rifle to point at Luis, and then to the man with the light.

Brent swallowed.

Luis glanced back at Brent. "Keep believing," he said to Brent.

"Sir, please step forward."

Keep believing? That he'll be okay? Or is that a goodbye message, to keep believing I'll find my family?

This was all happening too fast. Brent glanced at Jane and Emily, standing helpless, rifles aimed at them, the girl crying and clutching her mother, who could do nothing to truly protect her against men with guns.

Luis stepped toward the man in the light, but before he got there, he stopped, turned to the man in charge, and said, "I've been bitten."

Brent felt his stomach drop.

The soldiers all aimed their rifles at Luis in unison. The man in charge yelled into a radio in his mask, "We've got an infected!"

On the ferry, Brent saw four more men with guns appear, forming a barrier to prevent anyone from rushing onto the boat.

"When were you bitten?" the man with the light asked, keeping his distance from Luis.

"Yesterday, mid-morning."

"Jesus!" one of the soldiers said.

"Code red!" the man in charge yelled, panic in his eyes, and two soldiers rushed at Luis, rifles aimed, then shot him. Once in the head, a second shot ripped through his chest. Luis fell to the ground before anyone had a chance to protest. Another man in black came from the boat holding a large device which Brent didn't recognize until it shot flames which engulfed Luis' body.

Brent stared in horror, helpless, stunned, tears flooding his eyes, mouth agape.

Jane and Emily screamed, as the gunmen turned to Brent. He barely saw them, eyes transfixed on the fire.

"Have you been bitten?" the man in charge asked, snapping Brent's attention back to the threat before him.

"No," Brent shook his head, taking a deep breath. "I swear."

"Move forward."

Brent moved to the man with the light. As the man ran the light over Brent's feet, Brent stared at the burning man that had been his friend. And who had saved his life.

I'm so sorry.

A creeping fear burrowed into Brent's brain.

What if I somehow got infected by Luis? They'll just shoot me dead right here. No questions asked.

And I'll never see Ben or Gina again.

And that's when he remembered the truck in his pants pocket, which was now gone with the clothes, sealed up in a bag, destined for God knows where.

Stanley Train!

Tears now flowed down his face as his last physical tether to his child and the world before had been severed.

The light moved up, now at his knees. Brent held his breath, dreading the red lights or buzzing sound. The light was now at his waist, and the device made a noise that sounded like interference. Emily cried out. Brent closed his eyes.

Please, God, don't let me die here. Please, I beg you. I just want to see my family again.

The interference grew louder, and Brent swallowed, certain he was drawing his final breath as he stared at the fire that might soon take him.

The man lowered the light, then went back over the spot. No noise. He finished the sweep, then told Brent to join the others.

Brent released a sigh of relief as he walked to Jane and Emily and was given a blanket.

"We're going to Black Island Research Facility," the man in charge said. "You will not bring any belongings with you. You will be checked once every eight hours for infection for the next three days. If you show positive, you will be shot and incinerated. We cannot allow any infection at the facility, is that understood?"

Brent and Jane said yes. Emily continued crying.

"Let's get out of here," the man said.

As they moved forward, Brent looked back one last time at the burning corpse.

You were right, buddy.

* * * *

CHAPTER 14
JIM MARTIN

Jim was surprised to find himself missing television. Not that he'd regularly watched much TV to begin with. Though the blue light beamed from thin, black boxes in nearly every room in his old house, he'd never held much of an interest, even as a kid.

Sure, he loved the best the idiot box had to offer: *LOST* and *24*, plus cool cable shows like *Dexter*, *The Walking Dead*, and *Breaking Bad*, but most TV was crap and he knew it, made by producers who pulled the levers at the Crap Factory. Reality shows were cheaper than decent drama, and money meant more than legacy, so crap kept piling on top of crap until 1,000 channels were broadcasting little but stink.

Jim would rather read, or watch a good movie. He loved stories, adventure, the never knowing what would happen next. TV was too predictable. Sure, movies were mostly formulaic, too, and so were books for that matter, but the thing good books and movies had that bad TV didn't were the quality of the questions they asked.

Even the cheesiest sci-fi books, done well, left you with questions of who we are and where we came from, or even better, where we're going and how we might get there.

But Jim wasn't craving questions now; he wanted pure, unadulterated junk TV like sugary cereal on a Saturday morning spent watching cartoons — back when there were decent cartoons on TV, that was.

He made a face at the blank screen in his hotel room where he'd gone to try and take a nap even though it wasn't even 1 p.m. "Oh, TV, why hast thou abandoned me in my hour of need?"

Nobody was around to appreciate his humor, so he laughed at his own joke, then headed to the bar, to pour himself a drink. Then he thought better of alcohol, and headed toward the stairwell instead. Jim didn't care for drinking, not much anyway. Weed was much better. Alcohol usually made him sad, or sleepy. Herb expanded his mind, got him to ponder the size of the universe and his place in it. And other times, it made him laugh his ass off. But never did he have a bad weed experience or wake up wishing he'd not smoked so much.

Some comedian once said if weed were a legal drug marketed on TV, it would be called "Fuck it All" or something, which seemed appropriate — it helped him to ignore the shit that everyone else stressed out about, and think about bigger picture sorts of stuff. Important stuff.

Jim decided to head to the second-story window, which had the best view of the parking lot. *Might as well watch the sea of bleakers while enjoying a bowl or two.* As he climbed the stairs, he pulled the baggie from his pocket and sighed.

Shit, not much left.

Jim had enjoyed a steady diet of daily doses since he first turned 15 and Walter Hawking gave him a dime bag to celebrate. He had never even considered a future without weed. He would need to find more. And after that, he'd need to learn how to grow the shit.

Farmer Jim *in da house.*

Jim opened the door to the second floor and was surprised to find the window view occupied by Buzz Kill John Boy himself. *Fuck me.*

Jim had hoped to run into Will again, with whom he had shared some weed earlier and had a great conversation. The likelihood of John providing an interesting conversation was about the same as Jim running into a frightened supermodel in need of some companionship tomorrow.

John turned back to Jim and then back to the scene outside, without saying a word. Though it was lunch time, the world outside was darker than midnight. Heavy, swirling, black clouds churned low in the sky.

"That is fucking awesome," Jim said.

"It *is*, isn't it?" John said, with the hint of a smile on his lips. "So why aren't you eating lunch with the others?"

"Wanted to smoke myself into oblivion and take a nap if we're not leaving this place."

"Is that how that works?" John asked.

Jim laughed. "No, not really. But this latest stuff does seem to make me sleepy. It's called Jade, from my buddy Walter. He gets it from California because his older brother lives out there. He's trying to be an actor, or *was trying* anyway. He uses his medicinal marijuana card to make ends meet, including weekly shipments back home to Walter. Big business, at least for a high-schooler. They split the money, 50/50. Walter wanted to buy a car, but figured even if his parents were stupid, they weren't too stupid to believe he could afford a new X-Terra just from mowing lawns, so he's been stashing cash for two years. For all the good it did him."

John continued to stare, silent.

Jim sprinkled a few dried buds into the basin of his pipe. "Even though he always gave me a deal and a half, I was still one of Wally's best customers. Of course, looks like I'm gonna need a new hookup now! Oh shit, I should've thought to raid Wally's house! I would've had enough shit to last me at least a couple months. Hell, maybe enough for all of us, knowing what Wally had stashed away!"

Jim laughed and looked at John, trying to draw him into friendly conversation, but he may as well have been alone. John just stared out the window, casting an occasional glance at Jim, more curious than irritated, though laced with something else Jim couldn't place.

He'd seen the look before, mostly exaggerated on the expressions of bad guys in cheesy B-movies. Same look on John's face, but it didn't fit, like a turtle shell on a cat. The guy may have been anal with a capital A, and a bit of a douche the past few days, but he didn't have a mean bone in his body.

"You know," Jim said, "I'm not even really sure this *is* Jade. Wally always gets these cool names from his brother: Mace Windu, Blue Dream, Hippie Crippler, but hell, how would we know? I think his brother probably buys crap weed and changes the names. You really should give this a try," he offered the pipe to John. "I bet it makes you feel a lot better than you're expecting in less time than you imagine it could. *And* without the hangover." Jim smiled. "Temporary, but nice while it lasts."

Jim flicked his lighter. The quiet crackle of curling leaves sent a thin plume of bitter smoke swirling through the air. He drew the smoke into his lungs with a double barrel inhale, then held his breath for an impossibly long time, partly showing off, then blew the smoke in a frothy jet that settled against the glass like frost.

"Good ... shit." Jim said, pounding his chest. "Come on, man, *lighten up*. Give it a try. You've got no idea what you're missing. And seriously, this is the last of my stash. I should get a blue ribbon or medal for even offering."

John narrowed his eyes and held his gaze, long enough to make Jim think he was about to get a lecture. Finally, John held out his hand, palm open.

"What do I do?"

Jim grinned ear to ear. He should have handed John the pipe and pot right there, but that wasn't his style under the best of circumstances, and certainly wouldn't do when delivering the details of such an important process to a weed virgin.

"Believe it or not," Jim said, "there's a science to smoking. You want to get as high as you can with the smallest amount possible. Forget what you've been told by The Man; marijuana is a fucking miracle plant. You can grow it, chop it, make paper, wood, fabric or whatever. Plus, of course, you can smoke it, cook it, even simmer it in oil or steep it in alcohol to prime it for ingestion." Jim looked at John with professorial authority. "Now, it's not water soluble, so if you eat it raw, you'll only end up scrubbing your insides with a loofah you have to pay for by the ounce. Believe me, bro; a bran muffin is way cheaper. You ever smoke a regular cigarette?"

John took a second to think, then shook his head no.

"Too bad, because it's pretty much the same thing, except when you're done smoking ganja, you feel happy and creative, instead of swearing you'll quit tomorrow. I don't have rolling papers so I'm using this." Jim held the pipe between two fingers, then refilled the bowl with a few more dried leaves.

"Light it, then inhale. Like this." Jim drew on the pipe's stem, pulling the smoke into his lungs with another bottomless breath, then blew it out, turning his head and sending the plume into the hallway behind them. "Hold it in as long as you like, then let it out. When your mind starts swimming, it's time to stop smoking. Keep going, and it's just a waste of weed, especially when it comes to the hydroponic shit. Of course, there are a million theories about the ideal length of time to hold your smoke, how big a hit you should take, whether you should stand or sit, and just about any variable you can think of. But I like to keep it simple — breathe in, breathe out, and be merry."

If that wasn't a bumper sticker already, Jim thought it should be. *Breathe in, breathe out, be merry.*

Jim sprinkled a few more fresh leaves into the basin, then handed John the pipe and lighter. John put it to his lips, flicked the lighter and lit the leaves as Jim had done.

"Since you're not used to smoking, you're probably gonna hack a bit, no big," Jim said. "Just hold it in as long as you can."

Jim was enjoying the look on John's face, somewhere in the middle of ignorance and intrigue, when the bones beneath his face suddenly shifted.

What the fuck? Jim was startled, and jumped back, unable to hide his reaction.

This is weed, not 'shrooms. I have to be imagining things.

John blew a stream of smoke into the air, then placed the stem to his lips and lit the basin again, ignoring Jim's reaction. John was holding his breath for a few seconds when the bones in his face started to move in a wave beneath the surface of his skin a second time.

"Dude, what the fuck? Your face just ... "

Jim took a step back, staring at John.

"What ... the?" he stammered.

John's eyes widened, but his lips were sealed in a rising smile.

Jim fell back toward the hotel room door behind him, then turned and put his hand on the handle. He turned the knob, then heard a voice from behind him.

"Dude, what the fuck? Your face just ...What ... the?"

It was Jim's voice, as if the thing that wasn't John was trying it on for size.

Jim tried to scream, but the attempt died inside him as the thing grabbed him by the back of his neck so hard, he thought it would rip his spine right out of his body like in *Mortal Combat* or something.

Jim whimpered as the John the monster spun him around and pushed him into the hotel room, threw him to the ground, and fell atop him, hand crushing Jim's throat as Jim squirmed and struggled to break free.

"No escape," the thing that wasn't John said as it put a hand over Jim's head and sent a sharp pain through his whole body.

Jim wanted to scream, beg for his life, say something! But he was paralyzed, unable to move, breathe, or even swallow. Panic coursed through him like fire, lighting his entire body with a million messages to run, flee, escape, fight, breathe, but his body ignored them all.

His open eyes began to dry out as the thing that wasn't John bent down, picked him up, and threw him over his shoulders like a sack of laundry. Jim's face bounced off of John's back as he carried him into another room, then slung him into a tub. Jim's head slammed into the bottom of the tub with a loud echo. He couldn't feel the pain, but imagined there had to be a lot of blood.

He was fading.

As the world dimmed at the edges, the last thing he saw was the thing that was not John look down at him and close the shower curtain.

* * * *

CHAPTER 15
EDWARD KEENAN

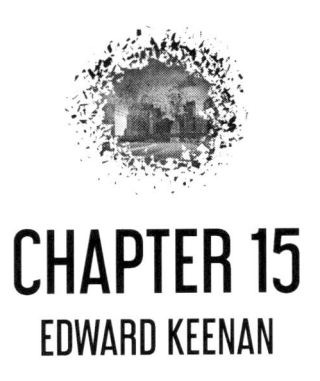

Ed's headache worsened while he sat and waited for the "answer guy."

His head pounded, and his memories continued to grow fuzzy. Mostly small things, like the street he lived on, the car he drove, his favorite brand of toothpaste. He could see them in his mind, but had to focus to draw them forth. However, the harder he focused, the more intense his headache grew. And the more his vision blurred.

He was beginning to wonder if he'd suffered some sort of head trauma in the plane crash. Unlike movies, where people were hit on the head and knocked out on a routine basis, with little to no lingering side effects, actual head trauma was different. A blow to the head could be initially dismissed while internal bleeding caused swelling in the skull, which could kill you.

I don't wanna die like this.
I want to see Jade. And Teagan.

Ed decided that no matter who came into the room to see him next, he would demand to see Jade. He had to know she was okay. And if Teagan wasn't nearby, he would demand to know where she was, too. And he wanted proof.

Of course, he was hardly in a position to make demands. But he'd make them anyway. He could tell by how they handled his interrogation, that he was better trained than these people were. Given time, he could win them over through persuasion. The only question was whether his touch would be gentle or firm.

Assuming, of course, that the killer headache went away. And that he had enough time to work his magic.

Alone time with the mirror had forced Ed to ponder some of the shit he'd done over the past few years. How he'd neglected his family. How he'd been ruthless in executing orders. How he'd let so much of his life pass him by with barely a memory set aside for posterity. And the worst part was, if anyone were to have asked Ed what things meant the most to him in life, he would never have said The Agency. Not if he were answering honestly.

The list would have comprised of his daughter, his wife, and living a normal family life. Not this shit.

He had no real past with Jade. He wasn't about to miss his opportunity to build a future.

If they could get out of this place.

The door opened, and Sullivan entered.
"Are you ready, Mr. Keenan?"
"Yes," Ed said.
Footsteps outside the door grew louder.
A man entered the room.
Ed's heart nearly stopped beating.
He stared in confusion, unable to look away.
In front of Ed was a man who could have been his identical twin, looking exactly the same, except for much nicer fabric that hung from his frame.
Sullivan spoke, "Edward Keenan, meet Dr. Edward Keenan."

TO BE CONTINUED …
IN
YESTERDAY'S GONE: SEASON TWO

WANT TO KNOW WHAT HAPPENS NEXT?

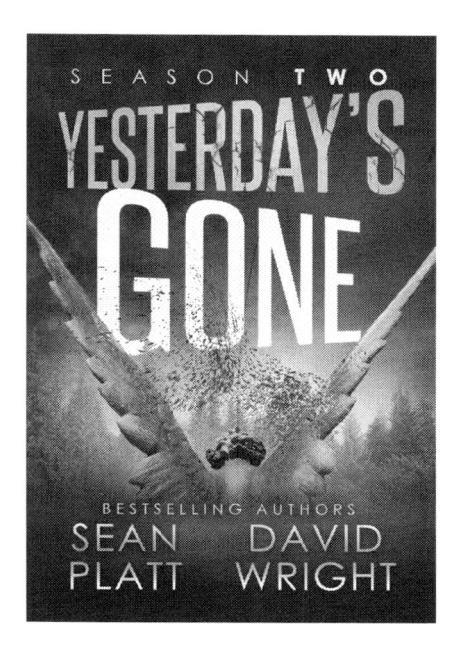

The story continues in *Yesterday's Gone: Season Two*
SterlingandStone.net/book/yesterdays-gone-season-two

AUTHOR'S NOTE: DAVID WRIGHT

When I was a child in 1979, there was a TV show on NBC called *Cliffhangers*. Each week brought you three 20 minute segments of ongoing serials. One story was a horror tale about a vampire, the other was a sci-fi/western hybrid, and the last one, a mystery. I don't remember the particulars of the stories. But I *do remember* how excited I got each week when the show was about to come on.

And how frustrated I got at the end of each segment when the announcer would tell you that the adventure would be continued next week.

"Arggghh!"

God, how I loved being teased and tormented by that show.

Of course, the network had the last laugh when after just 10 episodes, they cancelled *Cliffhangers* — before the series was even finished!

The ultimate, "ARGGGHH," but not a good one.

THE GOOD "ARGGGHH"

Anyway, we've all had those "Arggghh!" moments when our favorite shows leave us hanging another week to see what happened. Or, in the case of a season ending cliffhanger, we'd have to wait a whole summer!

"ARRRRGGGGHHHH!!"

Sean and I love shows like these.

I'm guessing *you* love shows like these.

Whether we're entrenched in *The Wire, Breaking Bad, Battlestar Galactica, LOST, X-Files, Game of Thrones, Dexter, Deadwood, Mad Men, The Walking Dead,* or any of the other great shows on TV, there's nothing better than serials and their cliffhangers.

In 1996, Stephen King released *The Green Mile* as six monthly chap books, each of them around 100 pages, the first five ending with cliffhangers. King had me hooked from book one. I remember going to my local bookstore the minute it opened on the release date of each new edition. Then I raced home to devour the story like a bag of chips or cookies!

And it was so awesome as I tore through the pages. But then, once I reached the end, I felt the same kind of guilt as when I'd eaten a whole sleeve of cookies in one sitting.

That's it? It's over? No!! I knew I should've taken my time.

And the wait would begin for next month.

While writers have been doing serialized fiction forever, and I'd read a few serialized stories in magazines (and comic books), *The Green Mile* was my first experience with serialized storytelling in book form.

You never forget your first.

As a writer many years later, I loved the concept so much that I wanted to write a serial. But the odds of Sean and I selling a serial to a publisher seemed next to impossible. Big publishers weren't publishing many serials from *known* writers. There was no way they'd take a shot on a couple of unknown authors.

SO WE WOULD HAVE TO FIND ANOTHER WAY...

Sean and I attempted to release our vampire thriller *Available Darkness* as serialized web fiction in 2008, posting chapters weekly on our blog. We drew a few readers, but most people emailed us saying the same thing:

"I hate reading on the web. When are you going to come out with a book?"

This was also the exact moment that we were drowning in work, trying to pay our bills. Putting a book out was not going to happen. So we reluctantly put *Available Darkness* on hold until we could finish it properly and release it as a book.

And then in 2010, eBooks and Print On Demand took off. Suddenly writers didn't have to wait to be picked up by a publisher — they could reach out and find their readers. In 2011, we decided that we had to finish *Available Darkness* and get it out to the few loyal people we left hanging.

But we released it as a book, not a true serial.

Then, as we looked around at the self-publishing landscape, we saw an opportunity to do what we really wanted to do — write serialized fiction. Not many people were doing it with e-books at the time, and we read from many people saying the format wouldn't work with the format.

We disagreed.

We saw e-books as the perfect vehicle for serials!

So we took a chance, and in the summer of 2011, we started writing *Yesterday's Gone: Season One*.

And unlike 1996, you don't have to drive to a bookstore to get the next copy. Instant downloads to your e-reader.

Our main inspiration in the page length and format was definitely Stephen King's *The Green Mile*. But we were also taking direction from another source — TV.

We approach serialized fiction just like our favorite TV networks — delivering weekly character-driven serials that bring you to the edge of your seat and leave you hanging, week in and week out. We wrote "episodes" ranging from 14,000 - 25,000 words and collected six episodes into "season" compilations.

Fortunately, our gamble has paid off so far. We've found enough readers who like what we're doing and are helping us keep our dream of writing serials alive.

NOW...

As I edit this introduction, it is now October 2013, and we've written six serials (with four seasons of *Yesterday's Gone* alone, so far) and released more than 18 *Dark Crossings* short stories.

The publishing world has changed so much in just two years, that now mainstream publishers are starting to take serials seriously again. In fact, based on reader response to *Yesterday's Gone*, Sean and I were signed to a book deal by 47North for two of our serials, *Z 2134* and *Monstrous!*

So, thank you, Dear Reader, for taking a chance on our serials. While the publishing world may continue to change, we believe that things like character driven storytelling and thrilling stories will always have an audience.

We're humbled and honored to have you with us on this journey.

Thank you for reading,
David W. Wright & Sean Platt
October 2013

* * * *

AUTHOR'S NOTE: SEAN PLATT

The first book I remember reading was *The Hobbit*. Not that Grover's, *There's a Monster at the End of This Book* isn't a real book, but *The Hobbit* lasted longer than a sneeze, I could feel its weight in my hand, and it left plenty of cool to ponder in the reader's afterglow.

I was six. My mom had gone on and on about Tolkien's masterpiece for as long as I could remember. She used words like magic, trolls, dragon, and elves, then insisted I'd love it when I "got older." She may as well have said:

"Hey Seanie, you should really read *The Hobbit* right now if you want to understand all those snake in the grass jokes your older sisters are always laughing about."

I found *The Hobbit* in our garage. My parents were in the house, my mom experimenting with new ways to flavor grease, my dad warming his hands in his pants in front of a ball game. I'd gone treasure hunting in the garage many times before, but this time was special.

I found two treasures: a hatchet minus its sheath, leaning against the rotting wall, and an old paperback copy of *The Hobbit*, wearing a thin sweater of filth.

Pretending I was He-Man was fun, taking the hatchet and swinging it into the trunk of the peach tree in our backyard, knowing that if I was caught, I'd be in a high heap of trouble. My adventures with the blade only lasted a few minutes. Though it wasn't because I was scared of getting in trouble. I'd been in trouble before, plenty, and I'd be in trouble again. But I couldn't stop thinking about the magic, trolls, dragons and elves waiting for me.

I tore through *The Hobbit*, understanding maybe half. I was used to this level of comprehension; it was a lot like listening to my parents argue. I read the book several times until finally setting it down two years later, where it lay untouched for two decades until I first heard that the director of *Heavenly Creatures* was adapting *The Lord of the Rings*.

I was eight the year I discovered Stephen King and became a different sort of reader.

My mom was an avid reader before I was born. That changed soon, though. Maybe it was the constant wiping of my ass which stripped her of the energy to tear through pages by the thousands as she once had, but she still saw herself as the reader she once was, or imagined a return to the good old days, so she bought the books to fit the image.

Though few were read, I believe in the early days, she never missed a single Stephen King. She started with *Carrie* and kept right on going.

I was around seven, laying on the floor in my sleeping bag beside my sister the first time I remember hearing the name Stephen King. Our parents were on the couch, our father flipping channels. Channel surfing was still new and therefore fun for the whole family. My father paused on a macabre scene of a woman, swimming in blood, being chased down a stairwell by another woman, obviously older.

"Why is that lady chasing her?" I said, more curious than frightened. I could feel my sister's discomfort beside me.

"Probably because she forgot to clean her room," my dad said. My mom suggested he change the channel, which he did immediately, but not before defensively saying to my mom, "*You're* the one who likes Stephen King."

"Was that *Carrie*?" I asked, pointing to the TV. My mom said yes. I have no idea how I knew.

I did know this – Stephen King books were scary and exciting. And after seeing seven seconds of Carrie, I also knew they probably had buckets of blood, which for all the swords and warfare, was something *The Hobbit* was seriously lacking.

I read *The Talisman*, fresh from the bestseller rack, still in hardcover about a month after my mom did. I took it from her room, transported it to mine, then twisted the landscape of my mind and imagination forever.

It took a couple of decades, plus a few major life changes before I realized I was a writer, but many seeds were planted in between the pages of my first stack of Stephen King books. Like *The Hobbit*, I rarely understood everything the first time through, but I never minded the return visits.

My parents had a small business, right around the corner from a Walden Books. Best babysitter I ever had. I devoured everything I could, hours swallowed hours and days ate weeks. That bookstore wasn't only the best babysitter I ever had, it was also my best teacher. It's where I read Twain and McMurtry, but it was also where I feasted on an endless supply of comic books and Blanche Knott's *Truly Tasteless Jokes* books. I was eleven when I read Anne Rice's *Exit to Eden*, which was a far more vivid lesson in sex than I'd ever get in school. My homework was often ignored, but by '88, I'd read everything Stephen King had ever written, with the exception of *Danse Macabre*, which I admit I've still not gotten to.

I grew up and was soon engrossed in film, preferring the bite-sized two hour adventures. I traded King for Tarantino and PT Anderson. The common thread was the same: well-told stories I couldn't break away from, with characters and dialogue that kept me smiling.

Most recently I've fallen in love with the golden age of television and the serialized delight from shows such as

LOST, Dexter, The Walking Dead, and The Sopranos. Great characters, open loops, and impossibly awesome cliffhangers.

These are the seeds which eventually sprouted Yesterday's Gone.

I expected my lifetime diet of books, movies, and TV would coalesce to help me tell a well-told story. After all, I'd been doing it as a ghostwriter for years. I love telling stories and knew Dave and I could write an exciting-to-read, impossible-to-put-down adventure.

What I didn't expect was the magic.

I started writing Yesterday's Gone expecting the first season to be fun, and maybe a little trashy. Though Dave and I wanted to deliver the highest quality experience we possibly could, part of what I loved most about his idea for the post-apocalyptic setting, was that I was confident we could write it fast and furiously (I'm a big believer that the faster you write, the more natural your voice, but that's a different author's note).

I was picturing the grind house experiences of the 70's, a trashy movie in a trashy theater that left you wanting more. I expected to enjoy writing the season, releasing it to an audience, then moving onto the next one. However, I didn't expect to fall in love with the story, or the characters.

I love everything about Yesterday's Gone, and after more than three million words written in the last three years, it's my favorite thing I've ever done.

And I never saw Boricio coming.

I can't wait for Season Two.

Thank YOU for reading. I'm looking forward to you and I having many more adventures together.

Sean Platt

* * * *

FIND OUT WHY READERS CAN'T GET ENOUGH
COLLECTIVE INKWELL

To see all our of our books, visit:
www.SterlingandStone.net/
collective-inkwell

ABOUT THE AUTHORS

Sean Platt is the bestselling co-author of over 60 books, including breakout post-apocalyptic horror serial *Yesterday's Gone*, literary mind-bender *Axis of Aaron*, and the blockbuster sci-fi series, *Invasion*. Never one for staying inside a single box for long, he also writes smart stories for children under the pen name Guy Incognito, and laugh out loud comedies which are absolutely *not* for children.

He is also the founder of the Sterling & Stone Story Studio and along with partners Johnny B. Truant and David W. Wright hosts the weekly Self-Publishing Podcast, openly sharing his journey as an author-entrepreneur and publisher.

Sean is often spotted taking long walks, eating brisket with his fingers, or watching movies with his family in Austin, Texas. You can find him at sean@sterlingandstone.net.

David W Wright is the co-author of several horror series, including the bestselling *Yesterday's Gone* and *WhiteSpace*, as well as the disturbing standalone books, *12* and *Crash*.

Dave is also the curmudgeon co-host of the weekly Self-Publishing Podcast, he invites listeners along on his journey toward better health on the strikingly personal The Walking Dave podcast, and regularly rants about his many

pet-peeves on the ridiculous podcast Worst. Show. Ever. (which should never be listened to by anyone, ever).

Dave is an accomplished and intermittent cartoonist who lives in [LOCATION REDACTED] with his wife and son [NAMES REDACTED]. Dave cultivates the perfect level of paranoia and always carries a decoy wallet in case he gets mugged. You can stalk him at dave@sterlingandstone.net or visit his personal blog at www.davidwwright.com.

For any questions about Sterling & Stone books or products, or help with anything at all, please send an email to help@sterlingandstone.net, or contact us at sterlingandstone.net/contact. Thank you for reading.